THE
TROUBLE
WITH
DROWNING

THE
TROUBLE
WITH
DROWNING

A NOVEL

HEATHER HACH

GREENLEAF
BOOK GROUP PRESS

Published by Greenleaf Book Group Press
Austin, Texas
www.gbgpress.com

Distributed by Greenleaf Book Group

For ordering information or special discounts for bulk purchases, please contact Greenleaf Book Group at PO Box 91869, Austin, TX 78709, 512.891.6100.

Design and composition by Greenleaf Book Group
Cover design by Greenleaf Book Group

Publisher's Cataloging-in-Publication data is available.

Print ISBN: 979-8-88645-125-2

eBook ISBN: 979-8-88645-126-9

To offset the number of trees consumed in the printing of our books, Greenleaf donates a portion of the proceeds from each printing to the Arbor Day Foundation. Greenleaf Book Group has replaced over 50,000 trees since 2007.

Printed in the United States of America on acid-free paper

23 24 25 26 27 28 29 30   10 9 8 7 6 5 4 3 2 1

First Edition

To my darling parents, Bruce and Muriel, who thankfully always knew their young daughter with a penchant for telling colossal whoppers would end up a storyteller and not in prison. Thank you for always believing in me, for knowing laughter is the glue, and for nurturing my wacky truth.

Dearly Beloved Reader:

HI. I'M SO GLAD YOU'RE HOLDING MY BOOK, and I'm even gladder you might consider reading it. Even if you put it down, it's a weird little triumph just to get that far. I'm literally doing a happy dance in my house right now.

I feel compelled, fair reader, to share that this book is about many things, but mental illness has a starring role. I am not for a moment trying to suggest all people who struggle with it will do questionable—or awful—things. Hell, I've struggled with anxiety for years, and I also have an OCD condition called trichotillomania (compulsive hair pulling, which is as charming as it sounds). I'm not immune. It seems no one is immune. We all battle our own demons, day in and day out. With that in mind, I feel I should warn those who might get triggered by—*spoiler alert!*—the inclusion of suicide. Suicide has unfortunately affected my life as well, and I know all too well the hideous despair it leaves in its wake. If you don't want to read about any of the above, I completely appreciate this book may not be for you.

I thought of this psychological thriller concept decades ago when I was a student at the University of Arizona. It's always whispered to me through the years but remained in my mind and not on the page. And then when the world shut down and seemed to collapse in on itself, I started reading obsessively. I've always been a huge reader but during lockdown, I was gulping books whole. I felt like I did when I first read *Little House on the Prairie* and Judy Blume as a little girl, and later as a teen when I devoured every single thing by Stephen King. With books, the world got so much bigger and better. I love stories and words, and I've always believed in their power. Today, I'm a screenwriter and Broadway librettist, but for me, it all began with books.

During COVID, I decided I wasn't doing much—going to Target seemingly a life-threatening proposition with a deadly virus raging—and I wrote this novel. I crafted and toiled and thrilled in spending time with these people. I couldn't wait to write each day. Even when I woke up in the middle of the night, I was excited to work out details just lying in bed. My lovely husband even let me sleep in, knowing I so believe in the power of dreams and the unconscious to forge creativity. It all helped form this novel.

I also wanted to comment on how our social media world has made us all navel gazers, comparing our realities to what we see around us and online. But as Theodore Roosevelt brilliantly noted, "Comparison is the thief of joy." He's right. All this sizing up is making us collectively miserable. Everyone's existence is different, and we all need to embrace our own truth and celebrate our differences. Don't miss your own life wishing you were living someone else's.

Despite all this gloom and doom speak, my intention with this novel was to craft something compulsively readable. Hopefully you can also see yourself in all the characters, however flawed they may be. I hope you enjoy it as much as I loved bringing it to life. Cheers and thank you.

AUTHOR'S NOTE

THIS BOOK CONTAINS TOPICS OF A SENSITIVE NATURE, including suicide. If you or someone you know is struggling with suicidal thoughts, please call or text the Suicide and Crisis Lifeline 24/7 at 988.

PART ONE

PROLOGUE

Two Years Ago

FUCK ME SHE'S BEAUTIFUL.

Kat nearly laughed at her thought, it was so positively lecherous. For a split-second she wondered if this meant she was, in fact, a lesbian after all. Never mind that she'd never had such a thought before in her entire life.

"That's me," the woman beamed, pointing to the sign in Kat's hands. Kat held up a flimsy handmade placard reading EDEN HART. The sign was so amateurish it was embarrassing.

"I'm Kat. I'll be your driver today. Your own *Uber extraordinaire*," she cracked, and instantly regretted the line—it was something an aunt would say to prove to her niece she was, in fact, pretty darn cool. Thankfully, Eden laughed, her smile so white it practically twinkled with a little star. Meanwhile, Kat was just glad she'd woken up in time to brush her teeth at all. "Alright then!" Eden said cheerfully. "So do you work at Antigone Books?"

"I do, yeah. I'm an assistant manager, actually. I started working there a few years ago when I moved to the area."

"Well, I'm excited to check out Tucson. I've heard great things."

"I would temper those expectations."

Eden grinned and pushed voluminous waves out of her face—it was so much hair to contend with, an absolute beast of honeyed magic. Self-consciously, Kat brushed her own locks behind her ears. She had deep, dark hair that was cut simple and practical—let's be honest, it was practically Amish—but Kat wasn't really in a position to invest in monthly salon treatments. Now she desperately wished her hair skills transcended the ponytail. She liked to think she was above such trivialities, but looking at Eden Hart, Kat realized most decisively she was not.

"Do you have luggage?"

Eden pointed to her light blue Away carry-on. "I pack lightly."

"Even for a book reading?"

"It's just two days, and it *is* Tucson. Bulky sweaters need not apply."

Kat smiled and started for the airport exit; Eden followed. "I have to apologize now for my car. It's not exactly a luxury town car."

"Thank god. I actually sort of hate being driven in them. Like I'm a Kardashian or something terrible like that."

"Oh, you'll be 'one of the normal people' with me, alright."

They walked outside into the unforgiving sunlight and punishing heat. "Whoa! Hello, Tucson!" Eden fumbled for her sunglasses tucked into her Chloé purse. They were oversized, almost clunky, and a weird lime green color but still somehow endlessly fashionable.

"You get used to the heat."

"I find that hard to believe. But . . . it's sort of nice, actually. The never-ending chill and rain in Seattle don't exactly do wonders for someone on anti-anxiety meds."

Kat stopped. *This dewy fawn needed medication?* Noting her pause, Eden explained, "Look, I believe in transparency. I assume you've read my book? I mean, it *is* called *Blue*."

Kat's face turned crimson, and her brow furrowed in self-doubt. "I did! And I loved it! *Loved.* I mean, I'm not a, you know, usual children's book . . . aficionado. But yours . . . was amazing. And the illustrations. Just . . . wow. It's no wonder you won the Caldecott."

"Thank you."

"And I'm sorry. About your fiancé, I mean." Kat popped the trunk of her stupid Honda with its dumb dings and scrapes. Eden set the luggage inside and closed the trunk.

"Thanks. It hasn't been easy. Which is putting it mildly. But art helps."

"Always."

Eden crawled into the front seat, recoiling from the molten, sticky heat. "Please tell me you have A/C," she pleaded.

"I'm not a monster."

Eden let out a robust chuckle and flashed another blinding smile, but this time Kat wasn't thinking about her own flaws. Instead, she was flattered and basked in Eden's brief attention.

As they exited the airport and pulled onto the freeway, Eden looked out the window. Kat forced herself not to stare at her profile. That nose! It was the sort of nose that you'd take a picture of into the plastic surgeon's office and say, "I want to look like that." Without thinking, Kat touched her nose, feeling the slight bump across the bridge. For a moment, she considered asking Eden if she'd had work done.

"What brought you to Tucson?" Eden asked, thankfully preventing Kat from making an even bigger embarrassment of herself.

"Oh, well, I'm a writer, too. Yeah. I just got my MFA from U. of A. on scholarship."

"Nice. Good for you! Great writing program, right?"

"One of the best. I'm also working on my memoir now."

Eden nodded, her face tilted once more toward the window, watching the desert pass by. "I see why people find it inspiring here. It's so . . . stark. And beautiful at the same time."

"I like it. Tucson is its own little strange creature of a town. And you're just gonna love Hotel Congress. It's super cool. Vintage and charming, good music scene, and a fun bar."

"I love a fun bar," Eden said, catching sight of herself in the side-view mirror and then frowning. "Speaking of bars—ha ha!—do you know of a nearby Dry Bar?"

Kat shook her head slowly from side to side, uncertain. God, how she wished she knew what a Dry Bar even was.

"You know, a hair salon? Just for a blowout. It's sort of indulgent and stupid—I mean, I doubt Joan Didion required this—but I try to get one before each reading."

"Of course! Duh! Well . . . I'm not sure, actually. Concierge will be able to help, though." Kat watched Eden loft her billowing blonde hair atop her head and nearly swooned. "But . . . your hair looks so nice. You know. Now."

Eden released her hands, her hair tumbling like a Disney princess, spilling onto her shoulders. "No, it's too much. Frizzy and crazy."

"It's beautiful!" Kat took a shallow breath, realizing the admission was too eager. She gripped the spongy steering wheel tight.

"You know how it goes, Kat," Eden said, digging into her purse for a tin of mints, pulling one out and closing the box with precision. "People always want what they can't have." She popped the tiny mint into her perfect mouth and stared out the window once more.

• • •

Antigone Books had no formal decorations for Eden's reading. There wasn't bottled water or wine, no table with platters of cheese and crackers.

Then again, Kat doubted they would have been necessary—no one was here for the light apps, they were here for the person behind this impressive debut. Kat had researched Eden Hart when she was assigned to pick her up at the airport. Two articles later, Kat was hooked. Eden had been a successful children's book illustrator in her own right—Kat recognized her work—but *Blue* had been Eden's first foray into writing herself. A piece in the *Seattle Times* chronicled how Eden transformed her experience of losing her fiancé to cancer into the bestselling story, which didn't seem like the most obvious inspiration for a new children's classic. But Eden handled the subject with honesty and skill, with both a light touch and a somber acknowledgment of pain. Kat agreed Eden's work skated the line of grief and madness, hope and despair. The book was embraced as a welcome addition in a parched field, and her work assumed kids could not only handle the truth but would welcome being treated with such respect.

The advance praise and shining reviews for *Blue* had generated quite a bit of buzz in the days leading up to Eden's signing. Hours before the event was scheduled to begin, there was an overspill of people out onto the sidewalk. Eager fans, young and old alike, clutched copies of her book, hoping for a few words with Eden, studying her with adoring eyes.

Kat watched Eden along with the others, similarly mesmerized, as she made her way to the dais and collected herself with practiced poise. It was obvious from Eden's shiny, blow-dried hair that she had, indeed, found a Dry Bar after all. After dropping off Eden at Hotel Congress—and Eden had cooed appropriately, charmed by the landmark hotel—Kat had gone straight to Creations Boutique on

4th Street and bought a sleek jumpsuit for the reading. It was chic and flattering, and she didn't want to look down at her stupid linen culottes with the tiny holes when Eden spoke. Kat had assumed the purchase would make her feel fabulous; mostly it made her just not feel terrible.

Eden read her entire children's book to the teeming room, her voice assured and lyrical, grief-stricken but melodic. Neither Kat nor the others would know that this was Eden's largest event to date, and she was, in fact, overwhelmed with nerves. The audience was particularly attentive, drinking in her words as if they were an exotic nectar. The laughs were appropriate; there were also distinct sniffles and muffled tears toward the end. Eden held them in the palm of her hand.

For the Q & A, hands shot into the air, waving with the mania of a hundred valedictorians. Eden happily called on her pupils, delighted by their thoughtful questions, noticeably basking in their perhaps-too-generous praise. She was very good at humble. She was almost convincing.

One by one, Eden answered each question, addressed each comment. Some people spoke about their own experiences with grief, others thanked her for "getting them through it." She listened to each one of them, keeping sincere eye contact and casting sympathetic gazes. She was an entity unto herself.

As Eden's hypnotic voice reverberated around the store, Kat momentarily forgot that she was at work. She should have been double-checking the signing table and making sure there were enough copies of the book. Instead, Kat was transfixed by Eden's voice, the personal depth she was sharing, and the adoration from the audience. Kat wondered what this all must feel like—to not only have a literary hit on your hands but also experience this praise in person. Eden had a following, and her readers genuinely loved her. There must be a special kind of pleasure and satisfaction in that kind of success, to have that kind of impact on others.

Kat reminded herself Eden *had* lost her fiancé. Life wasn't only green lights and rainbows for her. Eden had been through her own hell. Kat was embarrassed to admit it, but if she were being honest, now that she'd glimpsed what literary success felt like—it's all she wanted for her own memoir.

Kat would gladly suffer any loss if that's what it took.

Anything.

ONE

Present Day

KAT'S HANDS HELD ONE OF her favorite novels of all time—*Lolita*—but even the glorious, twisted prose couldn't stop her eyes from floating from the print and upwards to the kitchen window. She scanned across the pool, waiting for the outline of a person to appear.

Even the sluicing sounds of a glistening male body methodically swimming laps back and forth in the aqua water could not distract her from the kitchen window. Kat knew that Carol Walsh was due to return shortly with groceries, and she was determined to make the most of their introduction—assuming her nerves didn't get the best of her. Carol was a renowned author whose fiction had long been the beacon of contemporary feminist prose, and she was also now a professor at Kat's alma mater, the University of Arizona. Sadly—and shockingly—she had never gotten into Carol's class despite an eager attempt to do so. But as luck would have it, Carol was also the mother of Kat's new roommate Jess Walsh. So when Jess invited Kat to swim at the family pool, she jumped at the chance.

Which was basically why she was ignoring both Nabokov and the muscular swimmer, who she assumed was Jess's older brother, Jacob. Jacob always welcomed his younger sister's friends to share in the family pool. They'd peel off see-through beach coverups and apply lotion to one another's backs while cracking open hard seltzers. Maybe they discussed literature or the Jonas Brothers. Perhaps both. He

didn't know, and he didn't particularly care. Jacob loved the company and especially their tropical-colored bikinis.

Kat aimlessly reached over to pet Kahlo, the Walsh family's rescue Jindo who
had settled next to her as she reread the same sentences on the page she had still
not turned. Meanwhile, Jess was flipping page after page of *Shoe Dog*, the inspi-
rational memoir by Nike creator Phil Knight. Jess was a goofball, athletic and
punchy, looking every bit the part in her University of Arizona baseball hat, which
was faded with sweat along the brim from her time in the sun assistant coaching
the Lady Wildcat Cross Country team. Jess's strawberry blonde hair was pulled
through the cap into a long ponytail that fell past her shoulders. In contrast, Kat
appeared more like an earnest grad student truly unaware of her allure and not the
assistant bookstore manager and struggling memoirist that she was. She kept a tattered wide-brimmed hat over her dark, long hair to shield her sensitive skin from
the harsh Southwestern sun. The hat suggested a lack of interest in fashion that was
nonetheless on trend. As Jacob took final strokes to the shallow end of the pool, he
rubbed his eyes and looked over to the sunbathing girls, curious about Jess's new
friend. Intrigued, he noted how Kahlo—often more cat than dog—was uncharacteristically curled up next to Kat as she absentmindedly pet the dog's head.

Kat barely bat an eye when Jacob pulled himself out of the pool, shaking himself
off like a drenched Labrador, then toweling off his tanned torso like some kind of
Greek god. While not entirely obnoxious, Jacob wasn't exactly subtle about showing
off his body. He knew what he looked like, and it generally gave him an edge up in
just about everything. With a calculated degree of nonchalance, he glanced at Kat
laying on a chaise lounge and flashed his dimpled grin, which promptly gave way to
slack confusion. Expecting some sort of reaction from her, Jacob's brows furrowed
in dismay; Kat's eyes remained on her book and the kitchen window.

"I think my brother totally wants you to notice he just got out of the pool,"
Jess cracked, fully aware of Jacob's purposeful exit from the shallow end. She'd seen
the move a dozen times before.

Kat startled, looking first at Jess in confusion and then finally noticing Jacob
walking their way. He raked a hand through his wet hair and Kat gasped.

"Oh! Hello! Hi!" was all Kat could manage, clumsily waving her hand in the air.
Thank god for the oversized sunglasses she'd recently scored at Target shadowing

her face. Her eyes didn't know where to settle, every plane of his body was just ridiculous; sinewy but strong, tanned and dewy. How had she missed this?

"That's Jacob, my older brother. He's an idiot."

Standing over them, Jacob grinned and offered a dripping hand to Kat. "Hi there." Kat squinted into the sun and shook his wet hand. She felt faint with heat; god, he had already turned her into a cliché. He flashed a smile he knew would accentuate his generous dimples. "So you're Jess's new roommate, huh? The writer?"

Jess had told Jacob about Kat during a family dinner a few weeks ago. Her old roommate had bailed on rent at their two-bedroom at Sagewood Apartments, so she'd put up a flyer at Antigone Books, and Kat had seen it. They'd bonded over their mutual love of John Irving—Kat had named her Betta fish "Garp"—and Kat moved in the following day. Jacob had only been half-listening to Jess at the time, but now he wished he'd paid more attention when she'd told the story; he'd assumed this new roommate was just another woeful book nerd.

"C'est moi! Yes, that's me. I'm Kat. And I'm not, you know, officially a writer yet—published, I mean—but I do have an MFA in creative writing and—"

"From U. of A.?"

"Go Cats! But I'm still working on things and . . . yeah." This was a train wreck.

"Oh, boy," sighed Jess, who was used to seeing Jacob's predictable effect on her friends.

"I love that book." Jacob pointed to *Lolita*. "But doesn't it disturb you?"

Kat sat up straight and put the book down, tapping on the cover with a nervous finger. "Well, I'm troubled by the theme, sure, especially these days. But I'm dazzled by the language." She smiled, genuine in her literary adoration yet also desperately wishing her lips were glossed. "I've read it so many times. You know, Nabokov wrote this masterpiece in his second language and . . . that's not easy. I'm not exactly writing masterpieces in Portuguese or anything. So there's that."

Jacob laughed, and Kat blushed. Jess immediately shot her brother a warning look.

He promptly ignored her.

"Doesn't Sagewood have its own pool? Or perhaps you're just here for the outstanding company?" The beach towel fell from his waist. "Oops." He reached down and re-wrapped the towel, this time slightly lower on his hips.

"The pool's just . . . sort of nasty—it's filled with monosyllabic frat guys and deplorable club music," noted Jess.

"Perhaps you'd be right at home," Kat joked, her own smile now dimpled.

Jacob playfully grimaced. "Ouch! And for the record, I loathe house music. But I'm not above an occasional Coors Light. It *is* the banquet of beers. So when did you graduate, Kat?"

"Two years ago. Now I work at Antigone while I finish up my memoir."

"Can you believe she never had Mom?" Jess asked.

"Seriously? How's that possible?"

"Well, a few years ago, I *did* see your mother at her book reading for *Suspension of Disbelief.* I was in awe, but I didn't get to meet her—it's one of my favorites. She's so precise with her language."

Jess and Jacob gave each other a knowing glance. "Stick around. She should be here soon, and she loves praise. Writers are parched for it." Jacob grinned. He picked up a pool net from the deck and began dragging it through the nearly leafless water.

"Dude, you realize the pool is clean, right?" Jess deadpanned.

"Sis, it *is* one of my few duties so I can live in the guest house. Besides, I find sweeping up the leaves a bit Zen-like, sort of meditative."

"Yeah, it's super Zen to clean the pool so you can ogle my friends in their swimsuits."

To make his point, Jacob pulled a lone leaf from the net and held it aloft. "Just here to help." He leaned the pool net against the garage and walked back toward the converted guest house. "It was nice to meet you, Kat. Stop by anytime, and I'll inappropriately wander out."

Kat didn't respond, and Jess shook her head as Jacob closed the door to his quarters, a one-room villa behind the main house where he'd been living for the past few years, secretly saving up money for a down payment of his own. "Avoid that one," Jess warned, loud enough for Jacob to hear.

"He's . . . much too pretty for me."

"Which he's quite aware of. Jacob buys men's beauty products, which is apparently a thing. There's even some 'manscaping' involved. And he's constantly lifting weights and making those awful 'pumping iron' sounds." To illustrate his obnoxiousness, Jess loudly brayed and grunted with convincing levels of physical torture. Kat laughed at Jess's commitment to the impersonation; she truly sounded like a roid head.

"I don't sound like that," came a playful voice from within the guest house. The corners of Kat's mouth curled upward as she stared at the closed door with intrigue.

"He's going to ask for your number. Should I say he can't have it?"

"Oh . . ." Kat's face turned red at the thought. "I doubt he'll ask."

"He'll ask."

· · ·

Later, inside the modest yet stylish stucco family house decorated with an abundance of Southwest-inspired color and Mexican folk-art animal alebrijes, Jess was chopping carrots when Jacob saddled up.

"So?" he asked without preamble.

Jess didn't look up from her maniacal dicing. God, he was so predictable. Across the room, Kat was deep in conversation with their mother, but she lowered her voice anyhow. "Let me guess. You want her number."

"Well, she's cute AND she reads Nabokov. Of course I want her number."

"Why is it when a beautiful woman—especially a beautiful woman in a swimsuit—reads Nabokov it's this startling, glorious thing, but when a mousy woman reads literature it's just . . . *meh*."

Jacob threw a carrot at her. "Where's she from?"

"All over. She was apparently a foster kid."

Jacob's eyes bugged as he stole another glance at Kat whose eyes danced like she was talking to a lost Beatle and not his middle-aged mother. "A foster kid? I didn't expect you to say that. After-school special stuff, eh?"

"Something like that. Kat's . . . sort of moody. She's likely been through a lot, so . . ." Jess stopped chopping and glanced at her brother, who continued to study Kat like an anthropologist. Great, he was intrigued by the mystery, not turned off by it. Jess switched tracks. "No wonder she's a little weird."

But Jacob was barely listening. He watched as his mother routinely touched Kat's arm, she and Kat connecting like old friends, both gushing dramatically about Alice Munro. His bohemian mother lived in flowing skirts and believed art was the salient point to life. She seemed just as enraptured with Kat as Jacob did, though obviously for different reasons.

"My darling girl, how on earth did you slip through the program without meeting me?!" Carol's voice was high with excitement; she and Kat had already established a secret code. "How is this even *possible?*"

"You said she's kind of weird?" Jacob asked, lowering his voice as he turned back to Jess. He stole a carrot and popped it in his mouth; Jess playfully slapped his hand in protest. "Weird like how?"

"She obsessively watches World War II shows on the History Channel. Like she's an 81-year-old man."

"That's not weird. That's sort of awesome." He inched closer to overhear more of his mom and Kat's conversation.

"Really, dude? Now a thirsty interest in Nazis is cool?"

"I'll take history over those awful Housewives any day of the week. I still want her number."

"Of course you do," Jess muttered. "You always do."

On the other side of the room, Kat was still ping-ponging literary conversation with their mother who, when confronted with someone much like herself, always fell deeply in love. "Canada seems to breed phenomenal female authors—Alice Munro, Margaret Atwood, the list goes on," Kat gushed. "Canada's cold weather probably helps—literature *is* a rather indoor sport—though that doesn't exactly help me here in the desert."

"Arizona can claim Zane Grey!" Carol jubilantly exclaimed.

"And you," Kat added with a shy glance at the floor.

Carol beamed, then turned to Jess and called from across the room, "That other roommate had the personality of an eraser, volleyball player or not. I like this one."

"So does Kahlo," Jess said, gesturing to the family dog who was staring at Kat like she was a peanut butter-filled rawhide. "And Jacob. Naturally." Kat grew bright red, looked down.

"Sis. Now *you're* the idiot," Jacob playfully responded. He grinned as she leaned in and whispered, "And hey—we're all adults here."

"Said the buff dude still living in his mother's guest house." Jess watched as Kat and Jacob tried to avoid eye contact like middle-school kids on a museum field trip and knew she'd already lost the battle.

. . .

Kat was busy doing inventory in the back at Antigone Books—it was always crazier when a Stephen King book came out. She pretended she wasn't checking her phone, willing Jacob's call. Instead, she periodically looked up absurd quizzes on BuzzFeed and pored over *New York Times* news blasts—as if Biden's new energy policy could possibly distract Kat from Jacob. She'd nearly peeled off an entire gel manicure when her phone rang.

UNKNOWN CALLER

"Hello?"

"Kat? Hi, it's Jacob."

"Jacob! The pool-cleaner *extraordinaire*!" God. Why did she always throw in lame French when she was nervous?

"And owner of my very own cabinetry business . . ." Kat heard his voice and immediately pictured Jacob's dimples through the phone.

"Cabinetry, eh? Jess didn't mention any HGTV tendencies." Kat caught a glimpse of herself in a mirror on the wall—her smile was gigantic, the corners of her mouth reaching Joker-like proportions.

"Jess is likely extremely jealous of my expert architectural millwork," he joked.

"Well, that's very cool!"

"It was my dad's company. But I think we all know that's not why I'm calling," Jacob said, relishing in his flirtatiousness. "I'm calling because I wanted to see if you wanted to go to dinner sometime."

Kat did an excited little dance and realized Jacob had literally made her twirl. "What're you thinking?"

"Well, my brother Pete plays in a jazz band."

"Naturally. Former track star sister, jazz musician brother, acclaimed novelist mother, expert 'millwork'—is there anything you Walshes don't do?" Kat was secretly delighted with her own suaveness. Usually, it was only her words on paper that contained charm, and her track record with men was woeful at best. But with Jacob, she found a flirtatious rhythm that was at once foreign and welcome. It was shocking, frankly, considering the whole situation.

"Well, for one, we Walshes don't take 'no' lightly. How's this Friday sound?"

For a split second, Kat toyed with concocting a conflict, fabricating some glorious social necessity that would make her seem mysterious and elusive. "Yes! I'd love it."

"Great. I'll pick you up at seven."

"Perfect. You know where to find me."

"Yes. At Sagewood Apartments, among the house music frat bros, right?"

Kat laughed too loud. "I'm really glad you called, Jacob."

"And I'm really glad I wandered out of the guest house," Jacob returned, and Kat turned red with heat.

Friday could not come soon enough.

. . .

Jess desperately wanted her new roommate to avoid another awkward brotherly romantic intrusion from Jacob. He once briefly dated a member of her high school track team, Brynn. The quick romance and immediate break-up turned Brynn inconsolable, and Jess was tragically caught in the middle. She was pissed her brother had dipped his toe into her life and potentially compromised the track season. Even Carol had also been furious her son couldn't even contain his roaming eye at an innocuous high school track meet. Jacob could not understand the furor—he and Brynn (who was 18, for the record) had gone on one hike, shared one frozen yogurt. It was hardly a relationship, and the age gap was indeed too insurmountable. He promptly ghosted the colt-like high school senior.

Jacob had always been the most unstructured of the three children. He had also been the most naturally good-looking. That is, if naturally good-looking is synonymous with one-in-a-million levels of physical beauty. Each line of his body was almost a painting, vaguely equine somehow. His skin turned mocha under the summer sun, never burning like his siblings. His entire life, Jacob had been praised for his strong jawline and later, his imposing frame, which the family joked was "infomercial ready." His hair was sandy blonde, and despite being tousled any which way, always looked as if the effect was calculated. His smile was easy, his green eyes sparkled in the sun. Most attractive of all was his odd mind and infectious laugh. Jacob was a contradiction who threw everyone he met for a loop—his strait-laced Kennedy-esque physique somehow didn't square with his more esoteric life view.

Women never swiped left on Jacob. But it made things problematic.

Because Jacob genuinely loved them. Female eyes always found him, always traced his steps. And his gaze often found theirs. He got into probing conversations everywhere he went—the car wash, the grocery store, bars. Women's phone numbers were dutifully entered into his iPhone and at the time, he was genuinely interested in calling each and every one of them back.

Sometimes he did. Sometimes he did not.

He wasn't malicious; Jacob never meant to hurt anyone with his flighty indifference. Jacob simply enjoyed sampling life's buffet. And sample he did—on dates with Jacob, women laughed too hard at his jokes, leaned in a bit too much. They were entirely too willing to do whatever it took to make the date seamless. Truth was, he was often bored on dates by the time the appetizers showed up.

When Jacob pulled up at Sagewood Apartments to pick up Kat for their first date, he toyed with just texting her to come on down. He wanted to avoid his sister's toxic stare but knew such a move would be rude. He had to face the music.

Kat opened the apartment door and Jacob quite literally lost his breath. She had been make-up free and casual upon their first meeting, and he had not anticipated this transformation before him. Kat's face was perfectly done up and she brimmed with beauty. Time had been spent, and he was dazzled.

"Wow! Kat, you're . . . stunning."

"Well, I did more than brush my teeth this time . . . Shall we?"

Jacob opened the car door for Kat, and she slid in. "Thank you, good sir." Kat's hair floated past him and smelled of watermelon and summer nights.

"I have a reservation at Kingfisher. But I really should've asked if you like seafood."

"Hey, worse comes to worst, every menu has French fries."

Jacob laughed and found himself unable to stop catching glances at Kat who only occasionally looked his way. This nonchalance on Kat's part was something she'd vowed to do before he ever knocked on the apartment door. She'd seen enough movies to know indifference was apparently a big turn-on, and she wanted for once in her life to do this the right way.

By the time they got to the restaurant, Jacob was more intrigued than ever. Everything that fell out of Kat's mouth was a bit peculiar, and despite having a face that could easily sell women that they too needed a particular type of mascara or new toothpaste, she was genuinely interesting. Kat was altogether unexpected. Kat had lived in 12 states. She apparently didn't know how to ride a bike. She knew how to skin a rabbit. Kat was proving to be unlike anyone else he had ever met before.

Kat did, however, feel wonderfully familiar when she told him she wanted to be a writer because books were the only thing that made sense to her in the whole entire world. He had endlessly heard his mother say nearly the exact same thing.

Early in the date, Kat became shockingly aware that this Adonis somehow seemed to lap up her every word. Truly, she had anticipated quite the opposite. Had it always been this easy to achieve? Maybe so. And that gorgeous woman from the book reading years ago had been right about the professional blowout. For tonight, Kat had done the same, and her beachy waves were so transformational it almost felt like science fiction.

. . .

They had to wait for their table, but neither was disappointed to have to hang in the bar. They discovered both had an affinity for Moscow mules and quickly downed their first copper goblet. The restaurant was chilled to combat Tucson's heat, but Jacob and Kat both budded with warmth. Their feet touched under the table, their hands grazing. Conversation had a playful volley, a heady combo of light and dark. One minute they were discussing the latent hypocrisy of cancel culture, then they'd slide into a mutual love of Kurt Vonnegut, then land on a love of Comedy Central's TV show *Drunk History*.

Jacob lofted his drink. "I propose a toast."

Kat responded in kind, lifting her drink high. "So do I—'Here's to alcohol, the rose-colored glasses of life.'"

"You have a way with words."

"So does Hemingway."

"Of course you quote the best! . . . And for the record—'Beer is proof God loves us and wants us to be happy.' Benjamin Franklin. But I'm not here to toast literary lions. I want to toast you, *my lady*," Jacob said with a British accent as he clinked his glass with hers. He grew crimson and looked down, shaking his head with a grin. "*Well, blimey then.*"

"What?"

"*It appears you've inspired my rather unfortunate British accent. It only appears in moments of pure delight.*"

"*Bollocks, mate! And what's wrong with that?!*" she boomed and burst into hysterics, a dam of laughter pealing the restaurant. Jacob unsteadily laughed with her as he grew self-aware that heads were swiveling, curious to see whoever was behind this human hyena under a spell of inappropriate hilarity.

"*Steady there, you cheeky muppet,*" Jacob cautioned but felt the corners of his own mouth turning up in delight. Who was this unusual creature?

"*Cheeky muppet!* . . ." she gasped, pounding the restaurant's leather booth seat in appreciation.

"*It's really not even that funny, love.*"

"I know!" she howled in agreement. The incident was not particularly amusing, but this fact only heightened the entire thing. Kat's laughter was contagious, and Jacob cautiously joined in, incredulous she seemed oblivious to the scene she was creating.

But Kat knew all eyes were on her, judging her. And she was not okay with it. She was blowing it with this beautiful boy, she was blowing it all to hell. *Stop it stop it stop fucking stop it*, she thought feverishly.

Thankfully, Jacob laughed, surrendering to the moment. A brief memory came to him: in church as a kid with his brother Pete, stifling uncontrollable giggles in the pew. Just as it was then, now it was impossible to stop the weird guffaws.

"Well, this date is going well," a smiling waitress said as she approached, and Jacob and Kat burst into another bout of maniacal howling. "Do you want me to come back?"

Jacob shook his head no and dabbed his eyes. Kat reached for her napkin, wiping away the perfect smokey eye she'd spent entirely too long on, following along with a vapid beauty influencer on YouTube. They were calming down, catching their breath.

"Sorry. Pulling it together now. Okay." Jacob grabbed the menu. "Alright then, *my lady*. Do you know what you're getting?"

"French fries. And shrimp cocktail. And another one of these." Kat lofted her empty Moscow mule.

Jacob's face hurt from smiling. "Me too on the drink. And I'll take the branzino, please." The waitress took their menus, eager to escape their strange, secret world.

"French fries and shrimp cocktail?"

"I know. I'm, like, a seven-year-old boy. But I like what I like."

"Hey, you do you. And god, this is fun. I haven't laughed that hard in ages."

Kat took a long sip of water to recuperate from the exhausting laugh-fest, relief flooding. God, it seemed Jacob was actually charmed by her unevenness! It was miraculous. Perhaps Kat's weirdness was vaguely familiar—after all, his mother was an offbeat novelist. Surely Jacob would never be satisfied with a run-of-the-mill, dull beauty. Regardless, Kat felt so unlike her usual fumbling self she half-expected to lift into the air and float away forever. She flipped her hair over her shoulder, acknowledging her rare victory. This was the version of herself she wanted to be, always.

Kat was so otherworldly, so unique—laughter *was* his favorite language. And Christ, was she hot. Jacob leaned in. "Can I ask you something?"

"Of course."

Jacob reached for her hand. Instantly Kat's palm grew moist, and her stomach flipped. Should she squeeze it? Trace a sexy finger over his knuckles? "Jess said you were a foster kid. Is that true?"

Kat unintentionally pulled back. His intimate touch and the question itself caused an immediate whiplash in her confidence—it was as if a fire hose of cold water had doused her from head to toe. Sensing the shift, Jacob's smile fell. "I'm sorry. Too much."

Jacob tipped back in his chair, his hands fumbling with the silverware. Kat's heart raced in response and she knew she had to reassure him. She reached back for his hand and gave it a forceful squeeze. Her eyes met his again; she did not look away and took a deep breath. "It's okay. It is. I appreciate you wanting to know."

"Sorry, I don't want to pry—"

"You're not prying. You care." The sentence was a challenge, more question than statement.

Jacob inched forward; his eyes regained their twinkle. "I do."

Kat exhaled. "It's true. I bounced from state to state, home to home."

"That . . . that could not have been easy. And your parents? . . ."

Kat took a long sip. "I've heard so many stories. They were young. They were addicts. The only constant narrative was this . . . my family did not want me." She stated the sentence plainly, but Jacob felt the potency of her subterranean—and likely constant—pain.

Jacob shook his head, moved. His mouth attempted to form words but could not find them. His hand inched up her arm; he gave her forearm an intimate grip. "I'm so sorry. I . . . just can't imagine. Any of it. Life is hard enough when you're wanted and loved." Jacob wanted to toss a blanket around this vulnerable woman, protect her, coddle her. The feeling was new, and he reveled in his heroic impulse. "I didn't mean . . . to, you know, bring this date down. To get all serious and kill the mood. Frankly, this whole conversation feels like date number seven material."

"And will there be a seventh? . . ." Kat flirtatiously asked, lowering her eyes and then staring back at him.

"God willing." Jacob slowly lifted her hand and softly kissed it like they were in a cheesy Hallmark movie, and Kat unintentionally made a throaty sound. The room got woozy; her head swam.

Just then, a lanky man approached with a huge grin. Jacob got up and the two men fell into an easy hug.

"What's up, man? Didn't think I'd find you in such a swanky joint," the lean man said, his eyes equally as lively as Jacob's.

"I have to impress my date here," Jacob explained. "She's Jess's roommate, remember? Kat, meet my brother Pete."

"Hi. Mom mentioned something . . ." Pete extended a friendly hand; Kat shook it.

"Kat and I were just laughing so hysterically. Like, hold-my-sides dying."

"Oh yeah? Was it like our attempt at Catholicism?"

Jacob snorted a laugh in recognition. "Exactly! I was seriously just thinking about how you and I would always get in trouble cracking up like that in church." Kat watched them banter and found obvious similarities between the two brothers. Their faces were at once the same and completely different, but both had the same dimples.

"St. Ambrose did *not* want us back . . ."

"Hell no! We were heathens."

"Ungodly levels of sacrilegious snickering."

Clearly the two brothers fed off one another, ping-ponged from absurdity to absurdity. Kat soaked in their rapport; this is what she'd always hoped siblings could be like—genetic twin flames. Then again, why was she surprised? They were, after all, the offspring of Carol Walsh.

"We're actually hoping to catch your act. You're on tonight, right, Pete?"

"Yeah, yeah. The late show. I gotta head over soon."

"What do you play?" Kat inquired.

"Piano. Jazz piano, specifically," he clarified.

"My brother's amazing. Started playing at, like, three."

"I was two-and-a-half, dude. A child prodigy. A virtual wunderkind."

"Hey, I play mediocre lacrosse. You're not the only talented person in the family," Jacob teased.

"No, you just got all the fucking hair and heartthrob thing. No one exactly mistakes me for Rob Lowe."

"I haven't gotten Rob Lowe for, like, two months. Literally."

"Maybe I don't want you to come tonight after all," Pete cracked. "So what were you two laughing so hard about, anyway?"

"It wasn't entirely logical," Kat said as she and Jacob exchanged a coy grin. "But it all started with Jacob's British accent."

Pete shook his head. "Then that means one thing—my brother is gone. Stick a fork in him already . . . Alright, see you soon." Pete walked for the exit and turned to flash Jacob a knowing grin. Kat sensed the look suggested he approved. Jacob cast his eyes down, sheepish.

"He's right. I really had no idea tonight would go this great, Kat."

No other night in Kat's life had been so charged, so electric with possibility. She'd rolled her eyes at Lifetime movies, yet also still hoped for that kind of ending. Life had dealt her a lot of reality, so she wasn't easily convinced there was a Cinderella story in her future. Still, this was one of those moments; it was hard *not* to be optimistic. Maybe she wasn't the serious novelist or supposed intellectual after all—maybe she'd always been secretly pathetic and naive. Because four hours with Jacob Walsh later, she believed her life was finally about to begin with every fiber in her blooming rom-com heart.

. . .

Several hours later at the Dove Mountain Jazz Club, Pete slammed the piano with a wild authority—he was a man possessed, but he had complete control over his instrument. His brow beaded with sweat, his face contorted in concentration and delight. The jazz band let Pete bathe in the moment.

"Oh yeah!" the trumpet player brayed, as he closed his eyes and let his head roll back. A smile danced on his mouth as he shook his head from side to side in appreciation.

"Uh huh. Alright," the bassist blurted, head bobbing in time.

An occasional appreciative clap rang out from the audience, everyone spellbound. For Kat, the foreign sounds at once made no sense and all the sense in the world. She felt like a child who had just wandered into Willy Wonka's chocolate factory. It was an entirely new world, and Kat lapped up its newness.

Finally, Pete's solo crescendoed and concluded, and the joint erupted into applause. Jacob wolf-whistled with gusto, pride lighting his eyes. "God*damn*," was his only appreciative salvo.

A waitress wordlessly gestured for another round; Kat looked to Jacob. They were both tipsy and wordlessly concluded it was time to switch to water.

Jacob ordered a bottle of Pellegrino and the waitress trotted off. He leaned even closer, his lips grazing her ear in a near-kiss: "I want to take care of you, Kat." Electricity bolted through her veins, and she had to clutch the table to steady herself. Her groin bloomed and ached with such a near-violence that it scared her. It was too much.

Abruptly, she bounded up and high-tailed it to the restroom in almost cartoonish haste. Jacob watched in confusion, unsure what had just happened. His eyes swept the joint, and Jacob found he was not alone—most men were badly attempting to disguise the fact that their gaze was following the beautiful Kat as well.

In the bathroom mirror, Kat stared, gauging her readiness, and uncertainty clouded her eyes. Her prominent brows furrowed as she began to talk to herself, vaguely drunk. She wasn't sure if she was up for what was next. This whole evening was entirely new, and she was woefully unprepared.

Kat thrust her chin upward and inspected her profile in the mirror. Maybe she was beautiful. Maybe it was all okay. Didn't she want romance at some point? Could tonight be the "some point"?

"You're good. This is fine. Fine," she mumbled, then nodded, as if to comfort herself with the mantra. She swiped her lips with gloss, washed her hands. "Better than fine. You're *normal*. Okay."

She walked from the bathroom and found Jacob waiting in the dark hall. He reached for her, concerned, pulled her in. Kat melted into his firm chest; it would have been futile to resist . . . he smelled like pine needles and mysterious soapy goodness. He was safe.

"Hey. You okay?"

Kat aggressively nodded. "Yes. All good."

"I thought things were going a bit better than good." Jacob looked into her eyes and leaned close; she unconsciously pulled away.

Then without warning, Kat committed and impulsively leaned in, crashed her teeth into his. She retreated, horrified. It was her first attempt at true seduction, and she was a pathetic amateur. Now, surely, Jacob would lead her back to the car to end the date forever, her naivete so clearly exposed. But Jacob, like an experienced dancer who knew when to lead, gently held her face and guided it to his own, kissing her lightly on the lips. First it was gentle and kind, the way you kiss on a first date, but at this point in the night it felt like they'd already been on months' worth of dates. Everything deepened and Jacob nipped at her lower lip, playful but suggestive. From head to toe, Kat pulsated.

"'Thus, with a kiss, I die." Kat peered back up, holding his gaze.

"You . . . you're . . ." Jacob's words fell off, he collected himself. "You're wonderful."

"I'll take it." Kat grinned, wondering if he got her subtle nod to *It's a Wonderful Life*.

Without missing a beat, Jacob launched into the appropriate Jimmy Stewart soliloquy. "You want the moon? Just say the word and I'll throw a lasso around it and pull it down." The two smiled in total synchronicity. Jacob took her hand and led her back to the table, and Kat would surrender to the moment. Despite her recurrent fear she would blow the date, Jacob remained, attentive and apparently besotted. Kat's hungry lips nibbled on his neck, and she heard Jacob's submissive coos of pleasure.

It was like a goddamn movie. And, for once, it was her life.

• • •

After the show, Pete and Jacob held court in the patio courtyard bar. Kat had never seen two grown men laugh more. It was as if their very table had a currency of heat, a virtual neon sign pointing an electric arrow as if to say *Here, Here, Right Exactly Here* is the best place in the world to be.

At this point, Jacob had an easy arm around Kat as she sipped her water. Pete joked he was happy to pay for her "exorbitant bar tab." Just no Mountain Dew— he drew a line with the hard stuff.

"For the record, Kat, my brother is usually not this smitten," Pete said. "So don't go breaking his heart." Jacob shot him a playful stink eye.

Kat beamed, almost fearful to spoil the moment. She then pivoted to Pete, "Tell me all about how you got that amazing at piano. And please don't just say hard work and lessons!"

"She's officially my favorite." Pete clinked his glass with his big brother as Jacob took in the sum of Kat. She glowed in the courtyard strewn with twinkling lights, her mind equally electric with romantic possibility.

. . .

Jacob and Kat chatted with such easy intensity, they barely noticed when the sun rose hours later. They leaned against his parked SUV, making out with the heat of pent-up high schoolers, pausing only to laugh or occasionally comment. Their bodies were greedy; their lips tasted one another, and Jacob's mouth explored her neck. It was all new for Kat, and she was thrilled how comfortable she was with such overt affection. She wasn't just comfortable with it; she was actually thriving.

"Your tongue tastes like licorice," Jacob spoke into her ear.

"You smell like a lottery win," Kat responded, all dreamy and drunk on love.

"Lottery win beats candy every time."

The sun bloomed on the horizon, soft and subtle, then all at once. Along with it, loud sounds of cawing peacocks filled the air. Both fell into more incredulous laughter.

"Wait. Is that . . . is that a *peacock*?"

"Yes. I think it's a few, in fact," Kat laughed. "Maybe they're here just for us."

"Send in the peacocks *and* the lions," Jacob said as he continued kissing her.

"And the monkeys and elephants! . . ."

Jacob laughed and placed his forehead onto Kat's, staring into her eyes. "With you, the world's a goddamn circus! So. What are we doing tonight?"

Kat willed herself to pump the brakes. She wanted to preserve this feeling, this heat. She knew she had to be mysterious and feign nonchalance, she had to at least try. "Well, likely working on my memoir."

"And not going out with me?"

"Nope. You see, I *am* dedicated to my craft."

"So like my mom, I gotta say." Hearing his direct comparison to the brilliant Carol Walsh confirmed Kat had taken the right tactic. "How about Monday, then?"

Kat playfully studied him. "I'm curious. Has anyone ever said they just can't go out with you? That they're busy?"

"Well . . . I mean . . ." Jacob faux-humbly considered, pretending not to *quite* understand the question.

"I take it the answer is 'no.'" Kat paused and Jacob held his breath, worried she was pulling the plu g on their connection. "But don't worry. Your track record remains. I *could* do Wednesday."

Jacob's eyes raised, not used to being put off. "Wednesday it is."

They began to kiss again, and Kat was discovering she was not only good at it, but that she wanted to continue doing more of it as much as possible.

TWO

IN THE DARK, WHEN KAT TOUCHED HERSELF (which to be honest, was happening a lot more since meeting Jacob), she envisioned his taut body over hers, thinking of his name, letting go of any inhibitions and seeing herself as a primal, sexual creature. She wanted Jacob to look at her this way, to be transfixed by her confidence. She didn't want to be pitied or coddled in bed, to have Jacob treat her like a fragile amateur. Never mind she was, in fact, a virgin.

Sure, she'd done everything but the act itself, having been violated continually by horrid men over the years in the foster program. No one had protected her as a child, and men had often abused her trust to satiate their own vile impulses. So many moments were blurry. That doubt and shame was always there, and it was a wound that was always close to rupturing anew.

Sex terrified her, but it also mortified her to admit some of her prior abuse had felt good. Kat would never say that out loud and felt despicable for even having the thought. Only when she found an article online validating that these feelings were, in fact, quite common among sexual assault survivors did she truly believe perhaps sex *could* happen for her one day. The real kind, where you held each other's gaze, left inhibitions aside, and had the safety and freedom to go a little wild . . . even the silly kind where you giggle and laugh, teasing and taunting. Or at least that's what she'd imagined.

When Kat had first arrived in Tucson, quaking in fear and as uncertain as a stray cat, she could not believe the attention she got from men, some more subtle than others. A desert climate led to smaller and skimpier clothes, and Tucson put a lot of tanned flesh on display. So she bought fake eyeglasses and added a layer of fat to keep their leering eyes away. The clichés were all sadly true: dumpy clothes concealing a dumpy body with a mop of untended hair made you virtually invisible, which Kat liked. She wanted to focus solely on her work.

Still, Kat knew her body was potent. It was idealized and held power, her lithe torso, strong legs, and plentiful breasts, their damned floppiness. Kat found Reese's Peanut Butter Cups were the most successful food at layering on the doughy padding, but after a while, their tasty goodness disgusted her. Eventually, it just wasn't worth it, and she realized you could fake padding with looser clothes. She felt like an onion, sartorial and otherwise. Besides, the extra layer of fat was uncomfortable, like wearing a bad wig in the heat. Eventually she dumped the Reese's, and the extra weight fell away. Mostly, though, she did not want to be distracted from her writing.

Regardless of her fears—and perhaps because of them—Kat had always devoured romantic literature. Frederic and Catherine in *A Farewell to Arms*, Jane Eyre and Mr. Rochester. Kat knew love and lust fueled the human wheel, and she was more than interested. Especially if it was from a distance and safe, contained on a page and not in her bedroom.

But novels also confirmed what she already knew—chiefly, that peril was always around the bend. Kat did not have even one single example from her real life that she would remotely want to emulate. Relationships were entirely too murky, too painful, and besides—she had never met one man whom she wanted to risk it for.

Well, there was the house painter who was working across the street from her last year on Euclid. He was always shirtless, always a mess and covered with paint. His baseball hat was backward, he listened to music with ear buds, bobbing his beautiful head in time. His deeply tanned skin and lanky frame moved Kat; she would stare from the sealed safety of her apartment, feeling herself grow wet. She loved him and did not even really know why. All she wanted to do was cross the street and shake his ladder. He'd climb down smelling like the sweaty sun, and without even a "hello," they'd do things together under the shade of a palm tree. Kat had vague notions, nothing definitive, but it was aggressive and animal—she would be surprisingly adept.

Needless to say, Kat was a chaste kaleidoscope of speculation, curiosity, and horror, a virtuous and safe flower. Kat thought she had it all figured out, this tomb of security she'd built for herself. Indifference was the key. So was her writing and her complete devotion to it.

But then she saw Jacob, and all the lustful feelings she'd stifled for the house-painter bloomed anew. Most likely it was the knowledge he was the child of the great author Carol Walsh that allowed her to feel so much and wonder if it was time to thaw. After all, Jacob's brain was formed in Carol's uterus, an extension of her genius. Carol made his magical form, that holiday of a face. He just had to be good.

But there was always the chance Kat could never handle intimacy. Or that Jacob would recoil from her ugly past and rotten hang-ups, grow uncertain, and ultimately slip away.

But Kat had never actually wanted to take her fantasy to a real place before. She had clung to her virginity as a safety blanket, and she was anxious to shed its child-ish hold on her. She wanted to step into womanhood and life and sex and pleasure. She wanted her eyes to roll back in her head, delirious and dripping with lust.

Kat deserved that.

Maybe she'd been waiting for Jacob her entire life. Maybe it would all make sense.

• • •

Kat went to Sephora the day before her date with Jacob to buy a curling wand for her hair, hoping to replicate the beachy waves she'd had done professionally for their first date. Instead, she was so nervous she burned her arm twice and settled on a sloppy up-do. For the first time in her life, in anticipation of the night, Kat had shaved her pubic area. She wanted her vagina to look like it knew what was what. Even if that was basically a lie.

Jacob had suggested he pick her up to see a new Sundance darling of a doc-umentary at The Loft about this bizarre, sprawling retirement village in Florida. Carol was the one who had made the suggestion, calling it "troubling but darkly hilarious." If Carol gave it a thumbs up, that was all Kat needed to hear. Jacob was raised by an intellectual powerhouse, but still, he had his "dude" moments. It made Kat even more enamored knowing that he'd prefer an indie film to something with car chases and alien explosions.

Kat and Jacob each got a beer and found their seats. She'd forgotten how chilled theaters could be in Arizona and wished she'd brought a jacket. When Jacob saw her shiver he draped an arm around her, spreading heat with the friction of his hands. And when she settled, he kept his arm around her. Kat was glad she'd left her sweater at home.

In the near dark, their eyes kept meeting. Jacob stared at her profile, and she laughed, pointing back to the screen, chiding him to pay attention to the film. Still, her body was littered with ecstatic goosebumps. It had never occurred to her that *she* could, in fact, be distracting to someone like Jacob.

It was a fascinating movie, but Kat could barely follow. Somewhere in the middle of the film, Jacob's hands grazed her thighs and caressed her hands; she had to resist climbing on top of him right there in the theater. Even less attention was given to the film after that.

Jacob kissed her cheek and sexily whispered into her ear, "Let's get out of here." His breath was sweet, and her face bloomed with heat in the shivery, dark theater, and she followed. In the lobby, he explained he didn't want to watch eccentric old people—what was he thinking? He wanted to talk and be with her, not sit in silence. Kat hoped this wasn't just a line he used to get girls talking, vulnerable, and then into his bed; she didn't think so. It was everything she wanted to hear.

They drove out to Saguaro National Park to mess around and stare at the celestial sphere. In the inky night of the desert away from the city, the stars lit up the night like an absurd Lite-Brite board.

"It's beautiful." Truly, Kat had never seen stars twinkle quite like this before.

"I can't believe you haven't come out here before at night. I love it so much. My parents would always bring us. My dad would point out the constellations and Mom would tell us all the great Greek myths."

"That sounds magical."

"Yeah. When I can't sleep, I still retrace the constellations in my mind. Works like magic."

Gently, Jacob kissed her, and Kat looked into his eyes. "Your dad . . . He's not with us anymore, is he?"

Jacob exhaled. "No."

"I'm sorry."

Jacob explained his mom and dad had long been divorced when he'd fallen in Colorado hiking along a ridge near Longs Peak nearly 10 years ago. The fall was not uncommon; every year, the mountain claimed many people. The park rangers insisted it was a fluke thing, and Jacob said the untimely and strange passing had left a hole in his heart, a window of grief. "It never really leaves you, the suddenness of it. It's just . . . constantly this sadness. Mostly I just wish he was still here."

Kat's face shifted and her brow furrowed slightly as her eyes found the ground. Realizing his error, Jacob raked a regretful hand through his hair. "I'm so sorry. I shouldn't complain about losing my dad. I was lucky to have him as long as I did. I mean, just knowing what you've—"

Kat looked up, cutting him off. "Jacob. It's okay. Just because I never really had parents doesn't mean you don't get to grieve your dad. Of course."

Jacob exhaled and he pulled her close. "I know, it's just . . . I should be more sensitive." He paused. "I don't want to blow it with you, Kat."

"Honestly, I love hearing about families. I'm sort of a masochist about the topic. So. Was your dad as handsome as you?"

Jacob's dimples appeared anew; his eyes twinkled again in the dark. "Well, my dad was a big bear of a guy, truly an oddball. He'd, like, decide he wanted to make a documentary about beaver dams and would take off for Oregon."

"Seriously? . . . And did he?"

"Make a documentary? No. But he did learn a lot about beavers. He called them the architects of the forest. I think he felt a kinship with them, 'cause my dad designed furniture." His father had showed him how to build, and Jacob admitted he likely wouldn't be in the cabinetry business if it weren't for him.

"Oh, right—the *architectural millwork*."

"Yeah. I like it, of course, and not just because it gives me a lot of freedom, being in charge and all. I rent a workspace near campus and inherited all of Dad's tools, which is cool and full circle."

"Well, your father sounds bigger than life. Like you."

They continued to pepper one another with affection, alternating between playful pecks and luscious, deep kisses. "A documentary about beavers . . ." she joked-whispered into his ear. "Am I making you horny, baby? . . ."

"Insert very easy wood joke here . . ."

Kat doubled over laughing, then asked in a faux-seductress voice, "So did wood always feel right in your hands, Jacob?" He admitted it did—and not for the more ribald reasons. He recalled how he and his dad loved to design and craft impeccable tiny wooden boxes together. Kat nodded, lapping up anecdotes about her manly woodworker date. Jacob delighted in how they veered from jokes to seriousness in the blink of an eye; it was how his family had always communicated.

Jacob took a breath and leaned in close. "Kat . . . I just . . . I want to know you. If I overstep my bounds, tell me, okay? . . . Spray me with a water bottle or something." He was grateful for her snicker and knew it was code to proceed. "Did you grow up with a lot of foster families? . . . One in particular? It couldn't have all been terrible, right?"

Kat shook her head, swallowed hard. It was flabbergasting he found her interesting at all, but she felt him lean into her struggles, genuinely curious. She realized her pain could be a ticket to differentiate herself from all the others. "Chronicling my very strange childhood is actually the subject of my memoir."

"That's amazing. And healing, I'm sure."

"Yes. But it's not easy. I tend to think of my adolescence in terms of parentheses."

"Parentheses? . . ."

"Yes. The little couches we put around our life. The bookends of time that mark various passages."

Jacob nodded. "I like that. The parentheses of life."

"Right. Like, I had time with the Hippie Dippies. There was a lot of quinoa involved."

"Probably before quinoa was a thing."

"Ohmygod, so much quinoa. And then there were the Christian Soldiers, the Do Nothings, the Bitters."

"Please tell me there wasn't the Slap-the-Faces."

"Actually, there sort of was."

Jacob's smile fell, again doubt clouded his face. "Oh god. I'm sorry. Again. For being cavalier. But I . . . god, I'm bad at this."

"At what? Talking about real stuff? You're doing better than most guys."

"Well, the bar is pretty low. My mom insisted she raise me and Pete to be communicators, to be emotive . . . but . . . sorry, Mom." Just hearing a reference to Carol's name filled Kat with new light.

"Jacob. Your mother has done an impeccable job. Her talent is not only literary, obviously."

Jacob beamed with pride. "Thank you. And I gotta say-—this is so different, Kat. My second dates don't usually involve conversations about my dad dying."

Kat smiled and hoped her face did not broadcast how few dates she'd actually had—second or otherwise. To disguise her naivete, she lowered her eyes and urged him on with a sly grin. "Then perhaps we should talk less . . ."

Jacob nodded, his eyes eager in the moonlight. Conversation was over for now. He leaned into her with passion, kissing her deeply. Her tongue lilted and explored his mouth; she would have unhinged her jaw and swallowed him whole if she could. She felt vague pride—and latent fear—to realize Jacob's pants were straining with ropey heat. His hand gently found her breast and she moaned slightly as he caressed her. Kat's entire body vibrated with desire; it was pulpy and animal and everything she'd ever hoped for.

Kat was only mildly scared, the biggest surprise of all. She was mostly a throbbing green light. But Jacob intuitively knew she needed time, and he didn't push. Patience might have been an entirely new and satisfying turn for him, definitely one that was appropriate for Kat.

Finally as they lay curled up on the hood of his car, sunlight peeked over the horizon, illuminating the stoic cacti who stood at attention.

"Look. We did it again." Jacob gestured to the sunrise as the desert bloomed in orange.

"Beautiful," Kat exclaimed. They basked in the view, and their heat, savoring the delicious perfection of the moment. "I can't believe we stayed up all night again. And trust me when I say this—I don't miss sleep for just nothin'."

"Then . . . I'm glad I'm not just nothin'."

"Oh, you're somethin' alright . . ."

Their exhausted lips connected once more, tender and lovingly bruised. In minutes the sun officially crested; everything was awake. It was a new day.

. . .

Their third date lasted an entire weekend. The fourth date went longer. By the fifth, they stopped keeping track. Kat didn't have to pretend to be busy anymore, didn't have to play games. Jacob was helpless, so smitten and eager, verbalizing how different he was with Kat. Both Carol and Pete had commented Jacob was already altered by her. It surprised everyone.

Kat believed she'd always been waiting for Jacob. She knew—at least, wanted to believe—her relationship fears would dissolve with the right man. She wanted to taste the stuff of literature and had kept the beast of passion behind a locked door. But with Jacob it was so seamless, it was like he'd been there all along.

The most meaningful and welcome development that came as a result of their relationship was the utter transformation of Kat's confidence. As a feminist, she knew this was pathetic—that it would take a man's presence in her life to supplant her usual timidity with poise and certainty—but she also knew it was 100% true. Her nagging and often cannibalizing insecurity, something that had weighed her down for her entire life, was entirely dismantled as soon as she started dating Jacob. It was practically manic, the sudden joy she had about everything—she was most definitely the very worst person to be around. Always humming a song, finding the positives in just about anything, writing well, and enjoying her job. If it wasn't her life, she'd have hated that girl.

Of course, her confidence could dip—if not crater—at a moment's notice. Kat was obviously not without her hang-ups. The past didn't melt away entirely, and she still needed reassurance and patience. But she knew she could thrive with someone like Jacob.

And he loved the challenges—or, perhaps more appropriately, the complexity—of Kat. He respected how she was so devoted to writing, the unconscious way she reminded him of his beloved mother. And everything about her that should've turned him off, drew him in: she was mercurial, she said off-kilter things. Mania bubbled up in her but could just as quickly retreat. It was fascinating and he was never bored.

. . .

Once, Kat declared they were going to have "an 80s teenage John Hughes mall day." Jacob picked up Kat with her hair in a scrunchie, an explosion of Aqua Net holding it to absurd heights. They listened to Tucson's 94.7—"soft rock from the 70s to today!"—blasting Whitney Houston and Milli Vanilli the entire way to the Tucson Mall. In the mall, Jacob vowed to find Orange Julius. The entire day had a neon vibrancy, such an absurd charm, it practically needed a soundtrack. Jacob had never realized the way he could be weird with Kat was what he'd been subconsciously seeking for his whole life.

In Macy's, Kat tried on the ugliest and most absurd shoes for sale, hilariously modeling skyscraper high heels replete with bold graphic cherries, orthopedic sandals that suggested life was over. People turned to stare with bemused looks as Kat loudly assumed the character of each shoe, alternating her voice and demeanor to reflect the state of mind of every loafer, clog, and pump. Jacob was charmed, holding his sides in laughter, collapsing on the leather couches of Macy's shoe department in joy. Kat was channeling something that day, riding comedic lightning.

He was blindsided by how his sister's beautiful roommate could so quickly invade his heart.

Jacob also told Pete about some of what Kat had survived and admitted he'd never so respected someone he'd dated before. Would he have been as strong as Kat if forced to live the same reality? He wasn't so sure. Because who would Jacob be without the constant support of his family? Without his brother, his sister, the memories of his father?

For the first time ever, Jacob could actually envision the idea of another woman becoming his own tribe. Maybe Kat could be the family he'd choose.

. . .

Kat couldn't believe she was in this urban oasis restaurant—the hip sort of space featured in ads to sell life insurance and anti-anxiety meds, suggestive of an inspired life—awaiting one of her idols to arrive for lunch. She also couldn't believe she was dating Carol's gorgeous, brilliant son. Or that Carol Walsh, herself, had promised to arrive with thoughts on one of her short stories.

But it was all true. Carol approached their table, waving pages and smiling broadly. She arrived as if a long-lost friend, or the perfect aunt. There was nothing not to like about Carol Walsh: she was full of warmth, smiles, and a sassy streak that came out with a few cocktails. She was quick to cry and quicker to laugh. She could do a spot-on impersonation of a QVC pitchwoman and discuss Proust in the same conversation. Her writing classes at the University of Arizona always filled up quickly, and it didn't take long for her to develop a near cult-like following.

The two hugged; Kat inhaled her hair. "You smell so good!" she commented as they sat down at the table.

"Thank you! It's all my essential oils. I'm always slathering some miracle or another onto myself."

Laughing, Carol took Kat's hand. It was immediately intimate, so much so it almost made Kat uncomfortable. She reminded herself this was, in fact, a good thing, and leaned forward.

"I'm just going to cut to the chase. First of all, your short story is heroic. *Heroic.*"

"Really?!" Kat froze. She wanted to bury her head in her hands in disbelief. Beaming, Kat couldn't help herself: small tears formed from joy, relief, fear, or maybe just from smiling so broadly.

"Really. 'Darling Buds of May' is haunting. Your language is spare, melodic. And I did not see the ending coming. *At all.*"

"Oh I'm so glad! I'm so happy! Thank you for saying that, for reading it. For everything!" Kat reached for her water glass and nearly knocked it over. "Dear god. I'm shaking!" She held up her hand to show the tremor, and Carol grabbed it, clutching her with affection.

"You should submit to the *Kenyon Review*."

"I couldn't! Is it ready?!"

"I have a few edits, but yes. It's lyrical and timely. And I'm so relieved. I was worried I'd hate it, or worse, think it mediocre and have to fumble over bland compliments. So thank you for being so talented."

A hip waitress with multiple piercings approached with a sly smile and a shock of green hair. "Welcome to Nook. Can I get you something to drink?"

Carol beamed. "I would not turn down a buttery Chardonnay."

"Same."

"Coming right up . . ."

Carol turned her face up to the sun and basked in the rays. "God we're lucky. Do you know what the temperature is today in Detroit?"

"No. What?"

"Oh, I don't know, but it's not this." The two laughed as Carol tore into the breadbasket. "Now then. I want you to know that my son . . . well. Let's just say, he is *quite* smitten."

Kat looked down at her napkin, her giant stupid grin eclipsing her whole face. It wasn't just her mouth that was smiling. Her hair was smiling. Her knees were smiling. "He's not the only one."

"I'm biased of course, but Jacob's always been just a made-up boy, like a fairy-tale. Sweet, smart, gorgeous—good grief. It's all my side of the family, of course." Carol grew serious. "I'll admit: I'm usually so disappointed with whoever he's with. So you are a wonderful first."

On cue, the waitress set down the wines, which Kat quickly lofted to toast.

"To you, Carol. For creating such a masterpiece of a son." Carol happily clinked her glass. "And for saying my short story is worthy of *Kenyon Review*. I wouldn't be more thrilled if you'd said I'd won the Arizona lottery."

"Well, I mean every word. You're damned talented. Period. Now then. I wanted to get to know you better, separate from Jacob. I want some *girl time*," Carol trilled. "So how did you land in Arizona, anyway?"

Kat explained she'd received a generous college scholarship from the Live Out Loud Foundation, an organization committed to helping young women in need that she'd miraculously found online at her local library. Kat wrote an essay explaining her plight—bouncing from foster home to foster home, books her only escape—and apparently the board was so moved that several had cried. The foundation allotted funding for Kat's housing and living expenses, even awarding additional financial support for graduate work.

"Stop! Aren't the power of words a glorious thing?! . . . And does Tucson suit you?"

"Yes. It's so . . . other. But I actually like that it's so tough and rocky. Maybe it's weird to say, but I think it suits me."

"Like landing on the moon! That's what I thought when I first visited. There's a heartiness in Tucson I relate to."

"Right. It's authentic. Like you, Carol." Kat glowed, feeling the heady combination of the warmth from the Chardonnay, the afternoon sun, and praise from her literary idol.

"Oh, we're getting a big ole dessert, it's official. This is going to be a nice, looong lunch . . ." Kat bloomed with the knowledge Carol genuinely wanted to spend time with her.

"To be honest, I'm not sure I need any more sugar, Carol. This moment is already my dessert."

Carol clutched Kat's hand, cementing their burgeoning and rare bond.

. . .

Jess knocked over a glass of water trying to turn off her phone alarm. Half asleep, she awkwardly stabbed at the phone's buttons, making the noise stop. In no rush, she stretched across the bed, cat-like, then rolled out of bed and ambled for the door . . . already knowing the answer to her question.

Jess peered into Kat's room and found a made bed. "Once again," she said to the empty room.

Kat was too pretty to bring to the house to sunbathe. That was her first mistake. And Kat had been reading real literature poolside, which Jacob would love. Looking back, it was just stupid on her part. But Kat really admired her mother's novels and wanted to meet her, so she relented. Jess had hoped Jacob would be at the gym or sleeping off a hangover at some other girl's house. But he had made an appearance—a memorable one, at that—and now her roommate's bed remained empty night after night.

Basically, Jess lived alone now, something she did not like in the first place. She *had* rented a two-bedroom apartment and sought out a roommate for a reason.

Jess got up, threw her hair into a ponytail, and laced up her sneakers. It was a long run today in the morning heat for the University of Arizona Wildcat runners (the team she coached), and they got their miles in early. She would try to push this unfortunate development with her brother out of her mind. Besides, it was probably just a matter of time before her elusive roommate was blubbering all over Jacob. Goddamn her brother for being so attractive. Even she found herself startled by him when he entered a room sometimes, as if he was a new neighbor she'd spy on, and not her brother at all.

Jess wouldn't admit it out loud, but she almost secretly delighted in the knowledge Jacob was still struggling slightly to find his true passion. His custom cabinetry work felt like a pit stop on his way toward something else. He was handy but not in the same way their father had been. Over drinks a few years ago, Jacob had mentioned that when women found out he built custom cabinetry like his deceased dad, the girls either recoiled or simpered. It was decidedly blue collar, even though his high-end work went into some of Tucson's fanciest homes in the foothills. Still, despite Jacob's physical beauty and its predictable power, he hadn't yet found his true gift, not like she had with running or Pete had with music. But in a country that valued a face as much as a genuine talent, this seemed to be more than enough.

. . .

Jacob could not believe Kat had never spent the night over at a man's house before. It was shocking.

They had been together for a few months; weekends were always spent together. It was expected at this point. But Jacob understood why she'd mostly avoided romance. He was relieved to hear there had never been an actual rape, but the foster dad in Boise had touched Kat inappropriately, and the congenial youth pastor had done the same in Denver. The wife in Sacramento always wanted to watch her shower, claiming it was an effort to "keep her safe."

"I need your patience, Jacob," she said while they spooned next to one another in his bed. They were practically naked, warm flesh against warm flesh. She stroked the backside of her hand up and down the inside of his arm. "I want to . . . do things. To be with you. Badly. I do. But . . ."

"I'll trust you'll know when the time is right. I won't push, Kat. I'm not going anywhere."

Kat could not believe Jacob allowed her to just to snuggle into his warmth night after night. Even when they'd had a little extra wine and rationality might have been a little clouded, they honored what Kat's comfort level was. Of course, they'd fumble around, and she even grew to love how powerful giving him head made her feel. In that moment, she owned him so completely, and she started to crave the sense of control. Mostly, Kat loved to make Jacob so happy.

Eventually and ever so slowly, Kat allowed Jacob to touch her. The first time he slowly lilted her to climax, completely in touch with her rhythms, she had thundered with the release of a thousand sexless nights. The world blotted into color and Kat found herself so overcome she wept. Jacob held her close and whispered to her, reassuringly.

"Are you okay?" he said, moved, but also concerned.

Kat wiped her eyes, still seeing stars. "Yeah."

"Pretty good, right?"

Kat laughed, overcome. "More like *fucking fantastic*."

Jacob kissed her softly. "There's a reason it's a pretty popular concept."

Swept up in vulnerability and passion, Kat rolled on top of him and pinned his arms above his head. She looked him dead in the eye, her emerald gems flashing with mischief. "I want to, Jacob. I want to make love to you."

"Well . . . now? . . . You, uh, just . . ."

Kat encircled her hand around his stiffness. "I know you want to . . ." She moved her hand up and down, just slow enough to make him squirm, watching his eyes glaze with desire. He moaned. "I want you," she whispered in his ear, her tongue nibbling on an earlobe. She was emboldened, an absolute sex goddess of fire.

"Kat . . ."

She guided herself to him, slippery with heat as she steered Jacob, entering her ever so slightly. Then he suddenly pulled away.

"*What the hell?!*" Kat hotly barked, retreating from his embrace.

Jacob's eyes clouded with confusion, startled by her explosion. He quickly reached into a drawer and pulled out a condom in explanation. He slid it onto his eager penis.

Her eyes glowed with renewed warmth and desire, no longer confused. She pulled him closer, wrapping her whole arms around him, feeling the full weight of his body on top of hers. "I want you, Jacob. And . . . and I want you to know . . . That I think I'm . . ." Kat paused, then gulped. "I *am* falling in love with you."

He pulled back, just enough to make eye contact. "I love you, too, Kat."

Jacob guided himself to Kat, slowly, letting her welcome him. Her hips thrust rhythmically at first, and then all at once, feeling the whole of him. Kat gasped, one hand clawing his back, and the other gripping the side of his butt, clinging to the muscle there, waiting for the initial pain to subside. The sting soon dissolved, and she moved her body around him again in abject pleasure.

Kat was an ocean of desire. Her lust for him was all-consuming.

Jacob tilted her back so he could see into her eyes. *Are you okay? . . .*

She lowered her eyes, shy, but sexy, answering, *Yes yes yes*. She didn't know how to say it, the way this feeling was just so primal. She wanted to be filled by him, she'd break in half if she had to. It was a feeling she'd always needed, always craved, always wanted.

What began gently moved quickly to frantic waves, both in sync and each thrust more fervent than the one before. "More. More. More," Kat panted, and Jacob complied with her insistence. "Yes, yes, YES . . ." Kat's eyes closed in bliss, her head thrown back. Jacob reveled at her from above, this creature writhing in pleasure, this magical person. Her beautiful breasts rose in time, her skin already glistening and rosy from their fervor. He sucked her erect nipples. He could feel her slipping out to sea, liminal, he captured her cheek with his palm, letting her turn into him and bite his thumb. The other hand found her, rubbing her in time.

From the inside out, Kat melted. Her toes curled, legs wrapped around Jacob seizing, a sound lyrical and guttural coming from her, persisting until she felt like she might evaporate from pleasure itself.

Jacob climaxed just as Kat bit down on his thumb in ecstasy; groaning loudly and panting, exhausted with bliss. It was a thing of rapture, sublime and gratifying on a scale he'd never experienced. Overwhelmed, chests heaving against each other, they started laughing, marveling at the entire thing. Tears streamed anew for Kat as she wrapped her arms around Jacob's neck, pulled him tight, and inhaled. It smelled of Jacob, but different. She rolled to her side, facing him.

"How do you feel?" he whispered.

"Happy. Mostly, I'm just so grateful it was you, Jacob. And not just because you've been patient. I mean, not everyone has such a satisfying first time . . ." She blushed.

Jacob beamed back. "I know this is a big deal for you, Kat, and it is for me, too. I'm . . . well, 'honored' sounds sort of creepy, but I am. Sex is still significant, even when it's casual." He looked away with a winsome smile. "You made it so special for me, too." Jacob kissed her and she collapsed into his bare chest, her chestnut hair spilling across him.

Kat moved over him, kissed his mocha chest, and inhaled his scent again. "You know, this hasn't been as hard as I thought it would be."

"Sex? . . . I don't find it hard at all. I like to think of myself as a natural, actually." Jacob grinned down at her as she craned her head toward him to look into his eyes.

"Relationships, I mean. Love. Intimacy. All of it." Kat traced her fingers around his nipples, and he shivered. "It's because of you. You were the missing link, all this time." Kat snuggled deep into the crook of his arm.

"People are like puzzles. Some pieces fit together, some don't. It doesn't make sense, nor should it. Some people just feel like home."

"Beautifully put."

"Well, my mother is a novelist . . . And speaking of which, Mom said she had the best time with you at lunch—absolutely raved. Apparently I've finally made a good romantic decision."

Kat propped herself up on her elbow, eyes widening. "Really? Oh, I love to hear that! I just adore her. We did have the best time. And the fact she loved my writing? Fuhgeddaboudit."

Jacob grinned. "We all love you."

Kat leaned in again. No matter how many times their lips found one another, each kiss felt like the first kiss. Kat shifted until she was on top of him. Sitting upright, she stared down at him and gave a playful look. "How long do we have to wait until the next time . . . ? I'm not a virgin anymore, but I haven't had sex as a non-virgin either, so . . ."

Jacob smirked. "I think we can take care of that milestone right now." He reached up to her and playfully tweaked a nipple. "Only there's one thing . . ."

"What?"

"No more talking about my mother."

. . .

Kat was addicted. She started to crave him. To physically ache for him. Jacob would buzz in her mind like a persistent fly, and it was almost embarrassing. It *was* embarrassing. She would literally wonder if he was eating a sandwich. She would think about him eating a sandwich, and it would turn her on. Jacob liked a good turkey sandwich, and so did she. (See—right there, *So much in common! Turkey sandwiches! And he hated mayo, too!*) She wondered what he was dreaming. What he wanted to read next. She asked Jacob what his goddamn favorite color was, like a stupid teenage girl. He liked blue—cobalt to be specific—which she found very soothing. God, she was pathetic. It was a wonder she hadn't started dotting her i's with little hearts. It was all so predictably tragic.

Kat also couldn't believe how fascinating he found her. Of course, she had to be coy and not reveal too much, but her reserve worked in her favor. She left little breadcrumbs for him, offering just enough to keep him engaged. She noted which details he lapped up, which bored him. Granted, Kat's young life was fascinating, and in a macabre way, it was amazing how little she had to say to keep the embers of interest aglow. Kat was wise to only share limited amounts with Jacob. She told him about the foster father who liked to play the game "Everything But." Jacob recoiled and couldn't believe a child had to endure this. Where was the social worker? Where was the mother figure? Kat explained it was often the wife who cleaned up the mess and requested a transfer. It was hard for her to recall the bitter details, and Kat preferred to share them through her writing. Her spoken words stabbed at her heart. Still, the more Kat refused to divulge additional details, the more she felt her power rise with Jacob.

Weren't men supposed to not listen, to be aloof and terrible?

Jacob fed off her every word, eager for just one more story. He even pointed out when some facts didn't quite line up. And he was right.

Jacob leaned in. "So, who was like, the worst one? Who was the hardest family to survive? . . ."

"I think I've said enough today, Jacob," Kat said and grew quiet, pulling her knees up to her chest. He knew not to push more but still wanted all the details.

"And the drawbridge appears again . . ." Jacob traced Kat's graceful profile as they lay next to one another in his bed.

"I'm a woman of consummate mystery," she grinned.

"And consummate beauty," he added, and moved toward her so he could hold her face with both hands. He kissed her just a little too long, a little too fervent for it to have *just* been a goodnight kiss. She took the bait and nibbled on his lower lip, gently at first, then with attitude. They were naked immediately. She really was getting quite good at the entire affair.

THREE

JESS WAS EATING A BOWL of Grape-Nuts when Kat entered the apartment, all aglow. She was lit up from the inside and had never been more bewitching. In the past few months, her petals had bloomed, and she'd shed most of her chilly reserve. A small smile graced her lips. A bit guilty, but obviously enamored.

"So. You *are* alive after all," Jess said.

Kat sat down across from her, ready to finally discuss her relationship with Jacob. They'd skirted around the topic but had never actually had a real conversation about the development. "I realize I haven't exactly been around. But you got my rent checks, right?"

"Yeah, yeah." Jess took a long breath. "What's it been, a few months?"

"With Jacob, you mean? Nearly four months now."

"Wow. That was quick." Jess shook her head and grinned. "I knew taking you over to our pool was a bad idea."

"I'm really happy, Jess. And he is too. Honestly, I probably should thank you."

"Let's see how thankful you are when . . ." Jess's words trailed off, realizing she'd stepped in it.

"When what? He dumps me? I just don't think your brother is *that* flaky."

Jess took a long exhale. "Jacob's not a bad guy. Obviously. He dated Sienna for years in college."

"I've heard about Sienna."

"Yeah, she runs a Pilates studio in Scottsdale now; has two kids, hard-core conservative." She shrugged.

"Sounds dreadful," said Kat, and they both laughed.

"Look, I get it. Jacob's hot. I know he's my brother, and I'm not supposed to say that, but c'mon. He could sell shit all day long on QVC with that face and that charm. But he's also fun and cool as hell. He's also just . . . well, sort of aimless, right?"

"I think his cabinetry business is really coming along and he *does* have a plan," Kat countered. "He's also very well-read."

"He's Carol Walsh's child, dude! It's a prerequisite—Mom used to read us Shakespeare aloud when we were, like, four."

"Oh, I know that, too," Kat said with a confidence that suggested she knew Jacob better than his own sister. It bugged the shit out of Jess.

"It's just this, okay? You're cool. I don't want you to get hurt. That's all."

"Thank you for your concern. It's not like I wanna get hurt either," Kat agreed. "But both Pete and your mom assured me that Jacob is so different with me. We all had dinner; she made her carne asada. And your mom told us all about her Barcelona days. So amazing."

"Oh god, you got the Barcelona speech? . . . She had more than two glasses of wine?" Jess laughed.

"And a margarita. It was more 'speeches,' not 'speech.'" They laughed. "She was so happy to hear that Jacob deleted all his Tinder and things on his phone a while ago."

"Whoa. That is serious!"

Kat smiled, aware this was a victory and happy to prove to Jess her worries were unfounded.

"But does the guest house of it all bug you? You know, he basically lives with his mom?"

"Well, it is his own space. And your mother is amazing. I mean, *I* want to live with your mom." Kat grinned. "Besides, Jacob's assured me the guest house is temporary. He's getting his own place. He knows he's too old for it. And like I said, he does have a plan."

"Look. Live your life. Enjoy. My brother isn't . . . you know, *bad* . . . he's just . . ."

"—Jacob. He's wonderfully Jacob." Kat finished her sentence.

"So I see me protesting will do nothing anyway," Jess acknowledged. Kat slowly shook her head no with a grin. She looked down, blushed.

"You know he's my first boyfriend. My first real boyfriend, I mean."

Jess was gobsmacked. "Really? Dude . . . you're . . . what? 25?"

"Yes," Kat said embarrassed, the sun suddenly drained from her eyes.

Jess could tell she was hurt. "I'm sorry. I'm just shocked."

"It's okay. It's complicated, and you know a bit about my past. Mostly, I've just been focused on my writing. So it's not *that* weird," Kat said defensively.

"Jacob likes unusual. The unexpected. This certainly fits the bill," Jess observed.

Kat grinned. "We really do have a great time together, Jess." She softened again. "And trust me, no one is as shocked as I am."

"Alright. I'm happy for you. Knock yourself out. And I mean it," Jess said, her tone now warm and without reservation.

"Thanks. I admit . . . it's . . . well, heady. And new. But mostly, for the first time in my life, I just feel . . . *normal.*"

Jess nodded and grinned. "Oh—and I'm sorry about your fish. I noticed Garp was no more."

"Oh. Yeah. He got the flush."

"They don't last too long."

"It wasn't that. I knew I wouldn't be around much. So I just . . ." Kat mimicked flushing a toilet and waved good-bye.

"You just flushed him? Garp was alive?"

"Well . . . I knew I was mostly staying at Jacob's, and I didn't want him to starve or anything."

"I woulda fed him! He was sweet! He'd, you know, swim up to the glass when I went into the room. He was a friendly little fish!"

"Jess. It's no big deal. He was on sale for $7.99 at PetSmart." Kat got up and gathered her things. "Anyway, great to see you. And I'm glad we cleared the air."

She nodded but remained silent as Kat packed up and left the apartment. Jess was unnerved. It didn't seem normal to just flush a perfectly healthy fish down the toilet. Was she making too much of it? Jess realized there was little she could do, and within a few minutes, the fish had already swum out of her mind.

· · ·

In no time at all, Kat and Jacob were off to the erotic races. Kat's chilly reserve melted—she initiated, she was frothy, she was weirdly good. She even liked purchasing condoms at 7-11, looking the salesman in the eye, admitting her intentions. With Jacob, there was little fumbling, little hesitancy; she wanted him badly and let him know it over and over. And the feeling was mutual.

Kat laughed at how nervous she'd been. How unexpected and sudden the transformation had happened. It was a whiplash into desire.

"You sure you've never done this before?" Jacob asked, laughing. "You sure you don't have some, I don't know, a secret career in porn or something?" Kat playfully slapped his arm, grinning.

"I can't help it if I'm, like, a porn person."

"Porn star. Not 'porn person.'" Jacob kissed her shoulder.

"Thanks for helping me with my porn vocabulary. Porn star, got it."

"Just so you know—"

"I know. You're not into porn. You're entirely too sensitive for that. You have a feminist mother. You have a sister."

"I consider myself a feminist."

"Oh, c'mon," Kat needled. "That's just something men say to get women to sleep with them."

"What? No. No, it's not." Jacob sat up, his face inking with red. It was the first time he'd been the one retreating, and Kat was shocked by the strange shift. She sat up, too.

"Jacob, I—"

"—That was a pretty shitty thing to say, Kat." Jacob's voice was altered, unfamiliar to her. He sounded distant and it made her heart feverishly race.

They sat in unfamiliar silence, not the pleasant cloud of the loving, unspoken vocabulary they usually enjoyed. The air felt hostile. The axis had tilted.

"I'm sorry," Kat blurted. "But it *was* only a joke."

"Hilarious, Kat." His words were hot. Too hot. Kat grew more anxious, her hands fluttered in nerves. Words jumbled in her brain, unable to form coherent sentences. If she was new to coupledom and sex, she was more than new to the fights that tended to accompany them. No one had mentioned to her that logic didn't always play a starring role in adult relationships.

Jacob got out of bed and stared out the bedroom window at his mother's succulents and the pool where they'd first met. "But is that really what you think?!"

Jacob's voice rose as he searched for the words. "That I'm some douche who spouts progressive banalities to get *tail*?!"

"*DON'T! YELL AT ME!*" Kat thundered, covering her hands over her ears, clenching her eyes shut, surprising herself with the volume. Kat collapsed into a protective ball, rocking herself. The violence of her eruption was unexpected, and Jacob froze, knocked off his pedestal of anger, now more concerned with Kat.

Jacob was unmoored. He didn't know what was up or down. He watched Kat swaying back and forth, talking to herself, tears flowing. He saw her fingers dig deeply into her forearms, the skin puckering under her firm pressure. He instinctively went to her and tried to pull her hands away from her reddening arm. She flinched, as if his touch was acid.

"Hey. Kat," he said, trying to soothe her. "Kat. Look at me."

Kat's head stayed down; her rocking grew more violent.

"Kat."

Finally, she looked up, met his eyes. These were not sparkling emeralds of wonder, these were cold, unforgiving. Her black irises had gulped the green parts whole.

For an instant, Jacob almost backed off and let her go. He felt as if he'd gone to save a wounded dog on the side of the road, and it ended up snapping at him instead.

"Kat," he tried again, wanting to turn this around. He knew he was partially responsible for the tumultuous conversation, and he really loathed the unfamiliar tension. He wanted Kat back and to save her from herself; for this all to be cleared up. "It's okay, Kat." He really meant it.

"Is it?" she hissed. "It never is, you know. It *never* fucking is."

"What? . . . Kat . . . please. I just want you to know me better by now. That's all. That's why I got upset."

Kat paused.

"I guess . . . I guess you hit a nerve. I get so mad because a lot of people see me and assume 'douche.' I mean—I understand this is not remotely the equivalent of, like, the subjugation of women or anything . . ."

Kat's brow relaxed slightly, relieved to see Jacob retreat.

"Let me explain why I overreacted. And this is a small, maybe worthless, example—and frankly, this is just one of many—but . . . there's residual hurt, I guess." Jacob took a deep breath. "I joined this improv comedy troupe years ago and I was immediately nicknamed 'Quarterback.' And I was good! But everyone treated me like a fucking idiot because of my face. So finally . . . I just quit." Jacob paused. "And sure, in the history of universal wrongs, it's not huge, I realize. But it did sting, and I'm sensitive about it. I just . . . don't want people to think I'm a tool. It's one thing for other people to think that, but not you, too, Kat."

"Jacob, of course! . . . But again—I was simply TEASING about the feminist thing. Teasing!"

"I know. I do." Jacob reached for her; she clutched him back.

"Again, I overreacted, and I'm sorry." Jacob took a breath. "Mostly just know—I'm a feminist because everyone should want equality. Like that's complicated or something."

Kat smiled at him, softness emerging, finally. "Jacob. You're the best man I've ever met. I mean it." Her eyes twinkled once more with mischief. "A man with *so* many talents . . ."

Jacob grinned back at her, knowing full well what this meant. He moved his hands down to her breasts, lingering; her nipples immediately grew hard.

Desperate to get out of this funk, Kat pushed him back and tore off her robe, revealing only skin and a brief amount of silk. Jacob sat up, eyes dilated and heart pulsing. Never breaking eye contact, she stripped, laid down, and spread her legs.

And just like that, the fight was over. Their lovemaking was even more electric than usual, the kind of intense pleasure that upends marriages and instigates a total abandonment of rationality. Otherworldly. Neither of them was in a mood to do anything slow and gentle; for the first time Kat wanted to be fucked. They would be sore in the morning. Their mouths mashed together, fingers clawed into skin, they brought each other to the brink and then made eye contact—who would blink first? It was a bit of a tie, but Kat's orgasm was so loud, Jacob shoved his hand over her mouth to muffle it. Kat bit down, teasing, "I thought you said you were a feminist? Did you just put your hand over my mouth?" She couldn't contain her smile.

"My mom's making omelettes *right over there*!" . . . Jacob gestured to the guest house door as Kat writhed like an animal caught in a trap. Finally, her sensual gurgles and moans gave way to laughter, and they collapsed, entirely spent.

"Let's fight again as soon as possible," Kat panted.

"Yes, please," was all Jacob could say.

FOUR

SUNDAY NIGHTS TURNED INTO A regular thing for Carol and Kat, they didn't even have to confirm their gathering anymore. It was just a given they'd shop and cook together, first stopping at the Food Conspiracy Co-Op ("Everyone Can Shop. Anyone Can Join.") They'd putter through the produce aisle, a rainbow of organic goodness, God's candy on display.

"I like the misfit vegetables, the less obvious," Carol would say. She'd affectionately pick up a rutabaga. "You see? Give me a good rutabaga. Not quite cabbage, not quite turnip."

"That's what I say about myself—not quite a cabbage, not quite a turnip," Kat said, and Carol laughed, touching her arm. Another aging hippie grinned sheepishly at the duo, taking in their chemistry. Kat burned with weird pleasure that their relationship looked so intimate, it appeared they were a glamorous academia couple. Kat loved it if people assumed they were together. Carol, too, liked the unspoken energy, the silent acknowledgment their pairing was indeed special.

"I was thinking nothing too extravagant this evening . . . lamb meatballs, a simple salad, some roasted fennel?" Carol asked breezily. Kat looked down; something was amiss. "Did I say something?"

"Lamb. I'm sorry. I don't want to be difficult. But . . . I just can't. I don't eat lamb," Kat apologized.

"Darling! Half my friends don't either! I'm just a mean old woman out of a fairy tale—and I'm fine with that—but I want you comfortable," Carol cooed.

"Thank you, Carol," Kat beamed.

"Of course! Nothing to apologize for! I should be more sensitive myself but I'm a dyed-in-the-wool carnivore, an absolute dinosaur of a meat-eater."

"Mama Rex," Kat bequeathed.

Carol winked. "I like it! Feel free to call me that."

They continued through the store, the sounds of Lionel Richie's "All Night Long" filled the aisles. Carol joined in, singing with gusto. People turned to stare, some with charmed smiles, some less so.

Carol sang along, doing a little cha-cha, then looked at Kat expectantly, as if handing off a baton.

Kat so wanted to continue the moment but had never heard the song before. In desperation, she mirrored Carol's last line and repeated it. By some miracle, Kat had stumbled into the right beat, and Carol assumed Kat, too, was a closet Lionel Richie fan. Carol fell into hysterics, wiping tears.

"My, you're fun. I had no idea you're also secretly in love with the woefully undervalued dentist-and-grocery-store musical genre," Carol joked. "It's all so soothing, isn't it, after all this time, to still remember some Lionel or Mariah or what have you?" Kat laughed along but didn't really follow. "It makes sense why Jacob is so smitten. You're basically a younger—and let's be honest, more attractive—version of me. *Much* more attractive."

Kat's face turned crimson with delight. "Oh, thank you, but that's not true . . . And I could never achieve what you have creatively, you're—"

"Stop. Never diminish your literary talent. Your work is damned good. Precise."

"That's what I say about you," she offered shyly.

"And that's why Jacob is so gaga. But it's all predictably psychological, the boy latently searching for his mother in a partner," Carol explained matter-of-factly, nudging her knowingly. "I'm just relieved he seems to have slowed down. Enough with the SoulCycle vixens already," she said, rolling her eyes.

"Thank you, Mama Rex."

Carol put her arm around Kat. "Kindred spirits are not so scarce as I used to think. It's splendid to find out there are so many of them in the world."

Kat held back the hot tears brimming at the corners of her eyes. "*Anne of Green Gables*. One of my favorites."

Carol nodded and gave a knowing smile. "I *knew* you were my people, Kat."

Kat finally felt like she'd found her home, her family. Carol was her rightful mother all along, everything she wanted her to be—a literary hoot, alive and open, fun and affectionate. It was beyond Kat's wildest dreams. She wanted nothing more than to understand every single Walsh family joke, every turn of phrase, every nuance. With Jacob's family, there was an intoxicating swirl of intellect and whimsy, of love and warmth. Kat had never felt more at home.

Literature, of course, is filled with endless theories on family. Tolstoy famously stated, "All happy families are alike; each unhappy family is unhappy in its own way." Kat read that line under her bed covers for years and wondered if this Russian man could ever fathom just how lacking her family was.

But perhaps all happy families *were* alike—perhaps it was as uncomplicated as *they simply liked one another.*

Carol looked into Kat's eyes and could see she was having a moment. Knowing just how much writers feel all the emotions, she squeezed Kat's hand knowingly and winked. "Come on," she gestured. "We can have more emotional conversations in the wine aisle. We need a good cabernet for dinner."

. . .

Jacob was in his workspace, finalizing his latest commission and polishing a cabinet drawer to perfection. His clients had wanted to paint the cabinets a sage green, but Jacob had talked them into simply polishing the textured wood. The pecan's swirls of blondes and earthy reds and browns mimicked the serpentine patterning in their accompanying new marble counters. Concealing the wood's natural gorgeousness with color would have been a travesty, and Jacob gently convinced the clients to only paint the island. These cabinet doors would be allowed to dazzle in their existing naturalistic magic.

Jacob's phone rang, and he dug a dirty hand into his jeans pocket.

"Petey Pete!"

"Hey, man. You have a second?"

Jacob put down his sander. "For my only brother, sure. What's up?"

"An incredible opportunity just popped up. I'm so psyched. I told you about the jazz fest, right?"

"In Monterey?"

"No. Quito."

"Ecuador? I thought that wasn't a go?"

"It's back on! The Ecuador JazzFest this year is at the El Pobre Diablo Jazz Club. And they want me to come back!"

Jacob stepped outside, squinting into the sun. "Ah, excellent! That would be so cool."

"Yeah. And I want you to come."

"Seriously? Wow . . . I've always wanted to check out South America."

"Right?! You can tag along for free! I mean, you hafta buy a plane ticket, but don't you have a ton of miles, too? And we can share a hotel."

"But doesn't Maya want to go?" Maya had been with Pete for two years. She was a goofy, no-nonsense Black woman from Charleston who despised the South but adored the Southwest. Maya shared Pete's passion for music and loved babying him. She worked in marketing, but when she spoke about work, Jacob found it difficult to follow. Still, Maya was well-read and fit easily into the family.

"She's got a big deadline; work's a mess now. I just thought you and I would have the best time!"

Jacob *was* nearly finished with this big job . . . "Oh—you know what?! My buddy Mateo mentioned he went down to Oaxaca a few years ago and bought a ton of artisan pieces. Lots of stuff, but mostly those alebrijes, the Mexican folk art animals Mom loves. Anyway, he shipped a ton of it all back to Tucson and made a *killing*. Just went store to store and the buyers gulped it up whole. The mark-up was insane."

"So it'll be a business trip then!"

Jacob nodded, smiling, and realized it was already a done deal. When a trip plopped down from the sky, Jacob knew not to say no, and he relished the idea of one more mad quest with Pete while they were both young and unattached. They'd spontaneously journeyed to Belize a few years ago, and the entire trip was unforgettable. They'd even snorkeled with manatees, which to this day they both thought was one of the coolest things they'd ever done.

Jacob also knew soon enough he'd likely be best man for Pete and Maya's wedding, and who knew where Jacob's own life trajectory was headed. The window of opportunity for youthful flights of fancy and spontaneous travel would eventually come to a sudden close, and Jacob intended to suck the marrow out of life while he still had the chance.

"Okay, I'm in," he said. "But the first round of drinks is on you."

. . .

On weekends, Jacob and Kat always went to open houses. Whenever a placard appeared with a red arrow playfully pointing to a house with an open door, they stopped. Giant cheesy real estate agent smiles beckoned from the open house signage, arms crossed in a friendly stance as if to say "Please come in! Take a flyer, grab a bottled water, drop half-a-million dollars! It's a breeze!"

Jacob loved it more than Kat, but she played along. He liked to point out the polished brass finishes, the coved ceilings, the indoor/outdoor flow so desirable in Tucson. Kat nodded but didn't really get it—sure, rooms could be pretty, but all she needed was four walls. It was easy enough to get art from Etsy and fake a nice aesthetic.

But Jacob savored the details. He could talk shop with the real estate agents, and Kat saw they were impressed. In fact, Jacob spoke so smartly, they often asked if he was an agent himself.

"Just have a head for it, I guess," Jacob would say with more than a little bit of pride.

More often than not, Kat and Jacob would come up with roles before entering the house. Jacob was a retired hockey player; Kat had just arrived from Belarus and was his new young bride. Or Jacob had just moved from Pennsylvania where the jobs had dried up; Kat had asthma and the desert air served her well. Or Jacob had just won the lottery in Texas and Kat was his high school sweetheart; the turn of events had escalated their long-lost romance, and they both realized they wanted to be together. "I'd marry him without the money, of course, but now it's just easier, you know?" Kat said in a convincing Southern accent, mimicking Blanche from *The Golden Girls*. She really did love that show.

"You could say the lottery win *crystallized* things," Jacob noted to the real estate agent with a nod.

"I'll bet!" the spray-tanned agent chirped. "And a new house *is* in order, then! You get a lot of bang for your buck in Tucson, compared to Austin."

"So true, so true," Jacob twanged.

It was always a struggle to contain themselves by the end of the tour, and Jacob and Kat would giggle driving away from the house if they even made it that far. Kat loved that they had these little inside jokes, something that was just theirs. If she had read something like this in a book, she would have wanted to be them. And now she was.

Kat's memoir was difficult and plodding, but it was slowly taking shape. Jacob was a distraction of course, but he understood her creative process and valued it. He encouraged it and gave her plenty of space; he even offered astute observations about her pages. A voracious reader himself—even if his preferences ran in the more masculine direction—he was a helpful ally in every sense.

When Kat watched Jacob read her work, she held her breath. He would nod in appreciation of her craft. That meant everything to Kat.

"I like what you've done here. The detail with the neighbor in Idaho who owns the tiny horses is a nice, weird detail; it's very David Lynch," Jacob said one Saturday afternoon when they were still in pajamas.

"Well, that happened, of course. It *is* a memoir, after all."

"Right. But I like how you've given even the tragic a sort of lighter touch. These small, weird specifics that make it a more . . . satisfying, well-rounded reading experience."

"Very astute. I *am* trying to present the appalling with some humor. If that's possible."

"Augusten Burroughs proves it's more than possible."

"Well, I'm not quite Augusten Burroughs."

"But your talent *does* inspire comparisons." Jacob kissed Kat and she grabbed the back of his shirt collar, forcing him closer. She placed teasing kisses along his jawline, then started to move down his neck when Jacob moved backward, without explanation. He toyed at the ends of her hair as if nothing had happened, but when the two locked eyes, they recognized the inherent awkwardness of the moment. *Why had he pulled away?*

"Oh, uh, meant to ask you—Pete wanted all of us to go bowling. He and Maya take bowling very seriously, it's always a blast."

Kat was happy to see him re-engage. "I'd love that! I've never been."

"Really? . . . Well, it'll be fun. I'll figure out a time. You'll learn from the best."

Kat reached around his backside and gave his butt a wanton grab. "I already *have* learned from the best." Jacob grinned and leaned in, both slowly falling backward onto the sofa, kissing deeply.

Jacob sang her the chorus of "Afternoon Delight."

Kat's brow furrowed, not following.

"The song? 'Afternoon Delight'? . . ." Jacob cued. Kat shook her head, clueless, but desperately wanting to know the reference. "About sex in the afternoon? . . ." he continued, waiting for her to catch on.

Her brow smoothed immediately. A smile took its place. "You remember I didn't exactly get to listen to a lot of music growing up, right? . . . But this song, I think I could be a fan . . ." she said, teasing him, letting her robe slip past a shoulder, revealing bare skin.

"It's really quite iconic," Jacob said, playing along.

"Well . . . I can think of a few things that might make your *afternoon delightful*," Kat quipped back, chuckling at her corny pun. She grabbed at the drawstring on his pajama pants and pulled it free. Kat proceeded to demonstrate exactly how delightful an afternoon it would be.

The evening, too.

. . .

The following week was horribly busy, and by Friday, Jacob was spent. It had been a long day and his new clients were proving both demanding and indecisive—a horrid combination. All he wanted was a shower and a cold beer. And maybe a little solitude. An early night to himself would be ideal; he'd just started Haruki Murakami's latest novel.

Jacob stripped down, tossing his dusty work clothes into the hamper. After a quick shower, he went straight for the beer. He drank from the bottle and then took another sip. Laughter wafted from his mom's house—which was a pretty common situation, especially on a Friday night—and he walked to the window to check it out. On closer inspection, it wasn't laughter coming from the house, but sniffles interspersed with sobs.

The side door to the kitchen was open, and Jacob walked inside and followed the din of his mother's emotional cries.

"Jacob? Jacob, is that you?" his mother called from the living room, emotion thick. Jacob froze in response, his body tensed. "Your brilliant girlfriend and I are watching *Anne of Green Gables*. The newer Netflix series. Come, sit down!"

Jacob took a deep breath and had no choice but to join them. So much for the solitude.

. . .

Kat had been so thrilled to hear Pete and Maya had requested a double date. Kat quickly envisioned the two couples making their gatherings a routine affair, much like her and Carol's Sunday get-togethers. They'd all congregated multiple times at Carol's for family dinners but this time, Maya had personally reached out to Jacob, wanting to get to know Kat better. Maya was intimidatingly cool, but Kat was still hopeful they could fall into a sisterly pattern. It was another way Kat could show Jacob how much she was a natural fit for the convivial Walsh brood.

As the two couples entered the Cactus Bowl, it was obvious Pete and Maya were regulars, and not just because they brought along their own gear. The staff greeted them like beloved friends, even doling out a few hugs. Without having to ask, beers arrived for the two couples.

"We wanted to join a bowling league," Pete explained.

"It all just seemed so weirdly American, so kitschy somehow," Maya agreed.

"We had *Big Lebowski* hopes. Sadly, they were dashed."

Kat's eyes took in every detail of the couple, savoring the opportunity to study their body language and togetherness. Jacob had insinuated a marriage proposal was imminent, and Kat wanted any helpful information on becoming a Walsh. All education was appreciated at this point. Kat found Maya's general ease vaguely paralyzing. She was wholly confident in herself and seemingly her role in Pete's life. The two were always in contact, always in sync. *My god, they even had matching bowling shirts with name tags.*

"So what happened? With the league, I mean?"

"Oh. Too many practices. Truth was, I have weird hours as is, and we just didn't want to bowl at, like, ten in the morning on a Sunday."

Maya and Pete laced up their bowling shoes and pulled out matching teal bowling balls from their vintage carrying case. "We found this beauty at a garage sale," Maya said, gesturing to the case. "But we had to pay *cha-ching* for the balls. It was for Christmas last year."

"Monogrammed bowling balls!" Pete said in a Bronx-y, old-man voice. "It's the gift from the heart."

"For you, darling, the world," Maya said, laughing. She wrapped an arm around Pete and delicately removed a crumb from the corner of his mouth. Hopping up, she clapped to herself like a teacher about to start a lesson plan. "First, Kat, we need to set the stage! This is your first time bowling, so we have to make it memorable!" Maya linked arms with her and dragged Kat to the gleaming, modern jukebox, inserted a twenty-dollar bill, and immediately began flipping through the song selections. "Oh, E4 all day long . . ."

She hit a few buttons and the opening riffs of "I Wanna Be Your Lover" by Prince roared to life. Maya couldn't contain her joy and sang along. Kat nodded with a grin, inert. She didn't know the song but tried to fake it, mumbling garbled words with the hopes no one would notice she had no idea of the lyrics. Dark voices in Kat's head began to mumble to her as well, telling her she was full of shit and pathetic and would never fit in with the Walshes or anywhere else.

"You must love Prince. Everyone loves Prince," Maya yelled over the music.

"Oh. Yeah. 'Raspberry Beret'!" Kat croaked, grateful for the title.

"One of my lesser favorites of his. But . . . I guess 'Raspberry Beret' has its own charm. Put it in!"

Kat searched for the song and entered the subpar choice, hoping to appear breezy. "I mean, I get it, it's no 'When Doves Cry' . . ."

Maya smiled at Kat, narrowing her eyes in a challenge, singing the first line of the second verse of the Prince hit. Kat licked her lips and half-heartedly sang the second line, causing her voice to awkwardly crack, effectively ending the challenge with a question mark.

Maya laughed. "'Violets,' not 'violence.' But close enough! Get some juicy stuff going 'cause we are getting our bowl *on*!" Kat exhaled; the infraction didn't seem to lose her any points as Maya danced back to the team's lane. She then pretended to do some earnest stretches as if she was preparing for an Olympic event.

Kat entered every Prince song in the jukebox she could find and rejoined the crew. They cooed when each number started up and were impressed Kat had stumbled upon some of The Purple One's lesser-known hits. Kat had fumbled her way to a triumphant score. Pete and Maya high-fived Kat, and she felt the monsters of doubt retreat in her mind, dousing the inner beasts of self-loathing with beer and willful compartmentalization.

Pete handed Kat a bowling ball. "Okay, this one is latex for better grip. And we're gonna get you doing a mad 1-3 pocket soon enough."

"Be kind! You've got a virgin on your hands!" Maya called and Kat's face immediately colored with red heat.

Pete intricately laid out how the ball would spin and demonstrated his own technique, sending his bowling ball down the lane with thundering certainty, scoring a deafening strike.

"Whooo hoo! That's what I'm talking about!"

Pete gently guided Kat's hand placement. "Alright. Let 'er rip." Kat deeply inhaled, keenly aware all eyes were on her. She lined up and did her best to emulate what she'd just seen Pete do. Her ball landed with a horrifying thud and rolled immediately into the gutter.

Kat squealed and covered her mouth with her hands in mock horror, laughing.

Maya wrote a bold **2** on some paper and held Kat's rating up. "A slow start! Get back on that horse!"

Pete gave Kat more pointers as they patiently waited for her ball to clear the gutter and magically return via the underground tunnel. With the beer warming her insides and emboldening her psyche, Kat grabbed her ball and walked to the line with unearned confidence.

"Give 'em hell, baby!" Jacob called.

Kat took her time, analyzing her next move. Finally, she clutched the ball with both hands granny-style, sending the hot pink orb slowly down the lane.

"Giving exactly no thought to form, our intrepid Kat has a style that is entirely her own!" Pete joked in a winning British accent. The crew howled with laughter, anticipating with bated breath as the ball maintained a straight line, crawling toward the pins. Miraculously, the ball connected to the pins, sending them all collapsing, slowly toppling the entire set.

Kat jumped up in glee, bouncing madly, yelping up a storm. They all responded as if she'd just won Wimbledon. Jacob lifted Kat into his arms and twirled her triumphantly, placing a fat kiss on her lips.

"You see? See why she's so fantastic?!" Jacob excitedly asked his brother.

The game continued and the beer flowed. Kat found her granny style of bowling—while amateurish—was weirdly effective. She continually got strike after strike and baffled the entire bowling alley. Even others grew curious about the beautiful young woman's bizarre consistency with her atrocious bowling style.

At the bar they placed orders for just about every fried item on the bowling alley's menu; bottles clinked, and joy vibrated throughout Kat's body. Before long, her fears had ebbed. Her contributions to conversation were inspired and witty. She felt truly accepted, thrilled with the knowledge she had scaled an unspoken Walsh mountain. Kat's mouth ached from smiling so much. It didn't hurt that Jacob kept touching her knee, her wrist, her hand. He'd almost never been quite this affectionate in public before, and Kat drank the attention up.

"You guys are going to have such fun in Quito," Maya said offhandedly, smiling at the two brothers.

Kat froze. "Quito?! Wait, *what? You're going to Quito?!*" She turned to Jacob.

Jacob looked at Pete, then to the floor. He exhaled. "Yeah. Um . . . Pete and I were talking about, you know, maybe taking a trip."

"A trip? Um, okay. I'm a little out of the loop here. What's going on, Jacob?!"

Maya looked to Pete, confused, unsure if she was in trouble. "He didn't mention it?" she said to Kat.

"No! No . . . he *didn't* 'mention' it!" Kat hissed, realizing her response was far from the lighthearted ambassador of fun she'd just proven herself to be. "I mean . . . Jacob, what the fuck is going on? Where's 'Quito'?!"

Trying to keep things cool, Maya replied, "Oh, it's in South America. I can't go, anyway. Work's nuts right now. It's just gonna be a boys' trip; they'll have a blast and come back with cool gifts."

Kat's head spun to Jacob, her eyes boring into the side of his head. He turned to face her. "I was going to talk to you about it. I'm finishing up a big job, but I do have a window . . . It all happened pretty fast."

Awkward silence filled the once-happy space.

Pete cleared his throat and tried to play the diplomat. "Kat, I got invited to a jazz fest, and I thought Jacob might wanna tag along. He could stay for free and both of us can use miles for the flight. My brother and I have always liked to travel. We snorkel, hike. It'd be cool."

"Okay, let me get this straight—I wasn't invited but Maya was? Is that right?" Kat knew she sounded needy and pathetic, yet in the moment she was absolutely unable to contain her wrath and hurt. Her eyes flickered with indignant rage.

"Whoa. Calm down, Kat," Jacob said.

"—Alright, don't *ever* tell a woman to fucking calm down!"

"Wow." Maya got up. "I'm gonna go use the bathroom." She walked off, shaking her head. Jacob's jaw tightened in dismay.

Kat felt Jacob's ire and backpedaled, painfully aware she'd caused a scene, and wanting more than anything to erase their impression of her. "I'm sorry, I just . . ." Now lame tears gathered in the corners of Kat's eyes and she wiped them, furious they'd fucking shown up at all.

"Kat, I didn't invite Jacob to make you upset. And we won't be gone too long," Pete scrambled, sweetly trying to placate her.

"You don't have to apologize, Pete. Kat's out of line." Jacob turned back to face her. His face was cold; this wasn't the Jacob she knew.

"Jacob." The tears spilled from her eyes, and no matter how much Kat willed them to stop, they continued to stream down her face.

Maya came back to the table, her spine stiff, her prior warmth absent. "Kat, you really should be grateful Pete and Jacob have one another. Personally, I'm stoked they're such good friends." Her words were so logical they cut deep.

"Oh, I know! I know that! I just . . . didn't know about this trip, and it threw me, you know? And, obviously, I didn't get invited and you did, and—"

"It's not a contest, Kat. And it's not like Jacob wouldn't have told you."

Jacob didn't look up and maintained his frozen displeasure.

"I'm sorry. Can we just, you know, go back to bowling? . . ."

No one said a word or made eye contact. Pete studied his fingernails; Maya looked to the ceiling.

"It was so much fun. I'm sorry I ruined this. And I'm . . ." Kat's words trailed off, the futility settling in.

Jacob finally looked over. "I think we should just call it a night. Pete and I will pay up here and meet you at the car." It was going to be a long time before Kat would be part of the family.

. . .

The car ride home was chilly and painfully silent. Any connection or joy she and Jacob had previously enjoyed had been flushed into the atmosphere, seemingly gone forever. Kat kept catching frantic glances of Jacob's profile as he kept his eyes straight ahead, gripping his steering wheel with white-knuckled pathos.

"Jacob. I'm sorry. I'm really sorry," she whispered above the whirring car engine. His unresponsiveness was cavernous and deadly. Kat's green eyes darted, unsure where to settle. Panic was everywhere.

"Weren't you going to tell me, though? That you were going to *South America?*"

"No, I was just going to head to the airport one day and not mention it." Jacob snapped on the radio, affronted by the stale sounds of cheesy pop music, and clicked it back off. "Of course, Kat. Of course I was going to tell you. I literally was going to tell you tonight—I just had no idea you'd lose your goddamn mind."

Words floated above her head, bouncing off one another, incoherent and meaningless.

Jacob stared off into space at a stoplight, slowly shaking his head. "God, tonight was embarrassing . . ."

Kat reached for his hand and he flinched from her touch.

"I also didn't realize I needed permission. I mean, Maya was cool about it! She wants Pete to be happy!"

The thin scab of stability Kat was clinging to was scraped clean and the dam gave way.

"Well, of course Maya's cool! Unlike fucking *me* who's just this shit show of embarrassment and totally fucking wrong!" The words hung in a pathetic haze, her attempt to garner sympathy a pitiful display.

Jacob's car came to a screeching halt in front of Sagewood Apartments. "Tell my sister hi."

Kat wasn't about to leave the car. Not like this. "Jacob, Jacob, *please!*"

Jacob leaned over her and opened her door, causing the car's maniacal *ding* to start looping. "Bye . . ."

Her hands reached out, grazed his face, and Jacob held her firmly by the shoulders. "Kat, I'm serious. I don't want to talk now. I want you to get out of my car."

Her nose bubbled forth with snot, mascara staining her entire face. "Jacob—"

"*Now!*" he thundered, and she had no choice but to crawl out, a withered shell. The moment his car door thunked shut, his SUV tires lurched forward, racing away.

In impotent fury, Kat reached down and picked up a rock and flung it at his car. The rock smashed into his rear window and Jacob screeched to a stop. Thankfully, the window remained, and Kat gasped at the fact that she'd made contact at all. His taillights remained still, and then he peeled out once again, the red dots getting further and further away until they were gone.

She fell to her knees in the parking lot.

. . .

Kat entered the unfamiliar apartment, half-expecting to find Jacob's sister sitting on the couch with an I-told-you-so grin. Instead, the space was empty and foreign. Kat then remembered Jess had texted she had a cross country invitational in Nebraska, and she was grateful Jess didn't have to see her in this woeful state.

She couldn't bear it.

Kat paced as if in a jail cell, muttering to herself as she attempted to put the grisly evening's puzzle pieces together. Of course, the night had started clumsily as Kat fumbled along, willing her nerves to not capsize the double date. But Kat had pulled herself out of a potential doom spiral with Maya when she hadn't recognized the Prince song, and she'd not let the flub destroy her. So why wasn't Kat rewarded for saving herself from herself?

Kat pulled out her phone and stared at it, willing it to ring. All she wanted was for Jacob to call, to right this ship and get to the make-up sex. The two couples could even go out again for a "do over," and return to their earlier easy rapport, all past indiscretions forgotten. They'd laugh about the misunderstanding soon enough.

Except maybe they wouldn't. Maybe this was the beginning of the end, and Pete would talk him out of dating her—she was too damaged, after all. And then Jacob would meet some South American beauty who'd sweep him away on a cloud of international charm, never to return.

It was over now. It was clear. Jacob saw the truth, how unbalanced and stupid she could be. How disastrous she was. How Kat's past—once a charming tale of perseverance—would ultimately be impossible to circumvent.

Kat was too *unstable*. Just . . . too much.

She looked to the phone which seemed to stare back, mocking her with its silence. *Don't Don't Don't* her mind screamed as she watched herself reach for it, and she dialed Jacob. Immediately, it went to voice mail.

"Hey, you've reached Jacob. Leave me a message and I'll get right back to you. Thanks."

BEEEP.

Kat gripped the phone with such violence, it was as if she was trying to strangle it; then gave up and threw the phone into the couch and collapsed to the floor.

And that was where Jess would find Kat the next day.

• • •

"Kat. Kat!" Jess said gently, shaking her shoulder. "You okay?"

Kat looked up through bleary eyes and saw Jess's form kneeling above her with a furrowed brow and eyes squinted in worry. "Oh. Hey, Jess."

"Kat, uh . . . why are you on the floor?"

She slowly scanned the space, willing the room to become less foreign. Kat knew she had to project nonchalance. Jacob couldn't find out post-fight she'd hibernated in despair for almost 24 hours, an unmoving mass on the living room floor like a total freak. Kat could go from potentially being Jacob's future to becoming that woman he used to date, a forgotten relic from the past, an erratic blip in his life.

"Wow. I, uh, have low blood pressure. I guess I must have passed out . . ." Jess helped her sit up.

"Let me get you some water." Jess went to the kitchen and brought back a big glass. "I'm so relieved you're okay. I thought you might . . ."

"Be dead?" Kat said a bit too forcefully.

"Honestly, yeah. You scared the shit out of me." Kat thanked her for the water and downed the glass.

"Thanks. I'm fine, I promise. This has happened before."

"You sure you're okay?"

"Yeah. Totally fine. Hey, how was Nebraska?"

"Well . . . How is Nebraska ever?"

The two shared an ironic laugh.

"And how's Jacob, anyway? I haven't seen him in ages."

"Oh, he's good. We had a tiny fight. I'm sure it's nothing." Kat finished the last drop of water and shrugged as if it was all an afterthought.

"Well. Fights happen, right?" Kat nodded and Jess held out her palm. "I'll offer you a hand up, but not a hand*out*." Kat chuckled as Jess pulled her upright. "And could you please tell that brother of mine to not be such a stranger?"

"That's funny. I was thinking the exact same thing."

• • •

Later that day, Kat finally received a text from Jacob, and her hand shook with anticipation as she read it:

We need to talk.

Kat quickly typed back: **Ya think?**

Can you come over now?

Within the hour, Kat and Jacob were sitting poolside in their respective chaise lounges.

"The scene of the crime," Kat noted, gesturing to the pool and Carol's impressive succulent garden where they'd first met. Jacob nodded, noncommittal.

Kat had used her curling wand to achieve beachy waves and wore Jacob's favorite sundress. She smelled like sandalwood and hoped he noticed. She was terrified, but her face looked like she'd spent hours at a serene spa day. If she were to woo Jacob back, make him see the light, she had to be the epitome of grace and calmness. Everything was contingent on her maintaining an equilibrium of sanity. She gobbled up CBD pills like Halloween candy for insurance. She wasn't talking any risks. But Jacob had to see that last night was a misunderstanding. He just had to.

"First of all . . . you threw a fucking rock at my car," Jacob said hotly. He took a sip of beer as if to cool himself back down.

Kat leaned forward, incredulous. She'd practiced this look of sheer innocence. "What? You thought that was *me*?"

Jacob looked over with suspicion and nodded yes.

"God, I can't believe you'd think that. But Jacob—did you actually *see* me throw the rock at your car?"

He took a beat, and this time shook his head no.

"Because I didn't do it. Did you also see the two boys laughing from behind the fig tree?"

Shock spread across his face and Kat inched closer, eyes wide with purity.

"Jacob, I went after the boys who threw the rock at you. But you tore off so fast, you probably didn't see that part."

Jacob took a long pull on his beer. "Really?"

"Really. I would never throw a rock at you. *Ever.* Are you kidding me?" Relief flushed through her veins as he bought the lie. *Thank god he didn't actually witness it.* "I'm just so so sorry I behaved that badly at the bowling alley. I'm humiliated and embarrassed. I flew off the handle and acted like a child. Jacob, simply put . . . I screwed up."

Jacob looked over at her, thawing slightly. He remained silent.

"Look. You know I have literally zero experience with all of this. That relationships are all new to me. I have no role models, and I'm bound to step in it. And so I did. Big time."

"I haven't heard from Pete yet, but I can only imagine."

Kat cringed. "I want to apologize personally myself to him. And to Maya." She let out a deep breath. "But put yourself in my shoes for a moment. I heard you were going on a trip to South America, and I didn't know about it—and then I found out Maya was invited and I wasn't—and I felt like you were leaving me. Irrational, but true. My stupid fear kicked in, and I lost my mind. I embarrassed you, and I'm so angry at myself, I can't even tell you."

Jacob allowed a small nod. "I was pretty shocked."

"It all blew up so quickly. And we were having such a great time together." Kat reached out and put her hand on his. He didn't grip back but he also didn't flinch. "Of course you can go to South America. Of course you can have a great trip with Pete. Of course I want this for you."

"You really mean it?"

"Jacob, 100%. All I want is your happiness. That's it."

Jacob was stoic but seemed to accept the information. Finally he turned to her, his eyes softened once again. Grateful tears welled in Kat's eyes.

"Oh, Jacob. I just love you so much."

He studied her face and couldn't resist a moment longer. Who was he to doubt Kat's truth, to understand the hell she'd endured? Of course there would be residual messiness. That was life. And no one responded perfectly all the time; everyone deserved a second chance. Especially when that someone was as golden—and as tested—as Kat.

"I love you, too." Kat sprung from the chaise lounge and wrapped her thankful arms around Jacob's neck, peppering him with kisses in his hair and ears and mouth and neck.

From the kitchen window, Carol watched the reconciliation play out. "Thank you, baby Jesus," she said with a small smile. Jacob had come to his mother for advice, and in classic Carol fashion, she'd quoted Theodore Dreiser: "I believe in the compelling power of love. I do not understand it. I believe it to be the most fragrant blossom of all this thorny existence."

And with someone like Kat, as Dreiser had written, love *was* thorny.

· · ·

Kat was making progress on her memoir. The work was excruciating, of course, to not only recall her past as a foster kid, but to also breathe life into it. She had to watch her past unfurl in her mind, replay all the sordid events in intimate detail. Each passage was its own brand of torture. Every family and subsequent experience had left a handprint on her soul, usually for the worse.

Kat hoped the themes of rootlessness and survival would make a compelling tale. She'd toiled hard to seamlessly cast herself as the embattled heroine of her own life. She wanted her story to resonate, for people to read it and feel less alone—much like she'd seen with that stunning children's book author at her own book reading at Antigone Books years ago.

Kat wanted to finally step into the sun.

Jacob gave her all the time in the world to work on it. Because of his mother, he understood the process. He didn't want to read too much; he respected that she was still writing a work-in-progress and wanted to read the version that Kat had approved, the one she was most proud of. Still, all along Kat would close her eyes and envision the moment Jacob would read her published memoir on the chaise lounge near the pool, mouth agape, dazzled by her work. He'd clutch the pages to his heart with tears in his eyes and tell her she'd written a modern masterpiece.

Kat's hand fluttered when she found her fingers typing EPILOGUE and wrote the simple sentence:

"Kat Lamb survived the foster program and now lives in Tucson. This is her first book."

She stared at the computer screen and burst into incredulous tears. That was the last of it, the bow on top. All the years of thinking and writing and rewriting, and she was done.

She was truly done. There would be edits, of course, and she also had the agonizing challenge of finding an agent and selling her work before her, but Kat was going to savor and celebrate the victory of completion. So many people say they want to write a book but never do.

Kat could practically smell Carol's hair, with her lavender shampoo, when she'd lift Kat up into a giant congratulatory embrace, hearing she'd completed her memoir.

Jacob would take her out to dinner at some fancy restaurant in the foothills to toast the achievement, the city of Tucson glittering below. It would be a perfect evening, and the memory of their recent fight would be far off, a whisper of nothing.

Only champagne corks popped in her mind.

FIVE

NATURALLY, CAROL HAD PLOTTED AN elaborate Bon Voyage party for her two boys. The entire backyard—a space she had so lovingly worked on, having earned a reluctant green thumb through copious years of trial and error—was transformed. She'd purchased star lanterns in bubble gum colors that dangled from every cactus and tree. The tables were laden with her cooking, and she'd filled metal tubs with ice-cold beers and bottles of wine. The whir of the blender periodically filled the air, signifying the near-constant creation of margaritas.

Carol had even lit tiny flower candles and floated them in the pool, creating a dream-like mood, and a festive handmade sign hung between two cacti: BUEN VIAJE!

Kat put an arm around a glowing Carol. "You outdid yourself, Carol. What a knock-out."

"I do love to throw a good party! Don't have to twist my arm very hard . . ." Carol licked the rim of her margarita and took a generous sip, staining the side of the glass with her plentiful coral lipstick. "I just love the fact my kids want to travel together and explore new cultures . . . it's just a momma's dream come true!"

Across the yard near the pool, Jess chatted with Jacob. Both kept an eagle eye on the closeness of Carol and Kat, who were conferring as if they were sharing a secret. "Do you think they're doing it yet?"

Jacob playfully smacked his sister. "Jess, I do *not* need that visual in my brain, thank you very much."

"God, they're just so . . . *cozy*."

"Hey, at least Mom'll help keep Kat occupied and busy while I'm gone."

"Jesus, J., you're not going off to war. You'll be back in a couple of weeks."

"We'll see. I want this to be a business trip, too. I'm gonna look into buying artisan fare for next to nothing and selling it to shops around town. Apparently you can make a killing, and my nest egg is—"

"—Ohmygod, again with the 'nest egg'! What 20-something guy is so obsessed with his 'nest egg'? You're seriously like a 76-year-old man on the topic."

"Well, you won't make fun when you see what I have in mind . . ."

"Oh yeah? And what's that?"

"Patience, grasshopper. Patience."

Jess rolled her eyes and took a swig of beer. "Pete mentioned Kat went off the rails at the Cactus Bowl."

Jacob stiffened and his brow furrowed. "It wasn't exactly a good night."

"He said Kat was a total nightmare."

Jacob's eyes flashed with heat. "She wasn't . . ." he drifted off, fumbling for the right words. "Look, we all make mistakes. Kat's apologized. She *has* been through a lot in life, you know."

"Doesn't give her permission to be a psycho."

Before Jacob could respond, they both craned their necks upon hearing their mother's loud squeal reverberate over the pool.

"Congratulations!" Carol hugged Kat, spilling margarita down her back, oblivious Kat was now soaked. "*Someone finished their memoir!*"

Kat blushed under the party lights, looked down modestly, and tucked her hair behind her ears. "I mean, it's mostly a first draft . . ."

Jacob, having overheard the news, excitedly trotted over and hugged Kat, planting a kiss on her lips. "Why didn't you say anything?"

"I guess I was waiting for the right moment . . ."

POP!

"One with champagne, for example?" Jacob beamed and Kat laughed, nuzzling into him.

Champagne overflowed and it bubbled onto the patio's gravel floor as Carol held the bottle into the air. "We've got a lot to celebrate, people—and I didn't brave BevMo for nothin'!"

Flutes were distributed and soon most of the revelers were toasting Kat.

"Congrats. That's a huge accomplishment." Maya clinked her glass with Kat and the two wordlessly seemed to agree to move on from the unfortunate evening at the bowling alley. Kat resisted the urge to smother her with a hug, and she was grateful when Maya quickly exited, saving her from the embarrassment.

Carol refilled Kat's flute and leaned in. "Don't worry, son, I'm going to keep your girlfriend nice and busy while you're cavorting about South America. That is, if she'll allow me to edit her work . . ."

Kat felt herself nearly lift into space, her grin positively Cheshire. Grateful tears formed in the corner of her eyes as she hugged Carol. "You mean it? Oh, I'd be so honored!"

"I love this plan!" Jacob crowed. "Thanks, Mom."

"Now I won't pine and ache for you quite as much, J.—I'll be busy working with an acclaimed author, you see . . ." Kat grinned, letting the champagne's effervescence dissolve into her body, causing it to glow from the outside in. Across the courtyard, she spotted Maya and Pete conferring conspiratorially, whispering to one another and catching glances at Kat, then turning back to one another secretively. They pretended not to notice that Kat was watching.

Her beam dimmed as she was convinced they were gossiping with one another about her general mediocrity and doubtful literary talent.

She was fucking certain of it.

· · ·

Carol had propped herself up in bed and tore through *Foster Kid*. She read it in one lascivious gulp, consuming it as if in a trance.

Kat's memoir had a hypnotic spell. She laced words together with such staggering ease, as if her story had been there all along. All Kat had to do was reach up and pull it down; it was all so effortless. The language was not simplistic—far from it— but the words still virtually read themselves. More than once Carol looked down and saw her arms erupt into a constellation of goosebumps in the heat. Kat had made the terrible details of her childhood immediate and human.

Carol was awestruck.

She'd lost track of all time; it was so overwhelming. If the language and structure were one thing, the story was another entirely. Carol was in shock by the stark details, the cloistered hothouse of confusion and the ache of abandonment. Carol could *feel* Kat's rootlessness on the page growing up without an anchor. One family's ethos was a strange brew of vague Christian ideology, more of the brimstone meets QAnon variety. One brief stay at a foster house was normal—until the cheerful mother never returned home. Kat relayed her abuse sensitively, never blinking from the injustice. She made her own survival lyrical.

Carol knew very little about the foster program. She just knew it meant children couldn't be properly cared for by their parents, and she envisioned messy homes filled with rudderless kids. Still, she wondered if this image was just a lame stereotype she'd picked up from movies or television.

Kat's language heightened a mysterious but fascinating subject matter into a new immediacy. Kat had also brilliantly toyed with how memory itself can manipulate perception, and she carefully knitted the question of plausibility into the fabric of the memoir. Events seemed vaguely fluid, which animated the overreaching principle that the very act of growing up the way she did—with no basis in reality, like watching yourself in a fun-house mirror—had so fundamentally contorted Kat's mind, it caused her memories to float in an ambiguous bubble of *real or not*. As a writer, she was manipulative, meant to sway and engage her readers, all part of the secret to the memoir's originality. It was a brilliant hook.

Thinking more about the memoir's complexity, Carol pondered . . . Perhaps Kat, herself, was not even entirely sure what was really true or not.

. . .

It was a quiet afternoon at Antigone Books as Kat manned the counter. The lone customer was a friendly homeless man named Carl who came in a few times a week to discuss how everything terrible happened in April.

Kat saw her phone light up with the caller ID: CAROL WALSH. She snuck into the backroom to take the call, her pulse racing in her fingertips, her breath already shallow.

"Hello?" Carol didn't respond but Kat heard her inhale deeply.

"My darling. I am gutted. GUTTED by your memoir."

Tears immediately burst from Kat's eyes, her mouth exploding in a joyful smile. "*Really?*"

Carol blew her nose, creating a honk. "I'm absolutely dazzled—first of all, by your language, but second, by your STORY. For what you've survived."

Kat had to place the phone away from her face she was crying so hard.

Soon after, her boss Lucîa crashed into the backroom, her face a knit of worry having overheard Kat's emotional outburst. "Mi cariña! Are you okay, Kat, my darling?" Without knowing a single detail, Lucîa's eyes were already wet with her own tears. Lucîa was always dressed in flowy numbers in tropical colors; every detail of her being was vibrant, from her firetruck red eye-glasses to her nails to her lips.

"It's . . . it's . . . good!" It was all Kat was capable of getting out, her shoulders heaving.

"Oh! You're at work! I forgot! Listen—I'll let you get back to it, but just know I am in awe of your creation. I can't wait to get to dig in with you." Carol exhaled. "Now I need a drink."

Kat laughed and thanked her, said a silent prayer, and hung up.

"Tell me, tell me, tell me!" Lucîa exploded, pointing again to her moist eyes. "You see? I'm crying, and I don't even know why yet!"

Kat grinned and took a moment to collect herself. "Carol Walsh loved my memoir. Said it was dazzling." Kat broke down again saying the words out loud.

Lucîa bounced up and down, clutching Kat's forearms, squealing with joy. "Don't cry, my love! This is GREAT!" Her infectious spirit gripped Kat and she joined in, hopping with Lucîa in the back room.

Finally the two women fell into a happy embrace. "I am so proud of you! So proud!"

"Thank you. I can't tell you what Carol's words mean to me . . ."

"And Carol Walsh is one smart cookie . . . Take this moment and bottle it. Remember this day, these details. See my eyes, remember the light, the smell of the backroom where you got this important phone call. This call that validates what you do and your talent, which I have never doubted."

God bless Lucîa and her endless capacity for support.

Tears streamed down Kat's grateful face and she nodded, looking Lucîa dead in the eye.

"Um . . . *Hello*? Could anyone help me?" . . . A confused voice called from the front of the store.

Kat and Lucîa laughed and wiped their eyes.

"Coming!" Lucîa winked at Kat and exited to assist the customer. She took a second to follow Lucîa's sage advice, savoring the details of the moment. She closed her eyes, grace billowing through her veins. It was almost embarrassing how good validation could feel.

It was more embarrassing for Kat to realize one of her first thoughts about literary praise from Carol was how Jacob would respond.

Impressing Carol would impress Jacob, and there was nothing Kat wanted more.

SIX

A FEW WEEKS LATER, JACOB AND PETE were sharing an exhilarated look as their plane took off into the sky, knowing their South American adventure awaited them. Travel had always spiked their blood, and they adored watching nature and travel shows as kids, endlessly talking about all the places they'd like to see together. Each month, the brothers had pored over *National Geographic*, turning pages looking for women in traditional clothing, or hopefully, the lack thereof. They bought Dos Equis beers and toasted the trip ahead.

The Ecuador JazzFest 2022 was a burgeoning event and becoming a rising jazz staple in the music festival circuit. Pete was eager to be a part of it early on; he knew the jazz scene in Quito was gaining a reputation for a reason. He'd performed at the El Pobre Diablo club once before and kept in touch with the bar owners, hoping for this exact opportunity.

Pete and Jacob spent the days exploring and traveled to the beaches in Esmeraldas for snorkeling, giddy like kids. They were content to search the beach for shells, tapping into their younger selves. They toyed with chartering a boat to the Gálapagos Islands but decided there wasn't quite enough time. Darwin would have to wait until they ventured south again.

Watching his brother perform, Jacob was always so proud. He loved the way Pete's whole soul played the piano, the way he closed his eyes and floated away on a cloud of creation. Pete had always known exactly what he wanted to do. He also understood making it as a professional musician would never be easy, but he'd put in the work, and he loved it with every fiber in his being. Jacob was more than a little envious of Pete's complete professional clarity.

Before the brothers knew it, the Ecuador JazzFest came to a successful conclusion, and Pete stuck around a few days after, not exactly eager to return to real life. The brothers wandered through the Quicentro shopping district to find some local jewelry stores as Pete wanted to look at engagement rings, hopeful to get a great deal on a diamond overseas.

"Maya wants a yellow diamond. It's her favorite color." Pete inspected ring after ring as the staff brought the brothers champagne.

"I can't believe you're so close to this giant step! But I guess I shouldn't be surprised. Maya's amazing."

"It's always just been so easy with Maya. She's my best friend . . . who I also totally want to get down with," Pete cracked.

"It's really not more complicated than that, is it? Friends you fiddle?"

Pete pointed to a more vintage-looking yellow diamond with white diamonds encircling it like petals. "That one! Right there! *Sí!*" The salesperson delicately handed Pete the ring and he inspected it, nodding and smiling.

"Wow. That's a stunner." He could almost hear Maya already squealing. A smile crept over him as he saw the proposal in his mind. "You're positive she's the one?" Jacob asked.

"Oh yeah. I knew a few months in. Maya was it." Hearing Pete's assuredness, Jacob furrowed his brow.

"Do you feel that about Kat?"

Jacob looked away, exhaled. "Sometimes. We get along great. I mean, it's new-ish, obviously . . . but . . ."

". . . But Kat can be super unstable."

"Well. Everyone has their moments. Right?"

"Sure. I just want you to be happy. And I believe the biggest factor in any enduring marriage isn't more complicated than this—'Choose wisely.'"

Jacob grinned. "Was that in *Raiders of the Lost Ark*?"

"I only quote the best." Pete held the ring up to the saleswoman. "This is the one."

"Excellent. Your lady will be very happy, sir. We'll get it ready for you." She refilled their champagne, then took the ring and started the paperwork. Pete was vibrant, his smile wide and sincere. Jacob put an arm around his brother.

"Congrats, man."

"Thanks. I love that I'm buying Maya's engagement ring with you, my brother, on this trip. It means a lot."

"And tonight we'll drink way too much and hit a *super-cool discotheque*!"

. . .

After Pete headed back to Tucson, Jacob spent nearly a month in Ecuador, the majority of it in Quito. He loved nothing more than grabbing a nighttime trolley and rolling up the hill, the lights of the city spilling like shards of colorful glass below. He made in-roads with vendors at the Mercado Artesanal La Mariscal in the heart of town, a wondrous ribbon of booths teeming with South American trinkets and ornaments. Their handmade sweaters were gorgeous, and he bought them in bulk as if he was shopping at Costco. His haul was impressive, and he hoped Tucsonan artisans would gobble up his bag of toys just as they'd done with his friend Mateo. Mateo had raked in thousands selling Mexican wares, and Jacob wanted the same outcome.

Jacob went over the financials on napkins, projecting his profits. Ideally, he'd combine his prior savings with these earnings to secure a down payment on a house to flip. That had always been the secret intention, and despite years in the making, his goal always felt elusive. But for the first time, Jacob finally felt like it actually might happen. The entire business model could graduate from a lofty dream to an actual reality.

He also thought about Kat less and less. And he hated to admit it, but Pete's assessment of Kat—he'd routinely used the word "off" to describe her—had made him question her. Jacob trusted his brother's judgment completely. In the past weeks he'd spent as much time thinking about Pete's tacit qualms about Kat as he did missing her.

Jacob did think of her eyes, beaming with puppy-dog devotion, and her breasts, my god. They were fucking perfect. He also thought of her writing, how she was so meticulous in her craft, like a watchmaker building an intricate timepiece not with tiny gears but with words. He thought of her aura of mystery; how he would frequently catch her staring into space and wondered where she was. He thought of their talks in the dark. Kat was so different, so unexpected.

But she wasn't permanent. Here in Ecuador, where the subtropical heat kept him awake at night, he dreamt of a new home. Of calloused hands doing manual labor. Of stability. Of someone gentle.

He was fairly certain it wasn't Kat.

. . .

Kat was miserable. She cried in the grocery store over stupid sentimental songs piped into the produce aisle. She cried in her car when she spotted an injured bird on the side of the road. She threw her shoe at a stupid senator on TV with his impossible Southern twang and incoherent soundbite.

She texted Jacob entirely too much. Kat wrote all about the latest Margaret Atwood novel—he had to read it when he was back. Kat assured him she missed him *like mad* and tried to ride the line between devoted and pathetic.

Because she *was* pathetic. She knew it. She was lovesick, a teenage girl saying goodbye to her first camp boyfriend. She was obsessed, sick, filled up with one reality: Jacob.

Jacob. Jacob. Jacob. She saw his face everywhere. She'd touch her thigh accidentally and pretend it was his hand. Kat needed to taste him, to feel him, to have him fill her. She ached like a pulsing heart, constant and endless.

She and Carol got together to cook and work on her memoir, which was the only highlight. Still, she couldn't quite concentrate or find the right words. Carol would lay out intricate connections with her memoir, dissecting the chapters with a scalpel. Kat nodded but her concentration was hijacked. Now she had a dumb teenage brain, an endless loop of Jacob clouding any literary attempt. She wondered what he was doing, wondered if Pete had spoken ill of her, wondered if Jacob wanted to marry her. Because she would say yes and they could have the family she'd wanted to grow up in—loving, creative, good.

Kat didn't care about a ring—she wasn't into such trivialities. But she wanted to be with Jacob forever, to always feel this way, to always be a part of his family. He was her link to everything she was after, the antidote to everything she was trying to escape from.

Kat knew he loved her. He'd said it over and over. But she also knew she felt so much more powerfully than he did—she was not his first love, as he was for her—and that he had left for South America on vaguely questionable ground. Sure, they'd made up and she'd smiled, waving enthusiastically when he walked away at the airport, growing smaller and smaller until he was gone. But once he was out of view, Kat wept. Bitterly. People probably thought there was a funeral, a sudden death, some dark reason for her to be at the airport in such a state. They averted their eyes or gave Kat a little hopeful sad face as she wiped her tears away.

Because this could not be over. She and Jacob.

Kat would not allow it.

She had come too far to lose it now, to let this unspool into nothing.

SEVEN

WHEN JACOB TOUCHED DOWN AT LAX, he had to dash to catch a puddle-jumper back to Tucson. He was exhausted and knew he'd be home in the desert soon enough, his South American sojourn just a distant memory. He craved home, yet Jacob was also simultaneously—and weirdly—indifferent to his return.

And then there was Kat. He knew she'd be vibrating with anticipation to be reunited; he knew he'd be having a lot of sex again. That was good, it had been a long time. But he wasn't sure where he was going, where anything was going. He still needed to sell his plentiful wares, uncertain this investment would pay off. He was hopeful his plan would be fruitful, but until it was real, everything was only optimistic plotting on a napkin.

He also wished he could undo what Pete had said about Kat, wished he could settle back to the place when he didn't doubt. But the truth was, he had a nagging feeling something was not right.

Jacob stepped off the plane and went through customs, receiving another stamp in his well-worn passport. He loved this step, each imprint a vague triumph. He was close now.

Jacob made his way to the baggage claim, scanning for Kat. He spotted her, hands clasped almost in prayer. She saw him and squealed, ran to him. Kat even jumped into his arms and wrapped her legs around his torso. It was like a goddamn beer commercial.

Kat's lips coated his, he kissed back and inhaled her again.

"Let me look at you." Kat beamed, pulled her head back, eyes scanning.

Jacob's hair was lighter and longer, wavy and unruly. His skin sun-kissed. Small

lines formed around his eyes now; he'd lost weight. He looked wonderful and tragically different. She could see it in his face, feel the unease in his easy smile.

Instantly, Kat felt the hum of his interest had shifted. She pushed the pan-
icky realization down, banished it, but the intuitive worry still bleated out in her
soul. It croaked like a far-off frog somewhere in the forest. She couldn't see it,
but it was there.

Jacob took in Kat. He'd almost forgotten how beautiful she was. How could
he just forget like that? But he also noticed something new . . . Her light freckles
were blotted out, her eyes were more intricately lined, her eyelids shaded in deep
browns. Giant false lashes batted at him.

"You look great . . . but different." And while Jacob knew Kat had never looked
so beautiful, it was artificial somehow, like she was wearing a dramatic wig and pretending it was her real hair.

"Good different, I hope!" She had a baby-doll dress on that hung low on her
cleavage, displaying her beautiful bosom like the plump peaches she knew he
loved. He'd never seen her expose so much skin. "God, I missed you. I'm so glad
you're back." She kissed him passionately, he felt exposed and too public somehow,
but soon enough, her plush lips overtook his concern.

"It's great to be home." He grinned. The two stared at one another, smiling but
unsure of each other. "Well, let's go get the bags."

Hand in hand, they moved to the baggage claim and soon his enormous duffel
spilled onto the carousel.

"Your duffel is so Kerouac, by the way," Kat said and Jacob laughed, and she
was relieved to hear him respond with a chortle. Maybe it would all be fine. Maybe
it was as it always had been. Jacob flashed her his trademark light-bulb grin, heaving at the massive luggage. His tanned arms bulged at the effort. Kat made an
audible gurgle in her throat, already swimming in desire.

. . .

Jess was away at a track meet in Eugene, Oregon, and Kat had the apartment to
herself. Jacob was relieved—he knew the sex would be noisy and didn't want the
distraction of his little sister overhearing to complicate the pleasure.

Jacob and Kat went to strip each other right away. They clawed through buttons, overwhelmed to get to the next part. As if clothing was such a terrific hurdle to life, something to be banished with intense speed.

With Kat splayed on the bed, Jacob was as hard as he'd ever been in his life—positively high school levels of agony. She was so delicious, so tempting . . . so familiarly hot.

The time away had intensified the act to a cartoonish level. It was perfect, and the release was volcanic for both. Sweat drenched their bodies; they panted in the afternoon light peeking through the blinds.

"God. I missed this," Jacob cooed, running his hand through his sweat-drenched hair.

"This? But did you miss *me*?" Kat asked, too eager. The playful mood shifted, the molecules in the room lost their gravity. Jacob stiffened slightly.

"Of course. That's the point, right? I miss this . . . you, all of it," Jacob said, his smile not as full.

"Right! Duh. I just . . ." Kat climbed on top of him, kissing him all over. "I just missed you so much." She flicked her tongue around his nipples.

"I'm so exhausted, Kat. I've been flying for, like, two days. Maybe three."

"But it's only a nine-hour flight to L.A. from Quito, right?"

"Yeah," Jacob said. "Just feels like I've been traveling forever. I really need a shower." Jacob got up; Kat's eyes locked on his butt. "Promise Jess isn't here?"

"She won't be back until Tuesday," Kat assured him. "Need a partner?"

"Huh?"

"In the shower. Need someone to soap your back?" Kat asked playfully.

"Nah. Just wanna make it quick and sleep." Jacob grinned and went into the bathroom. Kat heard him turn on the shower.

"There's fresh towels and new soap for you!" she called. He didn't respond. Kat laid in the soft light of afternoon, anxious. Jacob was different. Fear plagued her again, floated up from her stomach, pissing her off with its nagging voice. She hated feeling so powerless.

Hamster wheels of worry circled in her mind and she pushed them out with authority: NO. Jacob was just tired. He was showering. He was so happy to see her. And besides, that sex was glorious, as always.

Kat blotted all subterranean fears from her mind by digging her fingers into her arm, relishing the cathartic twang of pain emanating from her forearm. She pulled her fingers away, observed the deep indentations in her skin. Kat was surprised there was no blood.

. . .

The yellow DHL van appeared right on time; all of Jacob's wares that had once lined the streets of Quito were jammed into shipping parcels. The items had passed through customs and were now official US citizens.

Jacob opened the goods, excited to see again the explosion of color. God, he needed this to go his way.

He loaded up the loot and drove all over Tucson. Each store's buyer greeted him warmly, men and women alike. Jacob was an easy salesman, his entire pitch never felt like a sale at all—it was as if everyone's best friend arrived with a pageant of goods.

The entire process was easier than he ever could have imagined. Not a single buyer turned him down and within a few days, he was empty-handed. He counted his profit and the amount startled him.

A few days later, Jacob lounged in the backyard near the pool when Carol approached, delivering a lemonade. She handed him the glass and sat down. "You're already too tan, you realize . . ."

"Ha. Just going over my numbers."

"So you sold all the goods, I take it?"

Jacob nodded, took a big swig of lemonade. "Mateo was so right—it was insanely easy. My markup was 70%. *Seventy*."

"Impressive." Carol traced her toe in the pool water. "So how's Kat? Lovely to be together again?"

Jacob wordlessly nodded, took another sip.

"You know, we worked wonderfully together on her memoir, which is truly a revelation. I was knocked out by it. Floored, actually."

"Yeah, she's told me that part about 12 times," he said with a grin.

"I'm going to help her get it into the world. I feel almost called to do this, I admit. Kat's truly amazing."

Jacob remained silent and again nodded.

Carol leaned closer. "Everything okay?"

Jacob shrugged, eyes scanning his mother's backyard of blooming succulents. "Son. What's going on?" Carol was level, steady.

"Just anxious, I guess. I'm excited . . . but at a bit of a crossroads."

Carol nodded. "You know, you've always reminded me of Hubble."

"The telescope?" Jacob wasn't following.

"Robert Redford's character in *The Way We Were*. Hubble. There's a scene in the movie where his English professor is reading his work aloud and everyone in class is shocked how bright he actually is. 'In a way he was like the country he lived in. Everything came too easily to him,'" Carol quoted.

"I remember now."

"You're Redford, Jacob. Most people would kill to say that, but it has its own burden . . ." Carol studied his face, felt how far away his eyes were. "You're on a metaphorical train platform, waiting for what's next."

"Yeah. Until my plans are real, it's all just sort of terrifying. And I wish I had that knowing everyone else in this family seems to have. You're the gifted writer. Jess, she's the incredible athlete. Pete is a freakin' jazz prodigy. And me? . . . Well, right now I make cabinets. And fill napkins and notebooks with plans I never seem to fully execute."

"You have so many skills. I'm not worried about you, J."

"I'm a little worried about me."

Carol smiled. "You're going to land on your feet. You'll see," Carol added, a bit uncertain how to proceed. She said it anyway: "Also . . . you know it's often hard to be in a relationship when you feel so . . . unmoored. But there's not a person on the planet who hasn't felt exactly the same way. Sometimes in life there's flow, sometimes there's static. The tension is there to teach you. To point you in the right direction. Lean into the discomfort. These are the times to ask yourself what truly brings you joy. Follow that and *listen*."

Jacob appreciatively nodded, put his arm around his mother. "You're a smart egg, woman."

"Yes. And I also know how to make great men."

· · ·

Kat and Jacob floated through the motions, mostly happy, sometimes bored. Their silence grew but it wasn't entirely unpleasant. Healthy stasis can be comforting as well.

Kat got promising news from a prominent literary agent, Jacqueline Caron. Carol had been so helpful with the daunting task of publishing. After she and Carol had finished putting the polishing touches on her memoir, Carol had secretly sent Jacqueline a few pages to whet her appetite. Before long, Jacqueline had called Kat to tell her she found her writing "brisk and original," which was like getting bathed in perfect sunlight. Jacqueline also found the entire subject matter of Kat's childhood intriguing and "rife with potential." She warned a memoir was more difficult to sell—upmarket fiction had a bigger market, Kat knew this—but Kat's voice had "a lyrical power worth exploring." The memoir wasn't entirely complete, but Jacqueline still wanted to read the first three chapters, which was a triumph.

The entire episode sent Kat into a tailspin of excitement. Jacob still warned her it could be for naught. He cautioned her how difficult publishing could be; he'd seen it himself. Once his mother got promising news on a novel only to be ghosted by the agent. He remembered her thick disappointment that clouded the house for weeks.

Kat was insulted. Can't he just be happy for once? Can't she be allowed to just bask in this great news? A prominent agent loved her writing. She didn't like it, she loved it. "*Loved.*" Her exact words. She wanted more. His own mother had greeted the news with champagne!

Instead of launching into a predictable fight, Kat pulled back and agreed he was merely being prudent. Jacob recognized she'd fought to tamp her hotness and hold her tongue. Once again.

This was getting increasingly exhausting.

· · ·

Weeks passed. Kat hadn't heard from Jacqueline Caron since she'd forwarded her first three chapters. She checked her in-box, re-checked and triple-checked to make sure her email had gone through. *Delivered,* her computer assured her. She wasn't assured.

Kat called Jacqueline's office in New York and got her brusque assistant with an indiscernible accent; she sounded like a Bond girl who'd be good at skiing and seduction. Kat asked if her chapters had indeed been received by Jacqueline; she didn't want a tech hiccup to get in the way—Jacqueline had been so *excited to read more*. The assistant took Kat's information and would let her know.

Days crawled by as if drowning in amber. Kat stared at her computer, willing it to deliver good news. Each time she sat down at it, she visualized seeing her In Box ablaze with **JACQUELINE CARON** next to the subject header: **I'M IN LOVE!**

Bold, all-caps-lock love for Kat's creation. Jacqueline would be dazzled by her brilliance, certain of the work's potential, critical and otherwise. Jacqueline would liken her take to *The Glass Castle* and want to rush *Foster Kid* into print.

In her fantasy, the media would pounce, salivating for Kat's true tale. Kat would insist on wearing yellow for her inevitable interview on *CBS This Morning* because it was Gayle King's favorite color. Maybe Oprah would watch and invite her and Jacob out for a weekend in Santa Barbara with Gayle to discuss Kat's memoir. They'd all hike in the purple foothills of the California Riviera, and while staring at nature's bounty, Kat would quote her favorite poem by Jack Gilbert about risking delight and having the stubbornness to accept our happiness in this furnace of a world. Oprah would clutch Gayle's hand to steady herself, overcome, tears in her eyes. She would applaud the line as the perfect thing to say at the perfect moment. Naturally, *Foster Kid* would have to become Oprah's next book club selection. Oprah would also have to call Reese to apologize, Kat having beaten her to the book club punch.

Except none of that happened. Instead, the days waiting to hear from Jacqueline turned into weeks, and Kat's mood went from absurdly hopeful to panicked to black. Jacob recommended many distractions from movies to Thai massages to museum trips. Kat rejected his requests outright or tagged along like a reluctant teenager. They were touring the Mini Time Machine Museum of Miniatures, pointing out the miraculous tiny sculptures on the tips of lead pencils. There was an impossibly small Statue of Liberty carved into a pencil that was doubly impressive under a magnifying glass.

As Jacob marveled at the detail in a minuscule Eiffel Tower, Kat's iPhone beeped with a message. She pounced and her face fell as soon as she read the email. The vaguely European assistant had emailed just three words: *Jacqueline received chapters*.

Nothing more.

Kat saw stars of rage, felt her blood drain.

"Kat, what is it?"

Kat held up her phone as evidence and stomped out of the museum, leaving the charming doll houses they hadn't yet seen in her wake.

Kat grew more than prickly, more and more irrational. She'd lash out at Jacob and then apologize, and the cycle would repeat again.

Jacob was getting weary. His mother was moody too, but it had never been at Kat's level. He wanted to gently steer clear of Kat, but he also knew she would always turn around and cling to him all the more tightly.

Jacob couldn't breathe.

He started taking longer and longer hikes in Sabino Canyon. He found other new hikes surrounding Tucson, driving further and further to take in the stark beauty of his hometown.

While walking, he could think straight. The heat lubricated his mind, the repetition of his steps released his creativity. The concrete details of his plan were taking shape on his desert treks.

Things were becoming clear.

· · ·

Kat was cooking in Jacob's impossibly small guest house kitchen, determined to have the chicken coconut curry turn out. She'd searched for "easiest chicken coconut curry ever" online but still found the recipe somewhat daunting. Nonetheless, she was encouraged by the aroma, which was heavenly.

"Wow. That smells great," Jacob said, inhaling the scent.

Kat was normally a disaster in the kitchen, but she knew she had to project some normalcy, some tenderness to Jacob. She simply had to reign in her volatility. Increasingly, she felt as if she had little control over herself, continually bouncing off a crazed pinball machine of manic behavior. An invisible wall had been building between her and Jacob, and she had to immediately put her thumb in the dam. Jacob wanted an erratic girlfriend about as much as Kat wanted to get a call from Jacqueline Caron that her memoir stank.

"Hey, 'A' for effort, right?" Jacob's kiss grazed her cheek and immediately it burned red in response.

Kat lit candles to place on the tiny dining table and bought a bouquet of wild-flowers from Trader Joe's. She felt relief seeing Jacob respond to her efforts and she felt a window open. It felt something like normal.

Jacob cooed about the food and even Kat was shocked she didn't manage to screw it up. The meal was terrific, as was the Pinot Gris she bought based on the pretty label alone.

"Listen. I wanted tonight to be a mea culpa. I need to apologize for how insane I've been lately. I can't take out my stress on you about my memoir. I'm really sorry I've been so difficult."

Jacob sat back in his chair and raked a hand through his hair. "We're both at a turning point, I think."

Kat worried that sounded ominous and had to reassure him. "I also reached out to a therapist today, Jacob. I need professional help to manage my moods, how to self-soothe and all that. I even downloaded the Calm and Headspace apps." She grinned at Jacob. "I'm gonna get more steady for both of us."

"My mom swears by meditation."

"I know. She demonstrated. A few times." Kat was thrilled to hear him respond with a chuckle. "Also—and call me a cliché—but I reread *The Prophet*, and I swear I felt this shift. Like . . . I've been wound so tight and losing my grip over something I cannot control, that my energy is doing the complete opposite of what I need. I can't give Jacqueline Caron the power to control my life and subsequently, damage me. Damage us."

"That's really healthy, Kat," Jacob said, looking into her eyes with hopeful affection.

"Thanks. It's even impacted my writing. Before, I'd read and reread and edit and re-edit my memoir, convinced I was circling the drain. Convinced it was all shit." Kat took a breath. "But with this new perspective . . . I don't know, I think it might be done. Maybe the trouble is my confidence and mind, not the work itself."

"Wow. That makes me so happy to hear. I had a feeling you were closer than you thought."

"I sure hope so. Anyway. Thank you for putting up with me."

Jacob just grinned and looked down. She reached for his hand. "Enough about me. I want to hear about *your* crossroads."

He looked up and Kat could feel him debating in his mind how to proceed and what to share. He finally reached for his computer and fired it up. A few clicks later, he swiveled the screen, displaying a photo of the most idyllically charming Spanish cottage known to mankind.

"Oh. It's divine! Where is that?"

"I don't know, actually. It's my screensaver on Pinterest."

"Pinterest? Puppies and houses?"

"Just houses. I think I want to flip a house. I've saved enough, and I'm gonna take the leap."

"You've mentioned it so many times . . . When?"

"I don't know. Soon. But enough with the daydreaming . . . Though it does have to be right."

Kat stared at the house on the screen, mesmerized by its complete ideal. It was quaint yet grand. She could see herself and Jacob someday cooking this exact meal in their own kitchen Jacob had designed. She could practically taste the entire scene. "Well, Jacob, I cannot wait until you show me your dream project someday soon. And remember, I'm here for you. We're a team. Right?"

Jacob nodded and looked down. "I'm terrified."

"You're supposed to be." They searched the other's face, both wondering what came next.

Kat leaned in and kissed him lightly, uncertain. The kiss grew in heat and she tingled all over when his hand found her face, his fingers combing through her hair. She moaned, so grateful for his touch. Kat led him to the bed, unbuttoning her shirt along the way. She tossed it and playfully tripped, immediately striking a cartoonish sexy pose.

"Oh, my goodness, it seems I've landed on a bed! I didn't see that coming at all . . ."

Jacob laughed and took his pants off, climbed on top of her.

"Hi." Kat's green eyes gave him that familiar suggestive look.

Jacob's response was a wet, full kiss that melted conversation. Their love-making was intimate and natural again, a reminder of their recent golden past. Afterward, both collapsed, happily post-coital.

"I've missed you, Jacob. And I can promise you from the bottom of my heart more meditation and sex."

"Not necessarily in that order." They kissed with such a thrilling ease, and Kat burrowed deep into the crook of his arms, even inhaling his vague body odor as if it was luxuriant. It was Jacob, and Kat loved it all.

. . .

Homes had appealed to Jacob since he was young. He was a Lego kid. He was fascinated by architecture, forever reconfiguring his own family's home layout. He loved exploring what mood a particular house delivered, wondered why certain homes made his heart swell, while others made him shudder.

He was even irritated with all the new reality TV shows featuring a new kitchen in 22 minutes, how easy the whole thing looked. As if mold damage could be cured by the time they came back from commercial break. Still, he watched them in secret, acknowledging the falseness but always dazzled with the end result.

Jacob had been riding his bike down 3rd Street a few weeks ago. It was a quaint road, filled with charming homes near campus, and that's when he spotted the dump. It was a ramshackle house amid rows of charming facades. He saw the potential immediately.

The location was fantastic. Jacob didn't waste time; he called the number on the For Sale sign. He remembered to act nonchalant, be all business. He assumed the part and asked the right questions. The price was a reach but doable. There was already interest, a few people circling, but the house had fallen out of escrow twice.

Jacob understood he didn't know as much as he should but trusted himself anyway. There was something about this property, something calling him.

Jacob crunched the numbers and thanks to the profits from his South American adventure combined with his savings, he had a healthy down payment. His credit was strong, and his offer was accepted.

. . .

Jacob did not share his news with anyone. He knew there would be push-back, inevitable sighing.

"He's always been my most unpredictable child," Carol would tell her friends at yoga. "I just hope this time he hasn't bit off more than he can chew."

Jacob would show them all. He knew this was a winner. He could live in the house, maybe rent it out, maybe sell. But his cabinetry business—which Jacob kept intentionally modest—had introduced him to many who worked in construction. His buddy Mateo was a contractor and always trying to convince him to join the fold. Jacob's friend Raj was an electrician whose Yelp reviews alone were the best in Tucson, and his buddy Karl's family owned the premiere plumbing empire of the Southwest. Jacob's odd collection of friends from all walks of life would serve him well. He always knew it would be beneficial to have an unusual Rolodex of allies.

"What do you mean, you bought a house? A house-*house*?" Carol asked in disbelief.

"Yes. On 3rd. It has huge potential," Jacob explained.

"What about your cabinetry business?"

"You forget I'm in charge. And I just finished a job, so I'll have the time . . ."

"Oh, Jacob, it's one thing to build a cabinet but another to flip an entire house!" Carol was exasperated.

"I bet Dad would understand. He'd support me."

"Oh, so now I'm losing arguments to the dead." Carol grimaced seeing Jacob flinch. "I'm sorry. That was below the belt. And you know I'm supportive, but this is colossal! It'll be financially very draining!"

"Mom, I've saved the money, I have a budget, I have friends with construction experience. Pete has most of his days free and could help out, too! . . . I promise you—someday soon, we'll be in the backyard of this house under those fairy lights you love so much, and you'll raise your Corona and tell me you were wrong." Jacob almost grinned. "You can even help me with the landscaping—xeriscaping—do it right."

Carol brightened. "Oh. I *would* love another project. Well. It's official, then! What did Kat say?"

"She doesn't know."

"Doesn't know? Were you going to tell her at some point?"

Jacob was silent. Carol sensed the tension. "How are things there?"

"Okay. We had a nice night recently. But she's a lot, Mom. You know that."

"Artists aren't easy sometimes, I agree. But I think we're worth it."

"I also think maybe with this new focus with the house, things will fall into place," Jacob surmised.

Carol took a deep inhale. "Well. Me, too. And I also hope to raise that Corona sooner than later."

Jacob lofted an imaginary bottle of beer and toasted the air. Carol followed suit, and they air-clinked.

. . .

Jacob had intentionally wanted to keep the reveal light. He and Kat had gone for frozen yogurts beforehand, and he'd insisted on topping his dessert with frosted animal cookies the absurd pink of a Barbie Dream Camper.

They'd watched college students enter the frozen yogurt shop. Kat and Jacob whispered to one another, speculating which sorority girl was likely having only sorbet for dinner. The evening was all going quite well.

When Jacob pulled up in front of his flip on 3rd, he looked for Kat's expression, hoping she'd understand and be encouraging that he'd finally taken the step on an investment. Instead, her face fell.

"What's this?"

"A dump that needs some TLC."

"Wait. Do you want my opinion on this investment??"

"Well, I'll want your opinion as I—"

"—*You already bought it, didn't you?*" Kat's eyes swam in burgeoning mania.

Fuck. Jacob knew this was a mistake. "Yeah. I did."

"Did you even *think* to run it by me first? Jacob, I want to be involved in your life!" She felt painfully incapable of any other response, barfing her emotions all over everything as usual, ruining it yet again.

"God, I'm really damn proud of this, you know?"

"Jacob, I thought we were a team!"

His head dropped. This house was his new start and right now Kat felt like the detritus of his past.

"I get this is a huge decision, but all I want is to be INCLUDED in your life! It's like I'm always this goddamn afterthought!"

He snapped his head up. "Jesus Christ, I'm telling you NOW!" Kat's stomach turned over, aware Jacob was retreating, cognizant he was at wit's end. She knew this couldn't continue, knew she'd blown it. Yet again. She dug her nails into her arm, and she attempted some calming breaths.

"I'm sorry. I—"

"—No. I don't want an apology. I don't."

Kat backpedaled, her face a mask of insincere pleasantness. Before he could say anything else, she popped out of the car to get a closer look, now grinning as if the outburst hadn't happened at all.

Jacob put his head on the steering wheel. "Fuuuuck." He looked up to see Kat approaching the house and opened his car door. He slowly followed, his hands stuffed into his pockets.

"Now that I get a closer look—it's . . . well, it *does* have so much potential. So much. And it's a great street, you'll do a great job, and it's gonna be just—"

"STOP! *STOP! STOP!*" Jacob breathed hard, overwhelmed. Kat was stunned silent. There was no going back. This felt different. "Kat. Don't . . . don't turn on a fucking dime. Please don't. I just can't take this. I'm already stressed out here, and—"

Kat ran to him and placed her hands on his chest, but he stepped backward. "Jacob, I know, I know, I do! And I don't want to . . . I acted badly. Again. I didn't think and—"

"You're. Not. Listening," Jacob said, his tone cold. Chills ran up and down Kat in the hot Tucson sun. "This needs to end." He took a breath. "More appropriately— *we* need to end."

Kat felt faint. Desperation flooded her. *NO NO NO* was the only word that flashed neon in her mind, frenetic as a hummingbird.

"I can't do this anymore. We're done." A final nail in the coffin. Tears pooled, Kat sank to her knees. She wrapped her arms around his legs. It was pathetic—she knew it—but she couldn't help herself.

"Don't, Kat. Please—" He tried to uncoil her fingers from him. "*FUCKING STOP IT!*"

Just then, a couple pushing a stroller passed by, and embarrassment crashed over Jacob. God, these were potentially his new neighbors. He resisted the urge to say hello and smile, as if this was all quite normal to have a woman wrapped around his leg like a petulant child who didn't want Daddy to leave for a business trip.

Everyone avoided eye contact and finally, they passed.

"Get up. Get up right now." Jacob jerked his leg away and Kat sobbed on the gravely mess of a front yard. He went to the car and opened the door. "Taking you home. Get in. We're done." Jacob went to his side of the car and was about to open it when—

SMASH! Glass shattered and Jacob was so shaken he couldn't figure out what had happened until he saw Kat reach down to pick up another rock and throw it at the house.

CRASH! Another glass window exploded.

In a flash, Jacob's mind went to their prior fight when the rock had slammed into his rear car window.

Of course it had been Kat.

"Excuse me . . . Um . . . do you need me to call the police?" an older neighbor yelled in a quasi-helpful voice from her front stoop across the street.

"Oh, uh—we're fine! No need! Just, uh . . ." Despite Jacob's woeful attempt at sounding breezy, venom filled Jacob's insides. He marched up to Kat who collapsed again, bawling on the hardscrabble yard. He grabbed her arm and looked into her eyes. "Listen to me. You are going to get off the fucking ground and get into my fucking car. Okay? Right now. Let's go."

He pulled Kat onto her woozy feet, her body a boneless doll. The neighbor stood watching the distressing scene unfurl. Jacob resisted an urge to wave pleasantly in an effort to undo the ugliness. Jesus Christ.

NO NO NO NO NO NO NO NO NO was the only ticker tape in Kat's mind, spooling endlessly.

"Jacob—" she gasped.

"NO. Nope. No more."

Jacob's eyes penetrated straight ahead, his jaw locked.

Kat knew she'd destroyed everything for the last time. Knew this was likely her last car ride with Jacob.

His car finally screeched to a stop in front of the Sagewood Apartments. Kat was numb, frozen to the seat. He idled the car and wouldn't look her way.

"I . . ." Kat stopped herself, knowing it was futile. Slowly, she opened the car door and weakly wheeled her legs out, then stood. She was still, blinking dumbly into the sun. Kat turned to him one last time, and Jacob's only communication was to hold her purse out for her to grab. She took it from his hand, defeated.

Kat shut the car door and Jacob peeled away.

It was over.

EIGHT

KAT APPROACHED CARUSO'S ITALIAN ON 4th Street, walking quickly. She saw the familiar neon sign inviting guests for SPAGHETTI, RAVIOLI, CHICKEN, VEAL, PIZZA PIE! Its homey décor, complete with red-and-white checkered tablecloths, made it a date-night favorite for Kat and Jacob.

When there was a Kat and Jacob.

It was still so impossible to process, to accept. Kat had never felt more hollow. Sadness radiated off of her like a cartoon, little hot sizzles of sorrow evaporating off her body. She took on the look of her emotional state—empty, depleted, gaunt. Food seemed meaningless; her thoughts were a garbled mess. She floated through a haze of despair, tried to put one foot in front of the other, but her footing failed her with each step. It was like those nightmares where you're being chased and you can't move, trapped in mud. Useless.

Carol had agreed to meet with Kat and had assured Kat via text she was "gutted, absolutely gutted like a fish." Kat was hungry for Carol, hungry to be told it would all be alright and that Jacob would return to her. Carol knew how fucking perfect they were. She got it.

Kat spotted Carol at an outdoor table near the fountain, already halfway through a glass of white wine. Carol rose to greet her and Kat felt her pity. It was obvious. Carol projected a winning smile; she wasn't about to be defined by her son's betrayal.

Kat kissed Carol on the cheek and the two women hugged. "You've wasted away to nothing! You're bones!" Carol said, startled, taking in Kat's new frame.

"It's the depression diet," Kat joked but the bitterness was clear.

"You have to take care of yourself, Kat. You were already quite small," she said, taking her seat. Carol shook her head. "I hate to see you hurting, honey."

Kat nodded, acknowledging her pain. "It hasn't been easy."

"It never is. And I know Jacob is your first."

"First everything." Kat wiped tears away. "I said I wouldn't cry."

Carol reached for her hand. "Hon, you're a human being. Human beings are allowed to feel things, to cry. It's okay. I'm here for you."

Kat offered a weak smile. "Thank you, Carol. I appreciate that. I'm just so sorry, so . . . *bereft* to be in this position at all."

"Well, relationships are complicated. Life is complicated. I mean, just take this house of Jacob's—at first it all seemed so shocking to me. And I don't want to call what he's going through a mid-life crisis, but it certainly seems like a quarter-life one."

Kat lit up. "Exactly! That's what I've been saying! He's not himself!" She was thrilled to hear Carol repeat her own perspective. They always had been so similar, twin spirits.

"He's not himself. But he's determined and seems . . . purposeful. Happy, even."

Kat's face dropped. Carol realized this was not what she wanted to hear. "I mean . . . let me re-phrase . . . Jacob just reminds me so of his father."

Kat remained quiet, still wounded.

"Matt was such a big force, a bear of a man, masculine energy going a million miles an hour. But my god, was he charming. When he wanted to be, that is . . ." Carol was caught up in the thought of him. "He wasn't an easy man to live with. Which is quite the understatement." Carol took a liberal swig of wine. "And you've always reminded me of myself, naturally."

Kat, flattered, said, "Because we're so alike, Carol."

"To be perfectly blunt, that's precisely what worried me about you and Jacob as a couple. There's a reason Matt and I would never have lasted in the long-term, even before the accident."

Kat withdrew again, could feel this too was falling apart and slipping through her fingers. Carol wouldn't be an advocate for her, wouldn't convince her son he was being a fool and making a huge mistake walking away from her. Kat felt it with cold certainty and the blood ran from her face.

"I just want you to be okay, darling. And you will be," Carol said, gripping Kat's hand for effect. "I want you to know I am here for you, always, and we will remain friends."

Kat nodded vaguely yes, but her smile was more tragic than not.

"Now then. If you Ubered here as I did, I say we order a nice bottle of wine and eat too much chicken parmesan. Because heroin chic suits exactly no one." Carol winked, then put her glasses on to inspect the menu.

Kat looked down; the words on the menu swam. She blinked back tears.

"You like sauv blanc, don't you?" Carol asked, though she already knew the answer to this question.

"Yes," Kat responded as she dug her nails into her thigh, piercing the skin.

. . .

Pete stood before the house, stunned. Jacob was beaming with pride, entirely too thrilled with the rundown abode. The paint had faded, the house was begging for attention, desperate for people to shower it with love.

"I can't believe this is yours," Pete said rubbing his jaw. "You've seriously been squirreling away *that* much money? To buy a house? AND have the money to make improvements?"

"I'm an international man of mystery," Jacob explained, then dangled the keys. "C'mon."

Pete followed his little brother into the house. It was trapped in the 70s. Linoleum, horrid cabinets, completely lifeless. The rooms were modest and it was chopped up into smaller, dysfunctional rooms. Frankly, it looked like the set of a Netflix documentary featuring some horrid 70s serial killer.

"I'm gonna open it all up, of course, but you see the potential, right?" Jacob studied his brother, uncertain if he was impressed or thought he was nuts. "I've already pulled some permits to start the work."

"Seriously? God, you'll probably have your own, like, HGTV show within the next month or something," Pete ribbed his brother. "But 3rd Street is such a great street. 'Location, location, location . . .'" He wandered throughout, inspecting each room. He peered into the backyard, taking in the junkyard vibe. But there was an underlying old-fashioned simplicity to everything, a modest space that could be reconceived.

"How are you gonna do it, though, dude?"

"Well, I told Mom you had time during the day to help . . ." Jacob admitted.

"Free labor. Naturally." He touched each knob, opened the mustard yellow fridge. Pete scowled and slammed the door shut.

"Wish Dad was here to see this," Jacob admitted.

"He'd be a good help, that's for sure," Pete observed. "And he'd be proud."

Jacob warmed hearing this. "Thanks, Pete."

Pete surveyed the scene, considering. "But I *could* see myself getting into this. A manly man, Grizzly-Adams-power-tools sort of project. Could be fun, actually."

"I'll feed you a steady diet of microwavable burritos and beer," Jacob joked. "I have a budget of 60k."

Pete whistled, impressed. "My god. I'm gonna stick around Ecuador next time and sell tchotchkes."

"I told you it'd work! And you know I've been putting money away for years. I feel just so charged with this challenge. It's a big jigsaw puzzle, you know? And maybe there's a reason I always end up befriending construction workers and plumbers—salt-of-the-earth, blue-collar types tend to be my speed."

"I'm glad you have a new focus." He paused, uncertain whether to say it. He blurted, "I was sorry to hear about Kat."

The sentence sat there. Pete regretted ruining the jovial mood with the mention of her name.

"Yeah. It was probably, you know, doomed from the get-go, right? Being Jess's roommate . . . just a bad idea. We had a lot of great times, but it had run its course." Jacob paused. "Kat's a lot of work."

"Mom just had dinner with her."

Jacob winced. "Of course she did."

"She said she made it clear to Kat it was over."

"I'm sure I'll hear all about it. You know, I keep feeling like Kat's watching me," Jacob admitted.

"Maybe she is. I did hear she was really having a hard time . . ."

Jacob looked up, silently pleading with him to stop talking. "Look, I tried to be gentle, blah blah blah . . . but she completely went off the rails because I didn't run flipping the house by her first. As if we're married already or something . . . The whole thing freaked me out yet again, to be honest."

Pete nodded; he got the message to move on.

"I'll call my old buddy Joaquin, he'll get you a deal on any tile work," Pete offered.

"Thanks, Pete." Jacob beamed at his little brother in appreciation.

"Just remember, lots of squatters hit construction sites, people who snatch tools and go. You don't wanna get ripped off. Make sure you lock up the house every time," Pete cautioned.

"Thanks, *Mom*," Jacob joked as he tightly locked up the front door.

. . .

Under the silver glow of the full Tucson moon, Kat studied Jacob's new unassuming house, holding up her fingers and squinting as if she were a land surveyor. She then closed her eyes in the warm night, willing the thick scent of the orange blossoms blooming up and down the street to soothe her.

The only movement was a cat crossing the street beside her. Kat hissed at it, and the cat responded in kind. Kat then walked to the back of the house, trying to jimmy open the windows.

Locked. Locked. Locked.

The backdoor, shockingly, was unhitched. She walked right in, sliding the ripped screen door aside. The air inside was hot, dense. It smelled of wet linens.

Kat laid down in the center of the small living room, making snow angels on the dingy shag carpet. She abruptly laughed. And stopped.

She looked around the room, her eyes dilating and getting accustomed to the dark. As her eyes came into focus, she saw the horrid walls were paneled with fake wood.

Her head swiveled to the front door. She closed her eyes and counted to 10, willing to see Jacob. When her eyes opened, she was so relieved to watch Jacob enter. He was in casual work clothes, carrying groceries.

"I got the steak," he called, lofting up the wrapped meat like a prize.

"Wonderful. I made a salad—the one with bleu cheese and almonds," Kat said out loud to the empty room.

"Yum. And I got a good pinot," he said, pulling out a bottle of red from the grocery bag.

"Rules can go fuck themselves," Kat said out loud and grinned to herself, satisfied. She closed her eyes, fell asleep, and would not wake up for nine hours.

. . .

Morning light flooded into the small house. The sun had risen hours ago, dust particles hung in the air like small stars, floating in space.

Kat heard the jangle of keys, then Jacob's familiar voice. "The key word here is 'potential,'" she heard Jacob say. Another person mumbled something in response. Kat's eyes grew to twice their size, cartoonish, and panic seized her body. Her eyes darting throughout the empty space, she scurried on her hands and knees.

"Still figuring out which key is which," Jacob explained, trying another key from the front porch. "And I'm so glad you're available, Mateo, to help out."

Kat bear-crawled into the nearby bedroom, crashed into the small closet, and slammed the slatted closet door shut. The cheap fake wood swayed with the violence of her movement. She pressed herself into the corner, gulping for air, taking deep breaths in an attempt to calm herself.

The front door opened. Through the tattered wooden blinds of the closet door, she watched Jacob enter. Her view of him was chopped up by the horizontal slats, like he was behind bars.

He was not carrying pinot noir nor steak.

He was not coming home to her.

Seeing him caused Kat's heart to race. She audibly gasped, covering her mouth to muffle her sounds. To blot out her existence.

"So as you can see, it needs a lot of work," Jacob explained.

His friend Mateo was a contractor, and he surveyed the scene. "Yeah. But it's got good bones."

"Exactly. I'd like to make this all one space, obviously, make it open concept." Jacob gestured as he spoke, laying out his plans. "Move this beam—I assume it's not load-bearing—and reconfigure the kitchen."

Mateo nodded, grinning. "Let me guess—custom cabinets?"

"I might know a guy." Jacob laughed, then paused. "Wait." He stood still, listening. "Did you hear that?"

Kat panicked and tried to pull her legs into her stomach to become a part of the closet wall.

"Maybe a rat? . . ." Mateo offered. As Jacob stepped out of the kitchen, Kat watched him move toward her room. She made a vague gurgle in her throat.

"That? . . ." Jacob asked again. Mateo shook his head no.

Jacob walked into the room, feet sinking into the deplorable shag carpeting. His eyes scanned the space, worry furrowing his brow. His beautiful, beautiful brow, his beautiful, beautiful face.

Kat held her breath, still like a statue. She pretended to be the faun Mr. Tumnus, frozen to solid stone in Narnia by the White Witch.

"I didn't hear anything," said Mateo from the kitchen and finally, Jacob turned. Kat let out a silent exhale; tears fell from her eyes.

She didn't hear any more of their words spoken, her mind an accordion of incoherent sounds, of reverberations. Inside her brain, a hum grew louder.

Finally, they were gone. Jacob locked the front door behind him, their voices getting fainter. She then heard Jacob's SUV roar to life—the one they had made out in so many times, the one he had driven with one hand on the wheel and the other on her thigh—and Jacob drove off into his day.

Into his day that did not include her.

Kat would stay in the closet, only crawling out at night when it was safe. She went to the bathroom and urinated in the filthy toilet. She did not flush.

NINE

JESS HADN'T BEEN TO THE apartment for a while. The Lady Wildcats' season was coming to a lackluster conclusion; she had been in South Bend at the Notre Dame Joe Piane Cross Country Invitational. It had been unseasonably cold; frost had laced the course. The whole thing had been a soufflé that never lifted.

She was exhausted entering her apartment, all she needed was a shower and her bed. Jess wanted to hibernate like a bear and not emerge for days. But immediately, she could feel the energy of the apartment, feel the coldness and the shift in the space. Her arms exploded into a galaxy of goosebumps.

"Hello?" Jess called. She knew no one was there.

She also knew Jacob had broken up with Kat and understood it had been bad.

Softly, she walked into the apartment. It was stark. Like walking into a cleaned-up crime scene.

Furniture was missing. Only a futon chair remained. The TV was gone.

"Kat?" she called, knowing it was futile. Jess stepped into the spotless kitchen. She opened the fridge. A lone jug of milk sat in the center. The cabinets were mostly bare. Only a wine opener and two forks remained.

Jess went into her own bedroom. Her bed was just as she had left it—unmade. Closet intact, bathroom untouched. She then walked down the hall, bracing herself . . . and looked into Kat's bathroom. It was sparkling white, clinical.

Jess continued down the hall to Kat's bedroom. It had been cleared out. Empty wire hangers dangled on the closet rod. The bed had been stripped of its sheets, nothing on the dresser. Jess noticed there was a lone piece of paper taped to the dresser mirror. Jess was chilled to the bone as she reached for it on the mirror, plucking it like a rotted apple from a tree. It read:

BYE.

Hands shaking, Jess reached for her cell phone, typed in KAT. The number had been blocked.

Jess then dialed her brother, who picked up across town at his home flip.

"Jess! It's been a minute!" Jacob said.

"J., did you know Kat moved out?"

Jacob didn't respond. Finally, "What do you mean?"

"She's gone. Everything's gone. Like, she vanished. All she left was a note that reads 'BYE,'" Jess said, still freaked.

"Jess, I'm so sorry to get you caught in the middle of this."

"Yeah, I'm never going to introduce you to a single friend of mine again. Ever. You are officially banned," Jess declared, pissed. Then it hit her: "Now I gotta find a new roommate! Great. Like I have the energy for that shit."

Jacob knew he was making his sister's life more complicated. "I'm sorry. I can help you look for—"

"—I'd actually rather avoid your help for a while, bro. BYE," Jess ironically emphasized the last word and hung up. She shook her head, still confused and fuming. She looked up and SCREAMED.

It was simply her reflection staring back from the dresser mirror. Jesus Christ. She crumpled up Kat's note and threw it at the mirror.

. . .

Despite mocking all the reality TV home flip shows populating cable, Jacob really had been naive. On some reptilian level, he *had* believed flipping a house would be that easy. But it was taking longer than 22 minutes.

The problems were endless. There was mold. Framing issues. The city was predictably slow for permits. The insulation was a mess. His money was going fast, and late at night he'd panic.

Still, Jacob found the overwhelming octopus of a project fulfilling. He loved that it was all on the line. He did copious research, found himself pulling over to construction sites to talk shop with workers. He pored over the Internet, watched YouTube videos, read a ton. He was a novice, but he was on the right track.

Mateo was a godsend, and Jacob was so relieved to find he worked beautifully with his friend who rarely bristled and always had a solution. They laughed a lot as friends, and the ease extended to the work site. Mostly, Jacob could trust Mateo, and both knew if the job went well, there would be others to team up on. Neither wanted to compromise the easy rapport and their potential future business together.

Pete did indeed come by the house often to help out and found the project equally fascinating. He declared it was like finally getting to build the tree house he and Jacob never got to complete as kids. Back in the day, they had drawn elaborate plans, interior and exterior scales, chosen the exact tree. Both parents distractedly nodded their approval of the plans, asked plenty of questions but took no further action. The absence of the tree house had haunted them both, and the two boys had spent hours fantasizing about the secret world they'd create. It had crushed them both that the tree house had remained in the planning stage, a pipe dream on a page.

Flipping the house on 3rd seemed to unconsciously undo this travesty.

"We got a head for this," Pete exclaimed one day as he tore down a cabinet with great satisfaction.

"This was *my* idea, remember, Pete. *My* brilliant idea," Jacob reminded him. "And I love that it's feeling like not just an investment, not just a hobby. More like it's my new thing, you know?"

"I'm happy for you, man," Pete said. "But just know, in the meantime—you're always welcome to stay with me and Maya," Pete assured him.

"I appreciate that. I've had about enough of Mom's guest house. At a certain point, you're nearly 30, and . . ." Jacob trailed off, laughed. "Besides, Maya's great. When are you gonna finally pop the question, anyway? You realize our family's generally terrible at secrets, and you *did* get that ring for a reason . . ."

"I'm thinking our anniversary. We've got a few months, and I'm sort of savoring it." Jacob nodded, welcoming the news, as Maya already felt like family.

One night for dinner at Pete and Maya's, Jacob made delicious scallops with English peas, and Maya tried to probe more about the creepy Kat story. Who just up and moves out of an apartment like that, only writing a note with the word "BYE"?

Jacob bristled at the topic. He and Kat hadn't spoken in some time. He frankly didn't want to talk about women for a while.

"Until you move into the house post-flip and some woman jogs by like an 80s movie, all slo-mo," Pete joked. Just then, Pete furrowed his brow and set down his fork, clearly struck by a thought.

"What's up?" Maya asked, spooning out more salad.

"It's just . . . I just realized something. Probably nothing. But . . . J., did you see anything weird at the house yesterday morning?"

Jacob considered. "You mean the water damage?"

"No. I thought I saw . . . when I first arrived . . . I thought I saw 'BYE' written in the dust on the floor." He paused. "I'm making that up, right?"

Jacob and Maya looked at one another. "I hope so. I didn't see anything."

Pete was lost in thought. "I'm sure it's nothing. I sort of did a soft-shoe over it . . ."

Jacob smiled, lightening the mood. "Please don't become one of those people who think your Cheeto's actually a tiny Jesus, Pete."

Pete laughed. "You're probably right."

"More wine, Maya? . . ."

"Are the Kardashians terrible?" Maya joked, and the wine flowed. Kat would not be mentioned again that night, pushed cleanly from their minds.

· · ·

Trudging into her job each day at Antigone Books had been agony. Kat was in a leaden phase, her feet trapped in concrete blocks. Each step was difficult, like moving through water.

The whole world seemed flat, grey. She watched herself move through life like a movie, hovering above, disinterested in the monotony below.

The pain she felt since Jacob shut the door was always there. It was a literal hum, pooling through her veins. She could hear it, like a savage tide in her ears. Sometimes the sound grew so deafening she saw people's mouths moving but couldn't hear, like someone had pushed the mute button on her entire life.

The thought of making a sandwich could make her cry, it was so overwhelming. Crackers were easier. She developed a huge affinity for ginger ale, soothed by the tiny bubbles. Jacob had introduced her to it on one of their first dates. It made her feel close to him, that night not so long ago. He had shown her so much, and she thought of her life in two halves: the part she had survived, and the part with Jacob, which now was a mystery.

Since moving out of the apartment with Jess, she had put her other items into a storage unit. She could write undisturbed in the library. Kat was also sleeping on a cot in the break room at Antigone Books. Kat had keys to the store; it had been easy to get away with. She joined the Y to shower.

When Lucîa found her sobbing in the parking lot, she wrapped an arm around her and asked what was wrong. "I'm an empath, cariña—your pain is my pain!" Lucîa cooed, relishing her role as the benevolent aunt.

It came spilling out of Kat like a broken dam, a torrent of emotion, incoherent in its execution but fully received in its severity. Kat was in trouble, Lucîa knew this.

Kat told her everything. At least, the CliffsNotes. Jacqueline Caron had never inquired further about her chapters. Jacob was the love of her life and had walked away. She had grown up in the foster system.

Lucîa was listening yet had drifted away—break-ups; are rough, Kat would survive—but she snapped right back into the story upon hearing about her childhood in the foster system. She was hungry for more details. Lucîa placed her hand over her mouth when Kat told her about one of her foster fathers who thought the US government was funded entirely by abortions. How had Kat never shared these harrowing details before? Kat had wanted to keep the premise of her book a mystery until it was more concrete, but this sordid tale was information Lucîa would have inhaled.

"I mean, I took some creative license, of course, but the bones are accurate," Kat explained through tears; her eyes swam in grief, nearly turquoise. "I've been doubting myself and convinced it's likely shit."

"Don't. A book like that would fly off the shelf at Antigone!" Lucîa assured her. "And can I just say—I really can't believe we never discussed your childhood before!"

"I prefer to write about it instead of talk about it."

Lucîa nodded her head, filled with total understanding. She also told Kat they must get together for tea, for a meal. She'd make her famous cauliflower tacos—people didn't even miss the meat.

Kat then admitted she had been sleeping in the break room on the cot.

Lucîa was shocked and felt betrayed by her own strong empathic powers. Immediately Lucîa offered Kat a place to stay at her house—hospitality was an important virtue of hers, and Lucîa would do anything to help. Besides, Lucîa had a Murphy bed in her cottage, and guests assured her it was quite comfortable.

"You can stay as long as you like until you get that book deal. And it's coming your way, cariña." Lucîa winked. "Isn't this the book Carol Walsh adored?"

Hearing Carol's name stabbed her heart, but she willed it away. Instead, she forced a calm—or something close to it—to cleanse her. Lucîa took pride in seeing her interaction had soothed Kat.

"I'm always here for you, you know. You're not just an employee to me, Kat," she said, her heart bleeding. "You're one of the most well-read employees I'm lucky enough to have."

. . .

Kat and Lucîa shared the cauliflower tacos—it was delicious, truly even better than beef!—and Kat managed a few smiles. After they opened a bottle of Albariño, Lucîa admitted to a torrid love affair she'd had as a grad student back in the day. "I will tell you, Kat . . . those memories never die. I can close my eyes and *still* feel Antonio's lips on mine. He had these ridiculous pillowy lips. I would have done that professionally, given the choice—just make out with him for the rest of my life. And it's been, what? 35 years? . . . I can *still* lose my breath. But a time will come when those memories are warm, not painful. *Trust me*." Lucîa gave Kat's hand a little squeeze. Older women seemed to love connecting with Kat.

Lucîa was right about one thing—the Murphy bed was more than comfortable. The cocoon of a room was off the laundry room. It was a dark, welcoming cave and gratefully, Kat found sleep.

Kat was thankful for Lucîa's presence in her life, happy to be under her wing. Lucîa even let her borrow a flowy embroidered long sweater Kat had long coveted. It was something a poet would wear, with generous pockets, as colorful as a circus. Lucîa decided the sweater looked much better on Kat anyway and insisted she take it. The sweater became a staple for Kat, and she wore it nearly every day, imagining it not a sartorial item, but more of a shield from the harms of the world.

She felt she was getting better, bit by little bit. Her heart still raced, and Jacob bobbed in her mind like a phantom limb, but she could write some again. Maybe she was climbing out of this muddy cavern of despair, the endless filth of it. Maybe she wouldn't slide back down into its gooey core.

She was improving; she was sure of it. That is, until she saw Jacob stroll past the store.

Jacob's perfect head, a crown of hair housing his delicious brain, walked right past, just like that.

Kat's heart fluttered like a hummingbird's. She dropped a heavy book with a crash. She tore to the front door and outside, blinking in the hot Tucson sun, and watched the man walk away.

It was not Jacob.

There was a shadow of Jacob there, but this man had a bouncy walk, not the wondrous slink of Jacob. His hair was actually meh upon further inspection, his brain likely not as sparkling.

No one was fucking Jacob.

She stood outside, breathing hard, her hands shaking. The hum in her head returned, the accordion of heartbreak. Kat closed her eyes, already saw herself sliding back into that hole, the one that beckoned for her and wanted to swallow her whole. That limitless cavity of utter despair.

Finally, Kat went back inside. Light classical music filled the space but she heard only the hum. The growing, deafening hum. Kat's feet went leaden as the store's resident cat Flaubert laced through her legs.

A small, bird-like woman stood before Kat. The woman's mouth moved, her horribly chapped lips smiling, teeth curling.

"What? . . ." Kat said, far away.

The woman exhaled and adjusted her thick-rimmed glasses. "I *said* I want to write a novel. I've had this idea for years and I was hoping you could recommend a good how-to. I tried Amazon, but every novel-writing guide I looked up had five stars, and that just can't be true."

Kat stared, unblinking.

"Well?" the woman huffed.

Flaubert meowed. Kat looked down; Flaubert blinked his giant gold eyes.

"Shall I ask the cat?" the woman queried in exasperation.

Kat felt a piano wire snap inside her soul. Everything went white.

"You want to write a novel?" Kat asked, eyes unblinking.

"Yes. Based on my childhood. It was *rather* unusual."

Kat laughed, closing her eyes. She exhaled a long breath and a heat overtook her body. Slowly, she opened her eyelids and found the woman's pinched face looking back at her in worried silence. "Alright. I'll tell you the truth, lady. The unvarnished, no bullshit *truth*." The woman's eyes grew in shock. "The truth is, no one cares about your childhood. It wasn't that unusual. I promise you."

"Well! I never!" was all the woman could get out.

"And tell me—how long have you had this goal, exactly? How many New Years have you told yourself that *this* year, 2015, 2017, 2021 is really, *truly* the year you're going to write your masterpiece? Huh? . . ." Kat was on a roll as the woman gaped like a carp. "How many times have you read a book, closed its cover, and shrugged, telling yourself you could do better? Huh? But have you ever ONCE woken up at 4:30 to write? Have you poured your SOUL onto the page only to have NO ONE GIVE A SHIT AT ALL?!"

The tiny woman was frozen as Lucîa ran up. "What's . . . what exactly is going on here?" Lucîa inquired pleasantly, trying to mask her horror.

"Your employee is berating me! That's what's *going on here*! I told her I wanted to write a novel, asked if she could recommend a guide—and then she lobbed obscenities at me! Told me no one cares! This is some business you've got here—" Angry spittle fell from the woman's mouth; other people were frozen, also shocked by the scene.

Lucîa shot Kat a panicked look. "Kat. I am very upset—no, *horrified*—you would treat a customer in this manner. I will speak with you later. Please take the day." Lucîa turned back to the woman, put an arm around her. "Now then. I will take care of you, and I am so, so sorry for this unpleasantness. I'm not going to attempt to excuse it. But I can offer you 50% off your entire purchase," Lucîa explained gently.

The woman perked up hearing 50% off. "Well. What do you recommend?"

Lucîa led the woman toward the WRITING section, whispering calm platitudes.

"I'm sorry," Kat whispered, watching the two women walk away.

Hot tears fell from her eyes. She realized the entire store was staring with looks of utter disgust.

Kat ran out and drove away.

. . .

Kat was all over the road, mind swirling, head bobbing like a ventriloquist dummy. Someone HONKED, she swerved, narrowly missing the car.

"Asshole!" a man screamed as he vroomed past.

Kat flipped him off, her finger stiff with anger. "Fuck you!"

Kat pulled over suddenly, another near miss, another screech of a HORN.

She put her head on the steering wheel and bawled, a tsunami of bitter tears. Her whole body heaved like a dying animal.

Kat was not fucking better.

Truth is, she'd always be a jangle of nerves, a worthless mess, a stupid idiot who preached about literature but couldn't get published. A woman who had lost love and would never find it again. A person so damaged, there wasn't a human repair shop available to put her back together. Her wires were hopelessly crossed, she'd never work properly. And mostly, she'd never get over Jacob. There was no point.

Kat would always be one step away from a total meltdown. The beast of imbalance was always pacing, and he would find his way out of the cage.

She looked up, could feel the heat of the desert sun. The stupid sun, mocking her with its endless loop. Why did people like the sun so goddamn much? Ceaseless, stupid rays of golden fever? What was the point?

And why in the hell did she seek out the desert, anyway? Its very plants were violent. Nothing could bloom here. Least of all her. Worthless, pitiful, inutile her. She'd give anything to unzip herself, shed her skin like a cool snake and step out into a new reality. Become literally anyone but herself.

Lucía would likely fire her. And if she didn't let her go, she would forever look at Kat with trepidation, never quite trusting her. The offer for the Murphy bed would be withdrawn. The bird-like customer would likely stomp back to her home computer to give Antigone Books a ONE STAR review on Yelp.

"AVOID ANTIGONE BOOKS UNLESS YOU LIKE VERBAL ASSAULT!!!!
I'd give ZERO stars if I could! I begrudgingly allow one star because the owner was

so horrified by my treatment, she did give me 50% off my purchase. Unbelievable what social media has done to us all!"

Kat wanted to see Carol. She wanted Carol to lift her wing and let her curl in, shielding her from the pain. She wanted Carol to whisper in her ear, tell her Jacqueline found her writing spectacular, truly *inspired*. She wanted Carol to fix her son, fix her life, fix it all.

Soon she was driving to Carol's. She didn't know what she'd say or do but she had to connect, like a magnetic pull. Her mind raced as she drove by the University of Arizona campus toward Carol's house. The very one that was home to some of the best memories of her short life.

She turned onto her street and sailed past Pete and Maya, driving the opposite direction. Pete's convertible top was down, jazz was blaring, and they were laughing. Laughing like a TV pharmaceutical ad for some horrible disease that looked like tremendous fun.

Kat screeched her car to a stop. She watched Pete and Maya park near Carol's house. Slowly, the top of the car rose into the air, sealing the jazz and people inside. They got out, carrying wine and food.

A family dinner.

Of course.

Jacob was likely to follow. Or he may already be inside. RIGHT NOW. Breathing and talking and living and laughing.

Then Kat saw Jess trot up, always on the verge of a jog. Her legs were powerful, strong. She carried a salad bowl and entered the house.

Kat inched her Honda down the street, parking from a close but safe distance. She killed the engine and waited. Finally—Jacob's silver SUV drove past. Right by her.

Jacob.

He parked, walked out, holding a platter of food.

Kat loved the way he walked. She loved the way he held a platter of food. She could smell him in her mind. She even loved his ironic T-shirt—an armadillo shaped like an Airstream trailer—*she had bought him that very shirt!* It was a very good sign indeed.

Kat held her breath until he slipped inside.

Hours passed. Or maybe minutes. Kat wasn't sure as her mind cartwheeled, imagining the various scenarios for how tonight could go. She saw herself approach the backyard. She saw herself warmly welcomed in one version, tarred and feathered in the other.

But Kat knew the truth. If she appeared in the backyard, she'd be treated like a disease, something you could catch, something that would poison anything good.

Kat got out of the car and inched closer. She watched and listened, got close enough so she could vaguely hear the conversation in the backyard. Their guffaws pealed through the desert air. It was so fucking easy for them, all that goddamn rapport. They couldn't get a word in edgewise, sentences overlapped, laughter exploded. Kat could make out some words now. Kahlo the dog chimed in with an occasional happy bark.

They were all on the back patio; the twinkly lights were on. Carol adored them, always told the same joke: "I feel positively teenage girl about fairy lights. I'm just one string away from happiness." The wine would flow, toasts would be made. Her carne asada sizzled on the grill. Kat could smell its deliciousness. Jacob was likely making his legendary guacamole. It truly was the best guac on the planet.

Kat was just outside the gate. It wasn't hard to hear their conversation. She heard her name and froze.

"Thankfully, my friend Nancy was looking for a place and she saved my ass. She moved in two days ago. But man, for a few days I felt so creepy. Scared to be alone in my own apartment. 'BYE.' What does that mean?" Jess trumpeted. Kat could hear the beer in her voice, the way it made her louder and more sure of herself.

"Anyway. I'm glad it worked out with Nancy. You know I felt so terrible," Jacob said.

"*Everybody hurts . . .*" Pete sang out the REM staple and the laugh track started up again.

"Kat is a fragile person. Complicated, and I do want to remain friends with her," Carol said.

Kat warmed slightly, snapped a bloom off a nearby cactus.

"Mom. Jesus. You don't have to be friends with all my exes," Jacob sighed.

"There's too many for that, Jacob! Kat is . . . special to me. We share a kinship," Carol explained.

"By kinship, do you mean nuts?" Jess joked. Carol clucked her tacit disapproval with a grin.

Kat was shattered. She retreated to a nearby lemon bean bush and hid among its rough foliage. She sat down. It was never going to be better.

. . .

Night had painted the sky a deep blue, the far-off stars and planets twinkled like Christmas lights. Kat had not moved.

Pete and Maya left first. They hugged everyone in the driveway, saying warm goodbyes, promised to get together soon. Jess jumped in the back of their car; they'd drop her off at her apartment.

Jacob and Carol hugged long and hard in the driveway.

"You sure you're okay? I mean about Kat. You can't blame her for having a hard time getting over you. You're pretty terrific," Carol noted with a smile.

"Thank you. But don't worry. At some point—maybe someday soon—I *am* going to bring a woman to the house, and you'll know at long last, I've finally met my match."

Carol hugged him, "I know that, J. I do."

A wrecking ball went through Kat's soul. Her heart imploded. She dug her fingernails into her thighs, felt them puncture, and her fingers pooled with warm blood.

Jacob climbed into his car and drove off, just like that.

He hoped to someday meet his match.

He had not yet met his match.

The hum grew deafening in Kat's mind and the metaphorical fingertips that barely allowed her to cling above the abyss gave way. She crashed and tumbled. She was gone, covered in thick hopelessness, anguished.

It was over.

She thought of Virginia Woolf. She had a room of her own and still she chose to fill her pockets with stones, walk into the river, and never return. She had been published. It wasn't enough.

Methodically and in a daze, Kat filled the roomy pockets of her long sweater with decorative rocks from Carol's front landscaping. She felt the cool of them, coated them with her bloody fingers.

Kat searched for heft, scanned for the larger stones.

Soon her sweater's pockets were teeming like a greedy child stuffing their pockets with chocolate.

She emerged from her hiding spot, her legs achy and pinched from the uncomfortable position she'd held for god knows how long.

Kat walked to the back gate, unsure what was to come. It was unlocked.

Carol had cleaned up most of the mess, bottles put away, plates cleared. The twinkle lights remained, willing the party to continue.

Kat inched forward, step by step, inching toward the pool—her march was catatonic. The water was speaking to her, calling her. It wanted her. It would end the pain, blot it out like an eclipse.

It would be over.

Kat stood on the edge of the pool, watched the light dance on the surface. There was here, and there was there. There was no in between.

She fell in, the water crashed.

Kahlo barked.

"Kahlo, hush." Carol hummed to herself inside the house, washing a big bowl, reminiscing on the fun evening. The mood had been particularly festive, the conversation especially engaging. Jacob did seem well, Pete and Maya couldn't keep their hands off one another, Jess was notably hilarious. It was a lovely night.

Kahlo barked again, more urgent. Carol paused, listened. It was still. Another bark, this time a whine.

Maybe that possum again. Kahlo and the strangely prehistoric creature had a love-hate relationship.

Carol moved onto the margarita pitcher when Kahlo's bark was menacing enough for her to stop and investigate.

"What's going on, friend, huh? What is it?" Carol slowly moved to the backyard, the sounds of Bonnie Raitt still playing on the sound system, lulling her into a half-step.

The backyard looked fine. The pool water did seem to be . . . undulating. An earthquake she hadn't detected? Was that possible? . . .

Carol walked up to the edge and peered down. She gasped seeing Kat, lifeless on the bottom, her chestnut hair floating, her eyes closed.

Carol jumped in, swam down, awkwardly pulled her up to the surface. Kat remained still, her eyes shut.

"Kat! Kat! My god!" Carol dragged her to the side of the pool and fought to lift her body onto the concrete lip surrounding the pool. Kat was lifeless, a doll without joints.

Carol screamed for HELP, begged neighbors to call 9-1-1. Lights came on nearby, neighbors appeared, horrified and shocked. Carol attempted to perform CPR, uncertain she was doing it right, overcome with emotion, crying.

Finally, Kat coughed, water exploding violently out of her. Carol pounded her on the back. "There, there. That's good. That's it. Alright," she cooed, forever the soother.

Kat's eyes fluttered open, far off and hazy. Her skin was a moonish blue.

"What happened?" her neighbor Maria asked from the other side of the fence, breathless.

"Call an ambulance!" Carol barked, too emotional.

They heard the wails of the ambulance in the distance, getting closer. It was the sound of salvation, of lives restored. It was the sound that everything could work out.

"You're going to be fine, my beautiful Kat. Just fine. Stay with me." Carol stroked her face as she took confused, shallow breaths.

"Sorry," Kat barely whispered, then started coughing.

"Don't be sorry. Don't be sorry. We are going to get you help. We all need help, sweet girl. We all do." Carol kept the encouraging platitudes coming, a chatterbox of consoling anxiety.

Kat appeared to pass out.

Paramedics swooped up, flew into action. It was a blur of helpers, a buzz of purpose.

"How long was she under?" an EMT asked, all business.

"I don't know! I didn't even know it had happened!" Carol said manically. "She's my son's girlfriend. Ex-girlfriend."

They quickly lifted Kat onto a gurney, rolled her to the awaiting ambulance. The ambulance lights lit up the neighborhood, a sea of strobing red and blue. Neighbors collected on the sidewalk, hands covering mouths in horror and concern, whispering among themselves.

Carol trotted next to Kat on the gurney. "I'm not going anywhere, Kat. I'm right here."

An EMT worker stopped her. "Ma'am, are you family?"

Carol shook her head no as she tried to enter the ambulance.

"You'll have to stay back."

Carol wasn't having it, indignant. "This woman needs someone! I'm her friend!"

"Follow us to the hospital," he said, and Carol flew back inside, grabbed her keys and purse. Running to her car, she called to a neighbor: "Maria, could you put Kahlo?—"

"Of course, of course, *GO!*" Maria insisted and took Kahlo by the collar back into the house.

Carol spotted Kat's purse laying near the front bush and frantically ran to nab it. She tore back to her car, chasing the ambulance as it wailed ahead, colors lighting the dark sky.

Kat was in and out.

"Stay with us," the EMT said amid the flurry of survival.

"What's the point? Brooklyn's expanding." Kat offered a groggy smile, then closed her eyes.

The EMTs continued their work, sharing a confused look.

The line was from the movie *Annie Hall,* a favorite of Jacob's. He had been so excited to share the film with Kat. They had laughed so easily together. She had felt herself bloom.

The ambulance roared into Banner University Medical Center's emergency wing; a staff awaited them in the circular driveway entrance.

Carol followed right behind, then parked erratically. She dashed up to the entrance, Kat's purse flailing behind her, out of breath. "How is she?"

The EMTs rolled Kat's gurney up to the hospital; Carol trotted beside them.

"She's not lucid. It's clearly a suicide attempt. She had rocks in her pockets."

Carol almost stopped but kept moving.

"We need you to stay out here, ma'am," the EMT instructed, and Carol froze. She watched the gurney and bevy of workers roll into the emergency unit, the giant silver doors sealed shut heavily behind them.

Tears rolled down Carol's face as she quietly quoted Virginia Woolf to no one, "My brain hums with scraps of poetry and madness."

PART TWO

TEN

WHAT HAPPENED NEXT WAS A BLUR. Carol stood numb outside the ER, tears spilling from her eyes, a complete sense of horror chilling her body. A panicked teenage boy with a bloodied kitchen towel wrapped around his hand screamed as he approached the ER, his frantic mother trying to soothe him. Carol thought she might pass out.

Carol waited a moment, then entered the ER like a zombie. She heard buzzes and beeps and screams, like a terror-fueled casino. She wandered around, lost, and finally found a vending machine. She placed coins into the machine, entered 7E. A metal coil swirled, releasing a Reese's Peanut Butter Cup from its grip. The candy fell with a plop and she snatched it up, opened it. Carol nibbled around the chocolate edges first, felt the wave of relief produced by sweet, glorious sugar. Reese's Peanut Butter Cups were her Achilles' heel, her Kryptonite. It was so fucking good. She and Kat had had a long exchange about the magical chocolate and peanut butter orbs.

The sugar hit settled her a bit, gave her some bearings. Then reality moved back in; she had to focus. Carol walked to the front desk. There was a flurry of activity, but finally a nurse looked up to see Carol's shellshocked face. She probably saw faces just like Carol's all day, expressions of disbelief, unrecognizable in grief.

"Can I help you?" the nurse asked.

"Yes. Um . . . I'm here for Kat Lamb. Maybe it's under Kathryn Lamb. With a K and a Y." Carol paused, added quietly: "It was a suicide attempt."

The nurse consulted her computer. "You're family?"

"No. A good friend. A very good friend. She has no family in town. She's very upset about my son. He broke up with her," Carol blurted. She went straight into bawling tears. She was overcome with guilt, as if this was her fault somehow. She hadn't done enough for Kat; she knew how fragile she was.

"If you could have a seat, I'll get back to you," the nurse stated clinically.

Carol found an uncomfortable vinyl seat nearby, needed a distraction and wanted to ground herself. She picked up a "Keto Over 50!" special issue of *Woman's World* magazine. **REAL WOMEN! REAL RESULTS!** it read. **KRISTA LOST 176 POUNDS! AND SHE EVEN ATE DESSERT!**

Krista smiled back at Carol, hands proudly on her hips, Mom jeans snug. Carol then noticed the chocolate that remained on her fingers and sucked on her thumb. *Fuck you, Krista. Fuck you and your sensible stupid bob and your fucking weight loss.*

Carol laughed out loud at her petty thought. She hated when women didn't support one another. Carol knew in real life she'd tell Krista she was proud of her, what an accomplishment to choose health as she did!

Then reality slammed into Carol again. She wasn't here in the ER to have thoughts about a Keto success story, she was here because her son's ex-girlfriend had tried to take her life in her own backyard pool.

Jacob would be devastated.

And Carol had to help Kat.

Antigone Books. Carol vaguely knew the owner Lucîa—she had had a reading there years ago. Maybe Lucîa knew more.

Carol dug for her phone, Googled the store, and called.

It rang and rang, finally a message played, "Thanks for calling Antigone Books, Tucson's favorite independent bookstore on beautiful 4th Street. We're not in or we're helping a fellow bibliophile find the perfect book pairing. Please leave a message and someone will get back to you soon! Gracias and have a GREAT day!"

BEEEEEEP.

"Hello. Hi. This is, uh, Carol Walsh, author—I've read at your store—and English professor at the Uni—" realizing, Carol cut herself off. "You know what? That doesn't matter. It's just that I know Lucîa Alfaro, the owner. Anyway, I'm . . . calling with disturbing news. I probably shouldn't . . . I'll just leave my number, hopefully Lucîa can call me back. Anytime. 602-555-1413. Thank you. Again, it's Carol Walsh. Okay, bye." Carol almost hung up, realizing she'd left out a key detail: "Oh, and uh, this is about an employee. Kat Lamb. Kathryn Lamb. Thank you. Bye-bye." Carol hung up, disgusted with her rambling performance. Could she be more incoherent? Then again, what *is* the protocol for discussing suicide attempts? Was Kat okay?

Carol's iPhone rang; she lunged for it. "Hello?"

"Carol. It's Lucía. I just got your message; I was doing some late-night inventory at the store. It's good to hear from you, but I know you don't have good news," Lucía said cautiously.

"I don't. At all. It's . . . quite disturbing, as I said. It's about your employee Kat—"

"Oh no . . ."

"Kat . . . won't be coming to work for a while. I thought you should know."

"Oh?" Lucía replied.

Carol took a breath, then felt herself ramble. "She was dating my son. They broke up. Rather, he broke up with her. And she tried to . . . well, she tried to take her own life in my pool tonight. I'm at Banner Memorial," Carol blurted. God, she was bad at this.

Lucía gasped. "I am horrified. *Dios mío* . . . Is she okay?"

"Honestly, I don't know yet. She did say a few words, though, so hopefully . . ." Carol trailed off, looked up at the ceiling, and shook her head.

"There was a terrible incident today. In the store." Lucía's mind scrambled, sifting through the details, her anger and dismay at Kat now replaced with a powerful wave of sympathy.

"What happened?"

"She bawled out a customer. It was . . . awful. So uncharacteristic." Lucía tutted softly to herself. "I hadn't fired Kat yet but likely would have. God, I feel so guilty now."

"So do I! It was my son's actions that drove her to this!"

"You know—it's not just that. Kat had mentioned a few times she hadn't heard back from the agent you recommended. She brought it up many, many times, actually. I saw a shift in her . . . the longer the wait went on, the more melancholy she grew. She was really doubting herself and her writing. I knew she wasn't well, but I had no idea. So you haven't talked to a doctor yet?"

"Not yet." Carol switched gears. "Jacqueline Caron hadn't circled back with her?"

"No. Kat was so distressed. I could see her coming undone. She was staying with me, did you know?"

"I did not," Carol admitted.

"Listen, if there's anything I can do on my end, *just say the word . . .*" Lucîa offered.

"Thanks. I'll let you know."

"Thanks for calling, Carol. We'll catch up properly at a more . . . appropriate time."

They said goodbye and cut the line. Carol's mind swam like an erratic, stupid fish. Her thoughts were interrupted when she heard an unfamiliar—

PING! Carol forgot she was even holding on to Kat's purse but saw her iPhone light up through the tote's gauzy material. Instinctively, she reached for Kat's phone and noticed a new email alert.

An email from *Jacqueline Caron*!

Carol's hand covered her agape mouth, her body one giant goosebump. Immediately, she put her reading glasses on to confirm that her eyes had not betrayed her.

And sure enough, there was Jacqueline's email with the subject line: FORGIVE THE RADIO SILENCE!!!

Carol futilely stabbed at the phone, attempting a few logins to no avail.

"Dammit." Carol's eyes darted about the hospital, searching for someone to help. She just had to unlock this missive to discover the news about Kat's memoir. Perhaps it was encouraging information that could buoy Kat in this grim time. Lord, how she hoped Jacqueline's use of three exclamation points— *three!*—in the subject line was an indicator of a positive reaction! It was somewhat pathetic to latch on to a trio of exclamation points, but Carol was desperate for something—anything—promising.

Carol charged up to the main check-in and leaned onto the reception desk, brimming with anxious expectation. The nurse was different from the other woman she'd spoken to earlier; perhaps she would understand the gravity of the situation.

"Hi. I'm here for patient Kat Lamb—she was just admitted—and I just found out something I think—at least, I hope—could truly help her." Carol smiled earnestly and the nurse weakly grinned back, silent. "I need to see her. Please?"

After a long pause, the nurse reached for a phone. "I'll see what I can do."

. . .

Carol was told to take a seat—yet again—and did as she was told, sitting in a woefully uncomfortable waiting chair. She was bleary and exhausted, her mind a whirling mess.

First off, she was assuming Kat was alive.

But what *if* Kat was dead?

What if she was horribly brain damaged?

That would be the most tragic of all—perhaps on the precipice of a book deal, dreams dashed by a compromised brain due to a suicide attempt. A brain that could no longer weave words together into a rich tapestry. A brain that could only pack bags at Walmart and collect pitying smiles from shoppers.

"Mrs. Walsh?" A voice snapped the nightmare out of her mind.

"*Ms.* Walsh. Yes?" Carol looked up, relieved to see a woman doctor.

"Forgive me. Long night. *Ms. Walsh.*" She gave a weary grin. "I'm Dr. Patel. I understand you're here for Kathryn Lamb?"

"That's right. So how's Kat?"

"What's your relationship, exactly?"

"I'm a friend. A very dear friend. She doesn't have family in town, and they'd be difficult to track down anyway. How is she now?" Carol asked, desperate to know *something*.

The doctor put her head down slightly; Carol braced herself. "Stable."

Carol exhaled. "Thank god. Will she be alright?"

"It's early but we are hopeful. How long was she underwater?"

"I'm not entirely sure. I didn't hear it happen. It was my backyard. But it couldn't have been for more than a few minutes. I'd just been outside."

"All it takes is a few minutes of oxygen deprivation to cause brain damage. After five minutes, brain damage is a certainty."

"It couldn't have been that long." Carol considered. "Or could it? . . . God, this night."

"We've cleared her lungs. She'd ingested a lot of water as well, and we have to be vigilant for hypoxia, which is low oxygen in the tissues," the doctor explained. "She's not very lucid. I'm sure you know the EMTs found heavy rocks in her pocket. We are categorizing this as a suicide attempt."

Carol looked down, forlornly shaking her head.

"She'll get a full psychiatric report. A toxicology report will be forthcoming as well. She's going to need a lot of help going forward, but we'll assemble a great team to help Kat as much as possible. We're just glad she's still here," Dr. Patel said, placing a sympathetic hand on Carol's arm.

"Yes. And I know why Kat's been so depressed." Carol brightened. "But I think I have good news I can't wait to share. It's on her phone. Anyway, I'd love to see her."

Dr. Patel furrowed her brow slightly. "Just . . . give me a beat. I'll circle back soon, but trust she's in good hands."

Carol nodded and watched her click down the hallway.

. . .

A search for Kat's family had led to nothing, so the staff relented. Carol would be Kat's contact. A nurse urged Carol to go home and get some sleep. Kat was under sedation anyway, comfortably resting. Carol would be more helpful if she was well-rested, the nurse assured her. Carol could come back tomorrow, perhaps even visit.

Carol dragged herself to her car, a wall of exhaustion slamming into her. The parking bill was exorbitant, but she did not particularly care. All she wanted was her bed. Only then could she recharge. Then she'd be helpful, could re-register this situation and plot accordingly.

She felt responsibility for Kat who was alone in the world. And Carol was sympathetic—she had had the vaguest whiff of suicidal ideations herself. Whispers of crashing her car into a tree often murmured in her ear, a strange and overwhelming impulse to end it all. Mostly Carol envisioned a heavily attended celebration of life ceremony complete with grieving students, literary fans, and . . . Once she saw in her mind her beloved family weeping over her sudden demise, the fantasy drifted away like sand, feeling selfish for having the thought at all.

She'd never do that to the people she loved the most. Never.

On the drive home, she saw the twinkling North Star through her car window on the corner of Speedway and Campbell, and she made a vow. She promised to the star itself she'd help Kat, no matter what. She'd nurse Kat back to health, like a featherless baby bird. The wheels in Carol's head churned thinking of the storyline. It would be literary catnip. Carol would help fortify Kat back to mental health, and Kat would be published thanks to Carol's benevolent introduction to Jacqueline. Carol would inevitably be hailed as a mentor with a heart of gold. Kat's memoir would explode, all possible because of Carol's care. The gesture would not be lost on the literary community. Perhaps it would lead to a new book deal for Carol herself. Maybe their books could be released in tandem—it was precisely the sort of story that the media would eat up. Truth be told, Carol's last novel hadn't sold as well, and this tale might prove to be a necessary ingredient contributing toward Carol's return to her esteemed literary perch.

Carol then realized how egoistical these thoughts were. They were also, sadly, astute. And she knew it.

Once inside, she let Kahlo out of her cage who charged her with a rush of concern, her desperate licks suggesting she knew the situation was grave.

A note from her neighbor Maria was on the kitchen counter:

CALL ME TOMORROW!
HOPE YOU'RE OKAY!

Kahlo followed Carol, uncharacteristically needy. "I know, Kahlo. I know," Carol cooed, collapsing onto her bed. Kahlo leapt up and Carol didn't fight it, she simply wrapped the dog up in her arms.

. . .

Carol awoke with a start; her head was foggy. She knew something important had happened but couldn't remember what. Had she drunk last night?

Yes. More than a few, the kids had come over.

Of course! She'd had to drive to the hospital, which hadn't been the wisest of decisions, considering the margarita and beer. But there'd been no time to think straight.

KAT.

Unblinking at the bottom of her pool. A reckless nod to Virginia Woolf, a poet she had only heard Kat casually mention.

The reality seeped into her pores anew. She knew she was going into emotional battle. She had to armor herself with courage and compassion, she had to be strong for Kat.

Poor delicate thing. Kat didn't know her own strength. She would soon enough. Carol would see to it.

Carol's impulse was to call Jacob. To call Jess. She wasn't sure what to do. Maybe she needed more information. Yes. She'd wait to see where things stood.

She threw herself together—hats were so ideal in these situations—and jumped into her car, headed back to the hospital. She'd grab bad coffee and a mediocre bagel there to face the music.

Carol started rehearsing phenomenal speeches in her mind, uplifting, perfect words that would be a balm to Kat's fragile soul. Aloud, she would read to her Jacqueline Caron's glowing email—at least she prayed that was the case—certain Kat's entire soul would then come back to life. Kat was likely to start crying, so relieved—finally, a reason to live.

Carol tried to think of writers whose suicide attempts had led to creative breakthroughs. She thought of none.

No matter. This would be her triumphant storyline of nursing Kat back to health. And after all, everyone loved all the painful admissions nowadays, there were no secrets anymore, only more and more radical proclamations of woke truth. Sometimes Carol thought things went too far—admitting to eating your own hair, proudly conceding to a secret meth habit. Carol was liberal—far to the left—but she was secretly irritated by the tinny sincerity of spilling "brave" revelations. The whole turn often rubbed her more like a fashion trend than a deeply held set of principles. She'd never admit this out loud.

But this wasn't that. Suicide was something that needed a spotlight. Multiple conversations. She'd heard a story on NPR that suicide had eclipsed car crashes in terms of mortality. It was appalling, and no wonder—everyone seemed so miserable nowadays. Carol would be doing society as a whole a service on some level.

Carol snapped on Tucson's easy listening channel for a hit of normalcy, willing Chaka Khan to be found. Some days, she just wanted to know all the words. It soothed her as much as anything else.

"Islands in the Stream" had just begun, which was a promising sign. Carol sang all the Dolly duet sections and vowed she would take Kat to Dollywood once she was well. Who else in America had the love and respect of drag queens and social conservatives alike? Dolly and Dolly alone, that's who.

She parked and the song concluded. "Dolly's a goddamn national treasure," Carol said to the car then killed the engine and steeled herself for what was ahead.

Carol knew the day was going to be more complicated than a Dolly Parton song.

. . .

Carol entered the bright lights of the hospital, accosted by the sterile lack of personality. The bland artwork, the fake ficus trees that offended her green thumb. Couldn't hospitals try a wee bit harder? Was color and good taste really that verboten?

She approached the check-in station, armed with Kat's iPhone which she just *knew* contained her salvation. A distracted nurse barely registered Carol's arrival.

"Hello, I'm Carol Walsh, here to see Kat Lamb."

The nurse consulted her computer. "If you could take a seat, please."

Carol sat and waited. Finally, Dr. Patel appeared, even more tired than before. Why were doctors—those who encouraged healthy habits—expected to maintain such unhealthy habits themselves?

Carol eagerly blurted, "How's Kat?"

"Better. We're hopeful. Your quick actions likely saved her life."

Carol swelled with pride. "Oh thank GOD. And I just did what anyone would do . . . Can I see her?"

"Alright. Come with me. But this will have to be brief." Carol followed her down the hallway.

They wound down the labyrinth of hallways. Carol peered into rooms, fascinated with the ghoulish display. All this desperation, all this pain. It was terrifying. She'd always despised hospitals.

They arrived at Kat's room, a placard on the door read Kathryn LAMB.

Carol entered gingerly; Kat was connected to tubes and monitors. She looked like a fragile science experiment. Kat was an inert, slack body, not the vibrant brilliant woman she knew. The contrast was startling.

Dr. Patel gestured for Carol to approach. "Five minutes. She won't be able to speak, but she can likely hear you." She turned and left. Carol gingerly approached. This was all so new; she didn't want to get this crucial moment wrong. It was all so fraught.

"Kat . . . Darling . . .," she said, peering down at Kat's face. Her eyes were closed, mascara still vaguely stained her face. She was intubated, and Carol scanned the slow green dot of her heart beeping on the monitor. Carol's eyes filled with immediate tears, but she willed herself strength, hoping her voice didn't crack.

"Kat, hon, it's Carol. I'm here, dear. And it's going to be fine. It will, it really will." She chastised herself for her bland platitudes. Wasn't she the writer? Couldn't she do better than "you're going to be fine"?

Carol brushed Kat's hair off her forehead, tucking it delicately behind her ear.

"Now you listen to me, Kat." Carol awkwardly gripped Kat's hand and worked around the oxygen clamp attached to her finger. "They won't let me stay for long, but I had to share something incredibly exciting, I know this is going to be so good for you. But guess who emailed you back? Would you believe Jacqueline Caron?!"

Carol looked to the monitor but Kat's heart rate did not increase.

Frustrated, Carol reached for the iPhone and then anxiously glanced around the room, almost as if she was about to steal jewels. Carol lifted the iPhone up to Kat's face, but it didn't recognize her with the tubes circling her swollen face. Gently, Carol then placed Kat's index finger on the password ID and miraculously, Kat's iPhone unlocked.

With hands shaking, she retrieved the Jacqueline missive.

"Now then . . . drum roll please!" Carol put her glasses on and carefully read the message aloud, praying that her faith in the exclamation points wasn't all for naught.

Kat—
First off, apologies again for the radio silence. I unexpectedly lost my mother recently and my life has been upside down. Regardless, I LOVED your chapters. I'd also love to read the entire memoir—you've got a keen eye and you are such a heartbreaking, sensitive, and precise writer! Talk soon, call anytime.
—Jacqueline

Carol lapped up the words as if finding an oasis in the desert. She even did a little dance, to which Kat did not respond.

"How about *that*, huh?!" Kat remained motionless as Carol awkwardly maintained her grin. "So here's what I'll do . . . I'll reach out to Jacqueline and explain that you're . . . temporarily indisposed. How's that? I'll be vague, but I'll see to it Jacqueline receives your manuscript. And I think you mentioned you actually thought your memoir was indeed ready. Isn't that right?"

Of course Kat did not respond and remained as slack as a sleeping baby. Carol felt her throat constrict and a maternal wave flood her veins.

"Listen. I won't tell a soul. So put that worry out of your head. I'm going to take care of you, the doctors are going to take care of you, and we're both going to put you back together again." Carol's voice faltered with emotion. "You've just had a terrible fall, that's all."

Carol gave Kat's hand one final grip, and Dr. Patel appeared again, signaling their time had come to an end.

ELEVEN

THINGS WERE COMING TOGETHER FOR JACOB. The entire living room of the house was gutted and open, allowing the space to be more clearly seen. Instead of vaguely creepy serial killer vibe, it now reeked of sheer potential, open and bright. The light flooded through the new updated windows, transforming the entire spot.

Jacob had started building the cabinets, and he'd splurged on kitchen knobs and discounted Moroccan tile. He found a knock-off light fixture on Etsy that would give the space an upscale vibe, a great focal point.

Mateo and Jacob had a total shorthand. Mateo had admitted it was like they'd been working together for years. It was so easy with Jacob.

"I'm serious, man. Not everyone is as great to work with. I haven't had this much fun on a job site since . . . well, since forever," Mateo gushed, flush with Fat Tire Pale Ale.

Jacob beamed. That's exactly what he wanted to hear. If this was going to be his new thing, he wanted everyone to have the same enthusiasm. Jacob never believed work had to be tortured; done properly, work could be enjoyable. He'd always seen that with his mother, even when the writing was hard. He was so relieved that this new venture was falling into place.

"Right back at ya. And thank you for making my entry into these waters so . . . seamless. I *love* this flip, man. I'm having a blast," Jacob admitted as he took a big slug.

"You have a good eye. You can't teach someone that," Mateo enthused. "The whole crew is psyched to work with you."

"Here's to many more," Jacob said, clinking his beer with Mateo's.

Pete was not shocked his brother had found his new calling. Jacob had a Midas touch, and even when a facet of the project exploded a bit, something got derailed, a hiccup emerged . . . Jacob found a way to calmly navigate it with Mateo. He patiently plotted it out, seemed to almost relish the conflict, the chance to extinguish tension. Jacob liked finding solutions.

When Pete complimented his brother on the ease of his new venture, Jacob scoffed. "Pete! You're the one that literally pounded on a piano as a preschooler and found your life's calling."

Pete shrugged, acknowledging this was indeed true. "And we all know how rich jazz pianists get overnight," he sarcastically added. "Why do I get the feeling I'm going to be seeing your face on those cheesy real estate bus ads around town, you wearing some stupid purple tie—'Call Jacob for a JUST PRICE!'"

"*Bus ads?* Oh no. I won't stop until I see *billboards* around town. You know, me with a baby tiger draped over my shoulders, 'FAST CASH FOR YOUR DUMP!'" Jacob laughed.

"Seriously, the house IS coming together. Think you'll move in soon?"

"Ahead of schedule and under budget." Jacob beamed.

"Naturally."

. . .

Carol read up on suicide, wanting to have the right vocabulary and tools. Carol had always been a stickler for research; information was power.

She arranged to meet with Lucîa at her house just off of 4th Street, near Antigone Books. It was a welcoming bungalow steeped in charm—and on some level, a mirror twin of Carol's home. Both places teemed with books, both had walls littered with colorful Southwest-infused and Mexican art. Carol instantly felt right at home.

Lucîa led her to the small space Kat had been using and gestured to the Murphy bed. "I joked with her it's like her own Manhattan apartment!"

Lucîa then offered her Kat's computer with great ceremony, holding it delicately. "Isn't it bizarre this small silver contraption contains everything? Our novels, our memories and photos, our *lives* . . ."

They shared a cup of tea, spoke in hushed tones of reverence that reflected the gravity of the situation. Lucîa wanted Carol to relay to Kat that they could discuss her job when she was back to full health.

"Also assure her, the offer for the Murphy bed remains! Make sure she knows that."

They vowed to do whatever it took to collectively help Kat.

. . .

Armed with Kat's computer, Carol scurried inside the hospital, accosted anew with the sterile air and general desperation. She had hoped to be ushered quickly to Kat's bedside but was instructed to wait. And wait.

And wait.

Finally, Dr. Patel appeared, even more exhausted than before. Carol knew as a non-family member, she had to tread lightly. Kat needed an ally, and she was determined to fulfill this role.

"Dr. Patel!" Carol said. "How's our girl today?"

"Improving. We did an MRI, and it appears there's no discernible brain damage, which is fantastic."

"Oh, thank GOD. She has such a brilliant mind," Carol said.

"We aspirated brackish water from her lungs, so we still have to keep an eye out for infection. When she's stabilized, she'll be placed in a mandatory 5150."

"A what?"

"An involuntary 72-hour psychiatric hold here at the hospital. She'll require an intensive psychiatric evaluation," Dr. Patel explained. "Anyone who attempts suicide must undergo a series of cognition and neuropsychological tests to explore if she has an underlying mental disorder."

"Oh . . . I see."

"We need to determine if she's still a risk to herself or others. You mentioned she'd gone through a rough break-up with your son. Had she ever threatened or hurt him before?"

Carol was aghast. "Physically? No, Kat's not like that." She considered. "Jacob didn't give me *all* the details, naturally, but I know their fights were . . . well, messy."

Dr. Patel nodded. "The more we know, the better. Also, Kat's lack of . . . family connection is unusual."

"All the more reason I need to see her—I'm like a mother to her. And I have her memoir right here." She lofted Kat's computer as if it was Simba the lion cub. "A top literary agent in New York is *very* interested in her work, and it's precisely the sort of thing that can show Kat there's so much to live for."

Dr. Patel considered. "Carol, do you feel guilty about your son ending things with Kat?"

"Well, my son's life is my son's life. I try not to interfere, but I admit . . . maybe I was hurt. I mean, I adore Kat. I really *do* relate to her."

"You just seem very invested in being her cheerleader." Carol studied Dr. Patel, unsure. "Which is fine, but keep in mind Kat needs someone who is around for the long haul."

Carol nodded enthusiastically, secretly worried her benevolence was transparent. "Of course. Could I see her now?"

. . .

Carol was startled to see Kat still connected to a maze of monitors and wires. If anything, she looked worse. Her eyes had deeply sunken, she had shriveled up even more overnight. Her skin was the color of a fetal pig.

"Kat, darling . . ." Carol said, gently stroking her hair. Kat did not stir. Carol edged closer. "Kat?" Carol touched her arm; it was cold and she pulled her hand away. She instantly felt guilty for being slightly repulsed and placed her hand back onto Kat's arm, then gave her an encouraging squeeze.

Kat's eyes barely fluttered open. She gave a weak smile.

"Kat! So good to see you! You look so well!" Carol lied.

Kat nodded, foggy. Carol pulled up her computer, displayed it proudly.

"Look here! I have your computer—and Lucîa wants you to know when you're well again, you still have a place with her."

Kat's eyes relayed vague relief.

"But here's the big news flash: we must get your memoir to Jacqueline Caron immediately. Immediately. Do I have your consent? She wants to read this NOW. Big things are in store, my darling, big things."

Kat nodded.

"Oh, Kat, it's happening! *It's all happening!*" Carol placed a celebratory kiss on Kat's forehead. "Now then. I understand there's to be cognitive sorts of testing—all routine, mind you—and I need to let you rest. You're going to need your strength when Jacqueline Caron calls to praise your glorious memoir."

Kat nodded again, mouthed, "Thank you."

"I'll be back tomorrow," Carol soothed, and left Kat alone in the sterile tomb of a room.

Once back in her car, Carol wondered if she was being too rash—was the shock of the entire situation and Kat's suicide attempt clouding her judgment? Was she jumping the gun—were the edits complete? But Carol just *knew* Jacqueline would have an enraptured response. She trusted she was doing the right thing and wrote a quick note to Jacqueline involving vague circumstances. She also asked that Jacqueline reach out to her directly as Kat was dealing with a health situation, and she would act as her surrogate.

Doing what Kat couldn't, Carol delivered Kat's sparkling words across the country with the touch of a button.

TWELVE

THE PAINTERS HAD ARRIVED AND Mateo was right—they were like a pack of ninjas. Two of Mateo's cousins were on the team, and it was thrilling for Jacob to see his paint selection of White Opulence slide into place, covering the original ghoulish grey.

Jacob had splurged for two giant curved windows in the front, and he knew the investment would pay for itself. The new domed portals made it look like an entirely new house—an exquisite Spanish bungalow brought into modern times. It was becoming a knock-out HGTV "after."

Jacob wanted to install a new gate in the front and personally build a curved wooden door to echo the curves of the windows themselves. He and his mom had been discussing the landscaping, and Carol lit up plotting the design. He knew she'd come up with general sketches that would be more than enough for landscapers to work with, and it would be a desert-hearty oasis.

Jacob had decided to convert the garage into another living space, and Mateo had helped him secure the permits with the city. There was already a car portico and a longer driveway for multiple cars; people wanted another bedroom or office nowadays more than parking. It was a gamble, but Mateo agreed it was the right step.

Jacob began to feel about the house as if it was more of a child of sorts. It was not just walls and a restored fireplace; it had a definitive heart. Jacob adored polishing something discarded into a true jewel underneath all that film of decay. He felt like an archeologist of sorts, an Indiana Jones of renovation, digging to discover the true sheen.

Excited neighbors chimed in on the progress, people slowed down on dog walks, strollers came to a crawl as they passed. Everyone was so relieved the prior eyesore was being slowly blotted out. What was once the embarrassment of the street was quickly becoming the showcase.

So it was no wonder when a red Tesla pulled up in front of the house and Phoebe Cane exited. She silently marveled at the work in progress as her Manolo Blahniks clicked up the driveway.

Phoebe Cane had been a top real estate agent in Tucson for more than two decades. She was a figurehead in the industry with a great reputation as tough but fair, and she had a sprawling team of agents. Phoebe had a face that Carol would have described as "indeterminate age." Phoebe had been buffed and injected, lasered and lifted, to a lustrous beauty, seemingly frozen in the mid-90s. She wore clothes almost cartoonishly out of place in casual Tucson, power suits and flashy jewelry that screamed *Dynasty*. For Phoebe, shoulder pads had never stepped out of favor, yet she made her throwback style look somehow modern.

Phoebe walked the site, peering from behind her Chanel sunglasses. Jacob recognized her immediately—it was hard to miss her billboards around town. He could see her smile grow as she took in the remodel.

"Phoebe Cane?" Jacob inquired, extending a hand.

Phoebe shook his hand, her grin only expanding. "Very good. Is this your flip?"

"It is indeed. I'm Jacob Walsh." He flashed his million-dollar smile and Phoebe studied him carefully.

"You've done an extraordinary job. This reconception is outstanding—just gorgeous! A colleague had noticed the wonderful revival when she drove by."

Jacob beamed. "Thanks. It's a real labor of love. I have a great team, led here by Mateo Arita." Mateo heard his name and approached, offering a hand covered in paint. He realized his error and laughed, retreating it.

"Sorry. Occupational hazard. I'm Mateo."

"Nice to meet you both. How long has this project taken you thus far?"

Jacob and Mateo looked to one another, unsure. "Six weeks? Seven? . . . It's been such a blast, I almost don't want the project to end. I'm not exactly trying to rush—and I want to do this right," Jacob admitted.

"Flips rarely get such high praise. But I can honestly *feel* the joy in the project— you're making the house so *happy*," Phoebe observed. "And people want to walk into a space and see their idealized selves in their idealized home living their idealized lives." Jacob nodded. "I'd anticipate multiple offers with a gem like this."

Jacob and Mateo shared an excited look.

"Are you going to sell it or enjoy it yourself?"

Jacob considered. "That's up in the air. I'm waffling on it. Other agents have stopped by as well."

Phoebe nodded, not worried. "I doubt the top real estate team in Tucson with the most experience has come by, because that's what I represent."

"I know who you are, Phoebe," Jacob assured her with a grin.

"This is uncharacteristically rash of me, but could I take you to lunch to talk real estate?"

Jacob was stunned. "Oh. Wow."

"Wow indeed. You're a natural salesman, I can tell, Jacob. And you can't fake a love of houses. I have a feeling about you."

"I had a feeling about this house."

Phoebe pulled out her card and handed it to Jacob. "I hope to hear from you."

. . .

Kat was moved to the hospital's psych ward, as her medical condition had stabilized. Her lungs were normal; there would be no permanent brain damage. Still, Kat was distant. She could not believe she had survived.

Kat was watching from above, numb. The attempt had at once been totally spontaneous and the result of years of suffering. She truly had wanted to disappear more than she wanted to die. But now that she had lived, she felt strangely little. Perhaps a part of her *had* been extinguished at the bottom of that pool.

Still, a flicker of hope glowed somewhere deep in Kat's belly, whispered that her future could change. Carol was being so attentive, and her words about her book did animate Kat's will. Perhaps this was her low EKG blip of misery, the worst life would lob her way. Her memoir could find a home and all the honeyed fantasies of literary acclaim might actually be realized.

Did Jacob know what she'd done? Carol had promised not to tell him, but she knew these things had a way of tumbling out. She knew once he *did* find out the truth, she could be seen as forever unhinged, a walking advertisement for mental incompetence. A walking suicide attempt.

Kat's team was sympathetic, some more clinical than others. But Kat felt that, to them, she was just another brain to analyze and prod. They assured her they were going to provide real solutions. "When someone is a diabetic or has a heart condition, we don't think twice about prescribing medication. And the same is true for mental disorders. We are here to help you *modulate* your brain and make your life more livable," declared an entirely too chipper member of her psych team.

Kat shrugged.

The psychological evaluation was exhaustive. The questions were shockingly rudimentary, but they assured Kat the test was strangely fool-proof. There were more than 800 questions and at the end of the marathon session, she was exhausted. Her brain panted, she wanted to hibernate for days. They could wake her up with the results that would inevitably confirm she was indeed mentally ill.

• • •

Carol had come to the hospital to meet with the psychiatric team for Kat's diagnosis with great trepidation. She was relieved to see Dr. Patel appear for the meeting, beamed like they were long-lost friends. Then again, they had been through something highly emotional together, a bit like war.

Carol realized she was being too sing-songy with Kat, and this disappointed her to no end. Carol wanted to meet the moment with the appropriate gravitas and poetic wisdom. But instead, she sounded as if she'd turned into one of those meaningless placards on clearance at TJ Maxx—LIFE ALWAYS OFFERS YOU SECOND CHANCES; IT'S CALLED TOMORROW!

Carol's smile was too plastered, too tense. Kat was slack and numb, her hair a sweep of a mess, her eyes far off. Her posture was exhausted, her spine curving into a lowercase R.

Carol winked at Kat. She *fucking* winked like a game show host. Kat barely responded.

"Now then," the small lead psychologist started. "We've gone through a battery of psychological profiles and neuropsychological tests. And Kat cooperated willingly, which isn't often the case."

"I'm super curious to see just how screwed up I am," Kat said flatly.

The team shook their heads and clucked. "Everyone has something, Kat, and we are focused on understanding your brain so we can properly manage your symptoms. Knowledge is power, and a diagnosis of the mind is no different than, say, a hernia tear or a bad knee."

"Everyone keeps reminding me of that." Kat wasn't smoking, but it sort of felt like she should be.

"Our team has concluded, Kat, that you have a bit rarer form of bipolar disorder—of the schizoaffective disorder bipolar type." It was said so pleasantly, you'd have thought Kat had been told she'd just come into some money from a long-forgotten aunt.

Kat nodded matter-of-factly; Carol's head bobbed in acknowldgement, as if this was great news. "Could you explain more about this particular variety of mental condition?" Carol said warmly.

"Certainly. Schizoaffective bipolar type is rooted in mood disorders, chiefly the manic highs and lows you're probably familiar with. This particular type of condition is also connected to psychotic symptoms, such as hallucinations or delusions, as well as symptoms of a mood disorder—bipolar in type and connected with depressive episodes," another doctor chimed in.

"In other words, nuts." Kat's words cut the air.

"Absolutely not," the lead doctor explained. "Nearly half of all adults will claim a mental disorder at some point during their lifetime. So you're not exactly in exclusive company, Kat. And we're going to set you up with weekly psychotherapy and good meds to modulate your moods. Talk therapy plus medication will give you a firm base to reorient your perspective and most important, your life."

"But it's not . . . schizophrenia *schizophrenia*?" Carol cautiously asked.

The Doogie Howser look-alike doctor nodded; Carol was uncertain if it indicated yes or no. "In schizophrenia, mood symptoms usually don't occur without psychotic symptoms. The psychotic symptoms are almost always present, but the mood symptoms come and go. In schizoaffective disorder, the psychotic symptoms may or may not be present during the times when a person is experiencing depression. The distinction isn't as obvious as the description suggests. Emotion and behavior are more fluid and less easy to classify."

Kat grimaced in confusion. "So . . . yes?"

"Yes. But bottom line is this—we now *know* what's at the root of your mania. And now that we know what we're dealing with, we will craft solutions to reinforce good life decisions. And frankly, considering how little support you've had your entire life, Kat, it's a testament to your will how far you've come."

"Yay me," Kat said, looking down, unconvinced.

. . .

Jacob spotted Phoebe Cane already at a table. She was before a vibrant humming-bird mural, and still among all that color, she stood out. Jacob envisioned Phoebe's closet, a cavernous space worthy of *Clueless*, a motorized sartorial display of pre-school colors. Phoebe saw Jacob approach and stood up to shake his hand.

"Hi, Jacob. Thanks for meeting," Phoebe said warmly.

"I love this spot," Jacob enthused.

"The jarred pumpkin blossoms are insane. And any place that has a mural of Anthony Bourdain is good by me," said Phoebe.

"Sir Anthony. I'm still grieving. He's sort of my hero," Jacob stated.

"You love to travel?"

"Yes. I got back from Ecuador a few months ago. I actually bought a ton of Ecuadorian wares and sold them around town," Jacob explained.

"A natural salesman. I knew it." Phoebe nodded, satisfied with her instinct.

"I also have a cabinetry business. My dad was pretty handy."

"You just get more interesting, don't you? . . . So. How's the house coming?" Phoebe inquired.

Jacob pulled out his phone and displayed some pictures. The kitchen was nearly complete, the flooring would go in soon. Jacob beamed with pride going over the details, pointing out his individual choices.

"You're like a proud parent," observed Phoebe. "And it's earned. This is a remarkable flip for a novice."

"Thank you."

"I want to talk about your future. Do you see yourself going into this as a career?"

"It's becoming obvious this should be my new focus. My cabinetry work has always felt sort of . . . like a pit stop, frankly. Obviously, I can continue with it for my flips, but this new step feels so natural. I'm also lucky to work with my friend Mateo, he's such a stand-up guy, as is his whole team."

"The universe has a way of falling into place when your heart and soul are aligned," Phoebe explained. Jacob could feel his mother clapping in agreement from across town.

"I'll cut to the chase. You know my real estate agency produces the most sales volume in town. My team isn't just a sales force; they're my family. I absolutely love real estate and facilitating people's dreams."

Jacob nodded in agreement.

"And I can tell you do, too. So I have a proposal. I'd love to sponsor you and pay for you to get your license, Jacob. Your first listing would be your house on 3rd. And if you wanted to continue with your cabinetry business, I don't see why not—our agency could put that to work." Phoebe leaned in. "Jacob, I want to mentor you, and this is just the start. I believe in you," Phoebe said.

"Whoa," was all Jacob could come up with.

"I think you're an astute person with a keen instinct. More than three decades in the business has afforded me this judgment." Phoebe leaned in. "So. What do you say?"

"I'd say . . . I'm flattered. And shocked, to be frank."

Phoebe nodded. "You should also know I've only done this once before. With Randa Thompson 12 years ago, and she's now my number two agent. I was right then, and I know I'm right now."

"It's a lot to process. I was sort of leaning toward moving into the house myself," Jacob explained.

"I would, too. But this is your start into this world. And I believe your future house is still out there."

Jacob was stunned, processing, buzzy with the possibility and offer.

"Think about it. Now let's have a nice lunch. I want to hear all about you." Phoebe handed him a menu.

"Thank you. And your belief in me. . . . It means a lot. Thank you again."

"Don't thank me. I'll thank you when you catapult to a top agent in Tucson."

Jacob was surprised by how well the lunch went, how seamless the conversation was. He had categorized Phoebe Cane as one of the sorts he and Pete would ridicule to no end—her billboards alone!—but had found her surprisingly refreshing. Phoebe grew up dirt poor outside of Phoenix and worked her way up. She preferred Tucson to Phoenix, claiming it was more truthful: "Tucson knows it's the desert and doesn't pretend to be a suburb of L.A." Phoebe related to the hearty scrappiness of the desert; her personal hero was Dolly Parton. And if Dolly could get away with wigs and lashes, she could continue with her shoulder pads. "Just because Dolly sparkles with rhinestones and has fake boobs doesn't mean she's not 100% authentic. It's a fair statement that I subscribe to the Church of Dolly." Phoebe winked. There was no way his mother could argue with Dolly Parton.

And Jacob wasn't even about to try.

THIRTEEN

CAROL HAD FOUND IT PAINFULLY DIFFICULT not to share the drama about Kat with Jacob, like not mentioning it when someone had a glob of spinach in their teeth. Of course you wanted to point out the obvious.

But Carol needed emotional support, too. Worrying about Kat was exhausting. She was happy to do it—eager, in fact—but at the end of the day, she was leaden with fatigue, weariness hardening in her bones.

She'd been up until nearly one in the morning poring over the Internet, going over everything she could find about schizoaffective bipolar disorder. The language online was so technical, so bleak. She found the initial rush of salvation she'd received from stepping in as a dutiful guardian had diminished. Now she felt overwhelmed. Kat had a major mental disorder that would take Herculean levels of effort to navigate for which there was no actual cure. And Kat had seemed so despondent at the diagnosis, Carol was not comforted. Kat had already been drowning, and the diagnosis wasn't exactly a life preserver of hope that had been tossed her way.

Still, she found many hopeful essays from those who lived with the condition. Carol dutifully printed the evidence to share with Kat so that she could see that people with her diagnosis not only survive, but they can thrive.

And then there was Jacqueline. Carol had received a text from her saying she looked forward to reading Kat's memoir, but she needed a bit more time. There was drama on her end as well, a nightmare of an estate to get through with her mother, details to sew up. Besides, Jacqueline liked to read submissions carefully and her headspace wasn't quite there. But soon, she assured Carol. Soon . . .

Honestly, the greatest glimmer of pleasure in Carol's life at the moment was helping with the design of Jacob's landscaping on his home flip. Plants had always steadied her, much like books. She found succulents to be so optimistic; she related to them somehow. The fact they managed to plod forward at all, to maintain a realistic beauty and even bloom in harsh conditions. Carol felt they were a perfect metaphor for modern life.

Jacob's immersion into his home flip project had been startling to witness. She didn't see this entire chapter coming, and she thought she knew her son well. He was so lit up with excitement. It filled her with trepidation—mostly, she worried he'd get in over his head financially—but she recalled her own parents panicked she'd never make a living as a writer. But Carol had shown them, and Jacob was showing his mother the same grit now. Carol vowed she'd be encouraging, helping with the landscaping was her unspoken amends.

She decided she'd stop by Jacob's project tomorrow with her new plans, hoping she wouldn't babble and reveal Kat's heartbreaking developments.

Really, though, Carol just knew it was a matter of time before Kat's truth came tumbling out. Because the truth was always there, always tugging at the pant leg, always wanting to be heard.

· · ·

Carol arrived at the site with extensive colorful sketches and ripped-out pages from design magazines. She hated to admit she had spent most of the week on Jacob's landscaping plans and dealing with Kat rather than her actual job teaching, and she hoped none of her students noticed how checked out she truly was. She canceled her office hours and besides, her own novel had hit a slow patch, anyway.

Jacob immediately understood Carol's joy with her designs and he was rightfully impressed with her vision. His mother had always been a rather strong artist, though she had no formal training. One of his favorite childhood memories with his mother was the two of them both lying on their stomachs in front of a giant sheet of blank paper—like Santa's Christmas list unfurled. Together, they wielded markers and crayons, drawing endless worlds and creatures, telling stories along the way. Her rule was there were no rules—Jacob could create anything he wanted to on the "white sheet of nothing where anything goes. If you want to draw a giraffe-dog, do it! Or design an apartment for bees!" His mom was a creative livewire, both expansive and patient. The two would build off one another's work.

These were some of Jacob's warmest recollections, something he wanted to emulate with his own family someday. The memory came crashing into him like a tidal wave as Carol excitedly laid out the scrolls of paper, showcasing her landscaping vision.

"How much coffee have you had today, Mom?" Jacob joked.

"How much cocaine have you had today, Mom?" Pete chimed in, and the two exploded in laughter. Carol playfully tutted, anxious to get back to her plans.

"I see two Italian cypress trees in the front—right there," she said, pointing to the spot. "They're so majestic, they'll give it that real Mediterranean flair. The front of the gate will be lined with lavender and succulents. I'd love to lace bougainvillea over the car portico—make the structure beautiful, give it some color."

"Oh, I like that, nice," Jacob marveled.

"Now, I know it's a *wee* bit over budget, but I firmly believe all houses should have a water feature. To incorporate Feng Shui design, a water element is essential," she explained.

"It's basically science," Jacob noted sarcastically.

"The sound of water is soothing, and it's an outstanding visual. I found incredible deals on Overstock.com." Carol pulled out her print-outs; the fountains were beautiful and attractively priced. "For the front *and* back."

"Budget *schmudget*," Jacob said, which strangely wounded Carol.

"Jacob," Carol said, shaking her head in irritation. "You realize I have other things I could be doing."

"Yes, like basking in your students' praise or scrolling through the Chico's website," Pete offered and the brothers laughed.

"Chico's? . . . Now you're just being mean." Carol was contemplating just walking off.

"Mom, c'mon, no one's above some Chico's Chunky Jewelry!" Pete offered, trying to lighten the mood.

"Chico's Chunky Jewelry!" Jacob sang. "And some slimming travel pants!" The boys guffawed at Jacob's non sequitur song.

Often with her boys, Carol felt like a tired substitute teacher of rambunctious students who just wanted to get back to instruction on the monarch butterfly's life cycle.

"Okay, do you want my help or not?!" Carol's tone was louder than she intended.

"Easy, tiger. We're just playing," Jacob said cautiously, still grinning.

"I know! You're always playing, constantly, like goddamn children!" Workers from the site craned their necks in the direction of the drama, then quickly pretended they hadn't noticed at all.

"Whoa," Jacob said. A weird stillness fell over the trio. "Mom. We're just 'consummate joshers.'"

"I know that! But I've worked very hard on these plans . . . and I just feel like you're being very disrespectful to the love I've put into these designs," Carol said, exasperated and a bit startled with herself.

"We get it . . . We do." Jacob paused, locked eyes with his mom. He could tell something was eating at her. "And I appreciate it. They're beautiful. I knew you'd come up with amazing designs. And you have."

Carol stiffly smiled, still reeling a bit.

"Is something else going on?" Jacob asked, looking her in the eye, now serious.

"No. No," Carol said too passionately. "I just . . .well, my novel isn't . . . *flowing*, shall we say."

"But I thought you don't believe in writer's block."

"Pete, goddammit!" Carol erupted again. After a strange moment, she thrust the drawings into Jacob's unsuspecting hands. "Here. Have at 'em. Good luck."

Carol stomped off. Jacob and Pete watched, frozen in shock. She jumped into her Prius and sped off.

Pete and Jacob simultaneously looked at one another, baffled.

"Dude. What the hell was *that*?" Pete asked.

"All I know is a Chico's reference doesn't usually end in fury," Jacob said.

"This . . . isn't about that. I don't know what is going on."

"And it ain't just the novel, either," Jacob added. Pete nodded in agreement.

"Guess you'll have to tell her at another time that she's gonna see her son's face splashed across real estate bus bench ads soon."

Jacob shook his head. "Which likely won't enhance the mood."

He stared down at his mother's designs in his hands, saw her illustrated red arrow pointing to an orange blossom tree in the front yard, accompanied by her tiny, excitable text: DON'T FORGET THE SCENT! MAKE A

GREAT IMPRESSION BEFORE SOMEONE EVEN WALKS THROUGH
THE DOOR!

Jacob grinned and knew he had to get to the bottom of his mother's atypical
conniption fit.

. . .

Jacob appeared at his mom's house bearing a beautiful succulent plant in a colorful blue terra cotta bowl.

"Knock knock," he said, letting himself in the back screen door.

Carol reached for the peace offering. "Echeveria, green sedum, and blooming
cactus! . . . Gorgeous!"

"I'll have you know, I selected these all myself," he explained.

"They're beautiful. I appreciate it, thank you."

"And I appreciate your great landscaping. I'm going to implement all of it.
Mateo's cousin is an incredible landscaper. His bid came in only slightly over budget, but I'm thrilled."

"Does that include the water features?"

"Yes, that includes the water features," he responded with a grin. "But you're so
right—landscaping *is* one of the first impressions people will have of the house."

"I'm quite smart, as it turns out."

"Indeed. But Mom . . ." Jacob moved closer, looked her in the eye. "Are you
okay? I mean—what happened back there at the house today? You're no stranger
to me and Pete joking around with you."

Carol nodded a bit too enthusiastically. "Oh, I'm fine. I am. And I'm sorry
for my outburst." She took a breath. "Like I said, I'm a bit stuck in my novel.
And I don't even believe in writer's block—Pete was right about that—only writers who don't know what they're doing."

"So what *are* you doing, then?"

Just as strangely and just as suddenly, Carol burst into tears. Big, dramatic
teenage tears. They were so abrupt, Jacob's mind wildly spun through reasons why
this was happening. She'd already gone through menopause, hadn't she? He had
no idea what it could be.

"Mom, are you sick or something?" Jacob blurted.

Carol shook her head no, kept sobbing into her hands. She could feel the emotion she'd been bottling on the verge of spilling out like a fountain, close to the precipice of blathering away. Containing this Kat secret was too much to bear. The truth was bound to be found out, anyway.

"Oh, Jacob," she said, and hugged her son. Her patted her back, still unsure what was afoot, eyes darting around the house, looking for a clue.

Kahlo the dog looked up at Jacob and whined.

"Jacob, it's awful. Awful," she whimpered.

"What is? Mom. Tell me."

She couldn't hold it in anymore. Carol collected herself, looked up to the sky. "This is confidential. But you know how I am with secrets."

"Terrible."

Carol nodded. "It's Kat. There was an incident. After you kids left."

"The dinner here?"

"Yes." Carol paused. "And . . . Kat tried to take her life. Here. In the pool." Carol immediately felt a tremendous weight lifted off her shoulders and also profound guilt for betraying Kat's secret.

Jacob steadied himself, leaning onto the kitchen counter. He ran his fingers through his hair, dizzy. His eyes blurred.

"What do you mean?"

"She was likely watching us during our dinner. I don't know. She snapped. Put heavy rocks in her pockets and tried to drown herself. Had it not been for Kahlo's barks . . ."

"Ohmygod," was all Jacob could manage. He slid to the floor. Carol knelt beside him.

"I'm sorry. I'm sorry for everyone."

"But . . . is she *okay*?" Jacob asked, wet eyes glowing with worry.

"She's getting out of the hospital tomorrow. No brain damage, thank god. She's been in the psych ward and got a full evaluation."

"Ohmygod. And? . . ."

"She was diagnosed with schizoaffective disorder bipolar type." Carol paused, studied her beautiful son's grieving face. "The good news is she now has a proper diagnosis and can get the help she needs."

Jacob was slack with shock. Waves of guilt crashed through his veins; he covered his mouth with his hands. "Shit."

"She doesn't want you to know. But . . . I couldn't just walk around with this secret forever, could I?! Besides, I knew you'd want to know." Carol considered her words. "Am I terrible? I shouldn't have told you."

Jacob shook his head. "No, that's a big secret to bottle up. You did the right thing. I'm glad I know. I just feel so guilty. So goddamn guilty." Tears pooled in his eyes. "Kat's one glorious mess, isn't she?"

"A gloriously talented mess. In fact, that New York lit agent is finally reading her work. I hope it leads to good for her. I'm trying to help. I have to. I'm sure you understand."

"Yes. And I hope the agent comes through. God, she's been through so much." Jacob was lost in his own thoughts. "Kat." He considered. "I felt like I knew who she was completely and also that I had no idea at all. If that makes sense."

"It does. I've just been so focused on being there for her. You know she has no one."

Jacob nodded. "Kat," he repeated. Suddenly, the room seemed to shrink, and he felt like the walls were inching toward him. He couldn't look into his mother's sympathetic eyes, he had to escape. He shot up.

"Where are you going?"

"Sabino Canyon. Gotta clear my head." Jacob scanned the room for his keys.

"Remember—this is between us. Do NOT reach out to her and violate the trust she's placed in me. But I thought you deserved to know. I may have done the wrong thing. I'm doubting myself now."

"I have to go."

Jacob exited, Carol on his heels, anxious. "You promise you won't reach out?"

"No," Jacob said, sliding into his car. "Just . . . take care of her, okay?" Jacob pleaded. Carol nodded yes and gave his hand a squeeze.

Jacob's SUV took off, and Jacob started to cry.

. . .

Jacob pulled into the Sabino Canyon parking lot, not having much memory of actually driving. His mind floated away, heavy with plaguing guilt. Walking would clear his head, the methodical one-two, one-two of steps always soothed him and assembled the disarray of his mind into a more cohesive order.

He knew Kat was tortured. Of course. Kat was volatile, up among the clouds one moment, as light as a meringue, then crashing to the depths of despair the next. In retrospect, her actions were not merely artistically erratic, they were driven by more madness. At first the startling shock of her intellectual ups and downs was unique, but by the end, he found Kat exhausting. Her lack of predictability—something he usually loathed in others, finding most people sort of dull—grew depleting.

The fact he hadn't diagnosed Kat with a condition himself made him feel stupid. It was so obvious.

Should he have been more sympathetic? Pushed her toward help? Therapy? Could he have helped her avoid this entire fractured turn?

Jacob knew that their break-up had decimated Kat. He knew she had given herself completely to him and that he was her first love. He should have been more sensitive to her delicate nature, but he had stormed off during that final break, furious, as if dealing with a querulous child. He should have been different. He should have been more human.

Still, it was not up to him to save Kat. He understood that. And he *had* tried. She was one of his longest relationships, and the truth was, once it was truly over, he felt little but relief. The longer it went on, the tighter her grip, the more he lost his breath and himself.

"*Hold on loosely!*" Jacob loudly and unexpectedly sang the .38 Special hit out to the cacti along the trail.

The absurdity of the song made him laugh. Where did that even come from? Everyone pretended to be adults, but everyone was just a fucking child. No one knew anything.

Around the bend, a young couple appeared ahead on the hike. The dad was wearing a baby in a sling on his chest, holding his pretty wife's hand. The dad saw Jacob and lit up.

"Was that .38 Special?" The dad beamed as they approached Jacob.

"Guilty," Jacob said, embarrassed.

The two parties crossed as the dad jubilantly said, "Words of wisdom" as they passed.

"Indeed," Jacob laughed over his shoulder.

The two parties were now moving in opposite directions. Jacob stopped and turned around, watching the couple as they marched back down to base, getting further away.

The couple laughed with one another, continuing with their banter. He heard them singing a bit more of the song and their merriment filled the desert air. You just couldn't fake that love.

God, it looked so easy. Why couldn't he just be like that? Why couldn't he just take a hike with his wife and baby and sing .38 Special? It didn't look hard.

But it felt impossible.

And he had always sought out the impossible, the Kats of the world. He made situations worse, he couldn't commit, he was so easily disinterested.

The irony was, Kat was so broken she had tried to snuff out her life in his mother's pool. But in that moment, he felt just as shattered, just as lost as Kat herself.

He wanted the orange dirt of the desert to give way and conveniently create a throat, grow horrid teeth and gobble him whole. He'd welcome the disappearance, the escape.

Jacob's pulse raced; his mouth tasted of blood. Sweat began to pool on his back, his head a wet mop.

He sat down in the middle of the trail, trying to catch his breath. The sun was setting, the sky was turning marmalade and lavender. Arizona's sunsets were the stuff of clichéd legends, paintbrushes of impossibility.

"Shit," he said out loud.

Just then, he heard his phone *PING*. Instinctively, he reached for it, then read the text:

Phoebe

So happy you've accepted the offer. Good things ahead! Onward! Phoebe

Jacob grinned at the irony, this proclamation of tremendous hope just as Jacob was cratering in on himself.

The phone *PINGED* again; his eyes darted down to see another text:

Mom

> I love you, son. XO MOM

Jacob closed his eyes, placed the phone on his heart, took a deep breath, filled his lungs with hot air. He exhaled deeply, tears running down his cheeks. Gratitude filled his cells.

"You okay?" a voice asked.

Jacob looked up to see a spry older couple staring down at Jacob sitting on the trail. He quickly wiped his eyes and gave an embarrassed smile.

"I am. Thanks."

"Okay. Had to ask. Not every day you see a young man just sitting down all alone in the middle of a hiking trail," the older man explained. His wife chuckled and readjusted her Diamondbacks baseball hat.

Jacob popped up. "Just had a moment" was all he could come up with.

"I've been having them my entire life," said the woman with a grin, and her husband laughed in response. They tipped their hats and moseyed down the path, holding hands.

Jacob watched them go until they were out of sight. "What's with all this fucking happiness?" he said out loud.

A loud voice reverberated in his mind, not Moses on the Mount, but also not his own: *TRY IT SOMETIME.*

Jacob looked up, startled. Above, a hawk made beautiful, lazy circles in the setting sun. It cawed out into the twilight.

"I will," he said, surprising himself with the immediate peace that eclipsed his prior angst. He inhaled gratefully, then turned around and headed back.

· · ·

Carol waited outside Banner Memorial, nervous. Lucîa was to join Carol to take Kat back home. Carol was secretly relieved Lucía had graciously offered to have Kat move back in with her; it removed Carol from a precarious situation. Jacob—who had since moved in with Pete and Maya, wanting more privacy and a fresh start—would not approve of Kat living in his old guest house. Frankly, it *would* be too much.

Carol saw Lucîa approach the entrance with a giant bouquet of cheerful mylar balloons. "Jesus Christ," Carol said under her breath. She waved hello anyway.

The two women hugged, exchanged pleasantries. Lucîa then nodded to the balloons. "Too much?"

"Well . . . Kat is leaving a psych ward, not joining a sorority."

Lucîa immediately released the balloons and the two women laughed.

"Goodbye, absolutely terrible idea," Lucîa said as they waved to the colorful orbs disappearing into the blue Tucson sky. "I'm nervous," she admitted.

"Me, too. And I think the best policy is to acknowledge the elephant in the room—this IS bizarre. For everyone involved. Let's just be honest." Lucîa nodded in agreement. "I've met with her team a few times. They're very hopeful that with this medication Seroquel, she'll find equilibrium. It can help the bipolar aspects of her . . ." Carol's words fell away, uncertain how to phrase it. "Disorder. Schizoaffective disorder. Is that right?"

"Oh, I have no idea. I've read a few articles online. I'm no expert."

"Clearly, neither am I. But let's just tackle this one day at a time, and vow to help Kat in any way."

They gave each other a little nod and proceeded into the gleaming silver hospital.

• • •

Carol and Lucîa were thrilled to see Kat in improved spirits. She did not have the thick film of depression and despair coating her entire being. She looked more like herself; her hair had even been braided. She gave both women a huge hug. Carol and Lucîa exchanged relieved looks, surprised by the turn.

"Thank you. I'd be LOST without you both," Kat said with a weak grin, tears filling her beautiful eyes.

Lucîa squeezed Kat's hand. "Hearing that is like listening to a symphony. And your smile is Mozart for my soul!" Lucîa took in Kat, happy to be together again.

"I can't exactly tell if the medication is working yet, but I am hopeful. Mostly I'm just grateful this whole thing's helped me realize it's NOT my fault. It's just wiring, and I simply need brain assistance to help me find my equilibrium."

"It's at once the most complicated thing in the entire world and the simplest, isn't it?!" Lucîa enthused.

"Lord knows hormones dictate who I am. *Jekyll and Hyde* is a classic for a reason," Carol said.

"Imagine that duality magnified a thousand percent. *That* was my reality," Kat said. "But now thanks to you both—"

"—And thanks to Kahlo's barking!"

"Thanks to my better angels—humans and dogs—I am here. Not many people are lucky enough to get a second chance." Kat gave both their hands an extra squeeze and the only appropriate response was a giant group hug, which happened immediately.

No one let go for a very long time.

. . .

Lucîa had made her famous sweet potato pie and Kat had two helpings.

"Fuck diets. I survived a suicide attempt, yo." Kat laughed, and the trio fell into guilty snickers.

"Oh, I don't need no suicide attempt to fuck diets," Lucîa wisecracked, and the women laughed again.

Carol got serious and leaned in. "Now. There's something I've been wanting to discuss. Something I've given a lot of thought." Carol took a long sip of her wine.

Kat leaned forward, intrigued.

"It's Jacqueline Caron. I know this entire episode is emotional. And I will honor what you want. But . . ."

"There's always a 'but.'" Kat grinned.

"BUT I could reach out to her and delicately frame this truth. This whole reality. How you have survived this attempt, and you are rebuilding your life, and—"

"—Wait, so *market* my suicide attempt?" Kat interjected skeptically.

Lucîa joined in. "From a bookseller's perspective, I see what Carol is suggesting. The storyline *could* be a selling point. The fact you survived your childhood, the fact that it *is* the subject matter of your memoir, the very reason you nearly ended it all—but you LIVED—now *that's* powerful."

"I WILL SURVIVE!" Carol sang out to the tune of the Gloria Gaynor classic and then took another sip of wine.

"My suicide attempt is also about a fucking boy," Kat said, this time more ice

in her voice. "And I don't know . . . using it like it's some noble triumph or something? . . . It's unseemly at best. At worst, it's . . . sort of gross."

An awkward chill filled the air. "Well. No one wants that. Or to make you
uncomfortable. And obviously, suicide is so, so complicated and awful; we all
know this. It's never about one thing," Carol cautiously said. "I guess what I'm
really saying is it can be powerful to be authentic. With your readers and with
yourself. After all, honesty *is* one of the most healing tools of all. Your words could
benefit a great many people, Kat."

Kat considered. Her eyes dancing with thought, she scanned the backyard,
processing her reaction. The moment seemed to play out for entirely too long.

"I see. And I *do* want to be candid. Especially if you think it could help others."

"With every fiber in my being," Carol said and then took a deep exhale. "It
could also sell a hell of a lot of books. Right, Lucîa?"

Lucîa enthusiastically nodded, unknowingly sloshing wine out of her glass.

Kat grinned, though she still felt hesitant. Then she remembered that beautiful
writer at the Antigone Books reading years ago who chronicled her fiancé's death.
Kat could do the same! She could also bare her soul and maybe she *would* connect
with people. Carol saw Kat's eyes dance with light and gave her hand a squeeze.
Kat nodded to herself. "You're absolutely right. Honesty is always the best policy.
Always. But . . . there's just one thing."

"Wonderful! And what's that?" Carol asked hopefully.

"I need to tell Jacqueline myself."

Carol kept her smile in place, careful not to reveal her ulterior motive behind
Kat's success. Hoping to further her own career on the back of someone else's
misery was, as Kat noted, unseemly. Carol peacefully let the mission float away,
confident she'd done her part, which was helping a friend in need. Getting Kat on
her feet was the point. And if Carol *was* literarily rewarded for her benevolence,
then so be it. Compassion was its own reward.

This was a cleaner break.

FOURTEEN

CAROL WAS DRESSED UP—AT LEAST FOR CAROL—and her lips were blood red. She only wore red lipstick for special occasions, and this certainly qualified. Carol had been on the board of the Tucson Arts Council for years—art being the lifeblood of a community and the reason life was livable—and she had fought for many years to bring the work of Kerry James Marshall to the city.

Kerry James Marshall was a prominent painter who depicted modern Black life with vibrant color and grace. He was Carol's favorite artist, and she felt his work was undervalued. Carol hummed with excitement awaiting her family for the opening night of his exhibit at the Tucson Museum of Art.

It was a warm night, and Carol was thrilled for once the air didn't feel so fraught. She could ease into the promise of goodness; Marshall's outstanding work tonight would usher in a new calm, a new joy. Kat was on her feet and seemed renewed, and it allowed Carol to also move forward with more peace.

One by one, her children approached. Her glorious cubs. It was such a joy to see them bound toward her again, like it was when they were small. To see these fully formed adults was shocking—these people she and Matt had created. They were such glowing, exquisite beings, and she secretly said grace whenever they appeared anew. Her books were her creations, but her children were her masterpieces.

Everyone was in great spirits; they knew how much the night meant to Carol.

"Oh, boy. Do I spy . . . *big night red lipstick*?" Jacob noted.

"It *is* a big night! A culmination of *years* of work! I can't *wait* for you all to see Kerry James Marshall's paintings in real life. The scale, the color . . . he's *extraordinary*! I find it all so moving."

"Mom'll be in tears," Pete checked his watch, "in approximately . . . 13 minutes."

Carol nodded yes with a smile. She was all emotion, a mass of feelings, and for better or worse, Carol had plugged her children into an artistic, if not messy, ethos.

"Shall we?" Carol asked, and they approached the entrance. Well-heeled patrons of the arts swelled the sidewalks; the museum pulsed with anticipation. Everyone grabbed a champagne as the trays were passed.

Once inside, Jess proposed a toast. "To our mother who loves art above all else—"

Carol saw her favorite Kerry James Marshall painting in the distance; tears instantly filled her eyes and she gasped: "There it is! *Club Couple!*"

Pete noted her tears, looked again at his watch. "Two minutes, ladies and gentlemen."

Carol marched to the painting as if pulled by a siren's call. Her hands were over her mouth in reverence, quivering in joy. The children followed, jockeying for a position in front of the huge painting.

It was a kaleidoscope of happiness, of color. A beaming couple with rich ebony skin sat in a booth, hands intertwined, leaning in close. Their smiles were infectious, you could feel their connection, the buzz of the romantic night, waft from the canvas itself. The couple had blue martinis next to them, the perfect absurd ritual for an absurdly glorious evening depicted in acrylic paint.

"It's my absolute favorite painting of his. Maybe of all time," Carol said, her voice cracking. "Just the joy. The . . . romance. The promise of a *good night out.*"

The children studied the painting, studied their mom. It was beautiful.

"I get so emotional that this subject matter is audacious. Why is it so rare to see Black love so beautifully depicted? White romance is splashed across every medium from Portland, Oregon, to Portland, Maine, but Kerry James Marshall makes the ordinary *extraordinary.*"

Pete wrapped his arm around his mother. "I love you."

Carol kissed his shoulder, and everyone intertwined, themselves a DNA link of tenderness as they studied the painting. Carol could already see herself years into the future, happily remembering this wondrous night.

They wandered for hours, taking in Marshall's work of sun-drenched lawns, flocks of songbirds, cerulean skies, and deep blue seas. Everyone agreed it was their favorite exhibit. Each child was also moved by the quiet strength of the subject matter, how Marshall elevated the everyday into the ethereal.

When Carol left for a bathroom, Jacob slinked behind her. When she exited, he pulled his mother aside.

"I had to ask you in private. How's Kat?"

"I've been dying to talk to you. She's on a medication now that seems to be helping. She is hopeful and sees a therapist weekly. I'm cautiously optimistic, though I admit I *do* intend to pull back on my end."

Jacob exhaled, hugging his mother in powerful relief. "Makes sense. I am so happy to hear this. So happy."

"You haven't said anything to anyone?"

"No. And I won't." Jacob looked her in the eye. "Now let's get back before Jess and Pete start to talk."

They joined them again, their absence undetected. Both Carol and Jacob shared a wordless vow of secrecy. The night unfurled with a magic found in Kerry James Marshall's paintings themselves. Sometimes when families gather, everyone's cranky, prickly with weirdness. Other times, the rhythm flows with a delicious familiarity and a total enchantment. This night was that.

The Walsh family was among the last to leave. Carol didn't want the night to end. No one did.

"How about a nightcap at the Owl's Club?" Carol offered.

"Yes! And I Ubered tonight, so I'm a big ole hell yes," Jess said.

The four wandered to Scott Street, finding the historic former Armory Park, which had recently been converted into the hip bar. The space was dark and cool, filled with late-night fun-seekers. The bar contained the urban promise of the very painting Carol had loved—a good night out.

They all decided on whiskeys. Jess grimaced at the first sip, declared herself "not a fan."

Carol silently vowed not to let the libations loosen her resolve to spill everything about Kat to her other two children. The situation was copacetic with Jacob, she would leave it at that. She was just terrible with secrets, and it killed her to sit on an amazing story, especially with Kat doing so well now. Still, Carol resisted.

"I have some news," Jacob announced, draining his whiskey and signaling for another. "Keep an open mind." Everyone shared looks of playful trepidation, but it was obvious Pete was in on the secret. "I have a great job offer. A real estate agent stopped by the flip and liked what I was doing. She has a feeling about me."

"Yeah, that you're hot," Jess joked, warming up to the whiskey.

"She knew I was a natural salesman, and . . . well . . . she'd even pay for me to get my real estate license."

Carol was frozen, uncertain. "Real estate license? So . . . *become an agent?*"

"Yes. Become an agent. You don't seem happy."

"I am! I just . . ."

"—didn't see a child of yours becoming a real estate agent." Carol didn't want to be a snob, but it was true.

"Mom, I'm not doing this so I can drive a Jaguar. Or be a douche. I just really think I'd be good at it."

Carol thawed. Of course she had to support her beautiful, smart son. She backpedaled. "I know that! Of course I know that!" she said too enthusiastically. It wasn't very convincing. "So! Which agency?"

"Phoebe Cane," Jacob said, and Carol was just tipsy enough to laugh.

"Phoebe Cane? With the billboards? Jacob—her blonde sales force is called the 'Candy Canes'!"

Immediately, the night cratered. As effortless as their rapport had been prior, it had now dissolved.

"You know what? I should go. I knew this would be your reaction." Jacob stood up, pissed off, and Carol reached for him.

"Stop. Jacob. I'm sorry. That was pretty shitty," Carol admitted. Jacob froze.

"It's actually a great opportunity, Mom," Pete said, defending his big brother.

"I want to hear more. I do. Please, Jacob. Sit back down," Carol pleaded.

Slowly, Jacob retreated, found his seat. The waitress offered him another whiskey, and he took a grateful sip.

"Okay. So Phoebe says it'll take me 90 days to get my license, assuming I pass. And I will. Phoebe's company will even pay to stage the house, allowing me to live there while I sell it. It'll be my first listing. She'll even put the power of her entire marketing behind it." Jacob stared his mother down.

Carol considered, then nodded. "That is a good deal. And I know how expensive staging can be."

"Mom, the reason you know who Phoebe Cane is isn't because of billboards. Her reputation's impeccable. Look at her Yelp reviews. You don't get thousands of five-star ratings for being a cheesy asshole. *And* she wants me to eventually cultivate a home flip division at the firm."

Carol considered this as she took a swig of whiskey.

"Also . . . Phoebe's hero is Dolly Parton."

Carol burst into a wide smile; she slammed her drink down. "Sold!"

Just like that, the night snapped back into focus, found its groove.

"I was a judgy wench, Jacob. Anyone who is a fan of Dolly Parton and sees your promise is fine by me. I trust you, I love you, I believe in you," Carol said with tears in her eyes. She lifted her glass to Jacob.

Jacob clinked her glass and Carol kissed her son on the lips, thrilled the night's magic was restored.

. . .

Kat stared at her bedside clock, shocked by the time. True, she didn't go into work today but she'd managed to sleep until nearly 11. A full 13 hours. Sleep—the once elusive beast—now welcomed her into its comfy, ambitionless cave. She loved the pleasant steadiness she found with the powerful Seroquel medication, feeling slack but oddly sanguine. She knew she had no business to be placid, considering what she'd been through.

I mean, my god, here she was in this crappy little room off a laundry room on her boss's Murphy bed. A few weeks ago, she had tried to end her life.

Still, belligerent optimism crackled in her veins.

Kat could even envision herself in the future at Antigone Books reading her memoir aloud to a big crowd, brilliantly answering questions from eager fans. Naturally, she would have her hair professionally styled.

"Is it true right before *Foster Kid* was published, you had tried to end your own life?"

Kat would grin bravely, nod yes. "It is true indeed. And I say this with a genuine reverence for life and gratitude I didn't think possible. Suicide is a leading cause of death in this country and only on the rise. But I want anyone out there who feels helpless to know it is TEMPORARY. But suicide can be permanent, painfully permanent. I want to usher in candor around the topic, I want to bring the subject of suicide out into the light. Let's diminish its power that feeds off of secrecy and shame! We have the tools to slay it completely, should we choose to face it with honesty *and* compassion."

Wet eyes would stare up at her in thick reverence, whispers of her brilliance would pepper the room. She'd connect with the crowd even more than that children's book author with the great hair.

Later, Kat would sign her books, and when a fan appeared with tears in their eyes, admitting that they, too, had suicidal ideations, Kat would write her cell phone number on the front page of her bestseller next to her autograph and tell them, "Call anytime. I mean it. Your life is worth it."

Her reading would be even more well-received than the one she'd witnessed with that genetically blessed wunderkind writer.

With a small smile on her face, sleep once again found Kat.

. . .

Carol turned on the twinkle lights in her backyard and poured a liberal glass of Sancerre when her phone rang. She answered, and all she heard were happy screams.

"Carol! She loves it! Jacqueline loves it!"

Carol lofted a triumphant fist into the air. Despite her attempts to disentangle from the Kat drama, she still felt grateful tears sprout in her eyes.

"She said *Foster Kid* reminded her of Karen Joy Fowler's *We Are All Completely Beside Ourselves*! You know I love that book!"

"Oh, Kat, I am so happy to hear that! This is extraordinary!"

"She has edits, of course. The ending's too muddy, blah blah blah. But you know I'll do whatever it takes!" Kat enthusiastically wailed into the phone. "Carol, would you be okay to help me edit?"

Carol knew this was her opportunity, the chance to give voice to a new boundary. It was also easier to deliver withholding news during a moment of jubilation. "I believe they'll have an in-house team, Kat. And you have to trust your voice! Jacqueline Caron certainly does!"

Kat's joy ratcheted down a beat. "Oh. But . . . you'll read some pages now and again, right?"

"Kat, let's not talk shop now! I'm just so excited for you!"

Kat giddily flipped back to her ecstatic celebration, exalting in sheer joy. Carol joined back in, the two wailing in delight, charged with relief. It was pure animal jubilance.

Carol saw her neighbor Maria peek her head over the fence with a look of bewilderment, grinning. She mouthed: "You okay?"

Carol nodded YES! Maria gave a thumbs up and shook her head, appreciative she had such a wacky, fun neighbor.

Finally, the high-pitched squeals turned to laughter and then trailed off, both ends of the phone still radiating in mirth.

"I love you, Carol."

"You, too. Enjoy this night. You've earned it."

FIFTEEN

CAROL HAD FILLED KAT'S HEAD with the literary legend of Jacqueline Caron. Her books went on to win National Book Awards and tore up the *New York Times* Best Sellers list.

Of course, Kat still had to firm up the ending, which terrified her. There was a reason Jacqueline identified her memoir as not quite done, and Kat was rudderless how to sew it up. Endings had always been her weak point as a writer. She usually circled the drain for so long nothing seemed to pass, just whirling in useless laps.

Kat rationalized it was because she herself hadn't entirely figured out what she wanted her message to be about the foster system. Was she resentful, weirdly grateful, or still terrified? All of the above?

Still, she somehow believed maybe ambiguity was the point. That maybe her lack of a definitive summation was honest. Kat also suspected it could just be philosophically flabby on her part. Lazy.

Despite all of Jacqueline's enthusiasm, Kat knew she had one last shot to dazzle her. For all intents and purposes, Jacqueline still hadn't officially agreed to represent Kat and take the book out to publishers. The uncertainty made Kat want to unravel the entire thing, and she started to doubt herself. She found herself tinkering to the point of insanity. She was terrified the new medication she was on made her entire being feel like a sheet of glass, a calm lake, but it had also decimated the edge of her words. She now had more discipline, but her language was soft. Common.

Her newly appointed therapist, Judith, assured her this was not true; madness was not connected to great writing or the creative process. That was sheer mythology. Kat simply was having a predictable "freezing of the psyche," realizing the heightened stakes. Kat was on the precipice of tremendous change, and the whisper of having Jacqueline Caron as her lit agent was an overwhelming thought. The enormity crippled Kat, buckled her knees.

Judith reminded Kat she was merely telling a story. That's it. There is a beginning, a middle, and an end.

Carol seemed a bit vague—she had some conferences coming up—but she had agreed to read Kat's final memoir before submitting to Jacqueline. Kat wanted her work to be so powerful that signing her and going out with her book would be the easiest decision Jacqueline would ever have to make.

Kat had never wanted anything more. Her future dangled just overhead, her fingertips grazing her impending fate.

. . .

Phoebe had been so instructive with Jacob. She had steered him toward his coursework and the required 90 hours of in-classroom training. She had happily paid all his fees, so believing in his potential as a future agent in her stable. The amount of work was endless, especially considering he was still knee-deep in his home flip. Jacob attacked both missions with equal zeal, working tirelessly.

He hoped in two months, he would take the state real estate exam and pass, thus ensuring that his first listing would be his own creation. He liked being a student again; he had the chance to do it right.

Carol ironically noted that Jacob and Kat both were involved with a final push, a Sisyphus climb up the hill that at long last would help both achieve a new station. While Jacob toiled on his house and real estate license, Kat was burrowed in the last throes of her memoir.

The laser focus had allowed both to blot out the drama of their lives; both were grateful to have a new target and purpose, to allow the past to fall away.

Granted, it was much easier for Jacob, as most things generally were. He was happy to move on, to leave behind the emotional detritus of his failed relationship with Kat. The guilt still plagued him, gnawed at him. Kat would pop into his mind like a neon thought bubble, and his heart would hurt, but he had gotten rather good at pushing it aside.

Kat was not at all as successful at moving on, of course. Jacob had altered her DNA, lodged into her on a cellular level, and the ache was persistent. She was grateful for Seroquel, her "little darlings" as she called them, which ironed out the kinks in her mind. Admittedly, it slowed her racing brain and made her lust for sleep, in which she indulged. But she'd take being groggy and tired over manically depressed. She found a quasi-peace humming in her veins now, a near-calm that was at once thrilling and a bit disturbing. She did not quite trust it and wondered if the beast was officially dormant or would rise again, hungry once more.

Talk therapy, as it turns out, was an unexpected gift. Kat found her sessions with psychotherapist Judith as comforting as a soft blanket. Kat was on the precipice of changes that would forever mold her into an idealized, healthier self.

Carol was thrilled Kat relied on her sessions more than her now. Of course Judith had the vocabulary to help Kat further—there was only so much reading online articles one could do. Kat needed all the assistance she could get at this crucial juncture, and she was grateful. For all of it.

After many, many weeks—much longer than anticipated, based on how exhausted Kat was most of the time and how flat her brain could often be—Kat had given Carol her final manuscript.

Carol owed her that much.

Late that night, Carol finished Kat's last page and set it down on her bed. She wept. It was the culmination of so much hard work and deep truth. In the end, as best she could, Kat had confidently embraced the ambiguity of her tumultuous childhood as a survivor. She accepted the slipperiness of it, cradled her reality, for better or worse. The experiences had formed her, smoothed her edges, and given her new depths. There would be no final summation, no tidy bow. Surviving was not done. It never would be.

But the memoir was ready, and Carol believed in Kat's unstructured conclusion.

She reached for her phone, texted Kat, offering to meet for lunch to go over the memoir. Carol rationalized this could be the true beginning of their end.

Naturally, Kat called back immediately and a date was set—her treat.

Carol decided before they met that she would barely bring up Jacob. Of course, he was still her son, her heart, and an occasional mention was appropriate. To pretend he had stopped existing seemed unrealistic. To deny Jacob was to deny everything.

At lunch, she did share the news he was working toward a real estate license and that he was going to sell his own flip once he passed the exam. Kat politely nodded, but Carol could not exactly tell if mentioning Jacob's name inspired a tsunami of emotion or a wave of self-disgust in Kat.

"It's just a bit ironic he is so close to finishing his new work, and you are so close to finishing your own," Carol noted, hoping to be transparent and breezy.

Kat nodded yes, afraid to give words to the scream echoing in her soul. "So much in common . . ." Kat said softly, not looking directly at Carol.

Carol took the moment to reach into her bag to hand Kat her finished manuscript.

Kat took it, felt the heft in her hands. Their eyes met. "Is it? . . ."

"Done? Yes. I think so. I really do."

Carol hugged Kat, looked into her eyes. "I am so proud of you. So, so proud."

"Your handprint is on every page, Carol," Kat said with tears in her eyes.

• • •

Later that night, Carol heard her phone *PING* and found a text from Jacob:

Jacob

PASSED! OFFICIALLY GOT MY LICENSE!

Carol took the phone and placed it near her heart. What outstanding news.

But how ironic. Kat was ready, as was Jacob. They were two spirits burning hot for their future that would share a parallel track but would not merge.

She called her son and would not mention this ironic duality between him and Kat.

Carol heard Jacob across town on the other end of the line, his voice warm with celebration. She felt his joy. Carol was so elated. It was true—you are only as happy as your least happy child.

While lobbing excited glee with Jacob, a text came in from KAT:

Kat

JUST SENT DRAFT TO
JACQUELINE!!!!!!!!!!!!!!!!

Carol placed a heart emoji next to Kat's battle row of excited punctuation. The world was truly falling into place.

PART
THREE

SIXTEEN

THE REQUESTS FOR EDEN HART'S book readings had stopped long ago. NPR didn't usher her into their studio anymore for a contemplative chat about her book *Blue* and ultimately, death itself. And Mac was still gone.

Eden's fiancé Cormac Pepper, or Mac as she called him, was a "rare egg." She described him that way because it was true. People had a hard time believing he was for real. But he was. An environmental lawyer, Mac called nature the greatest therapist known to mankind. He also loved Eden with his whole heart.

When Mac got his diagnosis of Hodgkin's lymphoma, Mac and Eden vowed to conquer it together. They had gotten engaged just six weeks earlier and hadn't even selected a wedding date when the first test of their union arrived at their door.

Still, the statistics were on their side. Medical advances had allowed the death rate to drop to only 4%—this cancer was highly survivable. Of course Mac would fall into this category; he was a healthy man who had climbed countless "14ers." This challenge would only heighten their joint commitment to health, and perhaps it would end up being the greatest teacher and gift they ever received.

Inexplicably, Mac got worse. He was accepted into trials. Doctors scratched their heads, couldn't explain why he wasn't getting better. It didn't make sense; Mac was so healthy. Where was the omnipresent luck that had always greeted Mac and Eden? Eden was horrified to admit she felt entitled to it. She gave this thought no breath, but it was there.

They went to experts. Traveled to the Mayo Clinic. Then to a shaman in Sedona. They ate perfectly. They prayed. Nothing worked. Mac got sicker and sicker and finally left the battle of life.

It was over before it began. The doctors said his case would be studied for its sheer improbability.

It was a terrible way for Eden to realize bad luck happened to everyone. She was not immune.

She had been so lucky to find Mac—they were meant to be, all those fables were true. On a flight to Chicago, Mac had sat down in 21A, Eden was in 21B, peeved to have gotten a middle seat. But it led her to Mac. They loved to laugh about how middle seats have their own magic; it became an inside joke. They shared a five-hour flight, breathless with their connection. When the plane landed, it felt like three minutes had passed, and Eden was sure she was in love. Just like that, in a giant metal tube in the sky, her life changed. It was sort of hilarious.

Sometimes, recalling all the specifics made her doubt her own allegiance to truth; surely this had to be made up? Had it all been a concoction, a fever dream? A bad Hallmark movie?

These were the thoughts that years later still roiled in her brain, still kept her awake.

For a brief spell, it seemed the gift of her book *Blue* had made Eden's grief make more sense. She'd willed herself to contextualize the loss, to forge it into meaning. The death of Mac had helped others with their own pain and, subsequently, dulled her own.

But out of nowhere, grief had again reared its ugly, unpredictable head. She started randomly crying all over again. Sleep became elusive too, like a familiar friend that had slipped out one night and never returned. Why was it all so shocking? Of course life would continue to deliver pain. *Blue* was about this very concept. Still, life *was* also supposed to go on, but Eden wasn't entirely sure anymore.

These bleak thoughts floated in her mind like buoys lost at sea, bobbing insignificantly. She saw Mac's face behind her eyelids, heard his laughter out walking in her neighborhood. It was eerie, to so *feel* someone who was not there anymore. She wondered all the predictable big questions—What happens when we die? Where do people go? She had no answers, only questions with the alphabet soup of grief sloshing in her mind.

She was supposed to be better by now, she was supposed to have "moved on." Whatever that meant.

Eden was pissed she couldn't snap herself out of it. She'd paid her dues.

Eden felt useless, hollowed out, just moving parts. It was all horribly familiar.

She didn't want to feel sorry for herself—she truly believed she'd been one of those brave women who faced pain with reflection, staring out at the sea with renewed resolve. Good god, she had a bestselling book as proof! But she wasn't remotely healed after all.

Eden wasn't exactly the praying type—though she'd certainly taken many swings at it while Mac battled cancer—and when she did so, she always felt like an imposter. She knew she was just showing up for the gift bag. Faith and God shouldn't be transactional.

Then one night, Eden found herself so low, so down, she was on her knees in grief. Literally had lost the use of her limbs. She looked up to her ceiling—the one that had watched her make love to Mac—and asked for help. From the depth of her soul, she begged for grace. For something. She'd served her time. She couldn't bear to go back to the well of unending grief.

The prayer was in her heart. She pleaded for calm and to move on with the dignity Mac had always projected in his life. She wanted not to feel so terrible. For it to end. It shouldn't be this hard to just live. Just to get up each day again. Please. She'd do anything. She'd be so much better, she promised.

As if pulled by a mystical force, Eden crawled into bed. She realized her tears had stopped; she felt a hum of calm soothe her soul. The sheets felt cool and perfect; she relaxed and breathed deep into her lungs. She drifted off with the pent-up release of a thousand sleepless nights. Slumber inked into her blood as if by an IV drip, cooling her, cradling her in a perfect embrace. Every muscle fell into symmetry, and she was out.

Eden slept for 14 hours. She did not wake once. She barely moved. This sleep was like a divine gift—it was so profound, so blissful, so necessary.

In her vivid dream, she saw endless blue. She recognized it, of course, as the healing blue from her children's book. It was the blue sky of infinite possibility, not just a summer day but a metaphor of cerulean plausibility. Of magic.

In Eden's children's book *Blue*, a girl named Hayden had lost her dog to cancer and the blues settled into her life. Everywhere she went, the blues followed. It was only an azure world of pain. Hayden saw a parachute of blue form around her head, blotting out any other color. She tried to hide in the dark of her closet, but when her eyes settled, it was a midnight blue. Blue would never let her go in peace.

Hayden then met a new dog who was, perfectly enough, named Blue. The dog was about to become a momma herself and Hayden was offered the pick of the litter. She named him Blue Blue. Hayden realized maybe blue wasn't terrible, maybe blue could be beautiful too.

In the dream, Eden followed the blue sky above and looked down to find a circuitous pathway. Much like Dorothy and the Yellow Brick Road, she followed it, crunching the pebbles under her bare feet. The path led to a darling house; it was a cottage of infinite charm. The house's arches made her heart soar. There was a lemon tree that smelled like the Garden of Eden—her very namesake! Honeysuckles and orange blossoms perfumed the air.

Through the curved, gracious window she saw a figure—a man—wave.

Was it Mac? . . . She couldn't see; the strong sunlight reflected off the glass, disrupting her view. She waved back to the familiar phantom in the window.

Eden inched forward, then stopped when she spotted two dogs on either side of a colorful hammock in the front yard. The hammock was draped between two lemon trees, and she crawled in. The dogs gently pushed the hammock with their noses like Tramp edging the meatball toward Lady, and the hammock started to rock slowly, like she was a baby in a crib.

Eden looked up into the sky, the impossible blue. It was so beautiful, all of nature in one absurd brushstroke. The beautiful blue was still there all along.

Then magically, the clouds in the sky took shape, lolling like puppies in the sky, then forming a word:

NEXT.

And just like that, Eden knew Next was her new tale. Of course you need a Next.

Eden awoke from her perfect amber slumber with a new peace and resolve. She had shifted, just like that, with this magical sleep. This trance of hibernation had been divine. She bound from her bed and went straight for her illustrator's drafting table, feverishly drawing the tale from the dream before it evaporated.

She spilled words as if under a spell, writing some, sketching more. She penned from her heart about the gift of NEXT.

And she would get to the next soon. Very soon.

. . .

In Eden's new book, the dog Blue Blue was all grown up. Hayden was older too, but now she had track practice. And dates. And homework.

Blue Blue was lonely and needed a purpose.

But then one day as Blue Blue looked out a beautiful arched window, he saw another dog walk by with the discernible word "NEXT" spelled out in her black fur, a word tapestry prominent against the dog's white coat.

Next had walked right by. Blue Blue realized you sometimes need a Next to stroll by. For hope to pass your door. For something to live for.

Triumphantly conquering grief and honestly addressing the thorns of loss wasn't enough. You had to get busy with the NEXT. You couldn't sit in your chair and just watch life stroll past.

So the next time the dog Next walked by, Blue Blue bounded outside, and the two forged a deep friendship, plotting new adventures and sharing their love.

. . .

Eden had sent a draft of *Next* to her agent, Thomas, immediately. It might have been rough, it might have come to her as a fever dream, but she believed in it. No project had ever come to her so easily. She had just reached up and pulled it down.

Thomas called instantly, gushing.

One thing Eden always wanted to achieve with her work, in addition to a peculiar vision and humor, was her firm belief that children are people. They are not stupid; they can follow complex thoughts. They can be deep, sad, and happy— children are simply more truthful than adults.

Eden always despised it when as a child, adults spoke to her as if she was mentally impaired. She vowed she would one day interact respectfully with kids, just as her favorite Uncle Mark and Auntie A. had done with her.

"*Blue* gave a language to grief," Thomas said excitedly in New York, overlooking the expanse of Manhattan bustling below. "But *Next* . . . *Next* is a powerful follow-up to the endless work of grief."

"Thanks. I had a dream—a powerful dream, Thomas, unlike anything I've experienced—and I hope *Next* captures the message that it's not enough to simply face pain. You also have to work it. To actively pursue the NEXT as a way to combat the beast of pain. The necessity of HOPE."

"And that's there, Eden. I can feel it. Your illustrations are one thing—stunning—but your words! Once again, such a poet!"

Eden thanked him, relieved.

"Let's craft the illustrations a bit more and get it out. The market will be thrilled with your follow-up."

Eden hung up her phone, gratitude pulsing. Hope was the thing with feathers, and she was also hopeful it was her Next.

. . .

Eden felt more sprightly now when she woke up. She went to the window and pulled back the thick curtain.

Grey. Clouds were thick and depressed, immobile. It was drizzling.

Eden grabbed her phone, hit the Weather app. She grinned to herself—she knew the answer. Rows of animated clouds with thunderbolts and rain popped up for the foreseeable future.

Granted, this was Seattle. It wasn't that shocking, this endless rain. Still, Eden felt the weather had changed when she and Mac had moved in together and they'd bought a cute cottage in the chic Queen Anne neighborhood. There was a view of the Space Needle and the water. It was green and rolling, and the weather had always been dazzling when she visited. Then they moved there, and the rain followed.

It was an easy inside laugh between her and Mac; they loved the irony.

It wasn't funny anymore. She was sick of the grey, sick of the wet.

"Okay, Google, play KCRW," Eden said out loud. Eden still leaned in to her favorite radio station of all time back in L.A., where she had attended the Art Center in Pasadena and got her degree in illustration. Eden felt that "Morning Becomes Eclectic," hosted by Anne Litt, was as essential as coffee itself. She played the coolest blend of funk, old and new—it was perfect. Some days she felt she and Anne Litt must be having a twin existence, she so often reflected Eden's mood through melody.

The opening refrain of "Under African Skies" by Paul Simon started up and Eden buckled in sweet recognition. Linda Ronstadt beautifully sang back-up.

Eden crooned along and her eyes filled with happy tears. Eden closed her eyelids, and in her mind she saw her younger self and her mother dancing in the kitchen to "You Can Call Me Al." Her mother loved the Paul Simon album *Graceland* with a feverish devotion.

Occasionally, a song will appear in your life as if by a miracle. A lyric will reach down from the heavens and grab you by the collar, revealing a truth. That morning, Eden felt the power of the moment as she listened to "Under African Skies."

She let the words pour over her very soul as she listened to the lyrics about a woman born in Tucson, Arizona, asking the lord to give her wings to fly through harmony.

Eden was in a fog; she sat down and stared out the window. The rain was coming down. The sky moved from a slate grey to charcoal.

She realized she not only needed Blue, she needed a Next. Of course.

And then she remembered her visit to the city with the endless cerulean sky years ago for her book reading. She'd loved Tucson from the moment her feet hit the tarmac, the way its heat accosted her, and the way it made her skin warm and her soul dance. Sometimes for no particular reason, a place just makes your soul feel good.

In that moment, Eden knew she was going to move to Tucson, Arizona.

There, with its sky a ribbon of endless blue, the sun ablaze with hope.

Tucson was her Next.

It made no sense and all the sense in the world.

SEVENTEEN

PHOEBE HAD POPPED A BOTTLE of champagne in the office when Jacob passed the real estate exam. "Of course you did," Phoebe said, handing him a flute of bubbles. The team had been shockingly supportive. Jacob had envisioned reality TV levels of competitiveness, but he had only been greeted with genuine warmth.

The house was nearing completion, the landscaping was going in. There was still tile to install, the bathrooms to finish up, last touches, but it was startlingly *there*. To see his sketches lift off the page onto a real space—a real house—was thrilling. He could already envision a young family in the home, already feel the memories the walls would contain.

Jacob had wrestled with whether to live in the house or sell it, but he knew the entire venture depended on obtaining financial security, and he had to see it through. He could already anticipate a big sale coming, and he'd be lying if he didn't admit it was entirely thrilling.

Jacob admitted to Phoebe that now that his project was complete, he felt a bit melancholy. He had so enjoyed the project and on some irrational level, he thought he'd never have to say goodbye.

"The good news is you won't have to. Not for a while. The stagers are going to set up shop this weekend, and you're welcome to move in while we get the marketing ready for the sale."

"Fantastic. One last embrace before we part . . ."

Phoebe laughed. "Design-wise, I'm thinking minimal, vaguely bohemian."

"Operative word being *vaguely*." Jacob grinned.

"Precisely. Jules at Foothill Designs does an outstanding job. It's like we have one brain at this point."

"I really do appreciate the offer to let me live at the house for a bit," Jacob said.

"Of course. You'll keep it impeccable so it can be shown on a moment's notice, that goes without saying. But we'll have to find you a new project STAT. I know you'll be happiest when you're tinkering away on another."

"That and getting my sales sea legs."

"Oh, I'm not worried about you," Phoebe assured him. "Everyone anticipates such good things."

. . .

Jacqueline called Kat with the great news—*Foster Kid* was a slam-dunk. It resonated on a deeper level, her writing was exquisite, and she now embraced the ambiguous ending. Jacqueline's team was excited to take the memoir out.

They were off to the races. Kat's whole being blazed forth with excitement; she was powerfully grateful to be alive. She *did* have so much to live for, Carol was right. The future did not seem so bleak, even if she felt as if her entire soul had been slightly flattened out with medication. For the most part, Kat felt almost sane.

Jacob was still an omnipresent reality, but the noise on the static had been turned down. Other thoughts could dance in her head now. She didn't exclusively throb with a neon sign of Jacob anymore.

Well, a lot of the time this was still true, but not always, and that was enough.

Carol had Kat over for a celebration BBQ—she couldn't help herself. She made her famous carne asada and margaritas. There were too many toasts to count.

"I am so proud of you," Carol enthused, flush with tequila.

"Carol. You've always been there for me. I owe you everything."

"Pish-posh. Don't think I'm just this benevolent healer. Selfishly, this has been tremendous fun for me, too, you know," Carol admitted, hopeful the comment absolved her of her prior ulterior motive to benefit literarily from Kat's rise.

Kat took her hand. "I wouldn't be here without you."

"And I would not be drunk on a Tuesday night without you. It's all your fault . . ."

They broke into familiar laughter and the twinkle lights felt very, very appropriate.

. . .

When Jacob walked into the newly staged house, he resisted an urge to cry. He could feel the tears creeping up, and he pushed them down. Good god, he couldn't start on this note.

Still, the emotion was warranted. The house was already outstanding. But the decor had elevated it to an absurd level of design magazine glory. It was the buttercream icing on top.

The wicker lights so complemented the natural reed window shades. The sage green kitchen cabinets were earthy and perfect, and Jacob's wooden floating shelving gave it a bohemian touch that was all the rage. The brass fixtures gleamed; the appliances shone. Jules the extraordinary stager had found a way to celebrate what was already beautiful—it was minimal, inviting, gorgeous. She had filled the walls with colorful Southwestern art and on the floors, handsome kilim rugs. A fig tree sat in the corner; the floating credenzas were sleekly beautiful.

It exceeded his wildest dreams. Instantly, Jacob was one of those weepy reality star folks who had just walked into their newly conceived space, hand covering their mouth, repeating "Ohmygod!" over and over.

"I take it you like it, then?" Jules the stager asked with a knowing smile.

Jacob nodded yes, but still couldn't find his breath.

"This is a home run," Phoebe gushed. "It's *adorable*. And that doesn't even begin to describe it properly."

The professional photographer set up shop, snapping the rebirth of the space, elevating it further for the marketing materials. Even the photographer had to admit this was one of his favorite houses he'd ever documented.

"And this is his first flip," Phoebe bragged. "You see why I took him on immediately."

Jacob's emotion was several things brewing at once—his happiness, his pride, his excitement. But he was equally sentimental he would not get to live in this perfection forever.

· · ·

"I have to put your father on the phone. This is just too much," Eden's mother, Cass, said in Boulder, Colorado, as Eden stared out at another grey day in Seattle.

Eden heard her mother's panicked mumbles on the other line and her dad, Herb, took the phone.

"June Bug! Now what's this I hear?" Eden's dad happily barked into the phone.

"I'm moving to Tucson, Dad," Eden said matter-of-factly.

"Tucson."

"Tucson."

"To what, pray tell, can we attribute this rather impulsive about-face?"

"I'm sick of the rain. The grey." Eden paced. "And I had a dream."

"A dream, eh?" Her father considered, and then he was off: "'I have a *dream*'!"

Eden grinned. "My dream wasn't *quite* MLK levels of eloquence, Dad."

"Nothing is, peach."

"But it *was* a powerful dream, and right after I heard Paul Simon's 'Under African Skies'—"

Her father sang the line about Tucson, Arizona, and Eden brightened. "Exactly!"

"Oh, for god's sake, Herb," she heard her mother say.

"And I know in my bones I'm meant to move to Tucson, Dad. I need blue skies."

"Don't we all," her father responded. "Well. I think it's a great idea."

"You do?"

"I do. Sometimes change for change's sake is exactly what you need. And hey—we all need our Next."

Eden's eyes welled with tears. She and her dad had always had a shorthand, a spiritual kinship. Of course he said the perfect sentence.

"And Eden—no one should ever disagree with blue sky."

Eden heard some commotion; her mother took back the phone. "You realize you're both irrational, don't you?"

"Yes, I do. Dad and I are the best irrational going."

Her mom considered. "I do love that song."

"I know you do. We used to dance to that album, Mom."

Her mother remembered completely, now instantly on her side. "Oh yes! The whole album is just . . . a poem! Isn't it?" She took a breath. "Well. I won't disagree anymore. Tucson it is."

"Thanks. And soon enough, you'll see."

"Blue sky for all!" Eden beamed in Seattle, knowing her grey reality was about to change.

. . .

Eden sat with her trusty pug by her side, compulsively going down the rabbit hole of Internet real estate. She loved the photo galleries, the breathy descriptions ("Imagine yourself in your own Italian vineyard, all within walking distance of U. of A.!"), the 3-D models.

Zillow was its own sort of porn.

She pored over alternative Tucson weeklies and blogs, researching for in-demand neighborhoods. Eden felt like she was already getting more of a sense of Tucson, but of course it was all still exotic and unknown. She'd never really considered the desert before. All that cactus and lack of greenery; it seemed hostile and arid. But she had found it intriguing during her brief sojourn for the book reading there, and it had seemed like a wealth of subtle beauty. It was harsh and sturdy, but gorgeous in its own right.

Endless shots online displayed the surrounding foothills of Tucson that were orangish red, crayons of impossible hues. It was the perfect backdrop for the postcard sky that beckoned her with its bewitching blue.

Eden found Phoebe Cane's real estate web site when it popped up after a quick Google search. Phoebe was clearly a force; her lacquered face and smiling team looked like an implausible spoof of the real estate world. Eden almost laughed to herself but continued scrolling.

At the bottom was a **COMING SOON!!** section.

Eden clicked. And there it was.

The most stunning Spanish cottage ever. It was dripping with charm and panache, it was everything.

Eden was cooing, talking to herself. "Are you kidding?" She clicked through multiple shots of the kitchen. "Come ON!" she joked to her pug, Don, who did not seem to acknowledge the depth of her emotion.

"Hello gorgeous! . . . Oh my god . . ." she kept mumbling hyperboles scrolling through the impressive pictures.

"Of course there's a separate studio!" She couldn't contain her excitement. "And of course there's a designated workspace, Don!" The pug snorted, bored.

Eden had to take a breath. Then, she spotted the hammock between two lemon trees and her eyes filled with tears.

The hammock from her dream. This was it.

Eden reached for her phone, called the real estate agent's number representing the property—**JACOB WALSH.**

Somewhere in Tucson, he picked up. "This is Jacob."

"Hi, Jacob. My name is Eden Hart. I'm calling you from Seattle, and I'm practically in tears—*tears*—over your house at . . ." Eden strained to locate the address.

"515 3rd Street?"

"Yes." Eden kept clicking. "I would eat this house if I could. Like, just hand me a spoon already."

"So the link is live! You are literally the first person to call about it! My firm must have just launched it!" Jacob looked it up on his computer, and there was his baby in living color. "Hey, hey! Thar she blows!"

Eden laughed. "It's ridiculous. It's practically porn."

Now Jacob laughed. "You're in Seattle, you say?"

"Yes, where the chance of rain is always and yes."

"Do you have a timeline for the move?"

"As soon as I can move into this house."

"I love your enthusiasm. It is special," Jacob concurred. "I, uh, actually, designed it."

"Shut up!" Eden crowed.

"True story. This is my first listing."

"Stop!"

Jacob found himself beaming. "When can you get here?"

Eden considered, overwhelmed. "Well. Be honest. Do you anticipate a lot of heat on this place? I mean, you must. Look at it."

"Yeah. Real estate is hot here. You know, there's a lot of people moving out of California and finding a really nice quality of life in Tucson for a fraction of the price."

"Everyone and their dog is going to want this house." Eden took a breath. "Though I must be honest—my dog is sitting right here next to me, not giving one damn."

Jacob chuckled. "Who's your dog?"

"My pug, Don Lockwood."

"Don Lockwood? Gene Kelly from *Singin' in the Rain*?" Jacob brightened.

"*Yes!* How did you know that? No one knows that!"

"My mom is an English professor. I was watching *Sunset Boulevard* and *Raging Bull* at, like, age six."

Eden grinned, staring out at the soup of ash sky. "I'm coming to Tucson tomorrow."

EIGHTEEN

WHEN JACQUELINE'S FINAL EDITS WERE delivered, Kat took a moment. It was a giant leap forward, and hopefully a new conclusion—and beginning—was near.

Kat went over the notes, tutting in approval. Jacqueline was indeed one smart cookie. The suggestion to collapse the two scenes in chapter three was brilliant.

Kat toiled mightily, molding the final project. Carol, unfortunately, was busy with her own work, but encouraged her to trust herself.

It was a Herculean effort, Kat having to push through her exhaustion and wait out periods of mental fog. Her brain was a spiderweb of turmoil, dull one moment, turbulent the next. Focus was a struggle and often her brain sputtered for words. Still, she flogged herself into submission and paced herself accordingly, despite her unpredictable mind and energy.

Finally, it was done. She was finished, she knew it in her core. Kat sent her work back to Jacqueline gleefully, expectantly.

And then she had to wait. Carol had warned her that waiting *is* often the hardest part of writing. Once again, Carol had proved her unending wisdom.

But a few weeks later, the final manuscript arrived like a magical present—nestled in a beautiful hat box—containing a printout of the final product that would be emailed to publishers. Kat's eyes grew misty seeing her name in large print—

FOSTER KID
by Kathryn Lamb

It was a dream realized, almost too good to be true.

Jacqueline assured her the buzz was strong among publishers. She also alluded to the fact Kat had written the book while living with a mental health disorder. Once people read *Foster Kid*, they, too, would understand Kat's plight and her valiant ability to survive at all. Naturally, Kat would be available to speak candidly about the topic during publicity for the book, should it be released. Kat's struggles could be a beautifully honest parallel track for the book release, publicity catnip.

Jacqueline assured Kat she would call immediately when she heard back and told Kat to "chill a bottle of champagne now."

· · ·

Eden sat with her head against the plane window, marveling at this turn. Normally, she was asleep on a plane immediately—a blissful cat nap always called her name. But not today. Eden was vibrating with possibility, excited by this unexpected shift. She was on a plane to Tucson, a city she'd visited for 48 hours once and now wanted to move to. She almost laughed to herself at the improbability of it all.

Jacob had agreed to meet her at the house at two. She'd Uber there from the airport, hoping her high expectations would not be dashed. Or worse—her expectations would be exceeded, and she'd lose the house to other bidders. She did not want her potent dream to be for naught; she still wanted to believe in her strong intuition. It had always served her well.

Eden knew she didn't have her finances in order. Her own house was not even on the market yet. *Next* was going to be submitted soon, but there was no guarantee of a big sale. Eden was hopeful there would be a buyer for the book—let's be honest, *Blue* was a giant hit—but a lottery win is never guaranteed, especially in publishing.

Eden approached the house from her Uber as Eduardo, her driver, inched to a crawl and she gasped. It was better in real life.

It was the house of her dreams, *from her dreams*.

"Thanks, Eduardo," Eden said in a daze as she climbed out.

"Do you wanna buy this place?" he asked. Eden nodded, grabbing her bags.

"Badly."

"Me too, man," Eduardo the driver laughed. "Good luck." He drove off right as Jacob pulled up.

Eden had her hand over her mouth, tears in her eyes. Could this be her future? God, she wanted a new start. She wanted it *right here*.

"Eden?" Jacob called out as he walked across the street toward her. Eden turned to face Jacob and was thunderstruck.

Shit. Jacob was one good-looking man. More like the best-looking man she'd ever seen in real life. And she was already feeling off-balance from the house itself.

Jacob extended a hand, beaming his movie-star grin. "Nice to meet you, welcome to Tucson! And you *do* work fast!"

Eden pointed to her teary eyes. "I guess this isn't me playing it cool, is it?"

"Believe me. I get it. When I first went through the house after the stagers set up the furniture, I was nearly a reality-TV-crying idiot. I'm not kidding."

"I get it! It's just . . . we need new words!" Eden marveled. Jacob grinned at her earnest appreciation, then scanned the space along with Eden's warm eyes as she traced the property. Jacob realized she was alone; he had half-expected to meet her pug.

"No Don Lockwood?"

Eden laughed. "Don is with Hector, my neighbor. He's a little obsessed with him. Don has a lot of fans."

"A pug you said, right? . . ."

"Yep. It's like owning your own Muppet." Eden repeated her favorite line about pugs and Jacob laughed. They stared at one another, smiles entirely too huge. Both had a sense of familiarity for the other.

"Well! Wanna take a peek?"

"Yes, please!"

Jacob led her to the outdoor front courtyard. "All eco-friendly, hearty and requires little maintenance. It's gorgeous, isn't it?"

Eden nodded, pointed. "Oh, what a beautiful fountain!"

Jacob grinned and bit his tongue. Eden then walked to the hammock hanging between two lemon trees and marveled at it. "May I?"

"Of course! Get comfortable!"

Eden crawled into the inviting hammock, then looked up at the crazy sea of blue above. The sun warmed her glowy cheeks, her smile was wide. "Okay, I'm gonna sound like a crazy person here—"

"—I come from a strong line of them, myself," Jacob joked.

"But I dreamt about this very house, Jacob. I did. This hammock in between two lemon trees. I'm not kidding."

Jacob was taken aback, ran his hand through his hair. "Really?"

Eden nodded. "It's wild. I'm almost afraid to go inside."

"I still think you should . . ." The two walked through the gracious front door and Eden marveled. It was from her imagination of wonder. Every detail, every curve, every precise everything.

"I love it . . . I *love* it," Eden gushed, walking slowly around the open space. "It's incredible."

"Thank you. I had a great team."

"So modest! Way to go team, then! . . . I just love the flow—the kitchen is so happy! And green cabinets, be still my heart."

"You like green, eh? Then again, not too surprising—you *do* live in Seattle."

"Not for long."

"But isn't the city green like Oz?"

"Yeah, but don't forget—all Dorothy wanted to do was click her heels and go home." Eden took a deep breath, basking in the house. She wandered throughout, oohing and aahing. She felt so at home, so at peace; the entire space colored her soul with the joy of the sun.

She stepped outside and followed the pebble path to the converted garage. It was dazzling and she was so grateful there was a separate workspace.

"It was a gamble to convert it as we did, but people want more space, more room. And hey—it's Tucson! You can park your car under the portico year-round, right?"

"Absolutely," Eden said, envisioning her draft table against the far wall; the light was heavenly for her illustrations.

"So . . . what do you do, again, Eden? I forgot to ask!"

"I'm an illustrator. And author. Not as used to that part of the title. I work out of the home."

"Illustrator/author? That's cool. What type?"

"Children's books, mainly."

"Wow! So great. Anything I would have heard of?"

"Do you, uh, have kids?" Eden knew the question had another layer.

"Nope. None that I know of, anyway," he joked.

"I illustrated *If I Don't Get a Puppy I Will Die* and *Hogarth's Hapless Vacation.*" Eden could tell he'd heard of neither. "I won the Caldecott for Hogarth."

Jacob nodded, not following. "What's the Caldecott again? Sorry."

"Basically the Oscars for children's books."

Jacob brightened. "You're kidding! How do I not know that?! My mom's a novelist. She'll be very disappointed I failed that Jeopardy question."

"And more recently, I wrote and illustrated *Blue*, which I'm grateful was so well received."

"*Well, ain't you just a fancy sort of lady, then?!*" Jacob barked in his stalwart British accent, and regret colored his entire face. "That was . . . just a really stupid sentence. Sorry." Thankfully, Eden laughed and turned her attention back to the property.

"Hey, I've been known to drop my fair share of stupid sentences, too. Anyway, I can so see my studio out here. I would *love* to work in this space."

"I'd, uh, love for you to work in this space, too." He followed her, grateful she'd graciously moved on from his middle school fumbling.

Eden looked him dead in the eye. It was difficult; Jacob was so handsome she had to really focus. His voice was pleasant on the phone but she hadn't foreseen this vision to accompany it. "Okay. Tell me the truth. What am I up against? Because I really want to live here."

"Well, we haven't even had our first open house yet. Obviously, I've already gotten a ton of calls."

Eden deflated.

"*But . . .*" Jacob continued. "If your offer was strong enough, we could conceivably take it off the market. I'd have to confirm with my team, but I do think that's an option."

"So it's $729,000?"

Jacob nodded. "It's on the high end, but there are similar comps in the neighborhood. And besides, I don't need to tell you how special it is."

Eden nodded, her mind scrambled. "I just wish this hadn't crashed into my life so unexpectedly the way it did. I know *my* house in Seattle would sell in a heartbeat—it's adorable too, in the Queen Anne section, views of the Space Needle."

"An all-cash offer would also be ideal."

Eden deflated even more. "I have savings but nothing close to that. Not without selling my house first."

"You could put in a contingency offer," Jacob explained.

"Contingent on first selling my house?" Eden clarified.

"Yes."

"But an all-cash offer is going to win every time," Eden said, heartbroken. "I just . . . this isn't rational, this whole thing, but I know this is my place. I know it." Eden tried to pull it together. "I realize I would do terrible at poker."

Jacob chuckled. "I feel like you're meant to be here too, for whatever it's worth."

"You built something really special here, Jacob."

Jacob grinned. "I'm happy to take you around Tucson, show you some other properties. I grew up here, and I really know the city." Eden nodded yes. "And this isn't the only cute home in the town, you know."

"Actually, I'm afraid it is."

· · ·

Jacob escorted Eden the rest of the day, pointing to various Tucson landmarks, filling her in more on the vibe of the city. Eden felt a strange calm and adored the completely new surroundings. It helped Jacob was so helpful, professional, and funny. The two felt like old friends, chatting amiably.

They stopped at several open houses. Eden perfunctorily nodded her approval; several homes were indeed lovely. But her heart was on 3rd Street, it called to her like a phantom limb.

Phoebe Cane rang Jacob in the afternoon to say the interest in the house was incredibly strong; they'd gotten more than 20 calls at the office about it alone, including several requests for early previews. Jacob confirmed he too had gotten serious traction. He knew this was spectacular news but couldn't help but feel a little sad. Jacob wanted Eden to nurture the house and have the chance to set up her new life there. Having an illustrator in the converted garage was a perfect fulfillment of the hopeful, creative space he'd been trying to create.

Besides, she was beautiful. He tried to pretend this didn't matter but it did. Eden was naturally stunning—her loose waves of honey blonde hair and her rich brown eyes were a potent contrast. But it was deeper than that. Her whole being was so recognizable, Jacob wondered if they had in fact met somewhere before.

Still, Eden was literally his first client. He knew better than to wade into anything romantic and compromise this new opportunity. Jacob was better than that. He was, nonetheless, vaguely humiliated that yet again he couldn't help himself from himself, and he pushed the potential of Eden out of his mind.

While Eden checked out a few houses, Jacob made calls and set up several showings on his house for the following day. He was certain the house would likely be snatched up by the end of the weekend.

Jacob offered to drop Eden off at her hotel once their search was complete. Eden had splurged on a beautiful resort in the foothills—La Paloma. She wanted the spontaneous trip to be a reprieve, a reward for all she'd been through recently. She'd even set up some spa treatments for the morning. Jacob insisted he take her back. On the way there, Eden said she just had to submit an offer on the house, even if it was a "fool's errand."

Jacob assured her that he'd do all he could; to him, the project wasn't just a money opportunity—though, of course, it *was* precisely that—but it was also the result of labor and love. He wanted the house to go to the right person who would celebrate it, nurture it like a treasured cub.

They went to the hotel bar to discuss the paperwork. Each got a glass of wine; Jacob made the exchange as easy as could be.

"This is literally the first offer you're submitting?" Eden gushed.

"It is indeed." Eden clinked her glass with his, then noticed the breathtaking sunset happening outside the mammoth window of the lobby. The light was striking the foothills with ridiculous shades of orange, lavenders, deep plums—it was a literal painting. Eden squealed in heady delight.

"Holy shitballs! We must go out and see!" Eden exclaimed, then grabbed her wine and headed for the outdoor patio. Jacob followed her, charmed all the more.

They stood outside taking in the changing sky, watching the magic dance of twilight on the foothills. "Please tell me that doesn't get old."

"It doesn't get old," Jacob agreed. "Arizona has the most beautiful sunsets, they're absurd."

"We so need that absurdity in our life," Eden said. She turned to him. "Be honest. Does my contingency offer stand a chance?"

"I'm going to set you up with our mortgage broker Joaquin. He's known to work miracles."

"But . . ."

"But a strong cash offer will likely rise to the top."

Eden nodded. She understood money spoke loudest in most matters. "Do you think I'm nuts? All the talk about the dream?"

Jacob grinned, shook his head. "My mom gets information from dreams all the time. Plot points for her novels, the works. She once bought a parrot based on a dream. An African grey."

Eden brightened. "Does she still have the parrot?"

"He flew away." The two started to laugh entirely too hard.

"Did he return?"

"He did not." The two started giggling like middle-schoolers on their first date.

"Hey, can you stay for dinner? I was going to eat alone here," Eden offered. "My treat for hauling my ass around town today."

Jacob considered. He didn't want to cross a line, but he also did not want to drive away from Eden. "Sure. I was just gonna watch the Suns game at home."

"Where do *you* live? I forgot to ask!"

"Right now? 515 3rd Street!"

"Stop it!" Eden squealed.

"I get to enjoy it for a brief spell while it's on the market."

"You lucky, lucky bastard," Eden joked.

"Well, you're buying me dinner, so I must be," Jacob said. As they walked back to the hotel, Jacob insisted he would, in fact, be paying for the meal.

"Business expense."

. . .

POP!

The champagne flowed into the three awaiting flutes. Carol, Lucîa, and Kat were ebullient, it was a group celebration, the result of collective toil. While Carol had significantly pulled back from Kat's life, rejoicing in her actual literary win was a no-brainer.

There was a bidding war for *Foster Kid*. Jacqueline had done her due diligence and delivered. Kat heard talk of three publishers—including Simon & Schuster!—and an offer of $80,000 for international rights and $90,000 for North American rights alone. At that point, Kat stopped listening, couldn't process, was so overwhelmed with joy.

FINALLY.

Finally, it had happened. Kat was on her way.

Pathetically, one of her first thoughts was that Jacob would be so dazzled, so impressed. How could he not be when he saw her glamorous black-and-white author's picture, read her lyrical words, saw the blurb from his mother on the cover? He would reach out to Kat offering congratulations, there'd be talk of lunch and—

"To Kat," Carol said, interrupting Kat's fantasy. "Who touched the bottom of despair and crawled back to triumph!" Carol lofted her champagne flute, basking in this victory.

"To you and Lucîa, my fairy godmothers," Kat said, clinking each of their flutes. "You helped me find my way back!"

"YOU found your way back. YOU," Lucîa enthused.

"Yes, but what did Mr. Rogers say about the helpers? Always look for the helpers?" Kat asked.

"Mr. Rogers, be still my heart."

"I mean it, Carol. You two are my helpers."

Carol beamed, then realized. "Are you supposed to drink alcohol on your anti- . . . your, er, your meds?"

Kat pondered. "No. You're right. But . . ." Kat's face burst into a big grin again. "*There's a bidding war . . . On my book . . . For lots of money . . .*"

The trio laughed, clinked glasses again. "I'm sure a little bit of celebratory champagne is *fine*," Carol agreed.

"Hey, Alexa! Play Stevie Wonder!" Lucîa called, and the happy sounds of the song "For Once in My Life" started in her backyard.

The three would boogie late into the night.

. . .

Eden said goodbye to Jacob and could feel the energy between them, the undeniable promise. She knew there was chemistry—their day together had zipped by—but she had to be focused on the transaction itself. She so saw herself starting anew in the house, cooking in the cozy kitchen, setting up her studio in the converted garage where she'd work at her illustrator's table. She already knew where she'd put Don Lockwood's dog door.

Jacob would do all he could to work miracles for Eden. Jacob also explained he was obligated to proceed with the weekend open houses—this *was* his first project, he had to dazzle his new broker, Phoebe, who had even sponsored his license. Eden understood, of course. But Jacob promised to do all he could to make it work. And if it wasn't this house, it would be another.

Eden went to the hotel's pool area to sit on a chaise lounge under the Tucson moon. The breeze was like a warm cocoon, it was perfect. The air was perfumed with orange blossoms, languid and heavenly. The sky was a Jackson Pollock splatter of stars. Just relaxing in this new city was calming, healing.

She exhaled. For so long her life had been dictated by what happened in the past. For the first time in years, she saw a future.

NINETEEN

EDEN PUT HER SEATTLE HOUSE on the market immediately. She wanted to sell the furniture if she could, wanted to move on. She would never forget Mac. But she also didn't want to be where she so felt his presence. It took her entirely too long to realize if Seattle no longer had Mac, she no longer wanted Seattle.

The real estate agent who had sold her the house originally reported good news—the house had appreciated handsomely; the Queen Anne area was in hot demand. The small improvements Eden had put into the house would more than earn the money back. Eden cleared out the space, took down all the personal pictures. She wanted an open house as soon as possible.

Coming back to grey Seattle was depressing. The gloom was too much to bear, she had felt her soul warm in Tucson along with the sun. She would trade the Northwest for the Southwest and not look back.

Jacob called a few days later. She was so excited to hear from him; she had been working tirelessly with their firm's mortgage broker Joaquin who did indeed know his stuff.

"Eden! How are you?" Jacob asked. Eden could feel his smile through the phone.

"Gloomy. I'd rather be in Tucson," Eden admitted.

"Well, you will be soon. And the good news is Joaquin says your credit is outstanding. And no debt—gold star for you."

"Great. My house has appreciated, too, like I emailed, and it's going on the market next week!"

"That's wonderful." Jacob paused, took a breath. "But . . . I just . . . I wanted to be honest on my end."

Eden took a gulp. Dammit.

"There's been so much interest in the house. Already two offers, not including yours. And we haven't even had the open house yet." Saying the words should have been cause for celebration, instead Jacob felt awful.

"Oh. Well. I'm not surprised. Cash offers?"

"One is, yes. The other is contingent, like yours. Though not as strong as your offer."

"Well, that's encouraging," Eden allowed.

"It is. And you know I want you to live there. Even though I doubt I'm supposed to say that," Jacob admitted.

"Well. We'll have to see how the weekend goes."

"I'd also love the info on your house, the asking price, etc., so we can include that with your contingency offer. It might help."

"Of course," Eden said. "I'll have my real estate agent get that to you immediately. I also should hear soon about my children's book."

"Yes! I'm sure it's going to be great news!"

"Fingers crossed."

"Eden. I want you to know—your dream wasn't for naught."

Eden grinned and hung up. She believed Jacob.

. . .

It happened quickly and all at once. Jacqueline encouraged Kat to take Random House's generous offer that included a two-book deal. It was almost too good to be true.

She was disappointed how much thoughts of impressing Jacob managed to maintain a stranglehold. Here she was, a real author—with a two-book deal!—and she was still pining for a *boy*. How intellectual was she, anyway? What a fraud. What a silly girl.

Kat was assigned a publicist and was more than willing to do whatever it took to promote her work. She knew she had to dip her toe into social media—something she had resisted—and also create a personal web site. Kat made it clear she would be incredibly candid about her life. They anticipated a lot of interest; her book and story were the human-interest stories morning shows lived for.

Her savvy editor planned a coordinated book launch for the following spring, even making sure it would release during mental health month. It was so close she could taste it.

Lucîa was already envisioning the over-the-top book reading; she declared it would be like "planning her own daughter's wedding!" She agreed to pull out all the stops: fully decorate and promote the book "into bestseller submission." Kat was touched by her enthusiasm.

With the money from her advance, Kat had started to explore other independent housing options; thankfully Lucîa understood an up-and-coming author shouldn't be sleeping next to the laundry. She needed a space of her own, just like Virginia Woolf! Instantly, Lucîa apologized for the reference; in her excitement she forgot the pockets full of rocks.

Kat found a cute bungalow off of 4th to rent. She *did* want a room of her own.

Her rent application was accepted. Kat had her own space now and her future was limitless. She wasn't sure why she didn't feel more fulfilled. The gnaw of unease was still fucking there, and sadly, Jacob still lingered. Her therapist, Judith, assured her discomfort was inevitable. There is no mythic "Now I'm better, now I'm cured!" moment, no matter how badly Kat wanted it.

Silently, Kat questioned how smart Judith was, anyway.

Kat was in charge of her life now—a soon-to-be published author!—and would ride the storms that might arise. She would embrace her truth, and only then could she find genuine inner peace.

Or at least its approximation.

Kat also was starting to question her "little darling" pills. She questioned the lethargy they summoned and she frankly missed how her brain used to spark. The hyper-erratic reality of her thoughts was forgotten in her nostalgic longing for more vibrancy. Slowing down her brain had also slowed down her body, and she was shocked to realize she'd gained 14 pounds. As much as she'd grown accustomed to her Eeyore languidness, she was worried her creative soul was also being snuffed out. She also hadn't written a word since she'd turned in *Foster Kid*. Kat was curious to see how she'd fare if she cut back on the Seroquel. Bit by bit, she let the pills start to collect, cut her dosage down, but still kept her prescription going, because you never did know . . .

. . .

Jacob called Eden; she braced herself for bad news. And it was.

"I'm so sorry. There were six offers on the house, four cash. It went for $85,000 OVER asking. I really wanted you to have it, you know that," Jacob said, exasperated.

Eden's heart sunk. It was like she had found the perfect dog to adopt, got to cuddle with it for a few hours, and then it was placed with a new owner. She was crushed, even though she had anticipated this.

"Shoot. Crap," Eden said.

"I know. If it wasn't my first sale . . ."

"Jacob. You had no choice. I didn't have my finances quite in order. I get it. It's not your fault."

"I still feel terrible. But I'm already on a quest for you. Gonna send you a link to a fabulous house that just went on the market right after we hang up," Jacob said.

"Cool. And just so you know, my house here is going on the market this weekend, too," Eden said.

"Keep me posted. And I *will* find the perfect home for you."

"I know you will." Eden hung up and cried.

. . .

That weekend, Eden stayed with friends all day, wondering how her open house was going. It was so weird to think of strangers traipsing through her home, peering into her closets, envisioning their own life in her space.

She got a call right after five with great news—there were three strong offers, one all cash! Seattle's housing market was surprisingly durable. The house had been flooded with potential buyers from start to finish, the response had been warm.

"And everyone loved your art!"

"That's the only thing I want to keep."

"The all-cash offer was interested in purchasing your furniture, too. She loved the whole enchilada! And the furniture's quite new, isn't it?"

"I bought it with Mac," Eden stated.

"Got it. And I understand wanting a fresh start. Let me work my magic, but I think we could have this wrapped up with a quick escrow. I'll call with more news."

Eden hung up and decided she would continue to have faith. It was all she could do.

TWENTY

A FEW WEEKS LATER, Eden's team called to say *Next* was warmly embraced. Knopf wanted to rush it into print and had submitted a handsome offer guaranteed to top all others. They were rhapsodic over the prose and felt it was a worthy follow-up to the mad success of *Blue*. *Next* was boldly human and gloriously hopeful.

"It has the potential to become a sort of *Oh, the Places You'll Go!* in terms of accessibility."

"Dr. Seuss is an excellent start, I'd say!" Eden enthused. Dr. Seuss had been her idol as a child, and Eden had insisted on writing "Dr. Hart" on all her elementary school classwork.

"We couldn't be more thrilled," a voice crowed from a conference room somewhere in New York City.

"And the illustrations alone. They're transformative. Healing," another piped in.

Eden's agent rambled platitudes as she stared out of her big window showcasing another dappled and depressing Seattle day. She sighed.

Eden saw Jacob's number come in. "I have to go, everyone! Thanks again so much, can't wait!"

People were still hurling exultant hyperboles as she clicked over to Jacob. She knew she should at least *attempt* to tamp down her enthusiasm.

"Jacob! And how is the fair sky of Tucson?"

"Cerulean."

Eden grinned. She nervously blurted, "I just sold my next book!"

"Congrats! What's it called?"

"*Next!* Which, you know, is my whole point of moving. NEXT!" The two fell into hysterics.

"Eden. It seems this is your day—maybe you should buy a lottery ticket or something."

"Why?" Eden asked, breathless.

"Because the house fell out of escrow!"

Eden screamed, almost dropped the phone. "Seriously?! What happened?"

"The financing fell through . . . blah blah blah. Anyway. I know you're further along—"

"I have the money now! Well . . . soon, when my escrow closes!"

"Are inspections complete?"

"Yes! It's all done!" Eden was worried her desperation was too much. God, she never had been good at faking anything, orgasm or otherwise.

"I said I'd fight for you, and I'm going to. Assuming you can match your original offer—"

Eden twirled, her dress petaling around the room. Don Lockwood watched, tilting his strange pug head. "I'll rob a bank at this point if I have to!"

"Easy, Bonnie." Jacob paused, realizing she might not know the reference.

"Okay, Clyde," Eden volleyed right back.

"Of course you know the reference. I'm so excited, Eden. This was meant to be."

Eden hung up and lofted her pug, eyes twinkling with tears. "Okay, Alexa, play Beyoncé."

The opening notes of "Love on Top" joyfully began and Eden set Don Lockwood down, then loudly clapped in hearty appreciation.

Eden sang along with Queen Bey to Don Lockwood, who looked a bit horrified and not shocked in the slightest by what was happening.

Eden sang along with utter joy, knowing each and every word, dancing with a style that at a bare minimum suggested a lot of video-watching in her past. She was passably fine, more than a bit awkward, but free and happy.

In other words, glorious.

• • •

A few weeks later, a U-Haul pulled onto 3rd Street. Don Lockwood sat next to Eden at the wheel. Eden hummed with excitement; Don Lockwood was unmoved.

"Here it is, Donnie! Our new home!" Eden squealed. The house was even more beautiful than she recalled. She parked, said a little prayer, and approached the gracious house.

At the same moment, Jacob pulled up in his SUV, one hand holding keys, the other a bottle of champagne. He bounded toward Eden who was beaming.

"Welcome home!"

"Thank you!"

"How was the drive?" he asked as he approached, and once upon her, Jacob awkwardly hugged her. The energy between them was strong.

"Not bad. I had a few books on tape," Eden explained as she stretched.

"Your keys, my lady." He handed them to her; she kissed them. "And a bit of the bubbly."

"Why, thank you. I never turn down champagne."

"Shall we?" Jacob led her toward the arched front door. She slid the key in, exulted, turned it. Eden had bought the furniture from the stagers she so loved the decor, and they offered a good discount on the lightly used furniture.

"I love it, I love it, I love it!" Eden sighed, plopping down in the comfortable couch. Don Lockwood was nonplussed.

"You seem a bit more excited about the house than Don Lockwood."

"Don is only excited about one thing: food."

"Don is no dummy. I'm so happy to know it's yours, Eden," Jacob shot back with a grin.

Suddenly, the truth hit Eden. "Jacob! I just realized—where are *you* going to live now?!"

"Oh. Don't worry about me. I've been crashing at my brother's again while I look for a new place. I'm just thrilled I get to leave here on such happy terms."

"Thank you so much for fighting for me. I mean it. You've been an absolute dream to work with. And there's a damn good Yelp review comin' your way."

"Hey, it'd be my first. I'd love it, especially from a professional writer."

Jacob put the champagne into the fridge, then rolled up his sleeves.

"Alright. Let's get you settled."

"You're going to help me *move?*"

"I really want that good review, Eden," he said, beaming.

• • •

Several hours later, Eden's U-Haul was cleared. Jacob was covered with sweat; he glistened. Eden tried to be nonchalant and not notice his almost alien attractiveness, but it was a bit futile.

Moving is always at the bottom of the list along with root canals and racist uncles, but Eden and Jacob chatted easily, laughing at their achy backs.

Her illustrator's drafting board fit perfectly in the converted garage; her plentiful art leaned up against various walls, awaiting their forever home.

Boxes exploded everywhere.

But it was real.

"What'd ya say? I think that champagne is cold by now," Jacob said.

Eden nodded and went to wash out two champagne flutes.

Jacob popped open the champagne, and Eden did a happy dance. "Greatest sound in the world, isn't it?" She then loudly mimicked the POP herself.

They toasted to the house, and then Eden toasted Jacob's tireless efforts.

"So are you freaked? Now that it's actually, you know, *real?*" Jacob asked.

"Maybe a little. It's strange—this whole thing—but I feel so good about it. You've made it such a lovely transition, Jacob. Coming here today like you did to help me move? Who does that?"

"Well, you *have* ruined me for all future clients. You're the best, Eden," Jacob gushed, realizing he might have gone too far. God, he had to tamp down his romantic intentions—they always got in the fucking way.

"Thank you," Eden said shyly. The tension was as thick as the smell of orange blossoms in the air.

"Well. You must be exhausted. I should leave you to it," Jacob said suddenly, decidedly more stoic.

Eden could feel an invisible bubble rise out of the air between them. Jacob was retreating.

"Okay . . ." Eden followed him to the front door, uncertain what she wanted to happen. Nothing, she knew, but also everything. "Hopefully I'll, uh, see you soon? Or . . ."

"Yeah! Sure! Call anytime! Okay, enjoy, bye!" Jacob gave her a formal hug and trotted to his car. Eden watched him drive away, waving out the window. Don Lockwood looked up at her with his usual weariness, then loudly snorted.

"Agreed, Don. Agreed."

. . .

Kat's plucky publicist Donna called, eager to get going on *Foster Kid* promotion. The publisher had high hopes for the memoir and felt it would be a fruitful entry into the "survivor" tales that were always popular among readers. Kat's admission of her struggles surviving a suicide attempt and battling mental illness was the perfect anecdote in the nation's "tell-all" moment.

"I really want to engage on the topic, I want to be available and open," Kat assured Donna.

"Fantastic. I think you're going to hit a chord with the country and become a face for this sort of guts—think Elizabeth Smart for a new generation. And everyone and their dog suffers from *something* these days—good lord, I'm a walking pharmacy—but you can be a human face on a real struggle. And your story will tell others if you can survive, then so can they." Kat beamed, thinking of her future self as a truth teller and soother. Jacob would be so impressed.

"Now then. I see you have virtually no social media presence," Donna said.

"I sort of hate it."

"Three words, darling: get over it." Donna laughed. Kat did not, and let her silence speak volumes. "Okay, lots of writers find the whole 'online presence' just as nauseating, but I would advise doing anything you can to increase your sales. That makes sense, doesn't it?"

"Sure."

"And a lot of reluctant writers find it's actually a beautiful link with their readers. Most of them end up thanking me for opening up their world. You get to be an extrovert without having to leave your house." Donna took a drag on her cigarette. "Did I mention it boosts sales?"

Kat was still not convinced; she viewed social media as culturally poisonous. Still, she thought, social media *could*, however, make her more open, more visible . . . and Jacob could follow her and see her *exactly* how she wanted him to.

"Sold."

. . .

Jacob was hustling at the office now that his first listing was closed. There was so much to keep track of, to learn, to figure out. Most of the agents had an easy shorthand. They were all accommodating and helpful, but underneath Jacob's smile he churned with uncertainty. Maybe the first house had been an inspired fluke.

Phoebe approached him at his desk, leaning on it casually. "So. Onto the next conquest, are we?"

Jacob nodded and grinned. "Yes. And I stopped by the house with Eden's new keys last night. She was so happy and just the most ideal first client. Ever." His smile fell a bit, then he cleared his throat. "And I, uh, also have a few other leads—"

"—Jacob." Phoebe pursed her lips, sensing something, and leaned closer.

"Yes?"

"Do you like this client?"

"Oh. She's amazing. An absolute joy to represent."

"Jacob. Do you *like* this client?"

His face pinked with obvious blushing; he offered a guilty smile. Phoebe matched the grin. "You know, Tessa married one of her first clients."

Jacob raised an eyebrow, looking over at the agent, Tessa, who chatted amiably on her phone. On Tessa's desk was a sea of adorable family pictures. "Really?!"

"Really. Your deal is done now, it's closed. As far as I'm concerned, we're all adults here . . ." Phoebe walked off and winked over her shoulder.

Jacob shook his head; happiness flooded his system. The sheer level of relief he felt was all the evidence he needed.

Jacob had to go back to Eden's, though he was almost a bit terrified to visit her again. He had a strong feeling if he did, his dating life would likely be over.

Eden was the sort of woman who changed everything.

TWENTY-ONE

DON LOCKWOOD BARKED, AND EDEN sighed when she heard the knock at her door. This was the third one today. Neighbors were so kind, delivering lemon bars, potted cacti, tips on good local Mexican food—but she didn't want to open the door, she was just tired. She had instantly felt at home with not just the magical space, but with the neighborhood and people as well. No one was pretentious; everyone casually strolled by in flip-flops. And wasn't it easier to be happy wearing flip-flops? Now she just wanted to finally relax.

Reluctantly, Eden opened the door, preparing a fake smile and forced enthusiasm, and instead found Jacob holding a hammer and a brown paper bag.

"Jacob!" Her happy surprise was definitely not faked.

"Hi." He kept it simple, smiled. *God, those dimples.*

Jacob handed her the bag, and she peered inside. "I brought you a professional picture-hanging kit. Complete with a leveling tool. I thought you could use some help hanging your amazing art."

Eden stepped aside, gesturing for him to enter. "It's just hard for you to say goodbye, I know."

Jacob spun around, guilty. "Oh! I realize . . . well, maybe I am coming on a bit strong here. Being back like this, obviously . . . because I don't, well, I just don't want to say goodbye to you yet."

The words hung in the room, neither of them knowing exactly what that meant.

"Oh. I thought you didn't want to say goodbye to the *house*," Eden quipped.

Jacob turned bright red and looked down. He ran his hand through his hair, nodded to himself, looked up. "No. Actually . . . I didn't want to say goodbye to you."

Eden burst out laughing.

"Really? That's funny?" Jacob joked hopefully, cutting the tension.

"It's just unexpected. You know. But I am . . . flattered."

"'Being flattered' is a kiss of death."

Eden considered her words. "I . . . I feel it, too, Jacob," she said quietly.

Jacob nodded slightly, warmed yet frozen in his tracks. He was usually way smoother than this.

"I want to . . . well, wait. Let me think." Eden paused; Jacob stood in agony. "Okay. I have loved being together. Talking with you. It's just . . . easy. You're such a gentleman, you feel . . . I don't know, weirdly familiar."

"I feel the same!"

"But—"

"There's always a but—"

"*But* I am here getting this new start for reasons I haven't gone into yet. So. If you'd like to hang out, you know, I would love that. I really would."

"Just don't try to kiss you, in other words," Jacob said with a smile but with obvious dejection.

"That's right." Eden grinned. "Not until I say it's okay, anyway."

Relief washed across Jacob's face; he glowed with possibility. It was enough for now.

"Of course," Jacob assured her. "Now. Let's get some pictures hung, shall we?"

"Awesome. I bought some beer and was going to order a pizza," Eden said casually, as if their loaded conversation had not happened at all.

"I think Scordato's is the best. What's your favorite topping?"

"Basil and chicken. You?"

"Basil and chicken." Jacob knew his smile was too wide.

· · ·

The next few weeks consisted of plenty of platonic meetings. Jacob was busy and so was Eden, setting up her new life, but Jacob always made time to drop by. Coming back to the house and spending time with Eden was more than soothing for Jacob—she was the emotional equivalent of a comfy sweater that never lost its shape.

Jacob took Eden hiking to all the great trails around Tucson. He adored watching her marvel over the beauty of the desert. She allowed Jacob to see his familiar hometown through new joyful eyes, a buoyant set of glasses to take in the world. It was easy to be infused with Eden's wonder.

They loved hiking Sabino Canyon together, sitting on the warm rocks at the top and inhaling the stunning vista. Their meandering conversations had a road trip quality to them—easily volleying from the light (they both preferred gelato to ice cream, both thought Wes Anderson's *Bottle Rocket* was seriously underrated) to the deep (they both agreed there was no definitive religion that had all the answers, both thought empathy the most important virtue of all). It was seamless, this finding one another. Eden was arrested by the ease with which she found herself considering romance again. But if she'd learned anything by losing Mac, it was that there was no clear timeline for anything.

As the sky turned to dappled hues of apricot and plum, electrifying the foothills in staggering splendor, Eden knew her resolve to keep their relationship simply friendly had reached its limit. For all the halcyon between them, there was heat. Plenty of it. She had to tell Jacob the truth.

"I need to tell you what happened before," Eden started. Jacob sensed the gravity of the moment. His entire being was listening.

"I was engaged to a wonderful man. Cormac. I called him Mac. We met on a plane, fell madly in love, and we were engaged months later. And a few weeks after that, he was diagnosed with Hodgkin's lymphoma."

"Eden. I'd be lying if I said I didn't know." Jacob paused. "I *did* Google you."

Eden dropped her head. Of course. She felt stupid for not realizing.

"And I cannot imagine what you've been through. Honestly, I've just been waiting for you to bring it up. I wanted you to be ready."

"Thanks." Eden looked up to the sky, then continued. "But I realized something recently, Jacob. The dream I had about the house . . . moving to Tucson . . . finding my next . . . It *was* Mac. How, exactly? I'm not entirely sure, but I know in my being, in my core, he wants me to be happy. I think he helped me here and wanted me to start over."

"I love that."

"And I think he would want me to be with you, too."

Jacob gulped and couldn't deny the high-wattage beam that was plastered on his face. Then a strange guffaw escaped from his throat.

Eden responded with a charmed, albeit confused, smile. "And what was that for? . . ."

Jacob flushed a bit as he fumbled for the right words. "Oh . . . just to hear you say your fiancé would *want* you to be with me. My ex, Kat,—and we weren't engaged or anything—but I seriously doubt she'd encourage me to find love again, especially with someone as golden as you. It's just a funny metaphor—your past is tender and sweet, and mine's sort of psychotic."

Eden cocked her head to the side. "Like . . . how psychotic are we talking?"

Jacob took her hand and offered a warm smile. "Let's just get back to Mac wanting you to be with me. I love that story."

Eden nodded with a grin and continued. "So I guess what I'm saying is this, Jacob—I am still grieving. I know it's been years, but it's true. And grief is not a linear line of good, better, cured. Grief is a slippery beast. A horrible monster. I am fine one moment, happy the next, devastated an hour later. I want you to know all this, understand and accept I will always love Mac. I will always talk about him; he will always be a part of who I am."

"Eden, that makes total sense. Of course. I'd never ask you to lie to yourself, to diminish what you felt or had."

"Thank you. But I need to trust myself here. Your gut is your God, all those bumper sticker platitudes are true. I believe that."

"So do I."

"And . . . Jacob. I want to be with you." Eden looked Jacob in the eye. "And I really want you to kiss me."

Jacob grinned, gently held her face, and did just that.

. . .

Eden had been a bit terrified to slip into another relationship, to do all the things she had done with Mac with someone new. She was certain Mac was the last man she'd love, the last man she'd sleep with. She was wrong.

She was also wrong to think it would be automatically awkward to be with someone new. It wasn't. It was—she had to admit—fucking fantastic. It made her feel a bit guilty, but it was also true. Releasing herself to the power of her feelings for Jacob was a rush of adrenaline, a flush of magic. Once she embraced Jacob, she was bathed in how right it felt.

Jacob loved the fact he now got to sleep with this virtual goddess in the very bed he had slept in prior. In the same room where he'd helped build and create. Their bodies fit together like lock and key, slippery with heat.

Once after an exceptional mid-day roll in the hay, Jacob turned to get out of bed for a water and found Don Lockwood staring gloomily at the sweaty post-coitus duo.

They both burst into laughter.

"Don Lockwood is FURIOUS," Jacob noted.

"Disgusted," Eden agreed. Don Lockwood then gave them both a you-people-make-me-sick sneer and retreated from the room. "God, I love him. Pugs just have the best comedic timing."

"I think I finally—and weirdly—get the appeal," Jacob admitted.

"It ain't for the smell."

"No. On a good day, Don Lockwood smells like a corn chip. On a bad, a shrimp boat." Eden had to hold her sides, repeated his new nickname aloud: "Shrimp Boat . . ."

Eden turned to Jacob and smiled, tracing his beautiful face. "God, this is fun. Where did you come from again?"

"I was thinking the very same thing myself." Jacob kissed her softly.

"You know my Grandma Minnie was widowed and found love again at age, like, 67. Maybe older. She met this handsome feller at the bank, and boy oh boy, she was IN."

"I already love this story so much." Jacob grinned, burrowing into her.

"She was this absolutely horny-in-love older lady. It was amazing—*amazing*—to witness." Eden beamed, remembering the story. "So, this one Thanksgiving, she had this new hairdo, all flowy grey glory, not her usual stoic bun. And she greets me and starts twirling in her foyer—*twirling like Maria in freakin'* West Side Story—she's so in love."

"Ohmygod. God bless Minnie."

"So Minnie pulls me into her bedroom at her new condo and points to the hot tub off her back patio. And she says, '*That is quite a playpen, kiddo.*'"

"NO!" Jacob delighted in her retelling, rhapsodic as he took in Eden's beauty.

"Oh, yeah. And I guess the point of this story is . . . love never stops. It can continue. And if you are lucky enough to have love arrive at your door again, open it." Eden wiped a happy tear. "I get it. *You go, Grandma!*"

"Or in her case, you COME, Grandma," Jacob interjected, thrilled with the bawdy turn. Eden swatted him, crumbling into hysterics.

"Please! Enough! I CANNOT talk any more about my Grandma's orgasm!" Eden's sides hurt she was laughing so hard.

"Hello ladies and gentlemen," Jacob said in his convincing British accent. "We are *MY GRANDMOTHER'S ORGASM!*"

Jacob hyperventilated with crazed guffaws. "Ohmygod! I am so gross! I literally PEED myself!" Eden wailed from the bathroom, though she was still laughing.

And I have never loved you more, thought Jacob.

He knew this was it. Eden was the one.

TWENTY-TWO

KAT HELD HER FUTURE BOOK cover art, her hands nearly shaking.

Carol whooshed open the door, ushering her in with ecstatic glee. Kat may as well have had a new baby swaddled in her arms.

She'd tried so hard to disengage from Kat and avoid further entanglement, but she couldn't deny Kat felt like one of her own cubs. And after all, they *had* been to war together. Besides, Jacob didn't have to know they still gathered now and again, but even he would likely understand if their gatherings were about Kat's memoir.

"Let me see, let me see!" Carol enthused, eyes taking in the book cover. "Oh, Kat. It's stunning. Truly!"

The cover art was stark—a lone child stood before the graphic of a house, staring up at it with fear.

FOSTER KID it said in blood red text, **by Kathryn Lamb** in black.

"I love the cover."

Carol nodded in agreement, putting her arm around Kat. "Look what you've done, Kathryn Lamb," she said, tracing her fingers over the bold author's name. "You did it."

"With your help. Oh, and thanks for the blurb."

"You're welcome. I can't wait until I'm staring at this on the shelf at Antigone."

Kat hugged Carol, smelled her soapy goodness. She was so grateful for her continued support, her everything. "Come. I think we have a bottle of something-something calling our name."

They chatted and ate and drank in the perfect warmth of the afternoon.

"I'm sure Jacob will be so excited for you, too," Carol admitted, then took a big sip of white wine.

Kat felt her face flush, her pulse quicken, her balance sway. "How is Jacob?" The nonchalance in her voice was quite convincing.

"So good. He even sold his first house."

"Really? That's great."

"And it seems . . ." Carol trailed off, caught herself.

"It seems what?"

"Oh. Nothing. Nothing."

"Come on. What? Carol, we are celebrating the cover art of my *published* memoir. I'm *fine*."

Carol took a breath, questioning her words even as she spoke. "It seems he's now dating the woman who bought it."

The light switch of energy went from warmth to inky cold. Kat's mouth curled nearly baring her teeth. "Oh." She took a liberal swig of wine, then wiped her mouth. She could feel her pulse behind her eyelids.

"Maybe I shouldn't have said—"

"—No, no, no. It's fine. Fine." Kat stood up, vertigo swaying her slightly. "I can't believe I forgot I have somewhere to be."

"Oh, okay . . ." Carol kicked herself for her predictable faux pas as she cautiously followed Kat to the door. "I'm, I'm sorry if I—"

"It's okay, Carol. I mean it," she said, this time sounding plausibly convincing. Kat hugged her a little too tightly.

"I'll see you soon. Thanks again." Kat's hand was on the doorknob, one foot out the door.

"Don't forget!" Carol scooped up the reason for this celebration—the book cover art. "Again, just so stunning, Kat."

Kat grabbed it and slipped out.

Her hands shook inserting the key to her Honda. It roared to life and she tore away, screaming at the top of her lungs.

. . .

Kat drove to 3rd Street, in a fog. Buildings passed, stop signs, spotlights. Nothing registered. Perspiration had collected on her forehead; her back was a sheet of slick sweat.

Why was Kat so thrown, so knocked off-kilter by this? She had been steady—relatively speaking—and now she was not. Everything turned on its axis, the rage and despair was clawing out of the cage.

"Stop it stop it stop it stop it," she said out loud to herself, tears filling her eyes.

She parked near Jacob's house. She had resisted driving by for so long.

Kat had been so good. So very good.

Taking in the fantasy of his Spanish bungalow was like a knife twisting in her side. Her breaths were shallow; it was so fucking perfect. Jacob had naturally done a glorious job; it was the sort of house that made people slow their cars when they'd pass. They'd coo with wonder, snap stealth photos, and post to Facebook with the hashtag #homegoals.

Then, she saw Jacob's SUV parked nearby.

YXP645. YXP645.

She would sometimes say his license plate number like a mantra while jogging, on a loop.

YXP645. Jacob was there. It was true. And he was with whoever got this house. As if it wasn't enough for this woman to live in Jacob's phenomenal domestic reimagining. She had to take him for herself, too.

Then Kat saw her. She was certain.

Kat's breath stopped, her blood chilled. It had to be. She stopped breathing completely.

Kat could never forget that cascade of honeyed waves, that aquiline profile.

It was the fucking perfect author from the fucking book reading.

Eden Hart. That had been her name—like a movie star. The very sight of her made Kat's body flood with wooziness. Knowing she was likely with Jacob now made her heart stop and the world swirl.

How could this be? The very woman who had dunked Kat into a vat of thick insecurity was actually Jacob's new girlfriend? It was a nightmare of such inconceivable proportion Kat could not ever process the turn.

She was in a light dress, something effortless and fantastic. Her hair was still a glorious crown. She was fucking stunning—like Jacob in female form.

Eden was walking a panting pug, and the dog had stopped moving in the afternoon sun, its strange face contorted in the heat, a floppy tongue distending from the side of its mouth. The overheated pug's permanent frown was now a smiling Chinese dragon of exhaustion.

She talked to the dog, then picked it up, cuddling, never stopping her conversation with the clearly beloved pet.

It was too much. The tiger of madness in Kat's mind batted its fierce claws.

Suddenly feeling eyes on her, Eden paused. She looked all around. Despite the heat, her arm erupted into a sea of goosebumps.

Kat ducked, her breath getting more and more fevered. After a few seconds, she looked back up, and Eden was gone. Kat only caught sight of the curved front door closing shut.

Then she put her head on the steering wheel and cried and cried and cried.

. . .

Eden entered the house, grateful for the blast of air-conditioning that greeted her, and she carried Don Lockwood into the kitchen.

Jacob overheard the dog's exaggerated panting. "Good lord! Is Don Lockwood okay?"

Eden set him down before his water bowl and he greedily lapped it up.

"Just not used to this heat. We can't go as far as we could in Seattle. Frankly, neither can I," Eden said, petting her baby. Jacob leaned over and added an affectionate pat to Don Lockwood's cobby backside. "He'll be okay."

Jacob's fingers traced Eden's back. "Do you always wear dresses?"

"Only because I'm lazy."

"Not because you're fancy?"

Eden laughed and shook her head. "Nope. It's just one piece. *One and done.* My Grandpa always wore a jumpsuit—sporty little numbers with built-in belts. He liked only having to figure out just ONE piece of clothing. His logic made sense, so—voila!"

Jacob hugged her, kissed her. "I'm so glad you're lazy, then. You look so beautiful in them."

"And you would look beautiful if they found you after 13 days in the forest, surviving on rainwater and beetles, covered in filth and dirt."

"Is that right? Rainwater and beetles?"

"Reeking of your own urine. And you'd still be hot."

Jacob laughed and smelled her hair. He then pulled back, looking into her bewitching eyes. People always raved about gemstone eye colors, but truly, the diamonds that sparkled in Eden's chocolate brown eyes were other-worldly. "I have to tell you something."

"You're pregnant," Eden said.

Jacob grinned, shaking his head. "Just tell me if I'm . . . around too much. Just say so, seriously. I don't want to impose myself here. Just because the house feels so familiar . . . I know you might need more space. And that's fine, just tell me. I'm a big boy."

"Oh, I like you here, Jacob. No—I love you here. I *luff* you here."

"*Annie Hall!*" Jacob nodded at the appropriate call-out from one of his favorite movies, then kissed her again. "And I do think . . . I do think I'm falling in *lurve* with you."

"I think I'm falling in *loave* with you, too," Eden said.

• • •

It was so easy to find anything online. Pop in a credit card, and you can excavate anyone's driving records, past felony convictions—you name it.

Anyone can research property records. Within a half hour, Kat knew even more about Eden than she did before. She combed through the information with shallow breath, her heart fluttering like a panicked bird in her chest. Each fevered tap of the keyboard seemed to punctuate her frenzied madness, her restless brain now creating its own rhythm, its own soundtrack.

Taptaptaptaptap.

Kat was chipping away at her reserve and commitment to be steady. She was letting it all fall apart now, feeding the monster in its sealed-off cage, tempting derangement to not only visit, but also make itself comfortable. Take things out of the suitcase. Put it away in the closet. Stay awhile.

Eden Hart. 30. Bought Jacob's dream house in fucking cash. No felonies, no misdemeanors. Of course.

She had lived in Seattle but grew up in Denver with parents who looked like the healthy older couple used in ads to sell active senior living communities. The sort you actually wanted to sit around a fire pit with, enjoying Pinot Grigio. They likely hugged Eden every chance they got, telling her over and over she could be anything she wanted to be! And they'd meant it.

Reading again about glorious Eden was like swallowing daggers all over. She had written several children's books and won a Caldecott. Kat had forgotten about the goddamn Caldecott! Oh, and didn't she look like that celebrity—Kat couldn't remember her name, the one with the stupidly great hair—accepting her award.

Naturally, Google was eager to tell her all about Eden's new book that was coming out in the spring.

To make matters worse, she'd forgotten how unique and adorable Eden's illustrations were—so much so, it made Kat's feet hurt. Eden's talent was epic and rare; she would likely have Judith Viorst-levels of success her entire life.

Kat's blood had turned to lava.

This was HER goddamn storyline! Kat's new book was coming out in the spring! Jacob was to see HER success, be dazzled by HER, not the impossibly new gorgeous femme fatale living in his house, wearing his shirts, smelling of his sex.

It was so unfair. Not only did Eden have the love of Kat's life eating out of her hand, but she'd already had yet another man who'd pledged his life to her, too. Sure, he'd died, but still. Women like Eden made men happily hang up their bachelorhood, made men envision children jumping at their feet, made women silently think to themselves they really had to get their shit together.

Eden probably didn't need deodorant. She probably smelled like lilies and shit fairy dust. She probably liked to exercise. She inevitably would donate to children and animals in need.

And she probably got a huge fucking book advance.

• • •

It wasn't exactly a slow process. Jacob had never really had to leave his new house, as it turned out. He had been staying at Pete and Maya's after it sold but found himself going over to Eden's place more often than not. At a certain point, he was barely at his brother's, and he and Eden had fallen into a comfortable routine. They were both meant to be there all along.

The whole relationship, the entire setup, had been so gloriously easy. Both felt their union was fated—the sort of thing Jacob had mocked and his mother had preached. Carol was always repeating one bromide or another, always whispering about the power of the universe, the unspoken forces in life. Jacob had mostly believed in science, concrete matters, facts.

With Eden, he believed in fates and oceans and destinies. Hadn't he been in the desert only months ago, on his knees feeling at wit's end, when he'd heard the voice commanding him to choose happiness? And hadn't Eden literally appeared right after?

Eden was more than happiness. She was a fairytale, the fulfillment of a million wishes on a million shining stars. Eden wasn't remotely difficult to deconstruct or analyze or wonder if it was right. She just was. Period.

It was instant couple, just add water.

When Jacob had been falling for Kat, it had been lovely, of course. At first, it had been mostly easy, too. But she was so unpredictable, such an enigma, he found her challenges thrilling. But he always had a worry, a whisper. A knowing it wouldn't work out in the end.

With Eden, it was only green lights, and it wasn't scary. Commitment had never been Jacob's strong suit, but now he welcomed it. Craved it. The easiest thing in the world.

It was shocking.

For Eden, too. Never in a million years did she think love would fall into her lap like this. She thought there would be years of processing the grief of suddenly losing Mac, more years of being alone, clawing her way back to contentment. She had Don Lockwood. She had a robust career. It would be fine, eventually.

But Jacob happened, and you can't deny love when it knocks on your door.

· · ·

Jacob and Eden had the family over for their first meal as an official couple. It had been weeks in the making, and it was about time.

Pete was astonished to see his brother so besotted with love. Sure, he'd seen Jacob fawn over beauties throughout the years, but this had another layer, another grounded component. He thought Jacob's very eyes would melt out of his head, the way he looked at Eden.

And her artwork! Eden had fantastic paintings from her travels and several of her own pieces throughout the house. Naturally, their mom squealed like a drunk chimpanzee. Even Jess's response was positively sorority, octaves higher than usual.

"I just finished this one, actually," Eden said, thrilled with the response to her latest painting that hung in the living room. "I went before dawn to Tumamoc hiking trail and just let my paintbrush do the talking. I honestly cannot get over the color of the sky. It's reason enough to live here."

Eden went on to give a beautiful soliloquy about color itself. The variety, the richness, the importance of it. That there's a reason Dorothy's world went from black and white to Technicolor in Oz. Eden believed color itself was at the core of life's meaning, a reflection of the human condition.

"Hence, your book *Blue*," Carol gushed.

"Correct!"

"I'm never going to see color the same way. Very cool, Eden," Jess said, still processing her thoughts.

Jacob put an arm around Eden, proud. "She makes me see everything so differently. So much more clearly."

Dinner flowed as easily as the wine, there was never a lull in the conversation. Eden got all the references. It was as if she had been there all along. At various points throughout the meal, everyone locked eyes as if to silently acknowledge the power of what was happening.

"So basically, J., you never really moved out of here?" Pete asked.

Jacob and Eden looked to one another and blushed. "Pretty much."

"It was just organic. And besides, he does give the best foot rubs, so . . ."

"And there's also my insane grilling skills," Jacob joked, and the two got lost in their own world again, stunned with one another, smiling silently. This had happened a few times throughout the meal.

"Okay!" Jess clapped her hands. "I stopped at Woops! Bakery for macarons."

"I thought I saw the green-and-pink box . . ." Carol said as the two got up and headed over to the kitchen.

Once a bit more separate, Carol and Jess leaned in to confer.

"Ohmygod. Put a fork in him. He's DONE," Jess said. "And I did not see Jacob falling for an older woman. At all."

"Oh, for god's sake, three and a half years isn't an 'older woman.'"

"But in dog years for dudes, that's, like, nine years. But kudos to him."

"It's . . . just . . . amazing, really, isn't it?! How quickly this has happened?" Carol looked over at the table; everyone was laughing. "Eden *is* divine. I see why he's so smitten."

"Oh, he's not smitten. He's in love," Jess stated and went back to the table, holding the box of desserts and plates.

"Sugar! Me likey!" Eden clapped, and everyone dug in.

The night came to an end. Eden and Jacob walked outside to say proper goodbyes.

Pete hugged his brother and whispered into his ear, "Hold on to that one."

"I intend to," he whispered back; the two high-fived, never far from their eight-year-old selves. Maya kissed Eden on both cheeks playfully.

Jess, usually the least effusive, hugged Eden. There was promise of another gathering soon.

Carol was the last to leave, embracing Eden. "My dear, I see why my son is all lit up! You are an absolute treasure! I've so enjoyed getting to know you and cannot wait to buy a copy of your book!"

"Thank you, Carol. You're everything Jacob has been raving about and more. It's so terrific to meet you," Eden gushed.

Carol hugged her one last time, giving one final squeeze.

Carol moved toward her car as Jacob and Eden waved goodbye, arms around one another.

Down the street, Kat sat in her car. Her white hands gripped the steering wheel, her jaw locked. Kat's eyes swam in fury, clouded in rage.

That was HER Carol.

Her Jacob.

Her life.

Kat felt the soldiers of mania marching through her blood, readying for battle, anxious to get back into the action. They could only be denied for so long.

These soldiers were a part of her. Why did she have to disavow them—and deny her *truth*? She couldn't believe she'd allowed herself to be partially drugged into a slack shell of herself.

Kat would go into attack, take her hands off the wheel.

Eden would not win.

. . .

Kat felt like a cat burglar, loving the thrill of being unseen, of the pursuit. It was an electrifying game.

She knew where to park to avoid getting caught, knew how to follow Eden's car with just enough distance to avoid suspicion. And besides, she was starting to know Eden's routine.

On Mondays and Wednesdays, she went to yoga. Of course. In the skin-tight leggings and tops that showed more-than-a-hint-of-a-belly Kat would never wear. Eden would pile her voluminous honeyed hair on top of her head carelessly, and each time it was a perfect sloppy updo. Every time.

Kat watched her stretch and do downward dog, her pert apple butt reaching for the sky. Eden dripped with sweat, causing her body to glisten like an 80s music video vixen.

After class, Eden would chat amiably with other women in the parking lot, all of them laughing. They'd sip their massive waters—good god, the hydration requirements of these women—and air-kiss their goodbyes.

Eden had them all eating out of her hand, she could tell. They likely wanted to include her in their dinner parties, wanted her cell number, wanted her to join their stupid book clubs to discuss stupid books that required no discussion.

It made her boil. And still . . . Kat could find herself entranced. Too often, Kat found herself marveling at Eden, the way she smiled, the way she stood gracefully with a hand on her hip, unconsciously drawing with her toe.

Kat hated herself for these thoughts, this momentary bewitching spell Eden cast. She loathed Eden's success, her face . . . still, she wanted to know what shampoo she used, found herself irrationally wondering if she liked smoothies, what music did she dance to when she was making dinner in the kitchen?

Who was Eden Hart?

And how could Kat get her life?

TWENTY-THREE

THE PUBLICITY DEPARTMENT AT KNOPF went into overdrive to help foment buzz for *Next*. Focus groups had responded so positively to the book's message, most wanted to pass along the book to others. It was a potential jackpot, another instant classic.

The team wanted Eden front and center sharing her tale about the continuation of her battle with grief and the necessity of hope. Eden gave words to the crawl of grief but also illustrated the belligerence of faith.

They encouraged her to build up her online presence, to engage with fans. Eden had a skeletal personal website that embarrassed her, it felt so boastful and narcissistic to promote herself. But the team rightfully pointed out this wasn't just publicity, this was also, in part, a civic duty. She could help people. She hadn't done so with *Blue*—the book's success being chiefly accidental, literary lightning in a bottle—and it was a missed opportunity. They gently told Eden her fans needed to hear from her.

Eden reluctantly agreed. She created an Instagram account and was a bit horrified to find the platform engaging and simple to use. She thought she was above the endless circle-jerk nature of it, but as it turns out, she was not. Eden loved volleying messages to her fans, secretly thrilled in their adoration and praise. All those exclamation points can be addictive.

Likes, as it turned out, were highly likable.

Eden all-caps-lock loved it all. Her embrace of social media was almost as shocking as finding Jacob himself. It was bizarre that the impersonal computer could, in fact, create personal connections and make the world smaller and—shockingly!—often kinder. Look what Lin-Manuel Miranda did with his Twitter alone. He was a poet of positivity, and she wanted to follow suit. If it was good enough for Hamilton, it sure as hell was good enough for her.

Eden was off to the races, amused with her foray into social media. Promoting her future work turned out to be so much less complicated than she envisioned. She found herself asking for more platforms, even paying someone to build out her website.

Kat gobbled up this new information, following Eden under an anonymous name. She could glimpse inside the completed house, see her fucking fantastic workspace—her rainbow of markers was so cool she wanted to vomit. Eden's dog was lovably pathetic and had a funny, weird name. Eden was racking up followers faster than a Russian bot.

Kat checked in daily. More than daily. She refreshed Instagram constantly, hoping for another glance into Eden's fabled existence. It at once made her burn hot with fury and filled her with paralyzing envy.

She studied Eden's face, traced her smile, zoomed in to get a better look at her hair.

Then Kat looked into the mirror, swooping her own hair up into an updo like Eden. She pouted her lips, which curled up, hoping to match Eden's grin.

Kat's mouth was a frozen sneer of a smile. Her eyes narrowed looking at her reflection. She blew herself a kiss.

. . .

Judith, Kat's psychotherapist, had left two messages for her. The first was breezy, "Just checking in!" The second was decidedly more panicked.

She hadn't been to see her in weeks. Judith really wanted Kat to call her back. When the third call came in, Kat picked up.

"Kat! There you are! How are you?"

"Well. Really well. My job is great; my book comes out soon. I am doing incredible," Kat said clinically.

"Wonderful. So much to look forward to! I know these are busy times but I'd love to see you—"

"I want my book to come out first, then I can get back into it. Super busy."

"Totally appreciate that. So . . . a few weeks or—"

"Yes."

"And your meds? All good—?"

"I could use another refill. Thanks for calling, Judith," she said and hung up.

Kat tossed the phone onto her car seat. Her veins rippled, coursing with power. She was in control now.

. . .

Lucía had begun planning Kat's book reading at Antigone Books; she and Carol envisioned a swanky rollout.

Of course they had to have an open wine bar. That was a no-brainer.

Lucía mentioned to Kat that Carol had been extremely busy lately and that she had not been quite as available to plot details for the book signing party.

Kat froze. "Extremely busy?"

"School, life, her own novel . . . It's fine. Carol and I talk all the time, and it's going to be a great night."

"But has Carol . . . been less available for a while? Or is this a more immediate thing?" she asked, trying to mask her worry.

"Not sure the timeline. I shouldn't have said anything. Don't worry about it," Lucía chirped happily, continuing with her inventory.

"NO! I really need to know, Lucía!" Kat said too loudly. Lucía turned, shocked. The truth was, Kat's tone scared her. "Is Carol suddenly blowing you off and refusing to help with my book signing?"

"No, it's nothing like that . . . She's just busy. Truly." Lucía scanned Kat's face, confused by her anger.

Kat realized she had been too forceful. "Of course. Sorry. I guess, you know, I'm just stressed about the book's debut!"

Kat left the backroom and went outside for air. She robo-reached for her phone, tapped onto Instagram, and instantly Eden Hart popped up.

Nauseating. It was a shot of Jacob from behind. He was in shorts and a baseball hat, standing tall on a giant rock taking in the spectacular desert scenery.

The caption read:

Pretty nice view. #sabinocanyon #74degrees #tuesdayafternoon #bluethebook #luckygirl #nextisnext

Kat's stomach churned, thick with acid. The bile started to rise into her throat, burning her esophagus. Her hands started to shake.

Jacob's backside was not Instagram fodder. He was more than that.

Kat could still feel his back on her hands, the way she'd claw at him, feel the heat of him.

The view was not fucking nice, Eden. It was mean as hell.

• • •

Kat was walking home from work, inert. She usually loved the ritual of strolling home. But today she felt chilly, distant—and she knew her reaction to Lucía had been too extreme. She had even spooked herself. Still, she believed she was doing the right thing by stopping those mind-stupefying pills. Kat had missed herself, truth be told, even her craggy, jagged edges. Sure, she'd have eruptions now and again. Didn't everyone? Besides, she'd learned those calming breathing techniques and knew how to manage herself better. She understood what she wanted now, who she was and how this was going to go. She knew she had to harness her power, not dull it.

When she heard her phone ring and saw Jacqueline's name, Kat pounced.

"Jacqueline!"

"Kat, hi. Listen, um . . . well, I'm just going to say it. It's not good."

Kat stopped walking. "What's up?" Her attempt at sounding breezy didn't even convince herself.

"The *New York Times Book Review*. We got an advance copy."

Kat paused. "Oh."

"We're very disappointed. It frankly pisses me off how much sway they have."

"What'd . . . what does the review say?"

"That your slipperiness of memory doesn't work as a device, it serves to only further muddy the water. Simply put, the reviewer wasn't particularly kind. I suppose it just wasn't for her. It happens."

"Huh."

"I'm sorry, Kat."

"But . . . what does this mean, exactly?" Kat asked quietly. It was like she was shot in the gut.

"We'll have to see. Great reviews don't necessarily mean great sales. And vice versa. It's just not the note we had hoped to start on."

"Can you forward me the review?"

"Sure. Just did." Jacqueline took a deep breath. "Call me if you want. And you know what they say? . . ."

"Fuck 'em?" Kat said with a little too much force.

Jacqueline laughed a bit unconvincingly. "Exactly. Talk soon and chin up. Your book *will* be in bookstores very soon."

Kat hung up and the sky turned from azure to onyx. Any remaining optimism seeped out of her pores, gone, floating up into the dark atmosphere.

TWENTY-FOUR

IT WAS A CRUEL JOKE. Kat and Eden's books were released within weeks of one another. One heralded as yet another modern classic, likened to *The Giving Tree*, one forgotten, marginalized as muddy at best, confusing at worst.

Naturally.

The good reviews didn't stop rolling in for Eden. Goodreads had endless five stars, and praise so glowy it was almost embarrassing. Kat had begun to wonder if Eden herself was blowing the entire Internet to secure the ovation.

The *New York Times* review for *Next* was lyrical in its accolades, calling the prose "graceful, searingly honest, irreverently amusing." *Booklist* said Eden's follow-up work was even more powerful than her first.

Kat couldn't take it anymore and vowed she had to stop reading anything related to Eden, the whole bloody thing. It made her pulse race and mind flare with wicked thoughts.

She never could have conceived how painfully this chapter would unfurl. And Kat was fairly good at that part already.

Kat felt like she had been physically attacked by her own life. She was honestly surprised her body wasn't littered with bruises and cuts.

Self-pity is a monster, but she fed it now. Tossed it scraps of meat, nurtured it by obsessing over Eden. Her mind used to hum with Jacob—and he was always there, too—but now he had his perfect girlfriend to accompany him in her brain. Eden's delightfulness was also now smeared onto the inside of her skull, layering Kat with a sturdy insulation of despair. And madness. This was an entirely new unique cocktail of frenzy lining her psyche, she knew that.

But Kat didn't fight it. Any attempt at controlling her fucking breaths to mitigate her mood was a joke. As if she was one yoga pose away from making this whole goddamn nightmare make sense.

. . .

Eden was starting to feel guilty. It almost felt as if she'd intended to profit from the pain of losing Mac. She'd be horrified if someone construed her loss as a business move. She knew this was irrational, but she worried. The success of first *Blue* and now *Next* had been quite unintentional, and several pointed out to her that's precisely why they worked.

It was because they were both from her heart. Her soul was on every page.

The requests started rolling in again. *Next* was charging up the children's *New York Times* Best Sellers list; movie producers circled the option. The book was becoming a library staple, another coffee table conversation starter.

When the Caldecott announcements were made in January, it felt fairly certain Eden's name would be on the list again.

It was all so gratifying—the interviews, the sales, the praise. But Eden had not predicted one of the most rewarding aspects would be interacting with her fans. She hadn't done it with *Blue* and was sorry she'd missed that opportunity. No matter, she was making up for lost time. Jacob had warned her not to get too sucked into the pathos of the tales; she couldn't save everyone. She agreed but still liked to try.

There was @blueskytucson who DMed Eden often. She had lost her husband only two months into their marriage and felt a kinship with Eden. Knowing Eden was trudging forward in life with joy had given her hope. This unlikely online friendship with a stranger had evolved, and soon they were sharing random tips about living in Tucson itself. They both loved the tacos at BOCA, both lived in Tucson for the endless poem of a sky. @blueskytucson promised to be at any upcoming book reading; they hoped to meet in person.

@blueskytucson

> Was feeling low, reread *Blue*.
> Again. Thanks

> Love it. Also try Pumpkin
> Pillsbury cookie dough.
> Equally appropriate.
> ♥

@blueskytucson attached a heart and clicked off.

As Kat closed her laptop, she rolled her eyes. *Cookie dough. Single-girl movie cliché bullshit.*

. . .

Lucîa still went forward with the book signing for Kat, trying too hard to project optimism. Carol finally showed at the last moment, and Kat was convinced her smile seemed clown-like and frozen.

Kat grinned weakly, but the truth ate at her. There would be no second printing for *Foster Kid*. Her story would end up in the bargain bin, and her books would likely be sent back to the publishers; the worst outcome of all. Reviews had been universally consistent in saying Kat's unreliable narrator device was confounding, making the reader question everything and ultimately trust nothing. Her very play on truth—an approach she and her entire publishing team had felt was so unique—had landed with a thud.

But looking at the spectacle of Antigone Books's party for Kat, you'd think she had a bestseller on her hands. Lucîa had purchased plentiful food and wine and strewn twinkling lights. She'd promoted it heavily.

But there were rows and rows of mostly empty chairs. For Kat, it was like seeing tombstones.

She scanned the space, searching for Jacob. Surely he knew this was happening. Of course Carol must have told him about it. Maybe, intrigued, he would show up to be supportive. But seeing the lack of attendance, Kat was relieved he wasn't there. And she sure as shit didn't want to see Eden hanging on his arm, another witness to her failure.

Kat read from the second chapter, trying hard to infuse her voice with emotion, to sound like the Audio Book masters. She doubted herself, looking up periodically to see a smattering of vaguely engaged listeners.

When she had finished, Carol and Lucîa applauded too eagerly from the back, like parents of a kindergartener who had managed to mumble two words in a school play.

"Thank you," Kat said as the audience clapped listlessly. "If you have any questions, I'd love to answer them."

A scruffy man raised a hand in the front row. Kat pointed his way. "Hi. Yeah, I read the book, it's super cool. Fuck the *New York Times*, man."

Awkward twitters filled the room, Kat laughed, appreciating his salvo. "Thanks. I wish more people agreed."

"Seriously—fuck 'em. But my question is—did you ever try to escape a foster family?"

"No. I had no other family, didn't know where else to go. I plotted my escape by writing—I literally thought I could write my way out. And I did, getting the scholarship to the University of Arizona. So here I am."

He nodded, satisfied. A woman behind him shot up a restless hand. Kat pointed to her.

"Yes, hi. What would you say if you saw your biological parents again?"

Kat took a beat. The room got white; the hum returned low in her ears.

"Um . . ." Kat felt eyes on her, knew she had to respond. Words swam in her head. She took a deep breath. "Wow, what a great question. I doubt they'd seek me out. And I also doubt anything I'd have to say to them would be pretty. In fact, I'm certain talking to them again would be quite ugly."

The answer seemed to satisfy everyone. The questions were done.

• • •

Afterward, Kat, Carol, and Lucîa sat in the back of the store, polishing off the wine. The store was closed; Kat's first book reading was now in the past. A gloom hovered over the trio, despite Carol and Lucîa's attempts to buoy Kat's mood, pretending what just happened didn't, in fact, occur.

"I'll tell you what—I never had a book reading for MY first book!" Carol enthused.

Lucîa nodded. "Word of mouth will matter a lot."

Kat slammed her wine back, felt the delightful buzz of boozy warmth envelop her body. "So did you tell Jacob the book signing was tonight, Carol?"

Carol and Lucîa shared a worried look as each took a delicate sip.

"Sweetie, I did not. I wanted this to be *your* night. I didn't want it to be awkward for you. And besides . . . you two haven't spoken in quite a while, you're both just doing so well, so . . ." Carol trailed off. It pissed Kat off how cavalier she was being.

Kat took another swig. "And how are things with Jacob . . . and *Eden*?" Her voice dripped with thick sarcasm.

Carol bristled, suddenly defensive. "How . . . how do you know her name?"

Kat looked up, smiled. "The Internet is a powerful tool."

Carol and Lucîa looked down, felt the waters get thick.

"Now, Kat. I don't think that is healthy for you. For anybody."

"Oh, no?" Kat grinned. "Can't a girl be curious?"

Carol and Lucîa did not know how to proceed. They wanted to steer this back into more pleasant waters but were also unnerved.

"Kat, dear . . . are you still taking your medication?" Lucîa inquired with the sweetness of a kindly aunt.

Kat stared at the two women with cold eyes, the corners of her mouth turned up in an indeterminate smile. "Lucîa. Of course I am still taking my medication. I adore my little darlings."

Lucîa and Carol breathed a sigh of relief but did not look entirely soothed.

"I guess I'm just down tonight because it wasn't quite what I'd hoped my first book signing could be. But I so appreciate your continued support."

Lucîa and Carol exhaled. "Oh, good. Good. Look, it makes sense you feel, well, a little down. I wish more people had shown up, too. But you have a BOOK. *A book on the shelves*. You have accomplished so much in your life and will continue to accomplish more," Carol pleaded. "*And you have a two-book DEAL.*"

"My future is *limitless*," Kat said. Her smile remained steady.

She knew she had to give the people what they wanted.

. . .

Eden was nervous taking in the sea of fans; this dwarfed the previous massive reading. It also was her first speaking engagement in her new hometown, and she wanted the night to be special. The giant stack of *Next* copies was dwindling fast.

Once again, Eden read the entire children's book to the teeming room. The audience listened as if she was sharing the meaning of life, the cure for cancer, and the secrets to Jennifer Lopez's dewy skin all at once.

In the back of the room hidden behind a bookcase and underneath a floppy hat, Kat took it all in. She was raging at the size, the reverence, the wondrous spell Eden cast. Kat dug her fingers into her arm, close to pricking the surface.

Kat's reading had hosted a motley collection of misfits, an accidental smattering of attendants. Eden hosted a rock concert. Kat was Jojo Siwa and Eden was Taylor Swift.

Eden handled the question-and-answer portion with aplomb. Naturally. Often, Kat would forget she was there in rage and let herself drift into Eden's blissful cloud, only to be furious she'd gotten caught up again in her magic. Everyone was powerless with Eden.

"Can I just say," a woman's voice cracked, "that your words gave my grief a voice. Your book helped my heart heal. So I thank you for that."

A resounding circle jerk of applause.

Jacob came bounding in the front door, more dashing than ever. Kat saw Eden spot him, watched Jacob mouth "I'm so sorry." Eden grinned and mouthed back, "It's okay." They had a secret fucking language even in front of others. He was late, dropped the ball, but it was fine. Of course. All she had for Jacob was understanding.

They were *so* going to have sex tonight.

Kat felt her head get light and she slumped slightly, breathing hard. She tried closing her eyes, attempting to calm herself, but her pulse only quickened. Kat studied Jacob as he watched Eden command the room with total adoration, then turned to see Carol mirror Jacob's worship. Carol may have been more in love with Eden than Jacob at this point.

The room burst into thunderous laughter, sounding more like the conclusion to a comedy set than a book signing. Kat's vision started to tunnel, everything slowed down. She knew she had to get out before she lost her breath completely and landed with a crash in self-discovery.

Kat slid out, the door shutting behind her, but the cheerful *ding-a-ling* of the doorbells themselves couldn't muffle the joyous reception.

endless support, his understanding of my creative process, has meant the world to me. I adore you, my darling."

Kat could see Jacob's angelic face beam in love, his dimples erupting upon hearing her perfect words.

She slid back into her clothes and tucked the Ulla Johnson masterpiece under her arm. She then slid out of the dog door on her belly. Don Lockwood followed her, barking playfully. Kat turned to him before slipping out the gate.

"Oh, don't worry, stupid. I'll be back."

. . .

Late into the night, an Uber pulled onto the street. Kat watched Eden and Jacob drive by, buzzed in the backseat. They got out exchanging loud pleasantries with the driver, and they were all over each other. It was a look of a celebratory night coming to an end.

The couple paused in the middle of the dark street, illuminated by a streetlamp, stopping to laugh. Eden held her sides; Jacob had a protective arm around her. They eventually found their footing and went inside. But not before Jacob grabbed at Eden's butt, playfully. She turned around and tried to swat at him—ending up wrapped in his arms, swaying with drunken pleasure. They kissed, then laughed.

Kat crept down the street on foot. She hid in the shadows of the palms, watching the couple through the giant curved window. They never closed a shade; the window didn't even have one. It was a convenient fishbowl.

Kat saw the couple erupt into confused disgust, holding their noses, calling out. She couldn't make out the words. She delighted in their shock, concluding the Reese's Peanut Butter Cup had worked its magic on the dumb pug.

Eden flew into action, terrified her beloved Don Lockwood was sick. Kat watched the couple scramble, Eden calling on her cell. They quickly cleaned up, swooped up Don Lockwood, and Kat saw an Uber turn onto the street.

Kat bolted for her car and climbed in, hidden. She watched the trio as they likely headed to the emergency vet.

Kat couldn't have felt worse realizing they were a united team. Even when presented with a literal shit storm, the power couple responded with quick action and compassion. She was going to have to rise to a different level. Or sink to one.

TWENTY-FIVE

KAT WOKE UP AFTER A fitful sleep and reached for her iPhone. She was on autopilot at this point, checking Eden's Instagram. Naturally, there was a witty post about Don Lockwood's diarrhea welcome home surprise.

> Don Lockwood for the win. Even his shits are heart-shaped.

The photo was a perfect heart of poo. There were already 16,782 likes, hysterically laughing emojis, and proclamations of hilarity.

Kat read the comments, everyone gasping for a status report on the beloved Don Lockwood.

> Don likely got into something, a.k.a. garbage toxicosis. On meds and eating chicken and rice for a while!!!

The news was met with breathless relief.

> Don will remain in doggie diapers to ensure new floors and rugs don't take another one for the team!

@blueskytucson added a GASPING emoji and *Stay strong, Don Lockwood!*

Kat tossed her phone, already irritated with the day.

God, Kat wanted her life. She'd eat broken glass to be Eden.

For Eden, even a diarrhea-infested dog was somehow a comedic boon. Imagine what she could do with a bestselling children's book and the perfect boyfriend.

Eden wasn't the only one entitled to applause, to success, to joy.

Kat would find her way.

. . .

Lucîa watched Kat at Antigone Books, studied her interactions with customers. There was a robotic distance to her now. She had seen this behavior before with Kat, but the mannerisms had intensified since her mostly disastrous book reading.

Kat rang up customers without a smile. Her eyes were dead, hollowed out.

Lucîa tried to pull her aside, gently probing if things were okay. How was her house? How was her second book coming?

Kat said all the right things, but her words were clouded with insincerity. It was not reassuring. Lucîa had a thunderbolt. "Say, I know, Kat! Why don't you treat yourself to a spa day?"

Kat vaguely grinned, nodded. Lucîa wasn't sure if she found the suggestion inspired or insipid.

"Or I know—how about you get a new haircut, something special?"

Now Kat's eyes really widened, nodding. She liked this idea, and Lucîa felt relief flood her body.

"You know what? That does sound perfect."

"Oh, I'm so glad. I know when I'm in the dumps, something as silly as a nice manicure can make me feel better. Say what you will . . ."

Kat would look for a salon after lunch. She really was looking for a change.

. . .

Kat researched online and found the premier hair salon in Tucson, replete with five-star reviews and gushing praise. The accompanying pictures of their handiwork were all the proof she needed—each head of hair a thing of shampoo commercial glory. The salon's specialty was color.

Kat was shocked to find they had a sudden cancellation—could she come in tomorrow?

The next day, Kat arrived at the slick studio that was decorated in a bohemian, funky manner, and it was heavy on ambiance. She was offered a Chardonnay right away and gladly accepted.

Her stylist Suzanne was a woman with glowing magenta hair and a perma-grin. She looked punk, but her demeanor was more home-spun mom. She cooed over Kat, gushed about how excited she was to "play with your hair!" Suzanne marveled at Kat's dark tresses but understood if she needed something new.

Kat admitted she had the hair inspiration right on her phone. She displayed Eden's Instagram profile photo, a glowing vision basking in a Tucson pink moment.

"Wow. Eden Hart, eh? . . ." Suzanne said, studying the photo. "I think I wanna be Eden Hart too, actually." Kat laughed ironically.

"So honey highlights, lighter in the front, a little ombre? And then big waves? . . . We'll give you volume with layers," Suzanne assured her.

"That sounds amazing."

"You'll be Eden-ified in no time." Suzanne velcroed a smock around Kat's neck. "You know, you're already really beautiful, hon."

Kat locked eyes with Suzanne, grateful for the encouragement. Tears almost sprung into her eyes.

Suzanne went to work with the focus of a skilled craftsman. Scissors whooshed in the air, hair flew. Suzanne painted thick goop onto Kat's hair, carefully folding the sections into aluminum foils. The whole process took hours. Kat had flipped through *US Weekly* and *People* four times, found herself re-checking Eden's Instagram and Twitter periodically. Nothing today.

Must be a slow day in paradise.

Suzanne blew Kat's hair dry and curled it with a rather violent-looking wand. Finally, three and a half hours later, Suzanne swiveled Kat's salon chair to face the mirror.

Kat gasped. She was breathless, almost unrecognizable.

She burst into tears, collapsing her head into her hands.

"Oh sweetie! Don't cry!" Suzanne cooed, placing an arm on her shoulder.

Kat couldn't stop. She looked up again, her eyes ablaze, incredulous.

"You're so beautiful!" Uncertainty now tainted Suzanne's voice. "Honey, do you not like it? . . ." she questioned.

At this point other patrons turned to stare at the woman collapsing in the salon chair. No one knew if she was pleased or despondent. The foiled heads waited with bated breath.

"I . . . I love it!" Kat awkwardly squealed, and the salon erupted into grateful laughter and applause.

Kat was shocked, realizing the cheers were for her. She smiled, basking in the strange turn.

"You look gorgeous!"

"Stunning! So beautiful!" chorused another. Kat felt her tears stop, felt her smile grow.

She found her reflection again in the mirror and basked in the effect. She looked so much more like Eden it was ridiculous. Kat had not expected the likeness to be that striking.

Kat pulled out her Instagram, displayed Eden's profile pic. At this point, almost the entire salon was invested, curious about Kat's tears. Several women ambled over to compare the aspirational Instagram photo with the actual end result.

"Oh, you're much prettier than her!" a woman assured Kat, who beamed, inhaling the praise.

"Stop! Eden's gorgeous!" Kat trilled.

"Sure, but you're just as stunning."

She clinked her empty wine glass with the woman's depleted goblet, and Suzanne realized they needed more. This was a cause for celebration.

Kat felt powerful, magical, dazzling. She held the salon in the palm of her hand.

Kat felt just like Eden fucking Hart.

. . .

Kat saw Eden's latest Instagram entry was a video, which thrilled her. She could really observe Eden, study her. Naturally, the post was racking up likes faster than a Japanese bullet train. It seemed Eden was really becoming a fan of social media— her posts were becoming more frequent, more intimate.

Kat clicked play, enraptured.

Eden held up a nonplussed Don Lockwood as Jacob clearly filmed, laughing off-screen.

"Ladies and gentlemen, I give you Don Lockwood. The pug who faces life with unshakeable reluctance and general disdain," Eden stated. Jacob was chuckling; the camera jostled in his unsteady hands. "For eight years now, Don Lockwood has faced his existence with subtle indifference and a general lack of a life plan."

Jacob guffawed, couldn't help himself. "Ohmygod . . ."

"Don. Anything to add?" Eden stared into Don's watery eyes. They relayed very little. He yawned.

"So we'd like to present a little home-spun theater this morning. For your Friday viewing pleasure, we present . . . The Many Moods of Don Lockwood!"

Eden held up Don for a closer view. "Don! Emote happy!"

Don stared off blankly.

"Don! Try sadness!"

Don licked his lips.

"Don! Give the good people some confusion!"

Don looked up at Eden, baffled with her, and seemed to shake his head. The response was, naturally, spot-on. Don could not have crafted a better comeback if they'd worked on the bit for weeks.

"Perfection. Ladies and gentlemen, the comedic stylings of one Don Lockwood. Have a great Friday everybody. From myself and Don Lockwood, make it jazzy."

The video clicked off, but not before Jacob burst into more laughter. It must just be a romp of bliss over on 3rd Street.

It was nauseating.

Kat clicked onto the video over and over, studying Eden's every detail. She began mimicking her words, her speech patterns, her gestures.

Kat looked up in the mirror and had forgotten about the hair. She was newly shocked to see herself so different. So Eden. Kat loved the effect, knowing it enhanced her appearance tremendously. Kat felt beautiful. She also knew it was dumb—good hair making this much of a difference—but it was also true.

"From myself and Don Lockwood, make it jazzy," Kat said, mirroring Eden's bubbly delivery. "Make it jazzy." Kat paused, repeated the line several times, nailing it, then plowed forward.

"We'd like to present a little home-spun theater this morning," she chirped. "Don! Try sadness!"

The cadence was spot-on. She was getting Eden's effervescent inflection down perfectly. Truly, it was a commanding performance.

Kat went to slip into the Ulla Johnson dress. It fell onto her body like a silken dream. Kat smiled at herself in the mirror, her lips curling like Eden's smile. "Ladies and gentlemen, I give you Don Lockwood. The pug who faces life with unshakeable reluctance."

Kat found a way Eden held her head, the way she tipped her chin just so. She was a goddamn chameleon. Who knew?

And then the bigger truth hit Kat like an electric spark—all of life is a pantomime. All of it. It's just an exaggerated exercise in trying on a persona and presenting truths and untruths to the world. People gritted their teeth, muttering "Go ahead, ass-dick" under their breath as they let someone into traffic. It was all a charade, a game of make believe. What was so different about masquerading to be chipper at work versus pretending to be Eden now? Life was projection, and some people were better than others. We try on various roles to see what fits, to see how the audience of the world will respond.

It was obvious as Kat leaned into her inner Eden that she had found a new authority and likability. She slid into the new skin with an ease that was at once shocking and familiar.

Kat was made for this role.

Granted, she was not entirely certain where the performance was to lead her, but she'd find out.

Kat would have the world wooed in no time. After all, it seemed pretty damn easy for Eden.

· · ·

Lucía watched excitedly from the back room as Kat interacted with customers. Kat was cordial, smiling—who was this version? Where was the angst, the gloom?

Kat looked good. Her new hair really seemed to bring out her features and tap into her joy.

Lucía called Carol who picked right up. "Carol, hi. I just had to share something *extraordinary*."

"Oh, yes, and what's that?"

"It's Kat. She's finally back to being more steady. Happy, even."

Carol furrowed her brow a bit, surprised. "How so?"

"You should see her! It's been a while, but she's lit up. She's smiling with customers, she's helpful . . . I swear, she's almost radiating!"

"Huh. Well, that is good news. Does she have a new beau?" Then Carol gasped, realizing. "God, is it horrid that's my first impulse?"

"I wondered it, too," Lucîa said. "I'll try to find out."

"I'm really relieved to hear she's well. I know we both had concerns," Carol added. "But I'll also admit . . . I just don't feel . . . well, as *comfortable* reaching out to Kat as much. I mean . . . look, we've all been through a lot . . . and I love Kat, adore her . . . and I invested a lot into her well-being."

"You sure did. Bless you."

"But . . . the truth is, she's not dating my son anymore. He's very much involved with someone else. And I don't think Jess has any contact with her either. It's just . . . complicated."

"That makes sense."

"I *do* want her to be well . . . I do. But I have to pull back."

The two women agreed this was best, but were hopeful Kat was on a new trajectory. They also agreed margaritas were calling their names and they had the latest Meg Wolitzer to discuss. A plan was made, and Carol could already taste the salty rim of the drink. She could go forward with a bit more ease with the knowledge Kat was finding her way.

. . .

Kat went through her closet like a surgeon, tossing most into a nearby garbage bag that was eager to gobble up the rejects. Kat's clothes had been bland and sturdy. She'd had to make economically sound choices when she'd first arrived in Arizona. Her desert wardrobe was all solids, functional mix and match. It was also devoid of personality. She lived in solid-colored flowy pants and T-shirts, plain shorts and T-shirts. She didn't give it much thought.

Studying Eden, Kat realized clothes were her costume. At least, they seemed to be for Eden. She always wore these gorgeously layered dresses, diaphanous fabrics that were uniquely timeless. Eden rarely wore pants or jeans. Still, her looks weren't fussy, but she always managed to look like a million bucks. It was doubly irritating fashion didn't seem to be a challenge for her; her look shouted a Parisian, I'll-just-grab-whatever vibe.

Fashion was confusing to Kat—both concepts weren't valued in her prior life. Clothes were all about utility. Did it keep you warm? That was the singular objective. But now she had to think differently.

Soon the garbage bag was bursting with her sartorial castaways. No matter—the pieces had been cheap to begin with; most of her clothes were falling apart.

It was time to start anew anyway.

TWENTY-SIX

THURSDAY WAS EDEN'S NEW FAVORITE DAY. Because at the end of it, she and Jacob would go see Pete perform with his brilliant jazz band at the Monterey Court. Pete was proud to score a regular gig there—the spot was legendary in Tucson. A neon sign that looked like throwback Holiday Inn signage summoned all with its retro kitsch. The entire gallery space was a beautiful urban brew of art, music, and hip retail offerings. In the warm cocoon of desert night and underneath the twinkling lights, the couple would join Maya for drinks and jazz. It was never anything less than wonderful.

Sometimes, Eden would marvel and just sit back, listening to the inspired conversation that inevitably followed Pete's set. She adored the backdrop, the scent of orange blossoms wafting in the air, her boyfriend, and his brother. She cherished this Polaroid snapshot of her life, the new world she had created in the desert.

Tonight would have been perfect, had she been able to find her favorite Ulla Johnson dress. She wanted to wear it and had always felt like a warrior in it—Beyoncé backup singer levels of cool. The dress was the perfect mustard hue and fit her as if it had been custom made. But it was nowhere to be found.

Maybe it was at the cleaners? . . . Eden didn't think that was the case. It was so puzzling. Like walking into a room and not remembering why you'd entered in the first place. No matter, it would show up. She wouldn't let one dress erase a night that held such joy.

Across town, Kat knew Eden and Jacob had this new tradition, knew they'd be out of the house for several hours. She also knew they were yet to install a home security system.

Don Lockwood began to look forward to her visits. Kat didn't want to repeat the diarrhea debacle to raise suspicion; she brought proper dog chews instead. Don Lockwood would wag his weird corkscrew tail when he saw Kat creeping through the dog door on her belly.

The house began to feel familiar to Kat. She knew where the laundry was, knew where they stored toilet paper. She knew Eden wore a 34B bra and owned lots of canary-colored clothes. Sunshine for Little Ms. Sunshine.

Their library was impressive. Their books were an eclectic mix of low- and highbrow reads. The whole wall was a piece of art unto itself, a confection of tomes organized in rainbow perfection.

Kat helped herself to a book each week.

And tonight, a pair of Eden's simple gold hoops. Those were stylish.

Their refrigerator was particularly fascinating, too. Eden was, of course, a naturalist when it came to food.

"No Coke Zeros in this fresh fawn's fridge," she said to Don Lockwood as he mowed on his new rawhide.

They were clearly a Trader Joe's/Whole Foods family, nary an additive in sight. Kat spotted the So Delicious Coconut Milk Creamer and sniffed. She knew Jacob drank his coffee black. This was Eden's. Kat spit into the creamer and set it back, then shut the door.

"What'd ya think, shithead? Is that enough?" Again, Don ignored her words. The idea came to her at once; it was almost as if the thought had been there all along.

Of course!

Kat had looked up her bipolar meds before she'd mostly stopped taking them and found unsettling information on the drug. Kat was so relieved she elected to triumph over the poison. It was horrifying, really—Canadian prison guards often gave their inmates Seroquel to soothe them, to numb them into obedient subservience. Apparently, the magic pills quelled the prisoners' violent instincts and made them docile dopes.

No wonder Kat had felt like such a slacker, no wonder she'd had to fight so mightily to summon the energy to just live and work. No one can thrive with that garbage polluting your body, mind, and soul.

Then Kat's eyes lit up. She reached into her giant purse for her stash. She was certain she still had some more of her tiny darlings.

Bingo!

Kat methodically crushed up three pills into a fine powder. She carefully dumped the noxious dust into the creamer, swilling the container like a potion.

She was thiiiiis close to doing an evil laugh. It was almost comical.

Why hadn't she thought of this before?

Glowy, dewy, honeysuckle Eden would be tamped down, her light blotted out like an eclipse. She'd be numbed into nothing, reduced to a bore.

Let's see how much Jacob worshipped her if she was a doll of dull.

Kat just couldn't wait to see that.

Tomorrow, she'd call her therapist Judith to get a proper refill.

. . .

Eden's agent had told her a few studios were circling the rights to both *Blue* and *Next*, but she didn't want to hear more about it until it was real. Otherwise, it was just wasted thought, wasted anticipation. Hollywood had a talent for dashing hopes; she'd experienced it before.

But the offer was real—Nickelodeon had been the highest bidder, and they wanted to combine the two tales. When Eden found out they were behind *Rango*, she was in. She adored the lovable gecko movie.

Eden only had one real sticking point—they had to use jazz music like Vince Guaraldi's in the film, just like in the *Peanuts* animated specials. Otherwise, the deal was off. She idolized Charles Schulz, who created a world of children who were textured and messy; a land where parents weren't even necessary. He had also introduced one of the first Black characters into his strip before anyone dared to do such a thing. He was a visionary and understood Vince Guaraldi was the only soundtrack appropriate for melancholy Charlie Brown. The cool jazz would be a lovely nod to one of her inspirations, and she also knew Pete would appreciate the call-out.

Jacob was so enthused to hear about the cash cow movie option. And he was doubly glad at least someone in the house was having financial luck. Jacob had two houses on the market that were nothing like the immediate sale of his flip. His listings were nondescript boxes. They'd languished on the market and he'd been worried Phoebe was disappointed.

Eden selling her books' movie rights was exactly the celebration they needed.

"Hey, what if we went up to La Paloma for the weekend? Couples massage, hit the links, and suck at golf?" Jacob asked, enthusiastic at the prospect of a staycation.

Eden surprised him by shrugging her shoulders. "Maybe . . ."

"Maybe? Maybe?! It's gorgeous up there—you loved it before!"

"Yeah, I know. I just love our house so much; I don't know why we'd ever leave. I'd rather not pay money to sleep in an unfamiliar bed when we've got a perfectly decent Tempur-Pedic right here."

"Well . . . Hotel sex, anyone? . . ." Jacob pulled Eden in close, kissed her. Her lips puckered, tightly shut. She shook her head.

"We have pretty excellent house sex here." Eden grinned.

"Perhaps you could offer a demonstration? . . ." Jacob smiled, his eyes flashing with desire. Eden smiled as he led her to the bedroom.

He slid her dress over her head, touched her breasts. Their love-making was always tender, always inspired, but Jacob felt a distance with Eden. She wasn't as vocal, seemed vaguely bored with the entire exercise. He usually knew exactly how to touch her that reduced her to shudders, but she didn't writhe once. Finally she told him to just finish, it was fine.

He did and rolled off her. After a beat, he looked over at her profile staring at the ceiling. "Hey. You okay?"

Eden turned to him, her deep brown eyes startling him anew. "Just . . . tired, I guess."

"But you slept, like, nine hours last night, right?"

"I guess I did. Maybe I slept too much. Who knows." Eden sat up. "I'm going to go get ice cream. Doesn't a sundae sound good?" She let her dress fall onto her body, then looked for her shoes. "With butterscotch chips . . ."

Jacob watched her, vaguely uneasy. Eden wasn't much of a dessert person. But a craving was a craving, so they headed out to The Screamery. Who was he to say no to butterscotch chips?

. . .

Jacob had been at his Sunday Open House for nearly four hours. It was almost 5:00; he was watching the clock. Only three people had walked through, nodding without enthusiasm. No one had signed in, no one requested a brochure. It had been a waste of a day.

He was startled when he saw a beautiful woman enter the front door. He was more startled to realize it was, in fact, Kat. He hadn't seen her for many months; she looked completely different. Almost unrecognizable.

Her hair was now honey, filled with voluminous waves. Kat wore a beautiful dress; frankly, she looked stunning. For a moment, he had thought Eden had stopped by to surprise him.

"Kat! Ohmygod!" Jacob said and moved in for an awkward hug. Kat walked into his embrace, hugging him tight. She pulled away, smelling of delicious citrus and wood. His mind pinwheeled trying to remember if he was not supposed to know about the suicide attempt. He vaguely remembered his mom making him vow to keep it secret. Not that he was anxious to dig into such unpleasantness in the middle of his listless open house.

"It's been a while." Kat beamed at him. She'd tamped down all that makeup she'd started wearing at the end of their relationship; this suited her much more. It was strange to see her again, but he felt relief seeing her look well. "How many months has it been at this point?" Kat asked warmly.

"I guess I've lost track. What . . . what are you doing here?"

"I was driving by, visiting a friend. I saw your sign and just had to pull over to say hi. Your mom mentioned you were kicking ass at real estate now," Kat explained. Jacob laughed, gestured to the empty house.

"Yeah. Pretty much crushing it." They snickered together. "So how are you, Kat?"

"I'm great. Really great. My book finally came out."

"Yeah, Mom said! Congrats!"

"Did she also mention the reviews were a big ole turd blossom?" Kat grinned relaying the sad truth. Jacob laughed unexpectedly at her admission.

"Really?"

"Really. Unless 'confusing' now means awesome."

Jacob found himself laughing yet again. God, Kat looked good. And seemed so . . . confident and sure of herself, despite the disappointing debut of her book.

She was different.

"I'm sorry. That must have been so frustrating. But hey—it is in bookstores, right?"

"It is. And I have a two-book deal, so I'm outlining a new one now."

"Oh, that's great! And I *did* buy a copy of *Foster Kid*. I'm acting a lot more clueless about this than I should be."

Kat brightened. "You did? That's so sweet, thank you!"

"I wanted to check out what you created. I've only read the first few chapters, but I'm totally engrossed. I recognized most of it from . . . well, you know, from before."

Kat smiled, played with her necklace, a tiny diamond horseshoe. "Jacob, I feel the need to apologize to you. I'm really sorry if I made you uncomfortable. For how everything ended. What a mess." She shook her head in embarrassment. "You were my first boyfriend, and to be perfectly candid, my first true love . . . But . . . I guess we all go a little mad sometimes, right?"

A devious smirk revealed her adorable dimples.

"Thanks. But you have nothing to apologize for. I could have been more sensitive, too," Jacob admitted.

"No. It was all me. And I hear you're seeing someone new."

"I am. It's going really well."

Kat's eyes teared ever so slightly. "I am so glad to hear you're happy. Well then. It's really nice to see you again."

"You too, Kat."

"Take care, Jacob." Kat walked to the front door, then turned around. "And if anyone can sell this house, it's you. It's a real dump." She flashed a sarcastic grin and walked out the door.

Jacob chortled as he walked to the living room window, watching Kat put on her stylish cat-eye sunglasses and climb into her car. The wind whipped her hair, a casual arm out the open window. Jazz music blared; she looked utterly cool as she sped away. So much more at ease in her skin than he ever remembered.

It was good to see her. How unexpected, how nice.

And had Kat's eyes always been that green?

· · ·

Jacob loved seeing her again, it was so strange, and not strange in the slightest. He was so happy Kat was relaxed. Apparently her medication *had* really made all the difference. He'd never seen her so effervescent.

Jacob tried to push her out of his mind, stuff the thought down along with his woeful open house. His stomach rumbled; snacking on open house cookies did not constitute lunch.

He bounded into the house and gave Don Lockwood a pat. "Eden? Hon? Hey, how about sushi tonight?"

Jacob saw Eden sitting at the patio table. He walked to the backyard.

"Hey," he said. Eden turned to face him, her lips puckered, sucking up spaghetti, splattering slightly onto her face. She had a ring of marinara sauce around her mouth, almost like a toddler. "Oh. You made pasta?"

Eden nodded. "Want some?"

"I was, uh, thinking we could go out for sushi."

"Oh. Sorry. I was starving. I think there's some more, though," Eden said.

Disappointed, Jacob went to the kitchen and looked into the pot. A few stragglers of spaghetti remained at the bottom.

"There's none left!" Jacob called. Outside, Eden ate her last bite, not hearing what he'd said. Jacob studied her through the window. Eden's hair was limp; she was in a shapeless dress, barefoot. She lifted her dress up to her mouth and wiped the spaghetti sauce away. It was the first time Jacob had ever recoiled at anything Eden had done. She got up and walked inside.

"What did you say?" she asked.

"The pasta. There's none left."

Eden looked into the pot, surprised to see it was now empty. "I thought there was more. I'm sorry."

"It's . . . fine. I'll just call Kazoku and pick some up, I guess." Jacob reached for his cell and walked back out to his car.

Eden picked up the remaining three pieces of spaghetti in the pot and ate them.

· · ·

Carol waited at one of her favorite lunch spots, Cafe a la C'Art in the arts district. The back patio was inspired by Monet's gardens, but she was mostly there for the berry cake.

Jacob dashed in, waved when he spotted his mother in the back. Carol smiled when she saw her son, he was so breathtaking. Jacob had always had a special hold on her heart. As a child, he had always asked her such probing, creative questions, always peppered her with endless adoration. He was such a loving child, and she was happy to see him hit his stride as of late.

"Hello, mother dear!" Jacob kissed the top of her head.

"Hello, darling son. You look well," Carol said, smiling fully, relishing this rare individual kid time.

"Thanks. Things are nutty, of course."

"Any luck on the listings?"

"No. They're not exactly multiple-offers-over-asking sorts of properties," he admitted, scanning the menu.

"Well. Someone will want them. You could sell fly traps to a fly."

"So you're saying I'm basically a sleazy car salesman?" Jacob smiled.

"Far from it. You're charismatic, but honest." Carol drank some water and fanned herself in the direct sunlight.

"Funniest thing at my open house last week. Kat stopped by."

Carol almost spit out her water. "She did? And?"

"And . . . well, she looked great, actually. Seemed to be doing really well."

"You know her book has been a real disappointment," Carol said cautiously.

"She mentioned that. But . . . she seemed alright with it."

"Well. I'm so glad to hear she's okay. I just feel . . . well, let's just say—I've pulled back. Now that you're with Eden." Jacob nodded. "Speaking of which, how is our fair Miss Eden?"

Jacob grinned. "Great. Usually people as interesting as Eden aren't consistently so easy to be with."

"All rose, no thorn?" Carol asked with a smile, and couldn't resist: "You know, I have two diamonds, one for each of you boys from your grandmother. When the time comes."

Jacob shot her a withering look and understood immediately why Pete had kept his impending engagement a secret. Carol would light up like the 4th of July and not let the topic die, likely ruining the surprise itself.

"Alright, alright, I won't bring it up again. But very nice stones. And why your brother keeps dragging his feet with his proposal to Maya, I have no idea . . ." Jacob grinned to himself as Carol put on her glasses to inspect the menu, acting too hard to be nonchalant. "Do you think, though, Eden is . . . you know, the one?"

"Mom. Come on."

"Can't a mother inquire as to the inner truths of her son?"

Jacob smiled. "Likely, yes. I'll never find someone like Eden if I searched the whole planet. Ever. And with her, I do feel . . . fated."

"The magic of the universe is real," Carol gushed, so pleased to hear her son speak this way.

"And so is science."

"Well, the *chemistry* between you two is scientifically observable," Carol said, knowing the joke would likely be met with a groan.

Jacob shook his head, playfully rolling his eyes. "Let's just put it this way, Mom—no one is in a rush. Especially considering what Eden's been through. We're just enjoying ourselves and no one's going anywhere."

Carol nodded, a bit disappointed. Jacob stared off a bit, lost in thought. She noted worry in his eyes. "What is it?"

Jacob caught himself, snapped back. "Oh. Nothing. Just . . . nothing."

Carol grabbed his hand, gave it a squeeze. "The diamond is a cushion cut. I won't say it again."

"You just did." The two grinned at one another as the waitress appeared.

· · ·

Kat was beginning to want a pug of her own. Don Lockwood really did grow on her. He was a curmudgeon but weirdly likable. He was always so delighted to see Kat crawl through the dog door, usually because she came bearing gifts.

Kat had systematically increased the weekly dosage of Seroquel—now she was smashing five pills into Eden's coconut creamer each Thursday. Tonight she intended to put six into her coffee companion.

Kat snagged a book from the green section of the rainbow library—*Little Children* by Tom Perrotta. She'd read another book of his—*Election*—and loved it, couldn't wait to read this one. Inside the book jacket was a sticker **From the Library of Eden Hart**. Jesus Christ. What adult uses stickers?

She then wandered out to the back and headed to the converted garage. Don Lockwood followed at her feet as she snapped on the lights. It was filled with colorful markers, paints, a drafting table. Sketches everywhere, the space filled with art. The office was so cool it made her breathless with envy.

She inspected Eden's latest animation attempts—a series of talking socks, trapped in the dryer. The socks were forlorn, bereft. Kat literally felt bad for them, wanted to weirdly protect them. They were fucking *socks*; how did Eden do this?

It suddenly hit Kat—how *was* Eden doing, anyway? Kat kept juicing her up, hoping to numb her into nothing, but she didn't know exactly how it was going. Drive-bys couldn't reveal the complete picture. Eden hadn't been going to yoga lately, which was a good sign unto itself but no serious confirmation one way or the other.

Considering Eden's luck, the pills would likely just make her energetic and lose weight or something.

Kat had to know. She tidied up and snapped off the lights, then headed for the dog door. She grabbed an anchor-shaped bracelet on her way out.

"Until we meet again, Don Lockwood."

. . .

Kat knew she was at risk of getting caught if she went to Monterey Court to spy, but she had to know if her plan was working. Then again, she could go there, it was a public place, wasn't it? Kat was a goddamn artist, too, and loved such venues. If Jacob spotted her, Kat would roll with it. She was getting good at channeling positivity and her role as an ambassador of charm. She'd had no idea she had this power all along. People loved it when you led with a smile. It was stupid how easy it was.

She parked her car outside of the arts complex, could already hear Pete's jazz band at work. It was a bustling night at the Monterey Court.

Kat inspected herself in the visor mirror, applied gloss. She could not believe how transformative her hair was. Blondes didn't just have more fun, they had another existence entirely. Kat had never felt so many men's eyes on her in her life, and she was fairly used to it at this point. She knew she had newfound power and relished it.

Kat wandered to the back of the outdoor courtyard through an enthralled audience of jazz purveyors. She spotted Pete happily pounding the piano, then saw his girlfriend Maya beaming beside Jacob and Eden at a nearby table.

Hell, if that even *was* Eden. Kat craned her neck to inspect—was Eden *asleep*? She had her head down slightly, looking like a drunk uncle at a Thanksgiving table trying to pass for awake. She looked puffy, too, less polished.

Kat could barely contain her glee. It was working.

Jacob—darling, sweet Jacob—was enraptured with his brother. Kat saw Maya nudge Jacob, point to Eden. Jacob realized Eden was snoozing. Jacob and Maya looked at one another and nonchalantly laughed, then shrugged.

Goddammit. NO. That was not the response. *Eden turns into a fucking dolt and she's still charming?* The woman could shit her pants running a marathon and she'd be celebrated as heroically determined.

"So good, right?" Kat was startled out of her thoughts by a man's voice. She looked over and saw a reasonably attractive guy grinning appreciatively.

"Oh. Yes. I love jazz," Kat responded, and the man raised his Fat Tire in agreement.

"Can I get you one?" he offered. Kat was about to refuse but changed her mind.

"Sure. I'll have one of those. I just love beer so much," she chirped with stupid enthusiasm. The man brightened and went to get her a drink. As the music crescendoed, the place erupted into wolf whistles and hollers. Finally, the band concluded.

"We'll take a 10-minute break," the lead singer said, and Pete and his band disappeared offstage.

Kat made her move, walked over to Jacob. Eden's head had fallen further into her chest. She was truly out at this point.

Jacob spotted Kat stride toward her and brightened. Once again, there she was. "Kat!"

"We meet again! I thought that was you!" Kat approached. "Hey, Maya."

"Kat, it's been a minute! Man, I gotta tell you—you look *incredible*. Seriously, girl," Maya enthused and Kat basked in the praise, could feel Jacob's eyes on her.

"Thanks so much, I appreciate that, Maya. You look amazing, too, as always. God, Pete is so talented, I almost forgot," Kat raved.

"That's my man!" Maya crowed.

"Who are you here with?" Jacob asked.

"Oh, uh—Kevin. He's—" Kat looked over and saw the man approach the space she'd just left, confused, holding a Fat Tire for her. Kat waved to him and put up a "one second" finger. "Right there. Anyway, just wanted to say hi. Great to see you both." Kat gave a critical look at the napping Eden.

Jacob blushed. "She's, uh . . . zapped." He shrugged, not sure what to say.

"Well. I guess it IS a school night . . . See ya," Kat said casually and strode back to her awaiting beer.

Maya and Jacob watched Kat saunter across the space, saw the way people noticed her pass. "Jesus. Maybe I should get dumped by you, too."

Jacob shot Maya a look but laughed anyway. No wonder she and Pete got on so well.

"Seriously though, J., was Kat always so . . ."

"No," Jacob asserted. Nothing more was said.

He found himself watching Kat flirt with the man who was responding to her attention like it was Christmas morning. She placed an intimate hand on his arm; they both leaned in and laughed. Kat put her head back, full-throatedly hysterical.

Eden woke up, her eyes fluttering in confusion and then embarrassment. "Oh man."

"Morning," Jacob said.

"What'd I miss?" she asked, rubbing her eyes.

Maya and Jacob looked at one another ironically. No one responded.

TWENTY-SEVEN

EDEN WAS IN A FOG. It was inexplicable, this molasses of melancholy she was swimming through. Every morning, her body awakened groggy, leaden after a long sleep. Her mind floated in a film of nothing. She didn't get upset; she didn't get happy. She was not herself.

Eden had not realized just how sunny she was until this bizarre turn. She'd always glided along with a hum of optimism, with a sense of wonder. Of course, she'd fallen deeply depressed following the death of Mac—and again in Seattle toward the end—but that made sense, it was the only proper response.

This did not. This melancholy was on a cellular level, unconnected to any reasoning. She felt like a much less interesting, much less active cousin had invaded her body. She fell asleep everywhere, her entire life now seemingly a big nursing home.

Nothing had changed but everything suddenly had, even though she wasn't doing anything different in her life. Eden knew she had to get her bloodwork done. Maybe it was mono? Wasn't that the virus her friend had faked in junior high so she could watch game shows and *The Brady Bunch*? Eden vowed to find a doctor tomorrow and get to the bottom of this—she knew this new reality wasn't an endearing look, this carb-craving dullard. Jacob would never have fallen in love with this version.

Eden was secretly terrified this was a latent response to losing Mac so suddenly. Despite the years since she'd lost him, perhaps she somehow hadn't processed it properly. Maybe her body was slowing down to pull her away from Jacob, as their relationship had happened so quickly, so unexpectedly. Could that be it? A primal self-protection, creating an invisible bubble of distance to tap the brakes on her and Jacob's future?

That didn't seem likely. With Jacob, it was only green lights. He was genuine, a rare man. Eden didn't want to jeopardize something so foreordained, something so wondrous.

She dragged herself to the car wash—it was always a spot she sought out when things felt like they were collapsing. Maybe your life was imploding, but you'd have a vacuumed, sparkly car. It was a hit of order, and she needed that.

Eden watched her car ghost-ride the car wash track, each step elaborately illuminated with lights and bubbles. The Vegas-ification of car washes felt like such an American concept, it always made Eden ironically smile. She loved it.

Her white Audi had a thick layer of pink foam when Eden heard the song. The tell-tale, groovy 70s sighs of the Bee Gees' "How Deep Is Your Love" filled the car wash.

How deep is your love? Eden heard Mac whisper into her ear.

The tears burst from her eyes as if they'd been lodged in the depths of her soul for years. They were violent, shocking—a blubbering explosion.

Eden covered her eyes and moaned, just let it flow. On the back of her eyelids, she saw it all again—she and Mac dancing in their living room, the Seattle rain pouring outside their big window. There was a time when the endless showers had, in fact, been romantic, not dreary. They loved the cheesy earnestness of the song, so much so that "How Deep Is Your Love" was their wedding song. Only Robin Gibb understood the depth of their intense emotion.

Her heart hurt. She couldn't breathe. What the hell was going on?

Eden looked up from her meltdown and saw the cashier pouting with a look of theatrical concern.

"Hon, you okay?" she cooed.

Eden was on another planet. Her eyes took in the car wash—the endless bags of chips, the painful collection of tacky greeting cards, the tree-shaped air fresheners. She felt like she was watching herself in a movie.

"Life can be pretty doggone rough sometimes, huh?"

She numbly nodded.

"Your car's ready, hon. You okay to drive?" She placed a hand on Eden's shoulder; it felt like a dead fish.

Her face streaked with mascara, she nodded and left.

The fog was getting thicker, each step was labored. She felt like a giant baby, struggling to find her footing and make her way to her car. She forgot to tip and drove off, worlds away.

Eden would call a doctor when she got home.

. . .

Jacob entered the house post-jog, sweaty. He found Eden laying on the couch, scrolling through her phone.

"Good run?"

"Yeah. I met Jess and we looped the Mall three times. She always kicks my ass. We're gonna go a few times a week," Jacob said, then asked if he could see her phone, which she handed to him. "I've been meaning to tell you—I installed this app Life 360 on your phone so you can always find me. See?" He pulled up the app and showed her. "If you'd looked 10 minutes ago, you would have seen a little moving graphic of me running around the Mall with Jess."

"Wow, I guess you must really trust me to install something like that," she joked.

"Damn straight. It's convenient—a few of the other realtors use it with their families."

Eden thanked him and then lifted herself onto her elbows, a new app far from her concerns. "Hey, I wanted to talk to you. I don't know what's going on . . . but I'm going to a doctor. To get bloodwork. I know you've noticed . . . I'm not myself lately."

Jacob sat down; they'd been dancing around the subject for weeks. "Yeah. I've been worried. When I brought it up before, you didn't seem too enthused to talk about it."

"Yeah, well . . . it's weird and . . . well, embarrassing to be honest. I don't get it. I do NOT feel like myself. Something is up."

"I'm so relieved. I'm worried about you, babe."

"Thanks. I'm worried about me, too. I just . . . hate how I feel. All of it. I just feel like I'm someone else, like I'm underwater . . ."

"You'll get to the bottom of it. And I'm here for you. You know that."

Eden nodded and grinned. She knew he wanted her back, the adventurous soul up for anything. He'd never want the blasé body who scrolled through Instagram and called it a day.

"I mean, truly, you should have more energy than Don Lockwood," Jacob joked, eager to get back to laughing. Don Lockwood responded on cue and farted.

Eden grinned. "I mean, at bare minimum, right? . . ." Eden leaned over and kissed Jacob; he delighted in the gesture. She hadn't initiated any affection for weeks. "Thanks, Mac."

MAC.

The name hung in the air like a polluted cloud. Any newfound closeness was immediately sucked out of the room.

"Oh, shit," Eden said, collapsing her head into her hands. She couldn't look at Jacob whose own head drooped, wounded as if he'd been punched in the stomach. "Jacob, I'm so sorry. I . . . I don't know what to say."

Jacob nodded. He didn't know what to say, either. It was a painful first. His silence stung Eden.

"Are you . . . Eden, is this . . . is this whole thing just too soon?" It hurt to even ask the question.

"No! No! Jacob, I'm sorry—I don't know where that came from. I just told you I'm a mess. That I'm going to a doctor. My brain isn't working." Eden tried to meet Jacob's eyes but he stared off. "Jacob, I love *you*."

Jacob finally looked over. His eyes were dulled with pain, a new confusion. He gave Eden's hand a tepid grip.

"You believe me, don't you?"

Jacob nodded and kissed her forehead, but she could still feel his hurt.

He got up to shower but Eden sensed a distance between them. It had always been so effortless between them, and now there was a chill.

Eden wished she could find sorrow to cry, but the release at the car wash had exhausted her tears.

. . .

Kat strode through the University of Arizona campus with a spring in her step. She liked to pretend she was constantly filming a perfume commercial, calling her imaginary scent Pleasure Kat. It instantly made her grin; it was all so absurd. Pleasure Kat smelled of potent musky sex and jasmine, and Kat was the shining face for the potion. It was a charade, of course, but it was almost embarrassing how well it worked. Project positivity, wear a confident smile, act as if you anticipate a stranger to approach with flowers. Expect good things.

It turns out mania could go two ways. One path for bad, another for good. Kat channeled all her fizzy frenzy for good. For electric, charismatic good.

She strolled into Carol's office hours, eager to share this vibrant self with her. There's zero percent chance Carol wouldn't tell Jacob how fucking amazing she was doing.

"Carol! Hi!" Kat trilled. Carol looked up, having just taken a big bite of sandwich. She mumbled a greeting through her egg salad. "Sorry—I caught you at a bad time!"

Carol shook her head no as she chewed aggressively, startled with the unexpected visual of Kat. Kat's hair was lighter, voluminous—she was stunning. Kat glowed with energy, but there was an edge to it that made Carol uneasy.

"How are you?" Carol swallowed the last of her sandwich, got up to hug Kat. She smelled so delicious. Carol wanted to linger in her hair.

"I'm great! Working on my new book, still helping out at Antigone . . . just keep on keepin' on!" Kat could feel Carol assessing her, could feel how surprised she was. "I was stopping by to see a few old professors and I had to say hello."

"I'm so touched you did! You look so great, Kat! Lucîa had mentioned . . . but I wasn't entirely . . ." Carol trailed off. Her resemblance to Eden was striking.

"Yeah, I wanted a change." Kat played with her hair like a weapon. "I'm supposed to look more like Jennifer Lawrence, but I think I missed that boat." Kat shrugged in an aw-shucks way, like when supermodels try to convince interviewers they're "really huge nerds."

"Well, I love it!" Carol grinned, studying Kat's transformed being. "Anyway, I'm so glad you seem so HAPPY."

"I am. And how are you? How's your writing, Carol?"

"Some days are better than others. You know. It's all a mess until it's suddenly not."

Kat nodded and beamed. She wanted to be the first to say goodbye. "Make sure you tell Jess I said hi."

"Oh. I will!" Carol watched Kat turn to exit and saw a colleague crane his neck catching a sideways glance at her.

"Bye Carol. Take care!" she sing-songed, heels clicking down the hall. Kat wanted to look back, but she didn't need to.

She knew Carol was watching.

. . .

Jacob saw Jess up ahead in shorts, ready to run.

"Vee vill run now," Jess said in an over-the-top German accent.

"Vee vill hurt now," Jacob answered back, his accent equally impressive.

The two started their loop slowly and gained steam. Instantly, they were puddles of sweat under the bruising Tucson sun.

"Think I got a nibble on a house," Jacob said, hoping to pass the time.

"That's great! A good offer?"

"I'll find out today. The family's moving from Des Moines."

Jess nodded, then had to ask, "How's Eden?" Jess had heard from Pete she'd fallen dead asleep at the Monterey Court mid-set.

"Well . . . truth?"

"No. Lie to me, bro. I love lies." Jess grinned.

"She's been . . . almost sick I'd say. Not herself. Lethargic—"

"Did she really fall asleep at Monterey Court?"

"Yeah. But she's going to the doctor. Gonna get bloodwork done."

"Good," Jess said. They continued on, only their breath between them. "Are you worried?"

Jacob considered. He knew the answer, of course. Yes. He was more than worried. "A bit. Yeah."

"Maybe anemic? Does she eat meat?" Jess inquired.

"Some."

"Well. I'm sure she'll figure it out. And you'll get back to being the same nauseatingly happy couple that makes all of us want to gouge our eyes out."

Jacob groaned.

"Just kidding. You can't help it if you look like the couple from the Target picture frame."

Jacob laughed, and Jess noticed he was out of breath a bit, yet *still* somehow made it look easy.

. . .

It was almost like a job at this point, sliding through the dog door to both see Don Lockwood and drug the Eden dolly into defeat. As she entered on her belly, Don Lockwood barked. Kat tossed him a rawhide.

"Hey, stupid." He went to town on the bone. Poor thing likely had to be subject to Eden's impossibly healthy eating himself.

Kat took in the house almost as if it was her place, it felt so familiar. She noticed each week it was decidedly less tidy, more disheveled—the house as metaphor for Eden herself. It warmed Kat's heart.

She strolled about but could feel a shift in the energy. Something was amiss, off. Like someone was watching her this time. It pissed Kat off that she felt a wave of fear. Pleasure Kat was terrified of nothing.

Kat had already pre-crushed her pills, she was all business. Ten this time. She grabbed the coconut creamer and carefully went to work in her kitchen laboratory, dumping the powder into the brew.

She paused, hearing something. Don Lockwood dropped the rawhide and dashed outside.

Shit.

Kat craned her neck—how did she not notice before?! The lights to the converted garage were ON.

Eden was home. Kat heard a door shut.

"Donnie boy, what's up?" Eden said, her voice approaching.

Kat panicked, tossed the creamer into the fridge, slammed it shut. She nearly ejected herself through the dog door, Eden missing the sight of Kat's feet just sliding by.

Eden did notice, however, the plastic flap of the dog door was swaying slightly. She started for the dog door, stopped. A rawhide was on the floor.

What?

Eden looked around the house, her arms prickled with fear. "*Hello?* . . ." She could feel the energy of the house, feel someone else there. She was terrified and felt incredibly vulnerable.

"Don? Buddy?" Don Lockwood trotted her way, oblivious, and instantly she felt better. She picked up the rawhide. "Where's this from? Huh?"

Eden went to the front door, stepped outside, peered around. The night was still.

Eden spotted a woman walking down the sidewalk away from her. "Excuse me?" she called out.

The woman stopped and turned. It was hard to make out her face in the shadows, she was on a phone. "Yes?"

"Did . . . did you see anyone?" Eden called feebly.

"Huh?"

"Never mind." Eden felt stupid. *Did you see anyone?*

The woman walked off down the street and turned the corner.

Eden had no idea what had just happened. She just knew she felt very, very scared. It was an especially warm night but her whole body had erupted into goosebumps. She needed a sweatshirt. Eden would call Jacob and beg him to come home. She did not want to be alone.

• • •

Jacob drove home as soon as he got Eden's call—it felt nice to be summoned to her rescue, to be needed. Eden had been so lethargic, it was refreshing just to hear emotion in her voice—even if it was fear.

Eden was on the couch when he arrived back home, clearly worried, clutching Don Lockwood. She threw herself into his arms, hugged him tight. He didn't let go.

"It was so scary," she said. Jacob kissed her.

"You're okay now."

"The dog door was swaying, there was a rawhide on the floor. Someone was here, Jacob," Eden insisted. "The house felt . . . altered. It even smelled different."

"Well, it could have been a skunk . . . another critter. Who knows. It's very unlikely it was a person, Eden."

"And the rawhide? I don't buy those; you know they're dangerous for pugs."

"Maybe Don found it outside and dragged it in?"

Eden didn't look very comforted. Jacob hugged her again.

"I'm sorry I made you come home early," Eden said, then smiled. "Thanks. I just . . . I just needed to see you."

Jacob felt himself brighten, thrilled with her words. "You needed me, eh?" He pulled her closer, kissed her neck. Eden was stiff, her hands crossed her chest.

"Jacob . . . I'm not really . . ."

Jacob kept softly kissing her clavicle, the way she loved.

"I'm sorry. No. I'm just . . . not in the mood."

Jacob retreated, hurt. He looked down, defeated. So much for being the hero. "It's just . . . been awhile."

"I know. And I'm going to the doctor Friday. I should have some answers." Eden could see he was still upset. "And hey, I miss me—and sex—too. But I'm sorry, being terrified isn't exactly foreplay for me."

Jacob nodded and grinned, hugging her again.

"Don't worry. We'll get back to being freaky-deaky soon enough."

Eden laughed. She so wanted this to be true.

. . .

Eden had always hated doctors. Or at least hated going to the doctor. It was filled with disease and needles and scales that instantly made you eight pounds heavier. And Dr. Beaver did little to convince her otherwise.

He strode in, peering down at his clipboard to make sure he had her name right. "Hello, Ever."

"Eden."

"Eden. What brings a pretty young woman like yourself in today?"

It took a lot to stop her eye roll. "Well, I just haven't been feeling like myself lately."

"And what are you normally like?" The doctor beamed, amused with himself.

"Energetic. Good. I don't know—productive."

"So in other words . . . human?" He winked. Wasn't he just a riot. Eden nodded. Get on with it already.

"Well, your blood pressure's 118/79, that's good. Pulse 68, again just fine. Let me take a listen." He pulled out a stethoscope and listened to her heart, satisfied. Dr. Beaver checked her reflexes, the inside of her mouth and ears. She wasn't going back to 4th grade here, she wanted herself back.

"Is anything especially stressful in your life? Beyond the average? Any new changes?"

"I'm new to Tucson. Just moved here fairly recently."

"Moving is very stressful. It could be—"

"—I need a blood work-up. A full blood panel, I mean," Eden said, wanting to cut the crap.

"Okay. We can do that. But you seem healthy to me. How are you sleeping?"

"Too much."

"Everyone should be so unhealthy. Appetite?"

"Too much," she admitted. "Apparently I've gained six pounds."

Dr. Beaver studied her, not entirely sure. "Well. Let's get the bloodwork results in and start from there, shall we?"

"Yes, we shall." Dr. Beaver sensed the edge, grinned, and left his nurse to take over. Eden looked away as the needle was inserted into her arm.

"So how long until the results come in?"

"Two or three days," the nurse said as the vial filled with Eden's blood, then leaned in conspiratorially. "We women know when something ain't right."

Eden smiled. "What's your name again?"

"Carrie."

"Carrie. Thank you and amen."

· · ·

Surrounded by torn and crumpled sheets of paper, Eden sat hunched at her drawing board, curled over in despair. Don Lockwood was lounging among the detritus of her creative attempts, the lone figure in a snow globe of frustration.

Her editor had been increasingly worried, even though she'd tried to disguise her concern, but they always knew. Eden feared they'd consider *Blue* just a lucky fluke and *Next* an interloper. The Garden of Eden had dried up. Nothing fruitful here.

Her mind was empty, just a pool of grey nothing. The problem wasn't that she was working with a blank slate; nothing was even coming to her creatively. Eden checked her email frequently, hoping to see her bloodwork results, willing there to be evidence, proof, of what was going on with her. Mostly, she wanted a cure.

Her phone pinged, and Eden lunged for it. Just an Instagram DM—she thought she'd turned off her notifications. Her fans were wondering where she'd gone, so was her publicity team, quite frankly. The message was from a familiar follower:

@blueskytucson

> Hey you! Checking in—you haven't posted much. Miss your hilarious missives! Hope you're okay!

Eden grinned, texted back:

> Don't feel so hilarious these days. But it happens, right?! Hope you're well.

Looking through her illustrations, she clicked off her phone. "The Secret Sock Society" was going nowhere. Apparently there were several other "missing sock" books. Eden was still allowed to explore the arena; her agent assured her if her take was unique enough, there could be a market.

Her take was not unique enough.

The message from @blueskytucson reminded her that she *was* alienated. She hadn't been reaching out, hadn't been connecting enough. Eden was barricading herself out of pity and embarrassment, wishing she would just get better. But she was also not doing anything to fortify herself. Maybe addressing the elephant in the room would free her? Wasn't honesty the cornerstone of all art?

She knew she looked like abject shit but grabbed her iPhone anyway and hit record. She didn't want to think it through too much, didn't want to rehearse her way out of this. She was done with thinking, she had to tap back into her instinct, to her heart.

She reached for her lip gloss, paused, and deliberately set it down. Eden went to check the lighting, shrugged instead, and hit "record."

"Hello out there. Whoever you may be. So listen . . . a follower of mine just reached out today and asked where I'd been. And it's true; I've been MIA. Hiding. Or wallowing is a better word. Drowning works, too. For a while now, I've just been so absolutely braindead, so tired, so NOT ME. I've been in a tailspin. I admit it. It's a new sensation. I feel like a lifeless shell of my former self. I've been to exactly one unhelpful doctor, but I am awaiting bloodwork. Who knows. I just wanted to tell the truth and let you know I am, in fact, okay. I mean, I'm crap, but I'm okay. We all go through things. And isn't that the point of *Blue*? That life is not one linear line to self-awareness? That we have passages that swim in gold and others where you trudge through shit? Well folks, I'm in the shit. And please baby Jesus, may this shit not be my permanent *Next* . . . But I love you. And I will get back to loving this ride. Peace."

Eden didn't watch it again; this wasn't supposed to be edited. There was no filter. She instantly uploaded the video to Instagram.

She exhaled. Deeply. From her gut and heart, and it was the most liberating feeling.

The truth was always best.

. . .

Kat read Eden's response to her DM. She was so happy she could cry. It was more proof positive her efforts were working on a grand scale. She was single-handedly bringing Eden back to earth, slowing her sparkle, anesthetizing her other-worldliness.

And Kat knew Jacob would never tolerate a mere mortal.

Kat started a frenetic happy dance, singing.

Then Kat noticed Eden had indeed posted a video. She clicked on it. At first, she thrilled even more seeing the decay of Eden, this new human version. Her face was puffy, her eyes tired. She was a half-life. But her admission was from the heart; she felt the humanity in her words. Frantic, she read the responses sprouting like Whac-a-Moles.

Aw, sweetie! Feel better!

You inspire me SO MUCH.

LOVE your honesty. LOVE YOU MORE!

> WE NEED MORE VOICES LIKE
> YOURS! KEEP UP THE FIGHT!

The messages were dripping with concern, compassion, rooting for Eden from afar. It was so nauseating, all this fucking support. Finally, Eden responded to her adoring fans—

> THANK YOU! ALL-CAPS-
> LOCK THANK YOU! I
> FEEL A RUSH OF MYSELF
> RETURN JUST READING
> YOUR WORDS OF LOVE!

Kat screamed and threw her phone into the couch.

. . .

After her admission of how much she was struggling, Eden felt a weight float up and away. The heaviness was still there, but she felt less burdened. Even if it was something as shallow as multiple Instagram likes, having a community of support changed everything. She wanted to go forward with more truth, and Eden was hopeful that it would help slay whatever invisible dragon she was battling.

She decided her sock idea would never be able to rise above what was currently on the market—she'd counted three titles on Amazon alone. Eden pulled out a previous idea she'd had about an abandoned Christmas tree who gets a new home underwater after being tossed onto a frozen lake after the holidays. Come spring, the tree would melt through the ice and serve as a spawning site for fish, giving the Christmas tree a whole new purpose. She'd named the tree Holiday Hank.

The illustrations of a forlorn tree were fine but nothing special, but she was inspired by this project and wanted this to be some of her best work. In the middle of drafting a new version of Hank, her phone rang, and she saw it was Dr. Beaver.

"Yes, hello?"

"Eden? This is Dr. Beaver. I have your bloodwork results here," he sing-songed.

Cut to the chase, man. "Yes?"

"All normal. Cholesterol of 192, that's good. White and red blood cell counts all within normal ranges, metabolic levels fine. Your hemoglobin and mean corpuscular volume were excellent."

"Oh."

"You sound disappointed! These are outstanding levels. We'll email them over to you. And *relax*—you're obviously doing something right!" Eden could feel his dismissiveness through the phone. He was fine with the results and wasn't inclined to go on a fishing expedition for something rare.

Eden knew continuing with this doctor was fruitless; she switched tactics. "Could I speak to the nurse Carrie, please? I need to schedule a mammogram."

"You betcha. Hold the line. And stay healthy." After a few clicks, a nurse came onto the line.

"Hello, how may I help you?"

"Hi. This is Eden Hart, um, is this Carrie?"

"Yes, I'm Carrie! I remember you."

Eden grinned with relief. "Wonderful. Listen. I remember you said something about trusting a woman's intuition? . . ."

"Yes . . . What're you thinking?"

Eden grimaced. "Honestly? I'm not entirely sure. But something is so off with me. I know my bloodwork is fine, but . . . I'm not. Fine, that is. I frankly feel drugged. I mean, I'm not on drugs—as long as you don't count my secret meth habit—but . . ."

Carrie laughed. "We could also do another full blood panel and maybe a toxicology report?"

"You think that's best?"

"Well," Carrie sighed. "I'm not entirely sure. But you're also not the only one with strong intuition."

That was all Eden needed to hear. When you know, you know.

TWENTY-EIGHT

JACOB, PHOEBE, AND MATEO STOOD inside the house, studying it critically. Only Jacob was taking in the heap as if it was a piece of art. Jacob again saw the unearthed potential, the thrill of the excavation. He knew this was a bigger job with more obstacles, but he welcomed the challenge. He knew more now, and Mateo also loved the potential of the property. Plus, Jacob desperately needed this distraction.

"It's an incredible location," he enthused. "The Dunbar Spring neighborhood is on the up-and-up, and it's great for families."

Phoebe nodded. "But you don't want it to be *such* a disaster it erodes the profit completely."

"Of course! But considering the comps in the area, we could net about $150,000 in profit. *Easily*. We're thinking we can do a solid flip for around 60K," Jacob said proudly.

"Not double that amount?" Phoebe playfully questioned.

"I have a lot of connections, we'll keep the prices down, ma'am," Mateo assured her.

Phoebe turned on her Manolo Blahniks and good-naturedly shook her finger. "Oh, I am not a ma'am. The day I turn into a ma'am, I will have dirt above me." Phoebe smiled, then shifted back to Jacob and asked, "And where is this lovely girlfriend of yours? She was supposed to be here today so we could finally meet. I like to think I *did* have a small hand in your union, you know . . ."

"Oh, yeah—Eden wanted to meet you, too, Phoebe. But she, uh, wasn't feeling so hot," he explained.

"Again? Is she alright?"

"Sure, sure, nothing but some allergies," Jacob said, eager to move on. "So. What do you think?"

"'I'll take the leap of faith with you. The firm will invest 25%; we'll split the profits accordingly." She poked a finger at Jacob. "And I also think I need to meet this ghost of a girlfriend."

. . .

It was taking too long. Kat was getting anxious, everything was either up or down, really good or really bad . . . all the time. It was chaos. She needed to steel herself, be focused. Otherwise her plan wouldn't work.

Kat made a poster-board detailing her efforts, declared it "My Jacob Vision Board." By embracing the truth, she felt the mania had less power. She was admitting she was painfully preoccupied with her ex-boyfriend. And what was wrong with that? Literature was filled with such examples. Gatsby and Daisy. Tom Ripley and Dickie Greenleaf. Humbert Humbert and Lolita.

If obsession was glorious enough for the stalwarts of literature, why was it so taboo for real life?

Yes. Kat was obsessed with Jacob. He was worth it—he was the sunlight she needed to flourish, literally, to live.

And yes. She would get him back.

She knew Jess and Jacob jogged three times a week around the U. of A. Mall. She knew when Jacob went to see his brother perform on Thursdays. She knew Eden was trying to start yoga once a week again.

Jacob also had a new house he was flipping—Phoebe Cane's web site had a photo of the mess of the home with a chyron underneath that read **FLIP COMING SOON—WATCH THIS SPACE!** Naturally, Jacob's photo was also included. But she was certain it was another sign from the universe itself, as his investment was close to her place. Strolling by could happen. Perhaps she needed a dog—some reason to be passing by on a frequent basis. But she didn't want the responsibility of a dog; it was too permanent and messy. Maybe she could be a dog walker. She paced the room, adding notes to the vision board.

Kat decided she had to move quickly in order to take advantage of the timing. She had to manipulate a way to physically be around Jacob. Plus, she was going to add more to Eden's creamer this week; this was the moment to make a big move.

Scanning her living room side to side, she landed on one of the many book-shelves. Kat walked over and instantly grabbed a James Baldwin title, pulled off the dust jacket, and took scissors to the publisher colophon on the spine.

She put glue on the paper and then pasted the image to the vision board. The Knopf symbol, a Borzoi dog. This was going to happen.

· · ·

Yoga had wiped Eden out. Downward dog and Vrikshasana had never exhausted her before; usually they invigorated her. She had been hoping for a similar effect if she could return to yoga; unfortunately, the opposite was true.

She crashed onto the couch. Don Lockwood plodded over to greet her. She realized she'd never had as much in common as she did now with Don—easily tired, lethargic, increasingly thick. Maybe her pens could cheer her up, color usually had a good effect on her mood.

Eden moved to her studio; Don Lockwood followed close behind.

"I get it, buddy. I get it," she said to him, watching his old body shuffle along.

Once at the drafting board, she couldn't get comfortable. Her back hurt. Her neck was strained. The chair wasn't at the right height. She needed water.

Even hydrated, Eden was gloomy. Her illustrations of Holiday Hank the Christmas Tree were nondescript, flat.

Her phone rang; she saw it was New York. "Hello?"

"Eden, hi. It's Thomas. How's Tucson? Impossibly perfect?"

"72 degrees, so yes it is!" she chirped, trying too hard.

"Wonderful. Listen, just checking in on Hank. We're relieved you've decided to abandon the missing sock idea."

"Yeah. Not the most inspired, I realize," Eden admitted. "Anyway, yes, I am working on some illustrations now for Hank the Christmas Tree. It's going well," she lied.

"Wonderful. Both *Blue* and *Next* continue to sell so well, we see no drop-off. Releasing a new book while they're both still hot could be a win for all," Thomas assured her.

"Of course."

"Want to send some mock-ups? Just have us take a peek?" he offered, as if this was the most helpful thing in the world.

"Just . . . give me a bit more time. A week or two. I'll have something soon."

"You got it. We know it takes time to create your level of genius. Just know we're always here for you."

Eden nodded and hung up, head collapsing backward and letting out a giant sigh. She stared at the ceiling, willing its blank space to provide inspiration.

None came.

. . .

Lucîa had been keeping a close eye on Kat. As of late, she was swinging like a pendulum between light and dark. Kat would whirl into work with the energy of a showgirl, electrifying the entire store. Other days, she'd slink in, possibly hungover, dark glasses disguising her hooded eyes. Half the time, Kat radiated the dreariness Lucîa was hopeful she'd forever left behind.

Customers would ask questions; Kat would yawn a response. When asked if a book was good, she'd shrug her shoulders. She was often late, and the gloomy moods were increasingly frequent and the upbeat days diminishing in frequency.

Lucîa had called Carol to discuss Kat, but Carol had seemed preoccupied and choppy on the phone, anxious to get off. Carol was done with worrying about Kat, and Lucîa realized Carol couldn't offer assistance at this point.

Kat was Lucîa's project now.

One day, Lucîa noticed Kat had placed Stephen King's *Misery* in the Staff's Pick section, complete with her personalized endorsement. Lucîa went to inspect what she'd written:

"*Misery* is a hell of a ride. The Annie Wilkes character is delicious and less of a villain than people realize. Her love for books and Paul is real, is that so wrong? 'I wasn't trying to be funny in a mean way when I named my pig Misery, no sir. Please don't think that. No, I named her in the spirit of fan love, which is the purest love there is. You should be flattered.' With a line like that, you can't go wrong. If you haven't read *Misery*, do yourself a favor. If you have read *Misery*, reread and delight again. And try not to see that Annie has a goddamn point.—Kat Lamb"

Lucîa inhaled sharply, goosebumps spreading upward on her arms—good god, Annie Wilkes was NOT the heroine of *Misery*. She spun around to Kat, who was at the register. Seeing that Lucîa had read her endorsement, Kat gave a thumbs up. "I'm so right, aren't I?!" she yelled over to Lucîa.

Having no words to say, Lucîa just stared, mouth open. She turned back to the display and debated removing the whole thing but weighed the probability of a devastating reaction from Kat. Lucîa was a spiritual person; she knew with certainty there was some kind of higher power operating in the universe. She took a moment to compose herself and pay attention—was this literally a sign on the wall?

And what in the world did Kat have planned?

. . .

Shortly after Kat added the Borzoi image to her vision board, the elderly couple down the street she'd seen before walked by with their actual—and rare—Borzoi. After they looped around the street, Kat stopped them, having just come home from work. They were an older Russian Jewish couple, and they'd just agreed to take in the dog, Boris, because their son couldn't take care of it anymore.

Kat explained she had just moved in one street over and was a huge fan of Borzois. She lied about growing up with one and said that she'd love to take their Boris for a walk whenever they'd like. The couple lit up; her knee was bad and his back was acting up. As it was, they had already been looking into a professional dog walker, but this was a much better solution!

For her first outing, Kat glammed up for her walk with Boris. She bought him a fire-engine red leash and a flowy gypsy-esque dress for herself to wear as she walked by Jacob's site. Kat thought the flowy dress would catch his eye, but still seem casual, boho-chic, and ultimately feminine.

Finally, Kat set off down the street toward Jacob's work site, pulsating with the knowledge every man she passed looked over his shoulder.

"Dammmmmn," Mateo said. He nudged Jacob who was inspecting some water damage at the front of the house. Jacob slowly looked up, irritated to be pulled from his focus, but gasped.

Kat.

Again. And *again*, she showed up looking like that with the weirdest and coolest-looking dog he'd ever seen. She looked like an esoteric perfume commercial—the thinking man's dream woman strolling past.

"Kat?" Jacob called. She stopped, looked about. Kat seemed genuinely puzzled to hear her name, but of course she had practiced this. Her face lit up when she spotted Jacob.

"Jacob?!" He waved. Then without thinking or having any control over his body, he found himself moving toward her, a moth to a flame. "What are you doing here?"

"What are *you* doing here?" he responded with a smile. "With this unusual dog?" Jacob pet Boris's head, who happily accepted his affection.

"I'm renting a house a few blocks over now! This is my neighbor's dog, Boris. I'm obsessed with Borzois—it's the Knopf logo, I can't help it." She pulled her sunglasses atop her head; her hair cascaded and framed her face beautifully. "So you're doing a flip? I mean . . . I'm hoping for your sake your work here is not done . . ." she said with a smirk.

Jacob laughed. "Flip number two. We've obviously just started . . . But you're looking so well, Kat." He realized he sounded too enthused, too surprised.

"Well, thanks. Not bad yourself." There was a wink in her voice.

"So which street do you live on, exactly?"

"I'm on 6th, right near the Community Garden, in a little pink house. Very John Waters."

Jacob smiled. "Well. Good on you."

"Yay me." Kat wanted to walk away first. Don't be the one lingering. And don't look back. Plus, she was confident he'd be getting a good look at her as she kept on walking . . . with a decent amount of hip involved. "I'll let you get back to it, then."

"Hopefully I'll see you again soon," he blurted.

Kat shot back a silent smile, put her sunglasses on, and walked off, Boris trotting amiably at her side.

Jacob rejoined Mateo, who had watched the entire exchange. "You know her?"

"My ex-girlfriend."

Mateo laughed. "Sure must suck to be you, dude." They both watched Kat turn a corner. "Please tell me she'll be back."

Yes, please, Jacob thought to himself, utterly surprised by his feeling.

· · ·

Jacob found Eden in her office, surrounded by crumpled sheets of paper. Frustration lay thick in the room and Eden had a large goblet of wine. That was new.

"Crackin' open the hard stuff, are ya?" Jacob joked, gesturing to the wine.

"Just looking for inspiration. Maybe drunk poets are onto something."

"Are they?"

"Not really." Eden rubbed her eyes until she saw stars. She then realized: "I forgot! My bloodwork came in."

"And?!"

"Nothing. Normal. Healthy." Eden and Jacob looked off, considering the impasse.

"Weird, to be disappointed with good news. But it *is* good, right?" Jacob asked. Eden nodded, unconvinced.

Jacob decided to move closer, put his arms around Eden's shoulders. She reached up, pulled him closer. He kissed the top of her head; she patted his cheek. Encouraged, he bent over and found her mouth, kissed lightly.

Jacob positioned himself closer to her; he felt her retreat. Again.

"Mac," Eden said, instantly realizing the massive garbage pile of dog shit she'd just stepped into. The word filled the room with tortured weight, anguished resentment. The entire world seemed to slide off the edge into the ocean.

Jacob pulled away, head down. She could see him shake his head slowly from side to side.

"Jacob, I'm sorry—"

He held up a hand, she fell silent. What magic he and Eden had built was now shattered, again, into so many shards of glass.

"Please—" Eden begged but again Jacob lofted his hand, silencing her. Finally, he looked up with wet eyes. Eden's eyes sprang with mutually pained tears.

"I'm sorry," she said softly. It was all she could say.

"I am, too." Jacob walked out the door, jumped into his car, and drove away.

Please tell me this is not how it ends. Please, begged Eden in her mind.

· · ·

Eden and Jacob danced around one another. The air had a frosty feel; walls had built up around them. They felt like strangers to one another. As quickly as they'd begun, they'd seemed to fall apart.

They tried talking about it, but Jacob seemed too pained. He said he wasn't trying to replace Mac, but he was convinced he was now the second favorite, a sad replacement. Would she ever love him as much as she had loved Mac? Again, it all seemed too soon. Perhaps they had begun in a flight of fancy to begin with.

Eden questioned their relationship as well. Perhaps she *was* still in love with Mac. Naturally, she would always be. But perhaps it was deeper than that. And how well did she know Jacob, anyway? Everything was upside down. It was all just too complicated to process, and her brain was still foggy and sluggish.

Meanwhile, she struggled with her Holiday Hank Christmas Tree and had started to illustrate him wielding a bloodied chainsaw and peering over bathroom stalls at unsuspecting Christmas Trees mid-urination. In other words, it was going terribly.

Jacob lived at his new flip and was busy showing other houses. He had sold two now, but he seemed to always have a showing or needed to "pop by the office." Their distance was straining; they were living in a chasm of uncertainty.

"I don't know, Mom, she's called me 'Mac' twice. TWICE," he asserted with pain as Carol poured them both a glass of wine. She considered his words.

"Well, you told me rather confidently you knew Eden would always love her former fiancé." Jacob admitted he had said these very words.

"But on top of that, she's . . . different. Tired all the time. I hate to admit it, but she's . . . well, now she's kinda boring."

"You said Eden had gotten her bloodwork done?" Carol asked.

"Yeah. Normal."

"That doesn't mean all is well. Remember, I had a doctor totally discount my anemia. Women have to self-advocate."

"Mom. What do I DO here?" Jacob pleaded, tortured. "And please do not mention the universe."

Carol smiled. "I can't tell you what to do. I can only tell you what I observe and what I know to be true. But you and Eden are potently connected. Creative, similar creatures with a bonded currency. You are rare. And I don't know what she is going through, but I would not give up so easily on something filled with unrealized promise. Don't end before you've barely begun."

Carol gave him one last look before taking a long sip of wine. "And women like Eden Hart do not just walk into your open house—*or your life*—every day of the week."

. . .

The needle pierced Eden's skin, again she looked away, grimacing. The nurse, Carrie, shot her a guilty grin. "Not a fan of needles, eh?"

"Is anyone?"

"Drug addicts."

Eden laughed. "I appreciate this, Carrie. For suggesting the toxicology report."

"Of course. And I said I'd run another full blood panel as well." Carrie placed a cotton ball onto Eden's arm and taped her up. She looked Eden dead in the eye. "Trust yourself and defend your life. You don't need a baby to be a 'mama bear.' Be one for yourself."

Eden nodded. She agreed with every fiber in her body.

TWENTY-NINE

TIME CRAWLED BY. THE CALLS from Knopf grew more frequent and less breezy. They reminded Eden politely but assertively that the public is fickle, and you can go from hot to not overnight. As if Eden wasn't aware of this.

Jacob's project was, thankfully, all-consuming. There were termite issues and plumbing problems; Mateo admitted the budget would have to be upped. The good news was there were several potential buyers who had lost out on 3rd Street who were eager to see another Jacob Walsh property. And he loved the way the title sounded—*Jacob Walsh Property*.

After dropping "Jacob Walsh Property" into so many conversations, his family had stopped indulging him and had gone straight to ruthless teasing. Pete joked over dinner one night that Jacob would be coming out with a fragrance. "*Reckless*. A new fragrance from Jacob Walsh," he chided, adding on a British accent for effect. Having just finished their meal, Carol looked at the piles of dirty dishes and quipped, "*Spotless*: A new dishwashing technique from Jacob Walsh." Jacob laughed at them all, but even in jest, it thrilled him a little too much.

Kat continued to walk by with Boris the Borzoi, an unlikely duo who turned heads wherever they went. Jacob found himself looking for her some days, always with an eye peeled for movement on the street, but so did the rest of the male crew. She'd walk by, giving an insouciant wave. Kat seemed a bit like Audrey Hepburn in *Sabrina*, when she came back from Paris at once the same, but also magically different.

Jacob didn't miss an opportunity to spot Kat and trot down to the street to chat with her, even if just for a moment. It was almost embarrassing—and utterly shocking—this role reversal. Kat was a bona fide spokesperson for what the right medication and therapy could do for someone. He even found himself wondering what could have been, had Kat gotten the help she needed. Perhaps he should have pushed more, taken better care of her?

Still, Jacob was fairly certain Eden was the most remarkable match for him. Their pairing was the stuff of magic and lifetimes.

And he also knew he had to be more patient, to work through this with Eden; do everything for Eden that he hadn't for Kat. Because if he wasn't careful, someday it would be Eden walking by with a renewed sense of self, and Jacob would kick himself all over for not trying harder. For letting the woman of his dreams slip away.

Still, every day that went by, the more time he spent looking for Kat, the warm harbor he and Eden had created together felt further and further away, fading into a blurry dot on the horizon.

· · ·

Jacob walked into the kitchen with a giant bouquet of dusty pink peonies, which were Eden's favorites. Her face exploded into a huge grin, and he felt himself melt just watching the joy reappear. He even insisted they watch *Amelie* again and knew Eden found it perfectly perfect.

The evening was, for once, lovely. Laughter filled their house again and Eden even leaned into Jacob on the couch. He stroked her hair exactly like he knew she loved.

Later, they found themselves in bed, cautious. As if they'd both been away for a while and had forgotten one another's rhythms. Jacob tenderly removed her top, touched her slowly all over. Their kissing was deep and fierce; she spread her legs for him. But even with all of the passionate crescendo, the act itself lacked a heat that had always really been there. The waft of detachment lingered in the room like a sample spritz of stale department store perfume.

For the first time in her life, Eden faked an orgasm. After, she turned to her side, disappointed in herself, hating this turn of events. At least she and Jacob had been intimate again. It was a start. But they both felt like they were still a long way from getting back to how they had once been; much less improving and growing back together.

In the dark of the room, Jacob asked if maybe they should go to therapy. Because it was, you know, *a lot*—what they were dealing with right out of the gate. Her fiancé dying, this new start together.

Eden appreciated the gesture, applauded his openness. These were the steps and tools necessary for a couple to grow together. But she just didn't want to be heading to therapy with a man she wasn't even engaged to yet. It felt doomed, moribund.

"I don't think we're there. Besides, I know I'm going to find out some medical reason—*something*—and I can get back to me, and then we'll get back to one another. Fully, I mean," she explained.

Jacob nodded into his pillow, felt solace in the dark, and eventually they both found sleep, only their toes grazing.

· · ·

As the days grew, so did the gulf between Jacob and Eden. They were polite with one another, sure, but Eden went to bed earlier and earlier each night. At least he got to watch all the sci-fi television she didn't like.

The house flip was a monster of endless problems, a Rubik's cube of unseen complications. Still, Jacob enjoyed the hiccups, loving the collaborations with Mateo that were needed to craft creative solutions. He poured over design magazines, eager to incorporate the latest bells and whistles. The house was at the stage, still, that looked as if it would never actualize its full potential.

Late one Saturday afternoon as the crew was winding down after a hard week, Jacob watched his crew doing a little grooving to the music, which was blasting a little louder than it had been throughout the work week. There was a sense of accomplishment, an acknowledgment that the past six days had been punishing. Everyone was eager for the weekend, even if it was only one full day off.

Kat rounded the bend on cue and Jacob found himself wiping his brow, futzing his hair. God, he likely smelled like ass.

She was wearing a bright red half-cape—she could have been in *Amelie*—and it was the color that caught his attention immediately. He smiled when he saw it was Kat. She was pulling a red wagon behind her, with a bucket filled with ice and beer.

"Do my eyes deceive me?" Jacob called. Kat lifted one of the bottles from the bucket into the air and the men cheered.

"Has it been a long week, boys?" Appreciative calls of "*Sí*" and "Hell yeah!" filled the air; the crew was clearly charmed. "Who wants a beer?"

A few of the guys ran to take the wagon from Kat and pull it onto the site. No one wasted time in cracking open a beer, raising their bottles to Kat in thanks.

"This is exactly what we needed tonight, Kat," Jacob said with a big exhale, cracking open a beer. Kat followed suit.

"What can I say? I was never a Girl Scout, but I'm pretty sure there should have been a merit badge for Construction Hydration Relief, right?" Kat grinned and Jacob laughed, clinking their bottles. "To Saturday."

"To you showing up like a mirage in the desert," Jacob added. Kat felt electric. *This was working out perfectly. He showed up. I have him.*

One by one, the crew dwindled and the beers ran out. The sun had officially set, with only lingering dusk hanging around.

Finally, Kat and Jacob were alone.

"So where's Boris?"

"Home. No Boris today. Beck's instead." Kat grinned, nodded to the beer. "So. And how is the little missus?"

Jacob took a long pull from his beer, finishing his bottle. She handed him another. "Well . . . How much time have you got?"

Kat flashed a sexy smile. "I have a date at 8:30."

Jacob raised his eyebrows, trying to act nonchalant, but he flowered with jealousy. "It's fine. We're good."

"Fine or good? There's a bit of a gulf between the two."

"Depends on the day." Jacob realized the beer was going to his head. "But trending more in the 'fine' territory."

"In other words, lousy." Kat got up and walked toward the house. "Are you going to show me the progress?" Jacob followed as she walked inside.

"Open concept, naturally. And eventual stainless steel appliances, white cabinets, pendant lighting, wood floors. Oh, and brass fixtures." Kat rattled off all the remodel trends as if she were the selling agent.

"No. *Polished* brass fixtures," Jacob corrected. The two laughed, stared at one another. New energy fizzed around them. Kat took a long suggestive pull on her beer, smacked her red lips. Condensation from the bottle fell onto her neck and dripped in between her breasts. Jacob felt beads form on his brow and above his lips, becoming light-headed watching her dab at her chest.

"Why . . . why are you wearing a cape?" It was all he could think of to say without revealing his lust.

"Because I look fucking hot in it."

Jacob felt himself getting hard.

Kat stared him down, eyes partially narrowed, assessing him. "I like it when you sweat, Jacob."

"I think you're liking *making* me sweat."

Kat leaned over slowly, dream-like, her painted lips parting. They were as shiny as the artwork on an 80s hair band album cover.

Jacob watched her mouth get closer; his mind went blank with lust. Their lips found one another, and they kissed softly, barely touching. She pulled away slowly and licked her lower lip. Jacob dove in with all of the pent-up desire from his dry spell with Eden. Their kissing was hot; it had always been perfect. Had it always been *this* perfect?

Kat could feel him pressing his body against hers and waited just a few more seconds longer before stepping back from him. "I have a date," she said, glancing at her phone's clock and straightening her clothing. She fluffed her hair, used her thumb to wipe a bit of lipstick from Jacob's face, then walked away. Jacob throbbed with confusion and uncertainty, thoroughly aroused, thoroughly guilty.

What the fuck had just happened? Jacob thought to himself.

Kat stopped and turned around, handed him the last beer from the ice bucket. "In case you need to cool down."

Jacob watched her disappear down the street and opened the beer, slamming it back in one swig, gulping for sanity. It hadn't cooled him off at all.

. . .

Jacob arrived home late, drenched in sweat and guilt. He had never once cheated on a girlfriend, and the guilt of the kiss felt like it was still burning on his lips. He'd had to scrub them clean from Kat's red lipstick with a wet wipe.

He'd entered the house a bit too enthusiastically with a "Nothing to See Here Folks!" grin. Making him feel all the worse, Eden had really dolled up tonight. She was in a beautiful dress, her hair piled high. She looked wondrous, smiling warmly.

"Hello there! Sorry I'm late! Things were crazy today at the site!" He spoke in perpetual exclamation marks, which did nothing to make him appear normal, much less like someone who hadn't just kissed their ex.

"That's okay. I was hoping we could go out for sushi? What'd you think?" Eden asked hopefully, coming toward him for a welcoming kiss.

"After I shower, you betcha!" When Jacob kissed her on the lips, he made a strange gurgle in his throat. "Let me get clean for ya!"

He strode off to shower. "Jacob?" He stopped, turned around, smiling brightly. "Yes?"

"Are you okay?"

"Of course! I just don't smell so hot. I'll be ready in a sec!"

Eden sat down on the couch, deflated. She hadn't put this much effort into her appearance in months, and he hadn't said she looked nice. Eden was wounded. Don Lockwood gazed up at her with woeful eyes.

"Huh. That's all I have to say, Don Lockwood. Huh."

They drove to a nearby sushi joint, Jacob this weird babbling version of himself, and Eden slightly petulant and wounded. He told a story about his co-worker Juan finding his eldest daughter making out with her boyfriend and seemed to find the story hilarious. It really wasn't.

After the last spicy tuna roll was consumed and they'd both drained a few drinks, Jacob sensed Eden's distance. "So. And how was *your* day?"

"Worked on some illustrations. You know."

"Anything good?" he chirped.

"Not particularly. I don't know—maybe the illustration with Hank celebrating Christmas underwater works. You know—why the lake twinkles at night . . ."

"Huh?"

Eden tried not to roll her eyes. "I told you—the whole point of the book? How Hank the Christmas Tree celebrates Christmas in his new home underwater with his fish friends, and that's why the lake twinkles at night? . . ."

"Right right right right! I forgot!"

"What is going on with you, exactly? You've been . . . so *off* all night."

Jacob had lost count of the beers. They probably should walk home and get the car tomorrow. "Off?"

"Yes. You sound so perky, like a game show host or something."

Irritation settled into his blood. He took a breath. "Game show host? Really?"

Eden felt the mood change from weird sunniness to raw indignation. "You're acting just . . . weird, I guess."

"That's funny. I was going to say the same thing about you for the past few months. But I don't get one goddamn night to be *off*?! *I thought I was being cheerful!*" He was almost yelling now, and a few people turned to stare.

"Jacob, shhh," Eden whispered, aware of the eyes on them and the escalating tension. "It's fine. Whatever. I just . . . I just wanted tonight to be nice."

"Weird fucking way of making it nice. Telling me I'm a goddamn game show host. Like that's not insulting." Jacob finished his beer, then slammed it down onto the table.

"God. Let's just go already," Eden said gathering her things.

Jacob rose and kicked back his chair. It screeched on the ground like nails on a chalkboard. The place was silent at this point, and Eden was horrified.

"I think I'm just gonna head to Pete's tonight." He started off. Eden followed, anxious, her mind swirling.

"Wait, what? You're—"

"—*I'm going to Pete's.*" Eden tossed a $100 bill on the table and followed him. There wasn't a set of eyes in the restaurant that wasn't following this action.

"Jacob, please! Stop! This isn't like you!" she pleaded.

"Yeah, well, lots of things aren't like me anymore. Just . . . give me some space, okay?"

"Jacob. Please come home with me," Eden said, attempting to be calm.

He turned, threw his hands up in the air. "It's not even MY home, Eden! It's YOUR home!" He threw the car keys at her and walked away. Eden stood motionless, tears flowing down her cheeks.

She feared they had just stepped into new territory, somewhere they were not likely to return from. It was terrifying.

. . .

To be honest, Kat was shocked how easily it had happened. *You literally just had to walk by a boy's house,* she thought. We never really age much beyond our adolescent selves, as it turns out.

Jacob had kissed her. He had wanted her; she saw it in his eyes—she knew the look well. And the heat between them was even more pronounced than before. But the best part? *She* had been the one to pull away. The one to walk off, and for a date no less. She had the power.

She was going to win.

The night was cause for celebration. Not only had she kissed Jacob, but she was also in charge of her mind. She was the captain of her ship; *she* knew what was best for herself. Doctors just wanted to numb her and then send her home. Kat wanted all of herself—the good, the bad, the impossible, the fucking irresistible.

Best of all was the weariness in his voice when she'd asked him about Eden. And as long as Eden stayed this way a bit longer—boring, a dolt, uninteresting— she'd be forced to let Jacob go. Then he'd return to Kat's arms without a second thought. He'd be back in her life again, and that would change everything.

If she closed her eyes, Kat could picture herself in Carol's backyard, laughing with the whole family again, Jacob holding her hand as they all lounged on the outdoor sofas and polished off wine. Everyone would be so relieved Kat was well; they'd want her back in the fold. Everything in its rightful place. Kat pictured the first night she'd see them; Carol, after too many margaritas, would coo how much she'd missed her. They'd edit another book together, this one an instant bestseller. She and Jess would jog the Mall together. Anything was possible.

Her endgame was so close now. The tension of what happened with Jacob was growing; Kat needed a release, some way to decompress all this sexual energy. She looked in the mirror, acknowledged her power, and grinned. "Hell yes, you do," she said out loud.

Kat grabbed her purse and headed to Club Congress. There'd inevitably be some band playing, inevitably some man who would buy her a drink, and inevitably she'd bring him back to her house. Like all the times before.

Which is exactly what happened.

Caleb was passably attractive, witty enough, and ecstatic to end the night in the arms of a nude goddess. Barely making it to the bed, Kat closed her eyes and ordered him about her body. Caleb followed each step like an eager student.

And when she came, she called out Jacob's name.

. . .

The longer Jacob stayed away at Pete's, the more nothing made sense. Perhaps their entire relationship had been a race to domesticity, a forgone conclusion. It seemed to Jacob that Eden was still in love with Mac, and he couldn't really fault her for that. But would it always be that way? Would Jacob ever be more important to her than Mac?

Maybe Jacob and Eden's union was an extended fling, a weird moment of vulnerability in which they'd found one another. Maybe they were just hot for one another and it had run its course. Jacob wouldn't have kissed Kat again if everything was fine. That wasn't him. He also knew his interest in Kat had reared its head in a strong way, which was an ominous sign indeed.

Still, if he got very quiet and really asked himself if Eden was the one, he knew she was. When he first saw her that day emerging from an Uber on 3rd Street, his immediate thought had been "There you are." He had never spoken those words out loud to anyone, but it was true.

Still, it was hard to be in love with a stranger, which is what Eden felt like now. So much less attractive, not as engaging—it was as if she'd had a lobotomy overnight. Selfishly, he wanted Eden to get back to how she was when they first met: sunny, bright, optimistic. But not for his benefit. He wanted this so Eden could return to herself. He knew this dulled version wasn't authentic. He could see that she was tortured.

If it all turned out to be something medical, he'd regret not sticking by her side. The uncertainty, though, was literally tearing them apart. Still, he had to try.

. . .

Eden and Jacob met in neutral territory, one of their favorites, the Sabino Canyon Trail. Eden walked as if in leaden shoes, and it drove Jacob nuts to be so slow. He was itching to trot up the trail like they'd always done.

Their conversation was circuitous and plotless. After they reached the top,

Eden needed to sit down and rest. She started to cry, dissolving into ugly tears. Jacob wanted to comfort her. He also wanted to turn and run.

"It just . . . it shouldn't be this confusing. Should it?" Eden asked.

"No. It shouldn't be," Jacob concurred.

"But I also know we can't judge this—judge us—when I am such an . . . unreliable narrator in my own life! I have no idea—NONE—what's happening right now. I don't understand why this hike—something that used to bring me such joy and was so easy—is now draining me raw." Eden wiped her tears in frustration, not even paying attention to the other hikers who stumbled upon the awkward scene and scurried off.

Jacob sat down next to her. "I don't know either, Eden. I don't." He put a half-hearted arm around her, and she leaned into him. "But we both know it's not working. Neither of us want to give up, but we're killing ourselves trying to make this relationship stay alive."

Tears pooled in Eden's eyes.

"Let's just . . . give it some space," Jacob said, exhaustion in his voice.

Eden nodded. "So . . . break up? Just end it?"

"Take a break. But, yeah. We've always said with us, there's no rush," Jacob reminded her.

There was nothing more to say.

Eden was depleted. A resolution—even a limp one—was preferable to the continued question mark, the endless confusion, the incessant loop of no answers.

Jacob hugged her, tears in his eyes, and kissed her head. "We don't have to figure it all out today. But just know—I already miss you," he admitted.

"I think I'm going to sit up here for a bit longer," she told him. Jacob nodded and brushed away the desert clay from his pants.

He moved deftly around boulders, descending down the climb, never looking back. Eden watched him through teary eyes until he faded out of sight.

• • •

Knopf was getting frustrated with Eden's progress and sensed her malaise. They pulled her from her own work and assigned a new book to illustrate instead. It was bound to be a bestseller; the buzz was strong.

It was another caterpillar entry, another discovery that life was filled with the cosmic ability for adaptation. Eden usually loved butterflies and caterpillars, the whole tale of rebirth, but these days it was just fucking redundant.

Still, she was eager for work. Eden wanted to get lost in the color of new drawings. Her mind was a combustible mass of negativity and she hated this turn. Maybe butterflies were exactly what she needed.

It wasn't easy. Eden found herself so newly heartbroken and shattered it was hard to focus. Her deeply desired tale of redemption and new love had gone bad, spoiled in the sun. There was little to tether her to optimism or joy.

Across town, Jacob was also losing himself in his work. Every detail of the flip was all-consuming and there were also other listings to manage, other showings to arrange. His life had exploded with commitments, and he was grateful. He didn't want to sit still for a moment and think about Eden. Think about Eden and her face, think about the face he would not return to tonight.

This flip was decidedly more complicated than the last. He knew this objectively, but the reality was another monster completely. Everything was going wrong. Everything needed attending to, so many new problems seemed to appear on a daily basis—he couldn't catch a break. But each time one did arise, Jacob was secretly grateful—he found purpose in every obstacle. And staying busy to the point of exhaustion meant less time being sad about Eden, and no time to look out the window for Kat.

· · ·

Eden tried acupuncture. She had heard raves about the Tucson Acupuncture Co-op and signed up for a package. Every few days, she had a mostly wordless Chinese man poke her with needles. Then he would leave her alone in the procedure room to decompress. It was such a curious space—a Costco-worthy level of paper towels sat nearby, next to a walker and a few bottles of Johnnie Walker. The decor was so discombobulated, it was almost amusing.

The needles did little, but she would often fall asleep after a few minutes, waking up groggy and sensitive.

Eden tried Reiki and professionally guided meditations. She found a psychic who told her she would marry a man named Kyle and would "get involved with birds." She found a therapist who asked her how she felt about that, as if parodying a Hollywood scene to demonstrate a tragically incompetent psychiatrist.

Her parents came to visit Tucson again, and their presence always cheered her up. They filled her house with flowers. Her mother hid inspiring notes throughout the house for her to find after they'd left.

It helped. But not enough.

• • •

Kat was so giddy about Jacob moving back in with his brother she was almost nauseous. Of course, she didn't know this for sure, but his car was never on 3rd anymore and always at Pete's. She never saw Jacob enter *that* house anymore. It was likely done.

Without the safety of a guaranteed night out, Kat worried she wouldn't be able to creep into Eden's house to contaminate her creamer. How would it work now that she was home more often than not? Turns out Eden was a solid sleeper, especially now. The Seroquel Kat snuck into her creamer turned out to be the very thing that knocked Eden out so completely for 10 hours or more a night.

Besides, when Kat broke into the house, she was electrified by the sheer danger of it all. It was her caffeine. And she desperately needed it to sustain her through-out the week.

Don Lockwood would inevitably come to meet her, used to the routine by now. Kat gave him kibbles, which he wolfed down with pug enthusiasm. She'd dis-solve the powder into Eden's creamer and slip out again, riding an adrenaline high. Kat stayed longer and longer each time, tempting fate and risking getting caught by awakening Eden. She also liked watching Eden sleep, how her chest gently rose and fell. And how one of her downy pillows could cover her perfect mouth and snuff out her breath, just like that.

Sometimes Kat worried about how this would end. But she knew the only thing that truly mattered was that she'd have Jacob. *That* would be the end result.

THIRTY

KAT KNEW IT WAS NOW or never. She'd created a window of opportunity to make Jacob a part of her life again, but it was going to close fast. She couldn't keep walking a Borzoi by his house forever.

She purposely stayed away from Jacob's site for two weeks. She wanted him wondering where she'd gone. She wanted him to crave her.

On Friday afternoon, as the sun was setting and the sky worked its Tucson magic, she leashed Boris up and headed to his site, vaulted sandals lofting her into the sky.

Kat felt the men's eyes on her, obviously noting her return. Undetected behind her red cat-eye sunglasses, she spotted Jacob and waited for him to recognize her. At once, he stopped his work, doing a double-take. She could feel his energy; sensed him coming alive.

"Hey stranger," he called. Kat stopped, petting Boris absentmindedly, pretending as though she hadn't been watching him. Kat felt a fizzle in her veins. She was perhaps too on edge, her mind a loopy hamster wheel. But she saw Jacob and her mind tunneled, coming into focus.

"Hey yourself."

"No beer today?" he joked, as Kat continued to let Boris walk forward, sniffing the grass along the way.

"Sorry. I am libation-less," she said over her shoulder casually. Jacob laughed. Kat started to walk on; Jacob followed her.

"Wait!" he called. Kat grinned to herself. She knew she had him. Kat turned as if he was interrupting her night.

"Yes?" she asked, feigning indifference.

Jacob beamed at her, then paused, raking his hand through his hair. It was obvious he wasn't entirely sure why he'd stopped her. "Um, you look well."

Kat nodded as if to say "And?"

"So. What're you doing tonight?" Jacob chirped.

"Well. That all depends."

Jacob grinned. "On what?"

"On you." Kat allowed a small grin, satisfied. She looked him in the eyes as if to call his bluff.

But Jacob just smiled back, a smirk really. He held her gaze. At this point it was almost as if they were testing one another as to who might back down first.

"Well, I *did* mean to tell you, my landlord allowed me to wallpaper my kitchen ceiling. It's a really cool print, a beautiful starry night. It looks incredible. It's sort of a new trend, and maybe since you're going to be decorating this place soon, you should come check it out? You know, for design inspiration."

"Interesting. Never seen that before," Jacob said.

"It's French."

"Of course it is," he said with a chuckle. "I guess this means I should stop by to see it in person."

"It definitely is one of those things you have to see to appreciate," she said. Walking a bit further away, she turned back to size him up, seeing if he'd take the bait.

"I might be wrapping up here soon . . . I could stop by, take a look?" Kat didn't respond immediately, letting him sit in the moment. "I could bring some champagne, you know, as an homage to your design theme? . . ."

Kat grinned. "Bien sur. 3315 6th Street, just a few blocks over. See you in a bit, then."

She sauntered off, could feel his eyes on her, drinking her in.

She closed her eyes walking away, certain this time he would topple her way. It was so close now.

Kat took a shower when she got home; it was even hotter than usual outside. She put on a flowy silk robe and tied her wet hair up in a turban, staging herself like it was all so last-minute, so casual.

A few hours later, there was a knock at her door. Kat took a pause to savor the moment, this flash of her and Jacob coming together again. Right here, right now, a Polaroid of bliss, the fruition of her endeavors.

She opened the door. Jacob had showered, his hair still damp and face glistening—a good sign—and held a bottle of Veuve Clicquot in his hand. *Ah, the good stuff*—an even better sign. "Bonjour," she trilled.

"Allo." Jacob entered as awkwardly as he felt, taking in the first glimpses of her home. It was an eclectic space, uneven but cool, vaguely French, definitely artistic . . . the sort of space you'd imagine for a Parisian salon with interesting quirks all around the home.

"Welcome to Chez Lamb. My own little heaven." Kat gestured to the space, proud. Jacob eyed her voluminous bed in the other room littered with pillows, fluffy sheets. There were bouquets of flowers in colored glass vases, interspersed with cacti, some modern mirrors and antique furniture; both kitschy and graceful artwork covered the walls.

"It's fantastic! I'm so proud of you," Jacob gushed, eyes roaming from room to room.

"Thanks. I absolutely love it . . ." Kat lead him into the kitchen and pointed up to the ceiling. "*La nuit étoilée.*" The rich blue wallpaper was littered with tiny pinpricks of stars. A sparkly chandelier perfectly complemented the wallpaper; it was a cozy, unique space. Jacob had never seen anything like it.

"It's so dramatic . . . I never would have thought to put wallpaper on the ceiling. Well done." Jacob handed her the bottle of Veuve champagne, smiling. "I don't want it to get warm."

"Alcohol! Yeah." Kat went to retrieve the champagne flutes. "You should probably pop that bottle, then."

Jacob laughed uneasily. "I could use some. It's been such a long week . . ." He tried hard to seem nonchalant, not quite knowing how to be with Kat or what was about to happen.

Kat appeared with flutes and took the sweating bottle from the counter, pouring the bubbly with ease, then offered him a glass. "Here's to tasting stars." They clinked glasses. Jacob gestured to her turban and robe.

"Are you, uh, getting ready to go out?"

"Perhaps."

"You were always a woman of mystery, Kat. But this is a whole new level, I gotta say." Jacob gulped down his champagne. He needed to steady his nerves, unsure of the path ahead. Without missing a beat, Kat refilled his glass. He took a sip, committing to asking the hard questions.

Jacob looked around the space and went into the living room, then sat down on the couch, taking his wallet out of his pocket and placing it on the coffee table. Kat followed and sat within easy reach of Jacob's hands.

"So how are you *really* doing now, Kat?" Jacob asked earnestly.

Kat leaned in; she smelled of lemons and soap. "Honestly, I have never been better. I'm more myself and centered, more at ease in my own skin. I think I've faced a lot of demons this past year and learned how to live with myself. And listen—I know I put you through hell . . . but the truth is, I put myself through so much more." She looked off, took a sip of champagne.

"That's great. I'm so glad. You just seem so . . . I don't know. Larger than life. But mostly at ease," he noted.

"My memoir failing so spectacularly was a strange, unexpected gift. It's hard to articulate . . . and the weirdest element of all is that I am also genuinely grateful I survived my suicide attempt. You must know about this. Your mother is incapable of secrets." She laughed, confidently, so pleased with her performance.

Jacob flushed. "Guilty. Why do you say that—about the book and the, uh . . . attempt?"

"Because both got me clear. Clean. I got diagnosed, and now I know how to manage myself, my expectations, my life. Gifts arrive in unpredictable packages."

"True. I think I understand what you mean." Jacob nodded. "I'm so glad for you. Here's to coming through life not unscathed, but smarter."

They clinked glasses, eyes locked, sipped the bubbly. Kat took her time crossing her legs and relaxed into the couch while maintaining his gaze.

Jacob exhaled, as if they both knew this was inevitable. He set his flute down on the coffee table. Leaning toward her, he cupped her face with one hand, his thumb tracing her jawline, pulling her in closer until he could feel her breath. It was a gentle kiss, light on the lips but teeming with what was to come. Kat kissed him back in kind, keeping herself in check, so it was Jacob who deepened the kiss. She could feel him melting into her, pressing her back into the couch, using both hands to pull her face closer to feverishly kiss her. Moaning, she ran her fingers through the back of his hair, and let his mouth find the right places on her face. Their kisses became frantic, hot, desperate; she writhed with desire and bit at his lower lip. Before long—and just like before—they wanted to consume one another.

Suddenly, Jacob pulled away, breathing hard. He was flushed with equal parts desire and confusion.

Kat sensed his sudden distance and wanted to reel him back. Her brain fizzed with panic; she stuffed the feeling, committed to her cool.

"Hey. You okay?"

Jacob shook his head. He didn't know if this was completely right or completely wrong. "Look . . . wait. I, uh . . . probably should get going . . . I don't think I should be doing this . . ."

"But why? I thought we always played together very nicely." Kat tried to tempt him with a sexy smile and leaned in. He pulled back.

"I'm sorry, Kat. I just . . . I need a beat here. This is, I don't know, pretty weird."

"And it *could* be pretty fucking fantastic . . ."

God, Jacob wanted to sleep with her. Of course he did. He pushed himself back away from her and held his head in his hands, running his hands through his hair, then straightening upward looking at her. Kat's robe was coming undone and she did nothing to pull it closed; her chest was still pulsating from heavy breathing. Jacob couldn't help but see the supple curve of her breast and her ruby-colored nipple peeking out. Jacob's head spun as he leapt from the couch and fumbled for the front door. "I can't be here right now, Kat."

Kat could feel the panic coming and she tried not to let it show. She followed him to the door, worried he could sense how frantic she was at the thought of losing him yet again.

Jacob's hand found the doorknob and he awkwardly turned it, tripped onto the front porch, then down the steps and into the dark. "Jacob," she said, mustering all her will not to scream his name. He paused, then turned back to her where she stood in the doorway. The sun had set long ago and now it was just black night. Kat was illuminated from behind by the dim front porch light.

She stood casually against the doorframe, robe still disarrayed, as if nothing had happened. "Don't be a stranger." Kat grinned and then turned away, the robe twirling with her and exposing her bare legs before she slowly shut the door.

Inside, the door clicked shut and Kat silently screamed in utter rage.

Through the window, she watched the taillights of Jacob's car fade away with clenched fists, then looked to the table next to her. Kat snatched the vase full of flowers with both hands and hurled it against the wall, shattering the glass and sending an explosion of petals across the floor.

. . .

Jacob was still shaking when he pulled up in front of his mom's house. God, he hoped she was home.

Carol opened the door, wearing her notorious "Your Opinion Is Not in the Recipe" apron.

"Jacob! Did you hear I'm making my famous chili and had to stop for a bowl?" she teased. Jacob didn't respond, walked inside, totally consumed. "What's wrong?"

Jacob paced around the house, wringing his hands. "Mom. I just . . . I have to talk to you."

Carol led him out back; the patio was twinkling with light from the strands of bulbs hanging above. She walked to the outdoor wine fridge and handed him a beer. He gratefully opened it and took a long pull.

"Thanks."

"Jacob, you're ashen. What's going on?"

"It's Kat, Mom."

Carol studied his face, a combination of confusion and guilt, and knew sex had to be involved. "And?"

"I'm not . . . look, Pete's out of town, I couldn't reach him. I don't know, I'm embarrassed—"

"C'mon, I'm not puritanical. Jacob, you can talk to me."

Jacob nodded, took another sip of beer. "I almost slept with Kat. Just now. I mean, I didn't, but obviously I could have."

Carol nodded. "Did you want to?"

"Oh yeah. Of course." He took another sip. "But not at all. If that makes sense."

"Kat's not well, Jacob. You know this."

"I get it! But . . . she's, you know, doing so much better now, and—"

"Then what's the problem? If she's truly just a walking advertisement for mental health these days, why not just get back together? What's holding you back? Hmm?"

The truth startled him; the obviousness of the entire thing struck Jacob immediately. *Good god, why had this even been a consideration?* Jacob's face turned red with embarrassment. "I'm an idiot."

"You're a human being. My list of unfortunate life choices is endless—and still, I regret nothing." Carol gave his hand a comforting squeeze. "Besides, you stopped yourself, didn't you?"

Jacob nodded, still reeling with how close he came to making a terrible choice. "I'll just call her and end this before it begins—definitively, I mean." He reached for his phone in his pocket and then froze. His face changed with realization and his stomach dropped. "Shit."

"What is it?"

"My wallet. I think I left it at Kat's." Jacob looked off in thought. "I'll just go and get it, look her in the eye, and tell her we will never happen again, ever."

"Do you want me to come along? I've always been a steadying force for her, just in case she's not in a good space, you know."

"Mom. I'm nearly 30. I can do this myself."

Carol hugged her son and they locked eyes. "You call me right after you're back in the car."

Jacob nodded, then walked to his car, knowing Kat Lamb should never be a part of his life ever again.

· · ·

Kat's mind was muddied, swimming through a fog of anger and desperation; she was still aroused, totally on edge, and in a sheer panic that she'd lost her chance with Jacob for good. She paced the house, talking to herself, furious with the turn. How could Jacob walk out on her? She'd done everything right; he'd been putty in her hands. Yet he still snapped and left.

Left her fucking again.

She poured another glass of champagne, chugged it, then re-filled.

A knock at the door startled her and she turned around, heart already racing. "Kat? Kat, you there?" Jacob. He was outside her house.

"Kat, I need to talk to you."

He'd reconsidered. *Thank god.*

Kat went to the mirror, grinned seductively, and smoothed her hair. She applied deep red lipstick and smacked her lips. Game on. She opened the door with practiced nonchalance and assumed a sexy pose, doing everything possible to appear relaxed and unaffected by what had happened hours before.

"You're back. So soon?"

But even through the darkness, she could tell Jacob's face was steely, his eyes cooled over with resolve and distance. A strong surge of unrest came over Kat, enough so that her mouth went dry and adrenaline made her pulse quicken. Clearing her throat, she did her best to seem calm. "Do you want to come in, Jacob? Is it your plan to give the neighbors something to talk about?" She forced a chuckle and winked. But Jacob shook his head and walked past her and into the house, determined to complete his mission.

"What happened here?" he asked, noticing the broken shards of glass, the explosion of flower petals, and the water-stained wall.

Kat kept her cool. "Oh, yes. Oops. I accidentally knocked it over before you arrived. I was just going to clean up."

He went to the coffee table and picked up his wallet, then turned around to face her.

"Listen. I'm so sorry. I think I've been giving you confusing messages. I mean, I know I have. And I admit, you have a power over me, Kat. You're gorgeous, you're smart as hell, and interesting . . . all of it. And we have a pretty explosive past, obviously. But—"

"Always a fucking 'but.'"

"*But* you and I are not good together. I mean—there are things we do well together, I think we all know what I'm talking about—but we are not going to work. I'm sorry for leading you on, but this is never going to happen. I think we both know this deep down, right?"

Kat remained still, a statue of inert mania.

"Look, that's why I panicked earlier—and I wouldn't have had that reaction if we were supposed to try out a relationship again. I realized this on the way home, and I wanted to call you because I don't think it's fair to keep flirting around something that isn't going to happen. Then I realized I left my wallet, so here we are. So I just came back for it, and I wanted to tell you I will always have affection for you and wish you the best, with all my heart. Okay?"

Jacob waited, but Kat said nothing. Words and emotions and panic tumbled in her mind; fury slowly consumed her body that was frozen in anguish.

"Are you going to respond, or?" . . . Jacob gave her a quizzical look, realizing Kat would likely remain frightfully silent. "Okay . . . Well, good luck with every-thing, Kat. I mean it. And . . . I'm really sorry." Jacob walked toward the front door, reaching for the knob.

Just then, his phone rang. He instinctively reached for it.

The caller ID read: EDEN HART.

Eden hadn't called in a few weeks, and Jacob's heart raced seeing her name. "*Eden?*"

"Ohmygod, Jacob. I knew it. Ohmygod," Eden frantically babbled.

Watching Jacob's whole being ache with concern for fucking *Eden* woke Kat up. "What's going on?"

"My toxicology results! They found Seroquel in my blood!" she blurted as if it were all one word. "It's an anti-psychotic drug—IT NUMBS YOU!"

Jacob turned white; his hands started shaking. "*What?*"

Kat grabbed a nearby snow globe and hurled it at Jacob. It slammed into his skull, crashing to the floor and shattering into tiny shards of glass. Jacob gripped his bleeding head and stumbled backward in pain, tripping on a chair and hit-ting his head on the edge of the side table. He landed with a crash, blood pooling onto the carpet.

"*Jacob?! Jacob?!*" Kat reached for Jacob's phone, hung up, and then threw it against the wall.

• • •

Lucîa had noticed the couple park an older VW van out in front of Antigone Books. It was almost too cliché, a 60s VW, chipped paint, pastel colored; a flower power mobile of hippie magic. And, as if on cue, an older "crunchy-granola" couple stepped out of the van. They began a series of intricate stretches on the sidewalk; clearly, they'd done yoga. They conferred, gesturing to the store, and Lucîa watched from her perch behind the counter as they entered. They seemed out of place, looking around like anxious time travelers. It was obvious they were in unfamiliar territory, having a hard time figuring out how to navigate the store. Lucîa guessed that perhaps they weren't garden variety aging bohemians after all; there was a rough edge to them, a dingy quality beyond just unshaved armpits.

They looked feral.

The couple wandered uneasily, blinking as if the lights were stadium bright. They stopped in front of the copies of *Foster Kid*—Lucîa always kept a prominent stack on display with a proud placard celebrating their employee and writer-in-residence. They touched the book, studied it, chatted in subdued tones.

Lucîa approached them. "May I help you?"

They turned, stunned, and stood in silence. Lucîa tried to warm her smile as much as possible, but she felt prickles of fear bloom on her arms and legs. The couple didn't blink.

"Can I assist you folks with something?" Lucîa repeated, this time frostier despite her plastered smile.

The man held out *Foster Kid*. "This is our daughter."

• • •

Eden was frantic—Jacob was clearly in danger. Her breath was rising again, panic spread throughout her whole body, blurring all rationality. Could this be about that psychotic ex he'd mentioned? Hadn't he mentioned the name "Kat"?

"No no no no no," she repeated to herself in a hysterical loop. Her eyes darted about, searching for a solution to magically appear. Still clutching her phone, she noticed the phone's battery bar was on red alert, nearly depleted. "Oh god! Shit!" But she had no time to waste and chose to ignore it. Her shaking hands found the Life 360 app, and she searched for Jacob's location, praying he hadn't removed himself during their break-up.

His name appeared, a blinking icon on 6th Street, and without hesitation, Eden ran for her car.

• • •

Kat immediately bandaged up Jacob's head, wadding up paper towels from the kitchen and securing them with an old Ace bandage. She caressed his head with an ice pack while she caught her breath, staring down at Jacob's sweet face. He looked as if he were just sleeping. She pulled him by the arms across the hallway and into her bedroom, awkwardly lifting him against the platform bed. Kat maneuvered him inch by inch until he was on top of the bed. Jacob grunted as she settled him into the mass of pillows, and Kat made sure he was comfortable. She stepped away.

Jacob was back in her bed. He was in their bed.

He was right where he should have been all along.

. . .

"I'm sorry?" Lucîa asked, stunned. There were no words.

"Katie. Our Katie Moon. Parson Nettles told us so."

"I'm . . . I'm very confused. You're saying . . . *You're Kat's parents? The ones who gave her up, or? . . .*"

They shook their heads no blankly. "We are confused as well. We never gave Katie up."

"But. You can't be! . . . How can I possibly believe you?"

The woman thought for a moment. "Katie was born under a full moon and has a horseshoe-shaped birth mark on the back of her neck."

Lucîa's face fell. Kat did have the exact birth mark; she'd noted it several times when Kat wore her hair up, which was often.

"Then . . . What's in the book isn't . . ." Lucîa trailed off. "Are you her foster parents?"

"No. We are her earth parents."

"And who's . . . Parson Nettles? Who's that?"

"Our sage counsel."

"Our enlightened master," the mother added. Her husband nodded.

"So then . . . a cult?"

The man shook his head. "We are a culture. Not a cult."

"We believe in the god of the collective, of nature," the woman said as if reciting from a brochure. "I know it's hard to understand, but I suppose it's easiest to say that we're more a *commune* than anything."

Lucîa was flattened with shock. "But . . . you're Kat's parents? Kathryn Lamb?"

"Yes, it's what we've been trying to tell you. Parson Nettles heard from the outside that Katie had a book. We went to Missoula and found it in the library. We need to speak to our Katie, to help her know her truth. So many years have passed since we saw her last. We've come a long way for this moment," the woman explained, her voice steady. Underneath the unkempt and dirty skin, Lucîa saw the outlines of Kat's face in her, a familiarity.

Lucîa had no idea how to proceed. The entire situation was just madness.

"Listen. Kat lives just around the corner and usually walks to work." Lucîa had no idea if this was the best course of action or the worst. "Just take a left out the door, another left on 6th. Cute little pink house, the only one on the block . . ."

Kat's parents nodded. "Thank you so much. We promise we aren't here to hurt her." Lucîa watched as they held hands, walking to their van, and then speeding away toward 6th Street.

• • •

Eden sat in her car at a red light, sweating through the blasting AC, tapping the steering wheel. "Come on, come on, come on . . ." Her eyes darted between the phone's nearly dead battery indicator and the stoplight, willing it to turn green. When it did, she gunned it, nearly hitting a cyclist.

"Fucking bitch!" he yelled as Eden screamed in equal horror, passing the angry spandexed man.

"I'm sorry, sorry sorry, so sorry!" Tears streamed down her face, and she said a prayer for her car to somehow find its way safely to 6th Street. And that Jacob would be okay when she got there.

• • •

Kat stared at Jacob, her mind a furious wreck. He was nestled into her blankets and pillows, breathing but unmoving. Kat leaned over and felt the scruff on his face; she placed her cheek against his and then turned to give him a gentle kiss.

She moved to the living room and hallway, practically sleepwalking, where shards of glass and the snow globe's tiny cityscape of New York littered the floor, in a pool of water, mixed in with the flower petals and broken glass from the vase. Kat reached for the glass and picked it up, inspecting the jagged edges, accidentally grazing her arm and drawing blood. She watched as the blood oozed, then looked back at the sharp corner and pointy ridge of glass and found her arm. Kat methodically nicked herself, finding a rhythm to the strokes. Each contact was stronger until finally the glass edge sliced her skin. Blood pooled and the glass dug deeper and deeper. She hit muscle and the cathartic, bitter release of pain bloomed, oddly soothing her tortured soul.

"Katie." A familiar voice stopped Kat cold. She froze. Her eyes shot to the front door, stunned to see the homeless-looking couple standing before her, silhouetted by Tucson's orange dusk sky.

Kat dropped the piece of glass, her arm red with blood.

"You're bleeding, Katie. You need garlic and limestone powder."

Kat started to shake. She rose and walked toward them, barefoot, stepping onto the glass but feeling nothing as it pierced her skin. "Papa? Mama? . . ."

"Katie. We came for you. We read your book, and we want to talk. In your book, you thanked Lucîa and Antigone Books, so we tracked you down. We went to the store and Lucîa sent us here. We came for you," she explained.

Kat nodded as if this somehow made sense, her eyes now a river of tears flooding down her face.

"Katie, we don't understand. Why would you lie?" her father asked with a chilly tone.

Kat didn't respond; instead, she just shook her head.

"Katie. Why did you lie?" he screamed.

"I . . . I . . ."

From the street, Eden's car screeched around the corner just as her phone died. It went black.

"No no no no! *NO!*" Eden slammed her car to a stop and frantically looked up and down the street—where was Jacob? Which house?

Up ahead, she spotted a man and woman at the entrance of a house, the door wide open. Instinctively, she hit the gas and squealed to a stop in front, strangely convinced this house was the one. Without thinking, she jumped out of the car and ran toward the front porch. Eden had to save Jacob. Or at least try.

Kat spotted the approaching interloper and exploded, extending a pointed finger.

"*NOOOOO! Stop right there, YOU BITCH!*" Kat thundered.

Like in a nightmare, Eden froze, her legs useless, her mind fritzed. "Jacob . . .
I . . ."

The man and woman turned calmly, surveying Eden with thick animus.
"Leave, wench! We have business with Katie!" The woman's eyes narrowed into
monstrous slits—she looked not human.

Just then, Eden felt a painful *THUD* on her arm, then heard shattering glass.
She looked down at her feet to find the dissonant shards of a snow globe, a plastic
Sydney Opera House, and pieces of glass. Soon another hard blow to her shoulder,
more glass, and a tiny Eiffel Tower. Eden called out in pain, then looked up to see
Kat wielding another snow globe, poised to lob again, her eyes manic. This had to
be Jacob's mentally damaged ex.

"*GO NOW!*" the woman hissed. Eden turned and ran back to her car in confused terror. Her hands shook as she dug through her purse for her car keys to
try to go for help. Receipts, a wallet, lip gloss. No keys. No fucking keys. *What
was happening?* . . . Eden's mind was a blank canvas of panic; tears dripped from
her face.

"Katie, why did you lie about Paradise Run?!" the man roared again, turning
back to Kat.

Eden heard the thunderous question and stopped cold, paralyzed with fear and
mordant curiosity.

"Paradise Run . . ." Kat spat the name out as if it was poison.

"The most glorious place in the world to grow up. 'Exultant of Self, Selfless to
Many!'" her mother said.

Kat laughed bitterly, the wheels of madness churning. "Selfless . . ."

Her parents looked to one another fondly, as if remembering a warm Christmas
morning.

The pleasant look they exchanged sent Kat into a white rage. The dam broke,
there was no going back. "You . . . you made me this way. You did! Don't you
see? . . . You RUINED me!"

"Ruin? We wanted to build you, form your constitution in strength and truth.
Instead, you chose lies."

Her father's eyes narrowed. "Katie. You still haven't answered the question.
Why would you lie about being a foster child?"

Eden gasped in shock. Her hands froze, stopping their frenetic search for the car keys.

"Because I FANTASIZED about being abandoned by you, of getting a new home! I thought it sounded great to have a revolving door 'til I found my real parents! . . . *Anything was better than fucking Paradise Run!*"

"Katie, ugly words," her mother responded. "I don't understand. Paradise Run was paradise. *Is* paradise."

Mania flooded Kat's eyes. Her arm and feet continued to leak blood; she was getting paler. "*Paradise?* It was HELL ON EARTH! Being forced to sleep in that goddamn tipi filled with rancid children?!"

"Ugly words," her mother repeated.

"Do you have any idea—ANY IDEA—what it was like to be left alone every day—cleaning lice from endless heads, slaughtering animals, seeing you trip on acid? Nearly freezing to death every winter sure was fun. I loved almost losing a toe to frostbite. I was bit by a rattlesnake and told to 'suck ginger'! And how about the filthy fucking 'Hands of Man' that found me in the dark every goddamn night?!" Kat breathed hard, chest heaving, eyes closed in pain.

"Katie, you wanted to leave, and we let you go," her mother said, unmoved by her daughter's words.

"When Parson Nettles informed us you left The Family for schooling, we mourned," her father added.

"Oh, for god's sake . . . You never 'mourned' me! You were never a parent to me! You handed me off to strangers, to kids younger than me, to men, to whoever. All that self-love of yours was all you had time for . . . There was no home, no love, there was NOTHING. A librarian took pity on me and taught me to read and write! I'd sneak off and walk miles and miles to get to the library, the only good thing in my LIFE! You neglected me into oblivion! I MEAN, I DREAMT ABOUT FOSTER HOMES LIKE IT WAS FUCKING DISNEYLAND! *FUCKING FOSTER HOMES!* I wanted to be the sympathetic foster kid, not the psycho who was brainwashed in a freak-show commune!"

Her mother looked down, shaking her head. "Well, this is unfortunate."

"*Unfortunate?* . . . Yeah, it was unfortunate YOU forced me to create another reality—or else I'd go mad! WHICH, BY THE WAY, SEEMS TO HAVE

ALREADY HAPPENED!" Kat screamed with such fury, and she unleashed decades of pain in a single moment. Unhinged, snot ran down her face, blood was oozing even faster now, she was getting paler and paler.

"We did not drive across the country for this abuse," her father answered.

"We did the best we could, Katie," her mother said hollowly.

The couple looked at one another and nodded.

"Journey on," her father said stoically.

"Journey on," her mother parroted.

They turned and walked away, unaware Eden had witnessed and overheard the entire wicked exchange. As the couple marched back to their van, Eden felt the blackness of their souls pass like a shadow, and she shuddered. She then looked up to the porch to see Kat.

Kat fell to her knees and screamed, howling like a trapped animal. The sounds she made were not human. It was ferociously primal.

The heartbreak and devastation were palpable. Eden felt an unexpected wave of empathy course through her system. She shocked herself with the impulse.

Then, emerging from the back of the house, Eden could see Jacob limping toward Kat. Relief brought her to tears once more; he was alive.

"*Jacob!*" She ran to him and crashed into his arms. Lifting her head to meet his gaze, she saw the bloodied bandage and bruises that were already forming. "Jacob, are you alright?!"

Jacob nodded. "We need to call the police."

"Jacob . . . no."

Jacob looked down at Eden's face, floored. "*No?*"

"No. She doesn't need bars. She needs help." Eden's eyes found his. "And she's your ex, isn't she?"

Jacob was stunned as he nodded yes. They both looked to Kat, no more than a decimated puddle on the floor, swimming in her blood, tears, and pain.

"Eden. Kat *poisoned* you. She did this!" he said, pointing to his bandaged head. "Kat's—"

"Unwell," Eden said, finishing his thought. "Jacob, she needs help."

"Okay . . . I *was* hit hard on the head here . . . I'm not following."

"You can do what you want, but I won't press charges against someone who's already been through so much abuse in her life."

"My god. You're serious, aren't you?"

"Yes. And . . . I'm shocking myself with this response, too. What she did to me was sick. And to you. It's inexcusable. Unthinkable. But . . ." Eden's words fell away when Kat let out another howl of grief, oblivious to everything around her. "But when she told her story . . . those awful details about her ghoulish parents . . . I couldn't believe it but . . . I just . . . I just felt so heartbroken for her."

"Eden."

"Hear me out. But Jacob—what if that untold bleakness was your life? What if you'd been 'neglected into oblivion'? Would you have survived it? Because Kat did. But it came at a cost. I just keep thinking—what if that was my childhood? Because mine was filled with unconditional love, stories that were read to me in bed every night, parents who told me over and over I could be anything I wanted to be."

Jacob paused, observing the miracle of forgiveness. Compassion emanated from Eden, and he felt humanity drip into his veins again. This was the woman he loved.

"What if those monsters were my parents? . . . Because if that was true, I don't know who the hell I'd be," Eden said.

"But . . . she's not even a foster kid."

"I know. But Jacob—*who would you be if you weren't loved?*"

Eden and Jacob locked eyes and after a long pause, they nodded in agreement. Their eyes spoke to one another, and they held each other's hands. Jacob whispered into Eden's ear, then they kissed.

Jacob leaned down, put a hand on Kat. Her maniacal eyes flitted, then settled onto Jacob. It seemed like she was starting to be present again.

"Kat. You're going to be okay."

"Jacob," she croaked.

Eden knelt beside Kat and met her gaze. "Alright, Kat. Listen to me very carefully. I'm truly sorry you've had to suffer in life like you have. I am. And while I *am* sympathetic, that doesn't mean I still couldn't go to the police and ruin you. It'd be the easiest thing in the world to prove what you did to me. I don't want that on my conscience. Obviously, you're not well. But . . . you don't deserve to suffer even more."

Kat's eyes widened with shock.

"Pay close attention, okay? You *will* go far away from here. As far as you can possibly go. And when you get far, far away, you're going to get help. Lots and lots of help. And I swear if you can't figure that part out—if any of this gets remotely confusing—I will come after you with everything I have in me to make sure you don't hurt anyone else, and that you'll rot in prison instead. So I'm giving you one chance—ONE—for redemption. And this is the last time I—or Jacob—ever want to see your face again. Is that perfectly clear?"

Kat nodded, her head bobbing like a doll.

"Mom mentioned that she and Lucîa were worried you might have gone off your meds," Jacob said.

"Is that true?" Eden asked.

Kat again nodded in affirmation.

"Meds start back up tomorrow, and you'll take them until the day you die," Eden declared.

"Yes," Kat squeaked.

"I'm sure we can get your information about your therapist and contacts at the hospital so we can help you get a solid plan in place."

Jacob and Eden gave one another a smile of understanding. "Alright, Kat. We're gonna get you bandaged up now." The two went about helping Kat with the wounds on her arm and feet. As they applied salves and bandages, Kat studied them; eyes wide with amazed wonder, absorbing their grace. Their care was akin to being swaddled as an infant—something she had been denied—and it was all so comforting and safe. As natural as breath itself. Love and hope warmed Kat's body. It was such a foreign—but delicious—feeling.

Why would anyone give this up?

EPILOGUE

YEARS LATER, EDEN AND JACOB pushed their baby stroller down 4th Street on a lazy Sunday that unfurled like a ribbon of blissful contentedness. It was unusual for Jacob not to have an open house and Eden reveled he had the day off. They wandered through stores and stopped for fish tacos while their baby, Harper, snoozed. She was only four months old; a gorgeous baby, coo-ey and perfect. Eden and Jacob loved her with feverish intensity; the depth of their emotion was startling. Jacob joked that for Harper he would not only jump in front of any bullet, or punch any shark in the face, but also voluntarily watch *Dora the Explorer*. He and Eden had made a glorious person together.

After lunch, the young family walked by Antigone Books and decided to amble inside. Eden had heard about a new cookbook on NPR and wanted to see if it was available.

Lingering behind her, Jacob saw it first. There, under "Staff's Pick," was Kat's book.

LIAR
by Kathryn Lamb

Jacob grinned. His mom had cautiously shared Kat's literary success some months ago, and truth was, he'd researched this development online, fascinated and gratified. Still, seeing it in person was haunting. A salesperson approached, having noticed Jacob clutching the book.

"The author used to work here!" the employee chirped. "Isn't that wild?"

Jacob smiled, nodding. "No kidding? . . ."

"Crazy. Yeah, it's all true. Really well-written. Her first book apparently was just littered with lies—her story was sort of a James Frey *Million Little Pieces* for a new generation. Anyway, in this one, she comes clean. She had this wild breakdown but came out the other side. Super interesting. I stayed up till two in the morning finishing it last week."

"That so?" Jacob asked. "I suppose I'll have to get it, then."

He flipped to the back flap and saw her author's picture, a black-and-white shot of Kat with a small, wise smile in a sensible white shirt. She looked beautiful, content.

Jacob read the inscription below.

"Kathryn Lamb lives in Portland, Maine, and takes her medications every day. This is her second novel."

Jacob grinned to himself, surprised to feel his eyes get misty.

"Beep beep," Eden said, playfully tapping Harper's baby stroller against his back. Jacob turned and handed her the book.

Eden studied it; her eyes bloomed in wonder. "Wow." She read the glowing blurbs on the back cover, then flipped to Kat's flattering author picture. Jacob watched her read About the Author. Eden looked up at him, her eyes were soft.

"Good for her," Eden said, with genuine sentiment in her voice. She flipped over the book and opened it from the front, drifting through the first blank pages and copyright info. Suddenly, she dropped the book and it landed with a loud THUNK.

"Eden? What?" . . . Jacob leaned down and picked the book off the floor. Eden wrapped her arms around herself, instantly cold, scanning the store. She felt eyes on her.

Jacob opened the book to the title page and saw a familiar scrawl:

MAINE WAS JUST TOO COLD
XO. Kat

A hum filled Jacob's ears as he slowly lifted his head, scanning for movement.

At the store's main entrance, the bells above the front door trilled as someone exited. The sweet chimes continued to tinkle, lingering. Jacob's arms were littered with goosebumps.

Rushing to the exit, Jacob opened the door and scanned down 4th Street, desperately searching the crowd of weekend shoppers. But he saw nothing. Still reeling, he turned back inside, making his way back to Eden and Harper. They lingered for a few more minutes and paid for the cookbook, a cloud of doom hanging over the young family. Leaving the store, Jacob—still anxious from reading the cryptic inscription—snagged the stroller's wheel on the leg of a "Free Books" table near the entrance. Something caught his eye, and his blood went cold. Jacob froze.

"Jacob, hon. What now? . . ." Eden asked in fear, noting his pause.

There, on the top of the pile, was a worn copy of *Lolita*.

ACKNOWLEDGMENTS

A BOOK IS CREATED IN solidarity. But it is also the result of a whole lot of community (in addition to chaos, joy, doubt, and caffeine).

There are endless amounts of people who have touched the pages of this book, and I hope I haven't forgotten anyone. It's more likely I have, because my brain can only do so much, and it also apparently has to remember all the lyrics to Milli Vanilli. Thank you to the Greenleaf Book Group for publishing my novel; you've been an absolute delight to work with from start to finish (though I am writing this midway through the process, but I know this will be true!).

My manager of 4,000 years, Alex Goldstone, you're such a mensch. I love when anyone asks who reps me and there's only one reaction: "Oh, I love Alex!" (Join the club.)

I adore the team at A3, from Valarie Philips to Adam Kanter to Sally Wilcox and David Doerrer; you're not only all good at your job but you're also kind. Thanks to my lawyer Robby Koch for taking care of the legal ho-ha.

I adored working with my editor Katie Gilligan, who told me things I needed to hear and made my book so much better. You fine-tuned this piano and hopefully made it sing, and I thank you.

My publicists, Kellie and Andrea, at Smith Publicity have been so smart from day one. Callie Cullen, thank you for making the Internets make sense and for making me kinda sorta social media savvy.

Gina Gomez, you offer such great advice and clear my energy with aplomb!

To my genuinely terrific and smart writing group of friends, Christie Havey-Smith, Kari Estrin, and Meta Valentic. Can't wait to read what you're cooking up next.

To my first readers, Carrie Stidwell O'Boyle and Kate Neale Cooper, thank you for your friendship and all the wonderful notes. And especially the praise. Your enthusiasm kept me going.

My parents. I dedicated this book to you both at the top and I'll thank you again. Thank you thank you thank you. I won the parent lottery with you two—you are the most fun parents, the most supportive people on earth, and I even forgive your perfect marriage that is impossible to live up to. I hope my kids want to be with me someday as much as I want to be with you.

My phenomenal children, Harper and Drake, you both have my heart. I love you and I like you, today and forever and the day after that.

Jason, my husband of nearly 20 years, you are my beautiful reward for saving all those orphans in another life. Thank god I was there to step in.

My brother, Bryce, and my sister, Haley, you are siblings I would pick out of a catalog if given a choice. You're hilarious, you're kind, you're wonderful. I don't know what my life looks without either of you.

I am grateful to the Walt Disney Company for selecting me as a Screenwriting Fellow back in 1999. I become a professional writer that day and it changed everything. My Grandpa Dean would just love that Walt Disney had something to do with my life. Andrew Gunn and Kristin Burr, I am so glad you were assigned to me!

Amanda Brown Chang, thank you for the gift of Elle and the gift of YOU.

Chanda Lam and Candice Edwards, you are both such magical people in my life and I am glad our kids were born at the same time so we could meet at preschool!

Kristin Harmel, you are the best cheerleader and such a wonderful role model for me, in literature and in life.

Tara Wachter, you are my soul sister, and Sedona awaits us for more weekends.

Thank you to my extended family—I am grateful my brother and sister married so well and my husband has such a terrific family himself.

Nancy T., Suzanne, Jennifer, Nicky, Shannon, Lisa, Laura Bell, Jill, Heather, Rebecca, Rina, Francesca, Mia, Nancy V.—do I know a lot of great people, or what? I can't include you all or this book would never end, but I'm so lucky to have so many exquisite friendships in this life.

I miss my friend Rachel who is a loose inspiration for Jess.

And before I forget, there's one person I actually *have* forgotten—thank you to that writing instructor at the University of Arizona who told me all those years ago I could make a living as a writer. Your words infused my very being, and I'm sorry I've rewarded your kindness by forgetting your name, but you really did make a big difference in my life.

ABOUT THE AUTHOR

HEATHER HACH is a screenwriter (*Freaky Friday* and *What to Expect When You're Expecting*) and Tony-nominated and Olivier-winning Broadway librettist (*Legally Blonde the Musical*). A graduate of the University of Colorado School of Journalism, Hach went on to become a magazine editor, an improv comedy troupe member, and, even weirder yet, a judge on MTV's *The Search for the Next Elle Woods*. She was a mediocre PA on TV's *Caroline in the City* and a truly terrible writer's assistant on *Dilbert*. Thankfully, in 1999, she won the Walt Disney Screenwriting Fellowship and has been writing ever since. She also wrote the YA novel *Freaky Monday* with Mary Rodgers. *The Trouble with Drowning* is her adult novel debut. Hach lives in Manhattan Beach with her husband, two kids, a charming golden doodle, and a weird pug.